Oh My Blessed Father

Book 1

A Coming of Age Novel

By

Ted Burton

Oh My Blessed Father

Book 1

A Coming of Age Novel

By

Ted Burton

Schooner Publishing

Ottawa, Ontario, Canada

Published in Canada by Schooner Publishing

Printed by CreateSpace

ISBN-10: 0993886809
ISBN-13: 978-0993886805

DEDICATION

Dedicated to the memory of Mary Veatress Burton who taught me the strength of love and the importance of the Golden Rule.

CONTENTS

1 ~ A New Life in Ontario

"Is Daddy going to tear down the Christmas tree this year?" Those words are one of my first memories, or are they really memories. When we remember something, do we truly remember it or do we only remember remembering it? I'm not sure. It was Christmas Eve in 1951. I was two years old. In March, I would be three. The year before, my father had pulled down the Christmas tree on Christmas morning and stepped and jumped on every bulb until none were left in one piece. My mother said I had not mentioned the incident since that day (not that I was a big talker). She had hoped I had erased it from my memory. So Mom and my older sister Claudia were amazed as these words came from my lips. Claudia was 20 and newly married and had come to visit for Christmas. As I said, I was not much of a talker. I had hardly spoken in the last year, and this was one of the first sentences I had put together. Mom says my first sentence was uttered as I looked out the window and saw one of my older brothers coming home. "Oh look, here comes Ernie," I said. Not up to Shakespeare's standards I know, but Mom was impressed just the same.

I had four older brothers, so I didn't see much sense in talking. I thought I could learn more by just listening to them.

In fact when I turned three, I got bored with the English language and decided to develop my own language. Water became 'cleo', Mom became 'Gawa', and many other new words were invented. Don't ask me where this came from; I don't remember any of it. Only Mom understood what I was saying. My Dad thought I was crazy. Others urged that I be taken to a doctor. But Mom understood. She had known that I had spoken normal before and would speak normal again. Was this my way of withdrawing and finding a way to talk secretly to Mom and shut the rest of life out? As I said before, don't ask me. I'm not much for that Freud stuff.

Anyway back to that Christmas – the Christmas tree remained standing until January the 6th. That was the day we always took down the tree and Christmas was officially over. We never put the tree up until Christmas Eve and it was decorated after we went to bed. That added to the excitement on Christmas morning. Not only did we wake up to see presents under the tree, but we had the additional thrill of seeing the tree decorated for the first time. So why had my father torn down the tree the year before, you may be thinking. That will become more evident as this story progresses; for that was not the last time he practiced that unusual Christmas ritual.

My actual first memory was from the summer of 1950. I would have been a little over a year old. We were in a car and I remember getting lost down some road and ending up at a dead-end lane looking at a lake. It was extremely dark. I asked Mom about it many years later and she confirmed that something like that had really happened. We were driving to Ontario from the Maritimes to start a new life. My father had become lost somewhere in Ontario and we ended up sleeping in the car overlooking Lake Ontario. Remember this was before the days of the 401, and Highway 2 was about as big as roads got.

I was born in Halifax on the Ides of March. I was three months premature and weighed around three pounds. Mom said I looked like a skinned rabbit. I guess it's a wonder that I lived considering they didn't have all the medical resources that they have today. I spent close to a month in an incubator. After I came home, I got sick again (weak kidneys, I think) and then spent another month in the hospital. Again, Mom thought I would die. But somehow I pulled through and came home to remain a healthy boy for many years.

Three of my brothers were also born in Halifax. My oldest brother Brad and sister Claudia were born in Newfoundland. Both of my parents were Newfoundlanders. Although my mother was born in Saskatchewan, her parents had only lived there for a few years before returning to their roots in Newfoundland. We were heading for Ontario for the better life. My Dad was always looking for something different, and we were always moving to somewhere else. We had actually lived in two different houses in Halifax between the time I was born and when we began our sojourn to Ontario. I am not sure where we were living when I commiserated about the tree, somewhere around Toronto perhaps. We had lived in Riverdale, Agincourt, and some other area of Toronto before I had my third birthday. We had left a house in Halifax, just letting it go back to the bank. We had also left behind the family dog, Sandy; for which my brothers had never forgiven Dad. We must have been quite a sight heading to Toronto with five boys in the car. Claudia had stayed behind in Nova Scotia to be near her boyfriend and soon-to-be husband, Tom Kilkenny. Dad told Mom not to worry about leaving Claudia behind, that she was old enough to take care of herself. But Mom was naturally upset to be leaving her only daughter in the Maritimes by herself while we went off to Ontario. Thus, I only knew Claudia from the few times she came to visit. I did not have the chance to grow up with her around me. My oldest brother Brad would have been about 14 at the time we moved. Mom always referred to Brad as Buddy. Apparently when Claudia was young whenever she attempted to say brother it came out as buddy; and the name stuck. Ernie who was next in age was six. Billy was four and Gordie was three. And bringing up the rear was Benny – me. After all those boys, Mom must have wanted another girl. I had long curly blonde hair with ringlets and wore jumpers that looked suspiciously like dresses. Luckily this style of attire didn't last too much longer.

Shortly after we arrived in Toronto, while driving along some side street, one of the back doors of our sedan suddenly flew open. Little Billy tumbled out of the car, and rolled across the road until he came to rest against the curb. My Dad slammed on the brakes; but before we came to a complete stop, Mom was running towards Billy's inert body. So she beat both Buddy and Ernie to the edge of the road. Billy just looked up and softly said, "Don't worry Mom, I'm OK." Mom picked Billy up and hugged him as if she would never see him again. Billy had a cut along the side of his head which was dripping blood on Mom's dress. He was also covered in scrapes and marks (which would soon be bruises) from head to toe. While Mom was crying, Dad looked at Billy and inquired about his condition.

"How you feeling, Billy?"

"I'm fine."

"He's OK, Mary. Let's get him back in the car," Dad stated as he started to round us up and guide us back into the car. By then a few people had gathered around to see what was happening.

"You better take him to the hospital, Mister," someone spoke.

"Shouldn't we take him to the hospital, Garf?" Mom pleaded.

"No, you heard Billy. You're fine, right Billy? See, he'll be as good as new."

We got back in the car and went on our way. Dad was right. Other than a concussion, two black eyes, scrapes, scabs, bruises, and an ugly gash on his head, Billy recovered quite nicely. One good thing that I can say about Dad in this situation was that I think he was just as worried as the rest of the family. Mom said he turned white as a ghost when he saw Billy fall from the car. Also, that was the last four-door car he would buy for close to twenty years.

My Dad would drink a lot and sometimes would drink anything. Onetime, someone gave him a case of hair tonic and he drank the whole thing. Another time he drank kerosene; but to be fair that wasn't on purpose. Dad kept some rum in an old bottle in the shed and somehow this bottle got mixed-up with one containing kerosene for a lamp. I guess he wasn't too happy about that. One other night, a few weeks after Claudia and Tom had returned back home to Nova Scotia, Dad came home late from a drinking binge. We were already in bed and unaware that a snowfall had completely covered our walkway. I woke up to hear Mom cry out.

"Leave him alone Garf, he's sleeping."

"Shut up you gray-haired old bag! You stay out of this. Get up you lazy son of a bitch. I just about killed myself on the fucking sidewalk. Now get up and shovel that walk now!"

"He can do it in the morning, Garf!"

"No! He'll do it now." I heard a loud noise like someone stumbling.

Then I heard Buddy say, "It's OK Mom, I'll do it now. Please, go back to bed."

"Get the hell moving!"

"I'm going, I'm going! Let me get dressed."

Again, I heard more bangs and crashes; then all was quiet except for the sound of a shovel scraping the walk. I got out of my bed to look out the window. I saw Buddy still in his pajamas trying to shovel the snow while it was falling and blowing all around him. I climbed back in bed, hoping I could fall asleep and that everything would get better. The next morning I found out that Dad wouldn't even let Buddy put his boots on. He pushed him out the front door in his bare feet. I didn't understand at the time, but I now know that Buddy didn't protest anymore because he wanted to protect Mom from further abuse. I found out later that the first crash I heard that night was Mom being knocked to the floor.

I will relate one last incident that happened before I take the story out of Toronto. I don't really remember this happening, although I do remember hearing about it many times over the years. Mom had been quite sick during our years in Toronto and was taking a lot of different pills. This is quite a wonder to me now. The fact that Mom had pills, I mean. As you probably already gathered, Dad was not much for doctors and we would have to be close to death before he would agree to us going to one. I guess Mom was much sicker than I remember. Dad had again come home late and drunk. Of course, he still expected his dinner to be served to him. Dad had sat down to eat at the table when he shouted, "What the hell's this? This looks like my hass'ole." At which point, he stood up and knocked all of the items on the table flying across the room. Ernie noticed Mom's pills spread out all over the kitchen floor. "Mom's pills, Mom's pills," he cried as he started to pick them up. While Ernie was upset about the pills and concerned about Mom's health, Billy reacted differently. He quietly got up from his chair, walked over to where Dad was standing, and started to kick Dad in the shins.

"You sonny bitch! You sonny bitch!" he yelled. "You pick up Mom's pills!"

Mom always said that Billy was the hot-tempered one.

2 ~ Maritime Life

At this point, I think I should tell you some information about my parents' background. Hopefully this will help you to understand things a little better.

After their unsuccessful turn at life in Saskatchewan, Bradley Simpson had moved his family back to Newfoundland to settle down in the fishing port of Grand Bank. Bradley and his wife, Jean, had four children – two boys (Sam and Gordon) and two girls (Rebecca and Mary). Bradley was a businessman who became involved in many enterprises – some successful and some not so. These included a few land deals which did not always turn out well. In fact, Bradley had still not collected all the money owed to him for the sale of his land in Saskatchewan. Another time he had bought property which had been surveyed as fertile farm land; however, it proved to be little more than bad soil and rock. Bradley always saw the best in other people and believed in trust. The Simpson family was based upon this love and trust. If you wanted to earn the respect of others you had to show respect and faith in their opinions and actions. And because of that, Bradley sometimes was the victim of bad deals. But somehow he always managed to keep his family amply fed and clothed. There were good times and bad times, but the good seemed to out-weigh the bad.

Ted and Ellen Cooper had lived in Grand Bank for many years. The Cooper ancestors were Newfoundlanders as far back as anyone could trace. Their family consisted of four girls (Annette, Eleanor, June, and Nora) and two boys. The youngest boy was Ben (my namesake) and the oldest was Garfield. He was named after President Garfield, who had been assassinated over twenty-five years before Garfield was born in 1907. Garfield was always known to his family and friends as Garf. Ted Cooper believed in strong discipline and he ruled the household with an iron-fist. Garfield, being the oldest boy, was often the recipient of this discipline. He was expected at an early age to help contribute to the labours of running a large family, and would feel the force of the back of his father's hand if it was felt that he wasn't pulling his weight. Garf was forced to quit school before he had finished high school, so that he could start earning his keep. There was no such problem for his brother Ben. He dropped out of school after getting tired of trying to get through Grade 3. Ted Cooper, like Bradley Simpson also tried his hand at many different ventures; but he failed to experience any of the mild success which Simpson had enjoyed. Still they managed to make enough to make ends meet.

The youngest Simpson daughter, Mary, was born in 1909. As a teenager, she was considered to be the best looking girl in Grand Bank. She had had a few boyfriends and had broken a few hearts. Mary and her older sister Rebecca (always called Becky) had different tastes and went in opposite directions. This was reflected even in their choice of music. Whereas Mary enjoyed the songs of the 'Roaring 20's', Becky preferred the classics and hymns of earlier decades. Becky had decided to become a teacher and worked hard to achieve that goal. She had no time for the frivolities of the modern age. Mary was more like her brother Gordon who was always looking for a good time, while Becky took after their oldest brother Sam who had taken a more serious approach to life.

When Mary announced her plans to marry Garfield Cooper, the Simpson household was not too pleased (to say the least). Her father, Bradley, was not too fond of the Cooper family, and Garfield in particular. "I saw him beating a horse," Bradley explained. "A man that is unkind to animals will be unkind to people as well." But Mary could not be talked out of the union and the marriage proceeded. This would have been 1930.

In the years between 1930 and the war in 1939, the Simpson family could have certainly said, "I told you so" to Mary. There were incidents of verbal and physical abuse which occurred almost exclusively after long bouts of drinking. Still during this period, the occasions of drinking were far fewer than they would become in later years. During this time, Becky Simpson had achieved her objective and became a schoolteacher. She began teaching in some of the isolated out-ports of Newfoundland that could only be reached by ship. She experienced a few harrowing tales in her early days of teaching across the island, before she settled down into a teaching post in Grand Bank. But that's another story.

In this period, the first Cooper child, Claudia, was born and a few years later she had a little brother, Philip. However, just over a year later, Philip had died from pneumonia. Mom, in later years, would refer to him solely as 'dear little brother'. In the middle of the thirties, Brad was born. Before the war began they left Newfoundland to go to Halifax and Garf joined the merchant marine. During the war Garf would return for a few weeks here and there, as his ship came back to dock at Halifax to pick up new supplies intended for the troops in Europe. So the war didn't stop the Cooper family from expanding. In 1944 Ernie made his appearance into the world. When Ernie was a year old, Mary was awoken in the middle of the night by a large blast which continued to rumble throughout the night. This was July 18th, 1945 when an ammunition dump on the east side of Bedford Basin had exploded sending the city of Halifax into a state of terror. My family and many others were evacuated from their homes to high points of the city, such as the Citadel. I remember Mom telling us about dragging Claudia, Brad, and Ernie out of their beds for the trek to safety. They had no idea what was happening. They weren't sure if the war had reached Halifax.

When he returned in 1945, Garf made up for lost time. First Billy came into the world, next it was Gordie, followed by a stillborn baby boy, and then finally came me. That makes me the seventh son, whatever that means. Mom would often say that the war changed Dad and that his drinking increased when he came home for good. Also she remarked that his verbal abuse became much more crude and vicious. By the time we left for Ontario, both of Dad's parents had passed away. All of Dad's sisters had moved westward to either Detroit or Toronto leaving Uncle Ben alone in Grand Bank. In 1949, the same year that I was born, Mom's father had died from complications arising from a fall from the roof of the house that he had built for his family in Grand Bank. Shortly after, Uncle Gordon left for California while Uncle Sam moved a few miles down the road to settle in the town of Fortune. That left only Mom's mother Jean and Mom's sister Rebecca (who was always known to us as Aunt Becky) behind in the house that Bradley Simpson had built. Mom's hair was now completely gray and she was missing her top teeth. Mom always said that the dentist pulled them out because they were crooked. I only found out recently that it was because of my Dad that they were crooked. Mom had a set of false teeth, but they were badly fitted so she never wore them. Also she was in bad need of glasses but couldn't afford a new pair of them either. Dad was looking to get a new job and to escape from creditors when he left Nova Scotia. Mom was only hoping for a better life.

3 – On the Farm

We moved from Toronto to take up the country life somewhere around the spring of 1952, settling at what was only referred to as Lowe's. This was the first in a series of places which we rented that I only remember by the owner's name. For the next ten years or so we lived close to the Orangeville area of Ontario. For those who need to know, Orangeville is about 60 miles north of Toronto. I couldn't locate any of these places now if my life depended on it. Some of these farms that you will soon hear about get kind of jumbled in my head. So I may have some of the stories take place at the wrong location. But, who cares? No one will notice anyway.

I'm not certain what Dad did for a living here, but I know it did not bring in much money. It had to be better than life in Toronto though, where things sometimes got so bad that Buddy and Ernie would scour the dumps looking for thrown out food that was still edible. I think that Dad did some chores around the farm for Mr. Lowe. The Lowe's own farmhouse was nearby and we only rented the house. I remember a pig that was like the family pet. I think we called him Curly. It wandered in and out of the house and even slept in our bedroom. One day Curly disappeared. I can't say what happened to him, but I know we ate well for a while afterwards. This reminds me of another incident a few months later. Mom and Buddy were sitting at the table discussing what we were going to do about food and where our next meal was going to come from. No one noticed Billy sitting on the kitchen floor. The conversation continued until Billy stood up, pointed out the window at Mr. Lowe's cattle, and stated his well thought out idea.

"Why don't we just go out and cut the ass off one of those cows?"

I remember that Grandma Simpson came to visit us on the farm. This was a good time for us, because Dad was on his best behaviour while Grandma was there – at least most of the time. Also Mom was obviously very happy to see her mother again. I do not recall too much about Grandma, only that she was always pleasant and loving to all of us boys.

The best part of living on a farm was that we got to have pets again. We acquired a new dog, which Buddy and Ernie named Lucky. Although Lucky was a mutt, he was mostly a collie. A white kitten that we called Snowball also joined the family. As I look at a picture of us boys with Mom and Dad standing by a car on Lowe's farm, three things are evident. The first being all the animals – including Lucky, Snowball, and a chicken! Gordie is holding the chicken. The second thing I notice is my hair – still long and curly; however, the ringlets are now gone. The suspicious jumper has now been replaced by overalls, thankfully. The last is my face – all screwed up. Gordie (and the rest of my brothers) always said that I could get the weirdest twists and contortions on my face. And they were right.

Ernie became familiar with some other animals at this time – bees. Ernie and Billy had discovered something which they soon found out was a bees' nest. By the time they had figured out what they were disturbing, it was too late. Billy was able to escape without too many stings, but Ernie was surrounded. They swarmed all over him, while Ernie ran as fast as he could towards the house. Mom saw Ernie go flying by the kitchen window with a swarm of bees hot on his trail. With Buddy's help, they got Ernie to strip off all his clothes, before he dashed into the safety of the house. Ernie had been stung from head to toe. It took him quite a while to get over that encounter.

Another incident happened while we were at Lowe's which illustrates that sometimes we could be taken to a doctor if the injury was considered severe enough. I thought I had better tell you, just so you don't think that we would never be taken to a doctor. This involved Billy again. We were out picking apples and Mom was knocking them from the tree with a rake while we boys picked them up. But none of the apples were big enough for Billy's taste. He saw a large apple on a high branch that he had to have.

"That one! I want that one, Mom," he yelled.

As Mom went to knock it down, Billy ran off in the direction where the apple would land on the ground. Just as the apple was falling to the earth, Billy tripped over a small rock and landed with his forehead smashing against a large boulder. As the blood began to run profusely from the gash in his forehead, Mom and Dad reacted quickly to get Billy and the rest of us into the car to take him to the doctor. Ernie, who had taken the time to pick up the large apple for Billy, passed it to Mom.

"Here's your apple, Billy," Mom said to my wounded brother who was sitting beside her in the front seat.

"I don't want it anymore," Billy cried as he threw it to the floor.

"Oh, Billy, what are we going to do with you?" was Mom's only reply.

Billy only required a few stitches and soon recovered from the wound. But Mom would never let Billy forget that day. She often retold the story and used it as an example to us about the consequences of greed.

We did not stay at Lowe's very long. Dad soon had a fight with Mr. Lowe and we had to move out. So by the fall of '52, we were on the move again. This time we moved just a few miles away to another farm. This place was known as Bullard's. There was one major difference between Lowe's and Bullard's. Bullard's had no electricity. This was the first house we lived in which had no lights or power. The heat was provided by a large wood stove and a series of stovepipes which circulated to most of the rooms. The source of heating was nothing new but having no electricity was definitely an adjustment for us all. We had an icebox in the back kitchen which kept things cool as long as it was supplied with ice. I remember the washboard washer and the hand-cranked wringer machine. Nothing but the latest technology for the Coopers. The cooking was done on the wood stove. At least it had a large oven. Light of course was supplied by lanterns. Entertainment was provided by five boys.

I have to admit that I fell in love with Bullard's right away. There was a white picket fence around the farmhouse. I thought we now lived in the lap of luxury. Forget that we lacked a source of energy; we had a picket fence. A white one too! Only rich people lived in houses surrounded by picket fences. Everybody knows that. The Bullard's lived across the road. They also lived without power. I spent a lot of time over at the Bullard's. Mom says she would watch me sitting on the tractor with John Bullard and I'd be wearing a smile from ear to ear. I would get up early and spend the whole day with John. Mom would ask John what I talked about. John replied, "Talk? What talk? I haven't heard Benny speak yet. Does he talk?" John was half kidding but there was too much truth to his statement. I was definitely a shy kid. The term 'introvert' did not do justice in describing my personality. When company came (such as one of Dad's sisters and family), I hid behind a large living room chair. Mom thought it was cute; that I was being proper and polite. I have worked hard over the years to change. Many people today can't believe I'm a shy guy. They think I don't shut up. Writing this book is my last step in exorcising the introverted ghost forever from my past.

4 – The Old Man

"Be careful Benny, the pit is full of sharp forks and knives."

"I won't fall, Gordie. Watch me go faster."

I sped up, running around the 'Pit of Hell' as fast as my little short legs would carry me. Suddenly, I stumbled and fell headlong down the side of the pit onto the sharp knives below. I was dead.

"Well, I guess you're dead now, Benny."

"Deader than a doornail," I shouted up to Gordie as I started laughing. "Whattaya wanna do now?"

"I don't know. Whatta you wanna do?" Gordie shouted back.

At that point, Gordie dove into the pit and died along side me. We both began laughing until our sides began to ache.

"That was fun," I said.

"Yeah," said Gordie, "let's do it again."

"Sounds good to me. Let's go."

It was March 1953, and I had just turned four years old. There had been a big snowstorm a few days earlier and where we were playing, beside the chicken coop, the strange twisting of the wind had created a large snowdrift against the coop.

We could walk right on top of the roof. The best part of this drift though, was that it was in a perfect circle. The middle of the circle was a deep hole with a rim of snow circled about it. A few blades of straw stuck up from the bottom of the pit. This was the perilous knives and forks. The infamous 'Pit of Hell'.

This is the strongest of all of my early memories. I remember that day like it was yesterday. This was more fun than I had ever experienced. I was now four. I was so happy. Gordie and I would have great times together. He was just a little more than two years older than me so we did everything together. Gordie was my best friend. Although I did not talk much to the rest of the world, I could talk Gordie's ears off. And he listened. And I listened to Gordie. I believed every word he told me. I did not need any other friends. I had Gordie and my other brothers. They were all the friends I needed, except for John Bullard of course. That was special. I loved my time with John. I certainly would be a farmer when I grew up. What could be more exciting than sitting on a tractor circling the fields all day?

So what was so special about that day around the snow pit? I'm not sure now, but it is such a strong memory for both me and Gordie. For me, I think it was the day I became sentient. What I mean; is that it was the day that I became aware of who I was. From then on, I can recall most of my life in chronological order. Before that day, I can only recount certain occurrences which are burned into my memory. I needed assistance in determining when and where things really happened. I have told you already about those. From now on, hopefully I will be a little clearer.

I now realized I had two fathers, the father who could be loving and caring, even the father who could be amusing. Then there was the other father. The one you've already been introduced to. The one I feared and wished would go away. From then on, I recognized that I did not have a 'Dad'. Beginning now, he will always be referred to as 'The Old Man'. That's what the rest of the family called him. It had only just sunk into my vocabulary.

A few weeks later, all the snow was gone. It was the beginning of April and it was a lovely spring day. Snowball was about ready to give birth to kittens, but she had disappeared a few days before. Then on that sunny day, she appeared at the door, back to her normal size. Mom looked at Snowball and said, "Where are your kittens? Go get them and bring them here." So Snowball turned around and took off towards our neighbour's farm. A little while later, we heard a meow at the door. We opened the door to see Snowball sitting there proudly holding a baby kitten in her mouth. She dropped the kitten and headed off in the same direction again. She kept this up until she had five kittens at our house. Shortly after, she took three of them away again. We never did discover where she took them.

Snowball was not the only member of the household that was expecting. Mom was due to have another baby in May. But she was getting very sick, so she went into the hospital in Orangeville to await the arrival of our new brother or sister. At that time Claudia, who was also expecting, was staying with us. Tom, who was in the Air Force, had been sent to Europe; so Claudia returned to live with us for a few months while awaiting the arrival of her baby. I must have driven poor Claudia crazy. She couldn't do anything right in my eyes. Whatever she did, I would say, "That's not the way Mom does it." When she made the bed, I said, "That's not the way Mom does it." When she washed my hair, it was, "That's not the way Mom does it." When she made us lunch, I complained "That's not the way Mom does it." I think she was ready to strangle me, by the time we learned that we had a new sister. She was a bit early arriving, it was still April. No one was more relieved than Claudia, when we heard that Mom would soon be home with baby Lily. Except for Mom, of course. She couldn't have been happier about having another girl after all those boys — not that she didn't love us the same; but, you know what I mean.

I remember the day they arrived home. The Old Man

drove into the driveway and parked in front of the white picket fence. Claudia was in the front seat with The Old Man, while Mom and Lily were in the back. All five of us boys were standing around waiting to get a look at baby Lily and to welcome Mom home. It was the longest that I had ever been away from Mom, so getting hugs and kisses from her just added to the moment. I never left Mom's side for weeks. Partly because I had missed her so much, but more because I was fascinated by the strange looking baby. She was quite lovely really, but I had never seen such a small baby before; therefore, she was strange to me. I wanted to help Mom do everything. I would run and get diapers, cloths, or anything else that Mom would ask me to do. We began to call our new sister 'Sis'. Later she would become Sissy. Have you noticed a pattern here? Everyone's name was changed to end in 'ie' or sometimes 'y'. Anyway, I was as proud as could be. I had a baby sister!

A few weeks later, I became an uncle. My new niece Elizabeth (Lizzie, of course) was born in the same hospital in Orangeville in which Lily had entered the world. Then not long after, Claudia and Lizzie returned back to the Maritimes to rejoin Tom.

Later that year, Grandma and Aunt Becky came to visit us on the farm for a couple of weeks. This was the first time that I remember meeting Aunt Becky. Although the two sisters were alike in some ways, Aunt Becky and Mom did not have similar personalities. Mom would say that they were as different as night and day. For example, one day Mom, Aunt Becky, Gordie, and I were sitting at the kitchen table, while Grandma was in a rocking chair in the corner with Sissy in her arms. Suddenly Mom said, "I guess Jingle-balls will be home soon." She was talking about The Old Man, of course.

"Oh my Blessed Father, Mary. How can you speak like that in front of the children?" Aunt Becky replied, accompanied with a look of utter shock.

"Don't worry, Becky. They've heard much worse than that many times, mainly from their father."

"Well! That doesn't mean you have to sink to his level, does it Mary?"

"Oh Becky, it's just a little saying I use for their father when I get tired of calling him The Old Man."

"Well, I'll just keep calling him The Old Man if you don't mind," Aunt Becky retorted.

Gordie and I were trying to avoid looking at each other. I was ready to crack up. If I had looked at Gordie, I probably would have fallen down laughing on the floor. I looked over at Grandma and Sissy; Grandma had a big smile on her face but didn't speak. If Aunt Becky had only known some of Mom's other pet names. And I don't mean just for The Old Man. I mean for all of us boys too. Just that morning she had said to me, "Come here Fart-in-strings, so I can brush your hair." Also she sometimes referred to The Old Man as 'Asshole-grinder'. Aunt Becky would have died of shock if she had heard that one. I'm not sure where some of those colourful names came from, but I must say they were unique. She had a few other singular expressions as well. Once when The Old Man commented about a dinner by saying "What am I supposed to do with this shit?" Mom only answered, "You don't have to eat it if you don't want to." Later Ernie said to Mom that she should have said something more in response to The Old Man. "Yes, you're right Ernie," Mom replied. "I should have told him to put his dinner where Fred Roberts put his ten dollar bill." I never fully understood that saying, but I loved it just the same.

The next year was a good time for me. I continued to ride the tractor with John most of the day and helped Mom with Sissy at night. I remember helping John collect sap from the maple trees on their farm. It was an exciting time watching the Bullards create maple syrup in large, steaming buckets over a hot fire. One time, they even made taffy. All of us boys had a great time pulling taffy. Then we got to eat some too. Other entertainment was provided by a big battery operated radio. We would listen to 'The Adventures of Sherlock Holmes' and other mystery shows on Sunday night.

I also recall all of us sitting around the radio listening to 'The Lone Ranger', 'Gunsmoke', and other westerns. Mom would listen to a few soaps such as 'The Guiding Light'.

I don't have any memories about The Old Man during that year; but I am sure there must have been times that he came home drunk yelling "I'm drunk again you gray-haired old bag! Who 'ave you been whoring around with today? What do you think I am an eight-day clock or a sewing machine? I've been around the world; I know the score. I wasn't born yesterday. You old bag!" I've heard those lines so many times that I could place them anywhere in this story and I would have it correct.

I do recall quite vividly an episode that occurred on a hot Saturday in the summer of '54. Gordie and I were playing outside in the yard. I was laughing about something Gordie had said when we heard doors slamming and loud voices. We looked up to see Buddy running out the front door; right behind him was The Old Man. The Old Man had been drinking beer in the kitchen all day.

"Come here you fucking bastard. I'm gonna kill you if I get my hands on you!"

Mom was right behind, "Garf, leave him alone!"

"I've got you now!" The Old Man shouted as he jumped onto Buddy's back bringing him to the ground.

As Mom was trying to stop The Old Man's blows from landing on Buddy, Ernie came running outside to help.

"Go get the Bullards," Mom shouted to Ernie.

Lucky appeared on the scene, barking and growling as he circled The Old Man and Buddy. Meanwhile, Ernie went running down the lane towards Bullard's house across the road. Billy and Gordie went to join Lucky around the battle. I just stayed where I was on the ground and began to cry. I think Sissy was having her nap while this was going on. Although The Old Man was not a big man, he had large powerful hands and arms. Yet, somehow Buddy was deflecting most of The Old Man's blows, but he wasn't fighting back. Mom was trying to pull The Old Man off of

Buddy; but, she just got knocked to the ground for her effort. Soon Ernie was running back up the lane accompanied by John and his dad, Frank Bullard.

"What the hell's going on here?" John yelled from about 50 yards down the lane.

By the time the rescuers arrived, The Old Man had ceased his fighting and was standing over Buddy.

"I'm sorry, Brad," he said. "I don't know what's got into me. It's OK John, Frank; I'm OK now. You can go home, I'm OK now."

"What's happening, Garf? What are you trying to do?" Frank questioned. "Are you OK Brad?"

"Brad hit me and I just lost my head for a minute," The Old Man argued. "There's nothing to worry about. You're not hurt, right Brad?"

"Yeah, no thanks to you, I'm not," Buddy spat out as he pulled himself up from the ground. "The cowardly bastard was attacking Mom. That's what he was doing! Show them your arm, Mom. He twisted it silly. I should have hit him harder."

Mom was standing a few feet away holding her right arm. "I'll be alright Buddy. I don't think anything's broken."

"What did The Old Man do to you, Mom?" Ernie inquired. "What did you do to her, Dad?"

"Jesus Christ, I was just holding her arm. I didn't do anything," The Old Man grumbled.

"Come on, Garf, let's go talk," said Frank as he led The Old Man back into the house. John followed them into the house as well.

Ernie, Billy, and Gordie all went to Mom to see how she was. Mom just said, "Don't worry about me. Did he hurt you, Buddy?"

"Nothing a few aspirins wouldn't help. Just a few scrapes and bruises. I think I corked him a good one. When I saw him getting up and the look on his face, I thought I better put some distance between us. Is your arm really OK, Mom?"

"It'll be right as rain in the morning. Don't worry, dear.

I've felt worse," Mom answered.

"That bastard!" Buddy repeated.

While all of this was going on, I had not moved from my spot in the yard where I had been laughing and playing a few minutes before. I was just sitting there and could not stop crying. Even Lucky had gone up to Mom and Buddy with a look that suggested an "Are you OK?" inquiry. But I could not move. I didn't want to move. I just wanted to hide, but there was no big chair to hide behind in the yard. Suddenly Mom noticed me on the ground.

"Oh Benny," she said as she came over and picked me up even though she had one very sore arm. "See I'm OK." "Benny, Benny," she chanted as she hugged me closer and closer to her chest. This was typical of Mom. She had been badly hurt by The Old Man, but she only cared about the effect on us kids. We were everything to her. It was only us that kept her going. I just kept crying and hoped Mom would keep me in her embraces forever.

5 – Apples and Soup

The next day, it was quiet in the house when I got up. Mom was in the kitchen with Sissy. The Old Man had not yet shown himself for the day. Gordie was still in bed as well. I wasn't sure where everyone else was. Mom's arm was beginning to turn blue in parts. I didn't mention the day before and neither did Mom, but I knew she was thinking about it. She was a lot quieter than usual. After a while, The Old Man came into the room. He sat down at the table.

"I've learned my lesson now," he began. "I shouldn't drink. I'm not going to touch another drop again."

Mom looked at The Old Man but didn't say anything.

"No, I mean it this time," he pleaded. "I know I've said that before, but this time I mean it. I'm hurting my family. I don't know what got into me. I'm a lucky man. I have a great family that I'm very proud of. No, that's it for me. I can't drink beer anymore. It drives me crazy. That's the end of it."

"I only wish I could believe you," Mom replied.

"I swear on my dear dead mother's grave. I mean it. I'm finished with that stuff. I'm a changed man."

"I know you mean it now, but will you mean it the next time you have a few dollars in your pocket?"

"Yes, I'm done drinking. It's going to kill me if I don't

stop."

"I think you better apologize to Buddy," Mom added.

"Yeah, you're right. I'll do that later. I'm going back to bed, I don't feel well."

The Old Man got up from the table and headed upstairs. "Do you really think Dad will quit, Mom?" I inquired.

"I only wish it were true, dear," Mom answered. "I only hope."

A couple of weeks later, there was another incident which required Ernie to run to the Bullards'. This wasn't due to The Old Man drinking, however. So far he had kept his promise, although I don't think he had any money anyway (and he never did apologize to Buddy). No, this was something different. Again, Mom, The Old Man, Sissy, and I were in the kitchen. The Old Man decided to give Sissy a piece of apple to eat. But he didn't remove the peel like Mom usually did. All of a sudden Sissy made a choking sound. Mom grabbed Sissy and tried to loosen the apple, but she just kept making a wheezing sound while trying to catch her breath. "Ernie! Ernie!" Mom yelled. "Go to Bullards'. Phone the doctor!" We did not have a phone then. Ernie came running into the kitchen from the living room.

"What's the matter, Mom?"

"Run quickly, go phone the doctor," Mom repeated.

Ernie could see the trouble that Sissy was in, so he didn't need to ask anymore. He headed out the door.

"I'll go too!" I shouted as I raced out the door after Ernie. As I went out I could hear Mom cry out.

"Oh my God, Garf, she's turning blue!"

Ernie and I ran faster than we had ever run before, but still it seemed a lifetime before we got to the Bullard's, explained the problem, and had the doctor called. We then ran just as fast back to our house with John following us. Before we got to the house, we could see Billy running towards us.

"Sissy's OK, she's better now," he yelled to us as we kept on running. Billy turned and followed us back to the house.

As soon as we ran into the kitchen, Mom said, "She's going to be OK. Sissy is fine now."

"What happened?" we all asked at once.

"Your Dad got the apple out," Mom replied.

"I knocked it out of her," The Old Man said. "I hit Lily on the back and the apple came loose."

We found out that shortly after we had left, Sissy started to turn blue. The Old Man took her from Mom, turned her upside down, and slammed her on the back with his open hand. They heard Sissy make a gasping sound as she seemed to catch her breath. Then The Old Man put his finger in Sissy's throat and pushed the apple out of her mouth onto the kitchen floor.

Eventually the doctor arrived at our house. He said that Sissy would have died if The Old Man hadn't acted when he did. This was one time I definitely didn't wish he would go away.

I should add that a week later The Old Man was drinking again. He came into the kitchen with his case of 24 beer. He sat at the table with the case beside him on the floor and did not get up until every bottle was empty. This became standard procedure over the years to come.

In September 1954, I began school. I was only five years old. I wouldn't be six until the next March. But somehow Mom had talked the teacher into letting me start Grade 1. I think Mom became so tired with me bothering her about wanting to go to school, that she found it easier to convince the teacher to ignore the rules than to listen to me whine anymore. I could be an excellent whiner when I chose. I felt I was ready for school. With four older brothers to teach me, I had learned quite a bit. Also Mom always read to me. I had the books memorized and would correct Mom if she changed any words.

"Why don't you read it yourself if you know the story?" Mom asked.

"I can't read, Mom," I responded. "Besides, I like the way you read it."

I went to the school with Mom to convince the teacher that I was ready. I remember that she asked me if I could count. When I got to 100, I asked if she wanted me to keep going. Then she wanted to test my alphabet knowledge. I recited my A to Z's with no hesitation or omissions. Mom was glad I didn't have any additions. Usually when I got to the letter after 'O', I would say, "Where's Poo?" But not that day. I was too old for that silliness now. I liked the teacher, and she seemed to warm to me as well. I would be in the same classroom as my brothers. This was a one-room schoolhouse in the middle of nowhere in the country.

Before I started my education, Mom took me to the barber to get my first official haircut. Mom had trimmed my hair at home many times before, but this was my first visit to a barbershop. Mom was upset when she saw me climb up on the board on top of the arms of the chair. She didn't want to see me lose my long locks. But I was happy; I was a grown-up now. I would have hair like my older brothers. I just sat quietly (there was no idle conversation from me) and watched the curls land on the floor below. They were no longer blonde; I was turning into a brunette. I said my good-byes and left the shop as proud as a peacock. When I got home, I looked in the mirror and started crying. "I don't wanna get old. I wanna stay home with you forever, Mom. I'm never going to get married."

The first day of school, Mom wanted to take me to class, but I said, "No thanks, Mom. I just want to walk with Ernie, Billy, and Gordie."

"Have you got clean underwear and socks on, Benny?" Mom inquired.

"Yes, Mom. Who would know if I didn't, Mom? I'm not going to take my pants off."

"You never know what may happen. You could get sick then they would have to take you to a doctor. I wouldn't want them to see you with dirty socks. One thing I always say, we may be poor but we're clean. I don't want people to think I don't keep good care of you."

"Oh Mom," Ernie said. "If Benny was sick the last thing you would worry about would be his socks."

"That's true as light, Ernie. But you all better have clean underwear and socks on just the same. Or I'll take you over my knee." Mom laughed when she said this.

The walk to school was several miles along country roads. And yes, it was uphill both ways. There was a big dip in one of the roads with a hill on either side. I don't remember too much about the early lessons at school except that I didn't learn too much that I didn't already know. Things like telling time (remember there were no digital clocks then). But I was already experienced in telling time. I could read the time early in the morning when The Old Man was up drinking. He would be blaring Country and Western music from Wheeling, West Virginia on the big radio.

A few weeks after I started school, I had an accident that I would just as soon forget. I can't tell you what happened, but I found out where that missing letter after 'O' went. And it's a good thing I didn't get sick and have to go to the doctor. Poor Ernie got volunteered to walk me home. He walked me home with mixed feelings. Ashamed of what I did, but happy to be able to go home early. So he didn't complain too much. I was afraid of what Mom would say. Would she take me over her knee? However, the only thing she said was, "Don't worry, dear. Accidents happen." Then Ernie said, "Did you have soup for lunch?"

"No," I replied. "Why?"

"You know what they say," he said laughing.

"Campbell soup, makes you poop.

Down your leg and in your boot.

Across the floor and out the door.

Don't you wish you had some more."

Mom and I both got a good laugh over that one.

Mom must have had fun making lunch for the four of us. We all had our own special way that our sandwiches had to be cut. Mine had to be cut horizontal so that it formed two rectangles. No fancy triangular shaped pieces for me. They didn't taste near as good. The four of us did have one thing in common though. None of us ate the crust. We didn't want it cut off though. That would be sissy. We just ate around the crust and threw it in the garbage after we finished.

On October 15 of that year, Hurricane Hazel hit our farm. I remember the terrible noise of the wind as it howled around us. You could also hear many creaks, crashes, and bangs. Then there was the rain. I had never heard rain pound down like that before, or since. We were one of the lucky ones, though. The storm blew the door right off our barn into a field a few hundred yards away, but that was the only real damage. Even our white picket fence was still standing. The Bullards didn't suffer too much damage either. Some of our neighbours had the roofs of their homes ripped right off. I couldn't imagine what it would be like to have that happen. Also, a few farms had some of their livestock killed. We had heard that the storm was coming, so the Bullards and The Old Man had spent the day shoring things up. But so had almost everyone else. We were just lucky, I guess.

In December of '54, Buddy left home. He had traveled down to London to enlist in the Air Force. It was called the Royal Canadian Air Force (RCAF) at that time. He had gotten accepted for officer training. The whole family was both proud and happy for Buddy. Still it was a sad day when he left for training in Winnipeg. I remember that Mom was especially upset that day. Although Buddy would miss us all, I think he was happy to be leaving The Old Man behind. He certainly must have had his fill of him by this time. But Buddy was feeling guilty. He was getting out, but he was leaving us behind. He had taken on the role of helping Mom look after all of us. He had also acted as the protector for Mom on several occasions (as I described earlier). Ernie noticed both Mom and Buddy's concern. He looked at them both and said, "Don't worry. I'll take care of things now." Ernie was only ten but he had to grow up fast. Later that year, I remember Mom looking sad on Christmas Day. I asked her what was wrong. She just said, "It's our first

Christmas without Buddy. It doesn't seem the same." And she was right.

A few weeks later, I found out that we were moving. We were moving to some place called Woodbridge. I had never heard of it. I didn't want to go. The Bullard's farm was all I really knew. Whose tractor could I ride on now? Who could John have daily conversations with after I left? It wasn't fair. Why did we have to move so much? Then a few days before we were due to leave, Snowball disappeared. I guess she didn't want to go either. We never saw her again. But we still had two of her kittens – Smokey and Snowflake. And of course, there was still our dog, Lucky. The chickens stayed behind.

6 – Hitting the Highway

Woodbridge is a small town along Highway 7. It too is northwest of Toronto, but not as far north as Orangeville. It turned out that we actually lived in a farmhouse about a mile out of town. I hated it! I hated everything about it.

In truth, I can't really remember the house now. Actually, I do remember a windmill beside the house which I thought was kind of neat. We had electricity now, although that didn't really mean much to us. We didn't own any electrical appliances anyway. We still used a wood stove for heat and for cooking. Snowflake and Smokey would sleep in a wooden box behind the stove. They knew where the warmest spot in the house was. We did have lights now though. So we didn't have to get dressed in the dark, better for distinguishing the clean socks and underwear.

When we went to school, the four of us boys had to walk along Highway 7 which I was not too fond of. Far too busy for me. The walk was not as far as I was used to, and it was flat (both ways). Not near as much fun. We would walk in the ditch, much safer than on the road. Lucky used to meet us about half way home. I'm not sure how he knew when it was time for us to come home, but he always met us about the same distance from home. I remember one day after a big snowstorm, we walked along the large snow banks which the plow had created for us. I think it took us well over an hour to walk the mile home, but Lucky still met us in the same place.

I didn't like the school. It was way too big. It had four classrooms. So I was not in the same room as my brothers. I would be alone. And I had a man teacher. I don't think he liked me much. He couldn't understand what a five year-old was doing at school anyway. This was in January, a couple of months before I would be six. At first he told Mom I wouldn't be allowed to attend. Mom argued with him, while I did my patented screwed-up face look and started to whine. I was in class the next day. Again I was learning how to tell time. But also I was introduced to that fun-loving couple of kids – Dick and Jane. See Dick. See Dick run. See Jane. See Jane run. You can tell by my writing style, that these lessons weren't wasted on me.

In April, only a few weeks after I turned six, we were told that we were moving again. I hadn't even finished Grade 1 yet and I was going to my third school. But I was not sorry to be leaving. We were going to another town, further north, back towards Orangeville again. Mom said that it was called Alton. I had never heard of it. I never understood why we left there so quickly, after less than three months. It was because either (a) The Old Man had an argument with the owner or (b) he wasn't paying the rent. Or even more likely – (c) all of the above.

It definitely had something to do with debt. Because a few days before we moved, The Old Man announced that we were changing our name. When we got to Alton, we would no longer be the Cooper family; we would be the Hoopers. He showed me his new driver's licence with his new name – Benjamin Hooper. I'm not sure what irritated me the most; the fact that I had a different last name or that The Old Man stole my first name. Well almost anyway. My name is actually Bennett not Benjamin, but it was close enough. I was named after my Uncle Ben who quit school after failing Grade 3, and

I was proud of it. Mom didn't want me associated with Uncle Ben so she made sure that I was always referred to as Benny. If you called me Ben you faced the wrath of Mom. I didn't want people to think I was named after The Old Man. Better to be named after poor, harmless Uncle Ben. The other more important document that The Old Man had his name changed on was his liquor licence. In those days you had to have a licence to buy liquor in Ontario. If you had liquor offenses, your licence was revoked. So The Old Man must have done something which caused his liquor licence to be taken away – hence the name change. The driver's licence name change was just for backup. Or maybe he had that licence suspended as well; I really don't remember. Maybe I never knew. They didn't explain everything to me, after all.

However, this was one time that Mom stood up to The Old Man. She refused to go along with his little ruse. She said that he could use his new name if he wished, but there was no way the rest of us were changing our name. How could she even register us for school if there were no school records for Ernie, Billy, Gordie, and Benny Hooper? It just wouldn't work. So in April of 1955, we moved to the town of Alton still recognized as the Cooper family.

A day before we moved though, Snowflake disappeared. This was just like Snowball all over again. But this time there was a difference. Ernie and Billy found Snowflake on moving day. He was dead along the side of the road in front of the house. He had been hit by a car. However, we had continued to think that Snowball was still alive; that she just didn't want to move. She must have gone off with her other missing kittens to live a life in peace. But not poor Snowflake. So Smokey would be alone now, except for Lucky and us, of course. This was just another reason why I remember hating that place. I didn't even look back as we drove out of the driveway.

7 – A Bed of Thorns

This time, we did live right in town. Right on the main street too. The school was only a few blocks away, also right on the main street. The house was a large two-storey frame house that had been divided so that two families could live in it. We lived on one side of the house and the Browns lived in the other half. There was a door in our dining room which led right into the Browns' dining room. One good point about this setup was that we thought it might curtail The Old Man's nightly activities. It did – for awhile at least.

The Browns had two kids. A boy who was six (a few months older than me), and a girl who was eight (a couple of months older than Gordie). I don't recall either of their names now. But I do remember some things about them. The boy had not started school yet, and that was quite obvious. He couldn't count to ten yet and the alphabet had no meaning to him. But the first thing you noticed about him was that he still wore diapers. His sister though didn't wear diapers anymore. In fact, she didn't wear underpants either. She would only have her dress on. To her a fun time was to look at us, smile, and then lift her dress up above her waist. I only found it weird, but Gordie found it quite amusing. Neither one of them looked like they knew what a bathtub was. Mom sized them up quite quickly and didn't want us to have anything to do with them. So she forbade us to go next door to play with them. It was no loss to me as I didn't want to associate with them anyway. Although the boy was my age, we didn't have a lot in common. To him a fun time was to kick a cat. So we made sure we knew where Smokey was at all times. Besides, I had Gordie and Sissy (and Billy and Ernie) to entertain me. What did I need anyone else for?

Again, the school was very large – it had two classrooms. One class was grades 1 to 4 and the other was for grades 5 to 8. So I was in the same room as Gordie and Billy. As I said earlier, I was still in Grade 1, Gordie and Billy were in 3, and Ernie in 5. Although Billy was close to two years older than Gordie, they were in the same grade for two reasons. Gordie had started school when he was five like me; they wouldn't let Billy begin his education until he was six even though his birthday was in October. The other reason was that Billy repeated Grade 1. When we moved from Toronto it was decided that this was the best thing and Billy didn't argue too much because that put him in the same grade as Gordie. Anyway getting back to Alton, the first thing the teacher (a woman again, yeah!) asked us was, were we related to Gary Cooper. This became the standard question over the years. Everywhere we went, someone would say, "How's Gary?" We got tired of it, and started to tell people that Gary was our father. I don't think anyone ever believed us, but it was more fun to say that. Everyone always thought that they were the first to suggest the relationship to Gary Cooper, but my Grade 1 teacher (my third one) was the first. The first for me anyway; I'm sure the others had already heard this line a thousand times before.

About the middle of May, Billy got Whooping Cough. He had to be quarantined in his bedroom. So Ernie had to move into our room and sleep on the floor. When we came home from school, Gordie and I would throw pebbles at Billy's window to get his attention. We could only talk to him through a window or a door. He ended up missing over a month of school. Just as Billy got well enough to return to school there were only a few days of school left. So he ended up not passing his grade. Mom was very upset that the school was not more understanding considering the circumstances. She went to the school to complain but did not get very far. They said that Billy did not do well enough earlier in the school year. But with all the moves and then the Whooping Cough he didn't have much of a chance. Besides, Billy was a notorious second term performer. I mean he always did better in the second term; but, Mom couldn't win this argument. This upset Billy because now he would be a grade behind his younger brother Gordie. He would miss the great fun they had together.

During the summer, The Old Man took us to my first drive-in movie. I guess it wasn't a classic. I don't even remember what movie it was. Gordie and I had another game we played that summer. We stood on the lawn of our house, as cars went by our house and down the Alton main street. In the country, we weren't used to seeing that much traffic. The glare of the headlights would cast large shadows of Gordie and I on the white two-storey wall of the house. We pretended that we were watching a drive-in movie. We called Sissy to come outside as well. "Hey, Sissy. Come here." She would run around on the lawn, while Gordie and I laughed at her large distorted reflection on the drive-in theatre screen. We tried to get Billy and Ernie to join the movie cast, but they thought we were crazy and refused. When The Old Man came outside to see what Sissy was doing, we watched him as well. If we went to different parts of the lawn, we could make lots of different interesting shapes appear on the screen — as long as a car was going by, that is.

A few weeks later, The Old Man came home with our first television. It had a small black and white screen, but it opened up a whole new world to us. Maybe seeing Gordie and I watching our shadows on the wall made The Old Man realize that he had better get us something to watch before we went completely insane. We had seen some television programs before. The Browns had a TV, but as I said earlier, we weren't allowed to go to their place. Also, we had watched some TV at our Aunt June's place in Toronto when we went to visit a few times over the years. At that time, we received three channels. There was a Toronto station (CBC Channel 6) and two Buffalo stations (NBC Channel 2 and CBS Channel 4). We were introduced to the new wonders of The Howdy Doody Show, The Mickey Mouse Club with the Mouseketeers, and I Love Lucy. On Sunday nights there was The Walt Disney Show followed by The Ed Sullivan Show. And of course, on Saturday night, there was Hockey Night In Canada. It didn't start until nine o'clock then, so you always missed the first period. Gordie, Ernie, and I liked the Leafs; Billy had to be different and cheered for the Habs. Mom was a Leaf fan too. We were very excited about finally seeing some of the westerns that we had previously only heard on the radio, especially 'The Lone Ranger' and 'Gunsmoke'. Sissy was enthralled by the television as well. She would sit on the chamber pot right in front of the TV, so that she didn't miss anything. As you can guess, she beat our neighbour out of diapers.

Later that summer, Smokey had six kittens. She gave birth while lying in the wooden box with a blanket by the wood stove. I had never seen kittens being born before. Snowball had gone off somewhere else to have her babies. One kitten was white like Snowball. I called her Fluffy and claimed her for myself. I watched the newborn kittens all day. I was fascinated by them. I got up early the next day to watch them again. But there was only Smokey and Fluffy in the box. I couldn't find the other kittens.

"Mom, where have all the kitties gone?" I yelled.

"Your father took them away. You know he wouldn't let us keep all those cats."

"When can I see them again?" I wondered aloud.

"I'm afraid they're not coming back, dear. You've still got Smokey and Fluffy."

"But, I want them all back," I cried as I ran off to my

room.

I found out later from Ernie that The Old Man had drowned the kittens in a pail of water in the kitchen after I went to bed. Mom had rescued Fluffy; or else she would have met the same fate as her brothers and sisters. Although I eventually understood why we couldn't keep six kittens, I could never understand how someone could drown an animal like that. And I still don't.

In the fall of '55, I started Grade 2. Billy and Gordie were still in the same classroom as me, as Billy was in Grade 3 and Gordie was in Grade 4. Ernie was now all the way up to Grade 6. Also the Brown boy from next door had started school. I was glad to see that he had graduated from diapers now. At least during the day. He still wore one when he went to bed. Soon after, he turned seven. I remember the birthday party. I was invited and this time Mom let me go on the other side of the dining room door to attend the festivities. I remember we had cake and ice cream. Believe it or not, that was the first time that I had ever had that combination. It was a real treat. We only had ice cream on special occasions. So to have it and get your cake too was a real extravagance.

Later in the fall, I had a riding accident. Let me explain. We had a bed with a metal (iron, I think) headboard and foot-board. By we, I mean Gordie and me. I never mentioned this earlier; but in a large family, you don't have the luxury of your own bed – let alone a bedroom. I was always in the same bed as Gordie, while Billy and Ernie shared another bed. Sometimes we had different bedrooms, and sometimes all four of us were in the same room. In Alton, Gordie and I had our own room. I was riding on the foot-board pretending that I was Gene Autrey. Gordie was on the headboard. He was Hopalong Cassidy. All of a sudden, I felt a sharp pain in my foot. I knew it wasn't a rattlesnake. I looked down and realized that a sharp piece of metal was sticking out on one of the metal posts. I had stabbed the bottom of my foot on it. It didn't hurt too much and I wasn't bleeding, so I just decided to put my horse away for the night and go to sleep.

In the morning, Mom called out, "Ernie, Billy, Gordie, Benny, rise and shine, time to get up and get ready for school."

I went to jump out of bed, but my leg wouldn't move. "Gordie, Gordie," I called, "wake up. I can't move."

"What are you talking about?" Gordie answered back.

"My leg, my leg, I can't move it. Have a look at it."

Gordie pulled back the covers to reveal a foot and leg that had swollen to twice the normal size. "Holy cow," Gordie said. "Mom!" Gordie yelled out, "Come look at Benny's leg."

"What did you do that for Gordie? Mom will just get worried."

"Did you expect to crawl down the stairs and off to school without Mom noticing?"

"Maybe it would have gotten better itself," I responded.

"Yeah, and maybe you'll grow another one too."

At that time, Mom came into the room and saw my leg. "Oh my God, what happened, dear?" she questioned.

So Gordie and I recounted the story of our horse ride the night before. Mom looked at my foot and then at the bedpost.

"Poor dear little Benny, I better get your Dad to cut that off." She was talking about the metal burr on the post, not my leg. This again was not serious enough for a doctor. Mom applied a hot poultice to my foot made from bread and boiling water.

"This will suck the poison out of your foot," Mom said. And she was right. Before the others returned home from school, I could move my leg, and the swelling had subsided quite substantially. I also soaked my foot in a bath of Epsom Salts. I ended up missing about two weeks of school. I could walk around the house again after a couple of days, but my foot still hurt to stand on it too long. Also Mom wanted to make sure the infection had gone completely before I went back outside. So the poultice and Epsom Salts treatment continued for a while. By the time I went back to school, there were only a few weeks left before the Christmas holidays. I was worried that I might miss something important at school and I would end up having to repeat Grade 2 – just like what happened to Billy. But it turned out that I had no trouble catching back up to the other Grade 2 students.

A few days before Christmas, Mom told us that we had to move again. After several incidents where The Old Man got drunk and started cursing and swearing all night, the Browns had complained to the owners. And we were asked to leave. I didn't bother telling you about these events, because they weren't anything special. Just the usual screaming obscenities in the middle of the night. Things such as "Get up you lazy gray-haired old bag! What the fuck are you doing in bed already? Get up, and get me something to eat." And now he had the TV he could blare at night, as well as the old radio. It really ticked Mom off that we had to move because of the Browns. Here was a family that kept their household like a pigsty in every sense of the word, yet they complained about us. Mom would have never thought about complaining about the dirt and smell coming from their side of the house. So just a few weeks after Christmas, we were moving again. Back to a farm in the country where there were no close neighbours to hear the goings on at the Cooper household.

8 – The Bridge of Sighs

The farm that we moved to was another that I only remember by the owner's name – Lemongello. We, of course, always referred to it as the Lemon Jello place. This house was one of those sprawling old farmhouses that had many different additions added to it over the years. Each new section was a different colour and constructed from different material. You could go from the house to a small barn without even having to go outside. In between there was a tool shed, a back-kitchen, and several passageways. Inside the house, the setup was kind of weird. When you went upstairs you walked up through a hole in the floor with no railings or banisters into a large room. Ernie and Billy got this room. Then off of this room, there were two bedrooms. The larger one contained Mom and The Old Man's bed plus Sissy's crib. The smaller room became the home for Gordie and me. Also there was another huge room that you could enter from Ernie and Billy's room. This large room had no source of heat and was naturally ventilated. The walls in this room were just bare planks with cracks in between – like a barn; so it became our playroom. It was a great playroom because there was so much area to run, jump, and tumble in. The other rooms were heated the same way we were used to – by stovepipes coming from the large wood stove in the kitchen.

The first day that we went to school, we walked down our long driveway, turned left along the road until we came to a highway, turned left again and walked what seemed for miles to our new school. This school was in the small town of Cataract, still in the Orangeville area. The school was another four-room school; therefore, I was in a class without any of my brothers again. I was not bothered by that as much now as I was the last time. Although I was still only in Grade 2, I was a school veteran. This was my fifth school and fifth teacher. Actually my sixth, I think one of my teachers left before I did at one school. I forgot that, sorry. On our way home, we realized there was a faster way to get to and from school. A little while after we left Cataract, we cut across a gravel pit beside the highway, over some wooden rail fences, across a few more fields, up a hill and down the other side into our farmyard. This cut the travel time in half, except when the snow was four feet deep and soft.

I didn't mention it, but the Lemon Jello place did have electricity. All of our places had electricity from now on; it was just a phone we were lacking for quite a few years yet. Assume we had no phone until I say otherwise. Television started to become a bigger part of our life. Mom enjoyed it because it was a good way to forget about other things (such as The Old Man) and to sink herself into someone else's troubles and/or adventures. All of us kids from Sissy on up to Ernie could watch it for hours. I was allowed to watch TV until 10:00 o'clock before it was time for bed. That was the same time Gordie had to go to bed too. That's one of the advantages of older brothers, you get to inherit not only their clothes but their privileges as well. Poor Sissy, who was almost three, couldn't understand why she couldn't stay up as late as us. But I had just turned seven and considered myself to be quite grown up now. I no longer hid behind chairs when we had company. No, I just sat there and said nothing. Unless I was spoken to, then I would say one or two words. On Friday and Saturday nights, we got to stay up even later.

On Friday night at 11:30, wrestling came on. We would all watch it, including The Old Man. I loved it when the midgets came on. Little Beaver was great! Mom liked Whipper Billy Watson. We all did. We would all boo Gorgeous George. We all knew it was fake, but we enjoyed it just the same. I thought it looked real to me; but Gordie said it was fake, so I believed him. As I said earlier, I believed everything Gordie told me. Except for one thing. He told me there was no Santa Claus. I didn't believe him for a minute. I just got Christmas gifts from him a few months back, didn't I? Anyway, Billy told Gordie that wrestling was fake. And probably Ernie told Billy. With older brothers you become a cynic about things faster. We could see that some TV shows such as Roy Rogers weren't nearly as realistic as others. We laughed every time Trigger out ran the Jeep. I preferred Gene Autrey; Gordie liked Hopalong Cassidy. Those were real cowboys.

I remember one show that I used to watch where there was viewer interaction. Let me explain. You had to order this plastic screen and special felt pens from the show. It was a cartoon show. You put the plastic on the TV screen and then when the hero got into trouble, the narrator would say, "You must help our hero escape. He needs a rope. Please draw a rope down the cliff." And then he would climb down the imaginary rope and get away to safety. I don't remember the name of the show now, but I thought it was great. I ordered the kit so that I could become involved in the outcome of the show. The day the kit arrived in the mail, the show was cancelled and I never saw it anymore. Another TV accessory that I wanted to order was a kit to turn your black and white TV into colour. I saw it advertised on the back of a comic book. My brothers talked me out of it though. It turned out that it was just these plastic screens of different colours that you stuck on your TV set. I think Ernie knew someone who had ordered them.

The TV wasn't always a source of distraction though. Sometimes it became the centre of an argument. I remember one night when we were watching television, The Old Man was in the kitchen consuming his case of 24 beer – probably Brading's Red Cap. The case was in the usual location at his feet. Dragnet started to come on. Usually this was one of The Old Man's favourite shows. But you could never tell what his likes and dislikes were when he was drinking. About half way through the show, he came into the living room.

"What the hell's this shit you're watching?" he bellowed.

Sissy who was sitting on the couch with Mom, looked up and said, "It's Dragnet, Daddy."

"I wasn't talking to you. I was talking to the old bag, your mother."

Ernie then looked up and said softly, "Quiet please, Dad. We want to see the show."

And then the storm started.

"Don't you tell me to be quiet for Christ's sake. This is my house. I didn't fight in the war for nothing. I don't need any gray-haired old bag and her kids telling me what to do. I've been around the world; I know the score. If I wanted, I could put my foot right through that TV screen. I paid for that fucking TV. Who the hell are you to tell me what I can and cannot watch? What do you think I am – an eight-day clock or a sewing machine? Trying to tell me what to do! What the fuck's going on here? You goddamned gray-haired old whore. Don't you tell me what to do? I'm going to put my boot through that TV set, now! I paid for it."

At that point The Old Man headed for the TV, and we all started to move away from the expected explosion. But when he got to the TV, The Old Man just changed the channel and sat down on the couch.

"That's better," he said. I don't recall what show he switched to. "I don't need to watch that other shit with the shooting. I lived through that in the war. What would those poofs do if they had a real gun pointing at them? Probably all run like cowardly pussies. Did I ever tell you about that time in Morocco when an Arab pulled a sword on my good friend Greg Rivers? A big fucking sword. He was going to slice Greg's head off. I got down on my knees and pleaded for his life. I don't know if the Arab understood a word I was saying, but he put away his sword and let us go. Greg wouldn't be alive today if I hadn't stepped in. I saved his life. I wonder what Greg's up to now. He's in Toronto now, I think. We should go to see him sometime."

The Old Man continued talking on, but we had all gone upstairs at this point. We then all headed off to our beds without any discussion. I climbed into the bed as Fluffy crawled under the covers beside me; at the same time Gordie got in the bed as well. We didn't say anything to each other. Lucky was out in the other room with Ernie and Billy. Smokey was probably still in her box by the stove. I listened as The Old Man continued to grumble and mumble about everything under the sun. Then I heard him turn the TV channel back to Dragnet and he turned up the sound. I just pulled the covers over my head and tried to go to sleep.

The next day, The Old Man again swore that he was done drinking.

"I've learned my lesson now. That's it, Mary. I'm a changed man. I'm not touching alcohol again. I guess I'm someone who can't handle his drink. I love all of you. You know that, don't you Mary? It's the drink; that's what it is. Don't pay attention to what I said last night; that was the beer talking. I didn't know what I was saying. I know now, though. I'm through."

Mom tried not to encourage or discourage The Old Man. She had heard it too many times before to believe a word of what he was saying. But she didn't want to appear negative so that he could use that as an excuse to start up drinking again. She knew he would, but she didn't want to be the excuse. This had become the regular pattern. On paydays (every two weeks then), The Old Man would buy his 24 beer and drink it all in one night. Sometimes he would go out to a bar instead, and sometimes he would do both. The next day, Mom would describe The Old Man's changed attitude as "Butter wouldn't melt in his mouth." At this point he would often give his remaining money from his pay cheque to Mom. Then he would be a fairly normal father until he had more money to spend. A few times there wasn't a lot of money left. Mom had to make due with what money there was, but we wouldn't have been able to get by if it wasn't for the monthly Family Allowance cheques for each of us five children. Mom had to use the money she got for clothes, rent, utilities, the finance company, and food. What The Old Man spent was just for himself. A few days or a week later, The Old Man would ask for money to get beer. He couldn't understand why she wouldn't have any left. For this reason, Mom made sure the shopping got done soon after she received the money. We always ate well although there wasn't much cash for food. We would have a lot of stews and canned meat such as ham and corned beef. These were meals that could be stretched a long way. My favourite meal was bologna and beans, though. Bologna is the great Newfoundland staple. Mom often made homemade baked beans. Mom was a great cook. Another meal that Mom prepared a lot was what she referred to as 'boiled dinner'. It was corned beef, cabbage, potatoes, and other vegetables all boiled together in water in a large pot. We all liked this dinner but weren't too fond of the broth. The Old Man called it liquor. He would pour the liquor from the pot over some bread and eat it that way. We would screw our face up as he tried to get us to try it. "You don't know what you're missing," he would always say. He would do this until the pot was 'hempty' (as Mom would say). For dessert, we would often have a stopper. That's what Mom called cookies – homemade cookies. To us, homemade cookies were a regular event. So store bought cookies were a real treat. On weekends, Mom would often make pies or cakes. Mom made great pies; but we still didn't eat the crust.

In the spring of that year, Gordie and I left the school in Cataract with a friend of Gordie's. I have no idea what his name was now. I'm not sure where Billy and Ernie were that they weren't with us. But for some reason they had already left for home. Just outside of Cataract, before you got to the gravel pit that marked our point of crossing, there was an old dirt road. Gordie and his friend decided that day to go down this dirt and grass road. I followed them down the road until we came to an old bridge. As we started to cross the bridge it became evident that it was not an easy crossing. The bridge was full of gaps that stretched between the old planks which spanned the river below. After going less than a quarter of the way across the bridge, Gordie told me to go back.

"You shouldn't cross here, it's too dangerous for you," Gordie said.

"I'm OK, Gordie. I wanna go with you guys," I replied.

"No. It's too dangerous. You better go back. I'll meet you on the other side," Gordie insisted.

"How do I get to the other side then, Gordie?"

"Just go back the way we came. Out to the highway, then just before the gravel pit turn right onto the next road. That leads to the other side of the bridge. This is just the old highway. You can't get lost. Don't worry."

I now took it as a challenge to prove that I could find the other side of the bridge. I was a big kid now. Gordie didn't have to worry about me. I could find the other side by myself.

"OK, I'll meet you on the other side," I agreed.

So I headed back across the rickety old bridge to the dirt road. I retraced our steps to the highway, and then walked along the highway. It seemed like a long way and I was afraid that I had missed the next road when I saw it just before our exit to the gravel pit. I turned down the road and then walked what seemed a long way before I came to the bridge. I could not see Gordie and his friend anywhere. I thought that I had probably missed them because the walk around had taken so long; so I ran back to the highway to look for them. But I couldn't see them there either. I then ran back to the bridge and scouted the area there again. There was no sign of Gordie or anyone else. So I decided to wait. I waited for probably only a few minutes but it seemed like an interminable time to me. After this wait, I decided to call out.

"Gordie, Gordie, Gordie, Gordie! Where are you? Gordie, Gordie, I'm here. Gordie, Gordie!"

I kept this up for at least ten minutes; but again there was no response. I then decided to go out to the highway and search for Gordie there. Yet there was no one around. I then resolved to go back along to the other side of the bridge. Yes, obviously Gordie had given up the crossing and was making his way back the same way that I had come a short while earlier. Thus, I walked back along the highway to the other dirt road. I eventually reached the bridge without running into Gordie or anyone else. When I got to the bridge, I looked down to the river below. It was raging by quite rapidly due to the recent melting of the winter snow. Still there was no Gordie.

"Gordie, Gordie, Gordie!" I cried. And I mean cried. Gordie, my closest brother, my best friend was gone. I kept shouting out his name, but still there was no answer. Then, I thought of one last hope. "I must have taken too long to get to the other side of the bridge. Gordie has already gone home. He is probably worrying about me. Which means Mom will be worrying about me. I better get home as soon as possible."

So again, I walked quickly out along the old road to the highway. I then headed up the highway towards the gravel pit. As I passed the second entrance to the bridge, I had one last look to see if I could sight anyone. But again there was no one to be seen. I took the familiar climb up the hill beside the highway and started across the gravel pit to the adjacent fields. I had now convinced myself that there was nothing to worry about. Obviously Gordie had already left for home, thinking that I had decided to go back to the Lemon Jello place rather than meet them on the other side of the bridge. So thinking about Gordie getting home and worrying about me, I sped up my pace across the pit to the fields beyond. Worse still, Mom would be worried to death. I had to get home as soon as possible. However, as I stepped over the old wooden fence rails into the next field, it started to get foggy. Soon the fog had become very thick, but I kept walking in the direction that I had walked many times before. I began to realize that I had no idea how far I had walked. Where was the hill that led down into our familiar barnyard? I started to toss in my mind whether I should be worrying about Gordie or about the rest of the family worrying about me. My eyes began to fill with tears as I continued with these thoughts. Shortly, between the fog and the tears, I could not see where I was going at all. What little I could see had no familiarity to me. Now I was lost and I started to panic. I ran off in the direction that I thought was correct, nevertheless I could not get oriented. Absolutely nothing was familiar to me. I wandered aimlessly and then began to run in this direction and then that direction. I had no idea where I was. And where was Gordie? I decided to calm down and keep walking straight. I had to eventually reach another road or house. Then I saw a light. There was definitely a light shining through the fog. I headed towards the light. I had walked way too far. That was the light from another farmhouse. I had no choice but to head towards the strange house and ask for help. I couldn't find my way back home in this fog. I began to run towards the light. I wanted this nightmare of a day to end. As I got closer to the light, I heard a dog bark. And then it barked again. In a few seconds, the dog was upon me. It was Lucky. "Oh, Lucky," I cried "What are you doing here, but it's great to see you." As I kept walking closer to the light, I began to identify some shapes through the fog. The barn, the house, and everything else started to look familiar. I was home, I thought; yet, how could I be? I never went over the usual hill that led down to our place. But there was no question, I was home. I ran into the back-kitchen door and into the house. The first thing that I saw was Mom and The Old Man standing in the kitchen. When they saw me, their faces showed a look of great relief. I also then noticed Sissy who was standing beside Mom.

"Benny, where have you been?" Mom questioned immediately.

"Where's Gordie?" I responded. "Is he home?"

"Isn't he with you, Benny?" The Old Man asked.

"He's not home? Are you sure?" I replied as my voice began to crack.

The Old Man answered before Mom could say anything.

"He's not home, Benny. What is going on? Why are you so late?"

I started to cry and I could not control myself anymore.

"Gordie is gone! Gordie, he must be dead. Gordie's drowned" My voice was cracking so much and the sobs were drowning out my words. I don't think Mom or The Old Man heard a word that I was saying. Mom put her arms around me to settle me down, but that only made the sobbing more intense.

"What's the matter, Benny? Whattaya crying for?" Sissy asked.

The Old Man spoke again. "Calm down, Benny. Tell us what happened."

"Gordie is dead; Gordie is dead!" I repeated. And this time they understood what I was saying. Mom could not speak, she was afraid to speak. So The Old Man put his arms around my shoulder and tried to make some sense out of my ramblings.

"Tell us what happened, Benny. What happened? Where's Gordie?"

"He's in the river. He's dead. He can't swim. He must be dead."

"Benny, what river? Where? Did you see him fall?"

"By the old bridge, near the school. Gordie must have fallen through the big holes. He's drowned."

"Benny, again, tell me. Did you see Gordie fall in the river?"

"He's dead. Gordie's dead," I cried.

"Benny, answer your father," Mom said softly. "Did you see Gordie fall in the river? Please, think, tell us."

"No, I didn't see him fall. I didn't see him at all. But he must have drowned. He must have."

"Why, Benny? Tell us what happened," Mom asked again.

So I told them the story about how Gordie and his friend had asked me to meet them on the other side of the bridge. I related how I had waited and waited and had called and called. How I couldn't find Gordie anywhere. So he must have fallen in the river. That's the only explanation.

Ernie and Billy had entered the kitchen sometime after I had arrived. I had not noticed them come into the kitchen.

"We'll find Gordie," Billy said. "Don't worry, Benny. We'll find him."

"No, it's too late; He's dead," I insisted.

"Come on Billy, let's get going," Ernie said. "We've got to find out what happened to Gordie."

"I'm going too," stated The Old Man. "Mary, you stay here with Benny. Try to get more sense out of his story. We'll find Gordie, you'll see."

At that point we heard the back-kitchen door open. I looked up through my tear-filled eyes to see Gordie stroll into the kitchen whistling. I ran to Gordie and embraced him in a strong hug.

"Gordie, you're alive. You're OK. How did you get out of the river?"

Gordie had a look that expressed bewilderment. He had no idea what was going on. He looked up at the faces of Mom and The Old Man and uttered only two words.

"Oh, Oh."

9 – Mother's Day

Gordie and his friend had crossed the bridge, and then decided to take off and play. They forgot all about me. Gordie just assumed I would go on home and there would be no issue. For that assumption, Gordie was grounded for a while. He knew he was in trouble when even Mom was angry with him. But I wasn't mad. I was too busy being happy to see Gordie to feel any anger. When Gordie realized how scared I had been, he was very sorry for the entire episode. To me that was all the punishment he needed.

It was a beautiful sunny Sunday in May. It was Mother's Day, so Ernie and Billy decided to go for a walk along the road to pick some wildflowers to give to Mom. Gordie and I said that we would come too. We both wanted to get something for Mom as well. I had never given Mom a present for Mother's Day before. The four of us told Mom that we were going for a walk and would be back in a little while. Sissy made a fuss about wanting to come as well; so Mom convinced us to take our little sister along for the walk. Thus, the five of us headed down our laneway accompanied by Lucky. We turned right once we got to the dirt concession road in front of our farmhouse. Soon we saw wildflowers on both sides of the road. Ernie, Sissy, and I went to one side of the road while Billy, Gordie, and Lucky went to the other side. I started to pick a few flowers when I saw dust rising a short distance up the road. I turned to pick a few more flowers when I heard Billy yell.

"Lucky!"

I looked around just in time to see a car speed by, and then I heard a yelp and I saw Lucky go flying in the air. We all ran to look. The car left a trail of dust off into the distance as it continued on at the same speed. Lucky had landed in the opposite ditch. Billy was the first one to the scene.

"He's still breathing. Help him."

Ernie went up to Lucky with the intention of picking him up, but before he could act Billy lifted Lucky up into his arms.

"I'll carry him, Billy," Ernie said. "Let's get Lucky home, so we can take him to the vet."

"No. I'll carry him," Billy insisted.

"How come the car didn't stop? Didn't they see Lucky get hurt?" I wondered.

"They saw him all right," Billy said. "They just didn't give a shit."

Ernie and Billy started walking back to our laneway. Lucky was cradled in Billy's arms. Lucky was not a small dog; as I mentioned earlier, he had mainly collie blood. In spite of Lucky's weight, Billy was walking faster than the rest of us. I grabbed Sissy's hand and said, "Come on Sissy, let's hurry." While we were walking, I continued to think about the people in the car seeing Lucky get hit while five kids were watching. And still they wouldn't stop to help. I couldn't understand it. As we turned back into our laneway, Lucky stopped breathing; but Billy kept walking with tears streaming down the side of his face. When we got to the house, Billy gently placed Lucky on the grass near the door. The five of us stood in a circle looking down at Lucky. All of us now had tears in our eyes.

"I guess Lucky wasn't so lucky after all," I observed.

"The bastards. They didn't even stop. Just hit and run.

Those bastards," Billy wept.

And we all had to agree with Billy. They were bastards.

Later that summer, we decided to have some fun. The grass on the hill overlooking the back of the farmyard had just been cut leaving piles of grass along the side of the hill. The Old Man told me that I could play with the grass if I wanted. So I took a small child's wagon out of the farm shed and went back to the hill. I loaded as much grass as I could onto the wagon and pulled it down the hill into the shed. Soon Gordie joined in to help along with Sissy. After a while Billy started carrying grass as well and eventually we even recruited Ernie. We got more containers out of the shed so that we could bring more and more grass into the shed. We kept this up for several hours until we had a large stack of grass in the shed that reached almost to the roof. I thought it looked great. Then all of us jumped into the pile and attempted to climb up to the ceiling. But we kept sliding down again. It was great fun. Before long, the entire shed was covered with grass from one wall to the other. At that point, The Old Man came out to see what we were up to. He entered the shed and had one look at the mess before speaking.

"What's all this? What is all this grass doing in here? Mr. Lemongello won't be too happy."

"But you said I could play with the grass, Dad," I protested.

"But I didn't mean the whole field, Benny. How did you get all this in here?"

"I had some help, Dad," I answered.

"I helped him, Daddy," Sissy volunteered.

"Well, you'll have to put it all back in the field tomorrow before Mr. Lemongello has a fit. But it looks like you're having fun anyway," The Old Man added just before he leapt into the middle of the large pile of grass. He did not stay long but we were happy that we could play in the grass for the rest of the day. The next day, we all gladly returned the grass to the side of the hill where we found it. The Old Man even helped us.

A few weeks later, I had another mishap involving my foot. But this time it wasn't a riding accident; it was a walking incident. While playing in the barn, I stepped on a piece of lumber with a nail sticking up out of it. I jabbed the nail through my shoe and half way up my foot. No big deal, though. Some more poultice treatments and Epsom Salt foot baths, and I was soon 'right as rain' – as Mom would say.

I was better before school started, so I was able to start Grade 3 on the first school day in September. Ernie was now in Grade 7 and Gordie was in Grade 5 (the Grade 5-6 class), while Billy was in Grade 4. Therefore, Billy and I were now both in the 3-4 class; and I was no longer alone. As always, I was the smallest one in the class. Not only was I the youngest in the class, I was short for my age. If everyone had been my age, I would have still been the smallest. All the girls were taller than me too. The teacher (a man once again) went down the roll call and after he called out "Benny Cooper," he said, "are you related to Billy Cooper?" The question threw me a bit; I was expecting the usual "Are you related to Gary Cooper?" So I hesitated a second before answering.

"Uh, umm, yes, Billy is my brother. Uh, umm, why?"

"I was just hoping that you're not going to be as much trouble as Billy, that's all."

"I'm Gordie's brother too," I volunteered.

"Yeah, he was no trouble; but it's Billy over there that I remember the most."

I didn't say anymore. I didn't want to get labeled one way or the other just yet. Let him judge me for myself. I never did really understand what it was about Billy that got his shorts in a knot. After all, both Gordie and Billy had passed their years. Billy didn't understand it either. I didn't tell Mom what the teacher said. It was just between us boys. Everyone told me that Grade 3 was the most difficult, and I soon learned that they were right. This was the year that we began Social Studies. That's what they called History and Geography combined into one subject. It was too much memory work for me. Also in Grade 3, arithmetic got more complicated. But I had no trouble with that. To me it was just common sense; I didn't have to remember dates or anything like you did for Canadian History. Furthermore, English became more involved. There was Literature (no more Dick and Jane), Grammar (I couldn't follow most of the rules – you may have noticed), and Spelling (not too bad as long as you crammed the night before). And now of course, there was homework. Yuck! I had too much playing to do for that.

Just as I thought that I was getting the hang of this challenging year, we were told that we were moving once again. It was about time, I guess. We had been at the Lemon Jello place for close to nine months. Enough time for The Old Man to wear out his welcome. As our next door neighbour in Halifax used to sing, "I'm moving on." Yes, I didn't mention it before, but Hank Snow was our neighbour, and Buddy used to play with his son. The Old Man, being a shrewd judge of talent, told Hank that he had better look for another line of work.

A few days before we were due to move, I walked into the kitchen to see Mom by herself crying.

"What's the matter, Mom?" I asked. I thought that she was sad about moving again, so I added "Don't worry, we'll be OK at the new house. You'll see."

"It's not that, dear," she responded. Then I noticed that she was holding something. It looked like a letter or a telegram. "It's Grandma," she continued. "Remember I told you that she's been very sick lately. Well, she's gone now, dear."

"Did she die, Mom?"

"Yes, I'm afraid so, Benny. You won't see her anymore."

"Just like Lucky, you mean."

"Yes, just like Lucky," Mom replied as I put my arms around her so that I could comfort her. Like she had done for me so many times before.

10 – Bullies and Ghosts

So in the fall of '56, we moved again; but this time the reason was different. The Old Man had a brand new job. The best part about this new job was that The Old Man now only got paid once a month which meant fewer times that he would be drunk. He had gotten a job with the telephone company as a lineman. His job was to climb telephone poles to repair and install lines. This task suited The Old Man to a 'T' because he could shimmy up a pole without a belt or climbing spikes. He usually wore the safety equipment but he didn't really need it. He said that his experience in the merchant marine had taught him how to climb up masts. And he had no fear. So The Old Man was now a telephone man but we still didn't have a phone.

We moved to another farm that was closer to Orangeville. Its address was R.R. # something or other Orangeville; however, we always referred to this place as Robertsons' – the owners of course. The Robertsons were two older women who lived on a farm across the road from us. The farm was larger than what I was used to. It was about 75 acres, but the land wasn't being farmed at the moment. There was a long tree-lined laneway which wound up from the dirt concession road to the house. Although we only rented the farmhouse, we had access to the entire farm including a large barn, a chicken coop, open fields, a small evergreen forest, ravines, and many other things that I can't remember just now. This soon became a grand playground for the Cooper boys and girl.

The house was an old stone farmhouse that looked fairly large from the outside. Although it was large, the four of us boys still shared the same bedroom. But it was a huge bedroom. We had the two double beds in that room – one for Ernie and Billy and the other for me and Gordie. Our bed was on the left with both of them facing towards the door; and in-between the beds was the ever-present stovepipe. On Ernie and Billy's side there was a window which overlooked the yard. Right beside my side of the bed, there was another window which looked down into an old storeroom that we were told to stay out of. It had a padlock on the door to ensure that we followed that rule. Of course, our curiosity made us wonder what could be hidden in this secret room. When we looked down into the room from the window we couldn't really make much out. It just looked like some old furniture and a clutter of junk. Sissy now had her own room even though she was still sleeping in the same wooden crib. It was a pretty small room though. Mom and The Old Man's room was a fair size but not near as large as our big bedroom. Downstairs, there was a large kitchen, dining room, and living room. Like most old farmhouses there was also a wooden back-kitchen attached to the house. In the dining room there was an old pump organ. Mom would occasionally play the organ. I had never seen her play before so I enjoyed that part, but I didn't enjoy the fact that she would insist on us four boys singing along to her accompaniment. She was very proud of our singing. I usually kept my voice low and let Ernie, Billy, and Gordie drown me out. I could carry all of my brothers farther than I could carry a tune.

The school was located a couple of miles up the concession road to the left of our farm. We were going back to a one-room schoolhouse which had a large pot-bellied wood stove at the back of the classroom which provided the heat on winter days. Our teacher was a young woman named Miss Evans who couldn't have been any older than her mid-twenties. She was also fairly short. She was extremely tall compared to me of course, but some of the Grade 8 students were quite a bit bigger than her. One of these students was a boy who was close to the age of eighteen and was well over six feet tall. His name was Woody. Poor Woody had trouble graduating from public school into high school. This was his third attempt at Grade 8. In Grade 5 along with Gordie, there was Henry. I'm not quite sure how Henry got as far as that grade. I don't know how old he was, probably around fourteen. But Henry definitely had a learning problem. And then there were the Wells – two brothers and one sister. All three of them were trouble, and if you tangled with one you had all three to face. The oldest was Allan, who was sixteen and in Grade 7 with Ernie. We quickly found out that Allan Wells ruled the playground at recess and lunchtime. He ordered all the other kids around, and they would do whatever he told them to do. His personal henchman was Henry; he would jump when Allan said jump. The one student that Allan didn't mess with was Woody. Woody towered over everyone including Allan. But Woody was a pretty quiet, gentle guy who did not interfere with Allan's escapades. In the middle, there was Donna who was in Grade 4 with Billy. She was eleven, the same age that Billy would be in a few days. She considered herself to be as strong as any boy, which was probably true. The youngest was Max who was in Grade 2, seven years old (my age), and only about an inch taller than me. He weighed quite a bit more than I did though. You could have called him chubby, but he was known as Mighty Mouse. Not that he was that tough however, because whenever he started a fight, Allan or Donna would finish it for him. I was regretting having to spend the next school year with the Wells and as it turned out with good reason.

A few weeks after we arrived at Robertsons' farm, The

Old Man brought home a surprise for us – another dog. He was a real mutt, the Heinz 57 variety. He was a medium sized dog that had no recognizable main bloodline. We fell in love with him right away. He seemed so excited to see all of us Coopers that he ran in circles, jumped, and generally played games with us.

"He's a right playful dog," Mom commented.

"What shall we call him?" I asked everyone.

"We should call him Happy," Sissy answered first, "because he's so happy to see us."

So we all agreed, and Happy became the most recent member of the family joining Smokey and Fluffy at Robertsons' – our new large playground.

It didn't take long to experience my first confrontation with the Wells. In the middle of October 1956, many of the younger students were playing Red Rover at lunchtime. We never went home at lunchtime as it was too far to walk home and then back to school in the hour allotted for the break. So during lunch, I always enjoyed my rectangular shaped sandwiches (sans the crust), and then it was time to play. We had to eat our lunch in the classroom and then go outside to play. Once we were finished eating, we had no choice but to go outside, even in the winter. On this particular day, I had already finished eating and was now playing Red Rover with a bunch of my classmates. When it became my turn, I took off as fast as I could to get through the other line. I certainly couldn't use my strength to break through; but because of my size, I could often sneak under their outstretched arms if I dove fast enough. So that's what I tried to do this time, however I didn't notice until it was too late that one of the arms that I was diving under belonged to Max Wells. As I went under the arms, I thought I had made it through when Max let go of his grip and jumped right on my back. One of his fat knees smashed into the small of my back causing me to lose my breath. I don't get angry very often, but when I do I don't care whom I'm facing. After I caught my breath, I jumped up and yelled at Max.

"You jerk, what are you trying to do? You cheated."

"Who are you calling a jerk and a cheat, you little shrimp?" was his reply.

I didn't respond, I just started to walk back to my own line.

"Shrimp, shrimp, you're a gutless shrimp," he taunted.

And then he started to come after me. I turned around just to push him away from me, but instead I ended up shoving him over the leg of another boy, causing him to fall flat on his back. He quickly jumped up and came at me with his fists flailing in all directions. I ducked and dove for his legs knocking him to the ground once more. This time he fell awkwardly and knocked the wind out of himself. He got up slowly, but this time instead of coming after me, he ran off in the opposite direction.

"You're gonna be sorry, shrimp. I'm going to get Allan. Now you're gonna get it good. You'll see shrimp," he sobbed as he continued running to the other side of the schoolyard.

I looked around, but couldn't see any of my brothers to help me. It was a fairly large yard with the schoolhouse located in the middle, so they could have been anywhere. Before I could locate any of them, Max was returning with Allan at his side. I heard Allan speaking to Max.

"Show me the kid that's been bothering you, Mighty Mouse."

"There, that kid there. The little shrimp."

Allan looked at me and laughed. "What, that little shrimp? You've got to be kidding."

"Yeah, he punched me in the face and jumped on me. Take care of him, Allan."

Before I could protest Max's version of the story, Allan looked at Max with a stern look on his face and spoke.

"If you want to be Mighty Mouse, you'll have to be a better fighter than that. I'm ashamed of you for getting beat by a little shrimp like that. Now, get out of here before I whop you a good one, too."

Max looked at Allan, but dared not say anything as a

rebuttal. He just turned and started to go away. At the same time, I saw Ernie and Billy heading towards us to see what had caused the crowd to gather around our corner of the yard. As I started to walk away as well, Allan stepped in front of me and spoke softly into my ear.

"I let you off easy this time, shrimp; but the next time you're dead. Understand?"

I just nodded my head to let Allan know that I understood only too well. By the time Ernie and Billy arrived, Allan had already left.

"What was that all about?" Ernie questioned.

"Oh, nothing. I'll tell you later," I responded as Miss Evans rang the bell to commence the second half of the day's learning.

A few weeks later, some strange things started to happen at home. I woke up in the middle of the night on a cold November evening experiencing that eerie feeling one gets when someone is watching them. I looked around the room as best as I could in the dark letting my eyes adjust, but I couldn't see anything. All of my brothers seemed to be sound asleep. So I turned on my side to go back to sleep when I caught something out of the corner of my eyes by the storeroom window. I then looked at the window to see the face of a man staring back at me! It was the face of a middle-aged man with a big black handlebar moustache and his face seemed to be partially illuminated. I softly called "Gordie," but he didn't stir. I was going to wake Gordie up when I realized that there was no way a man could look in that window. It was a second storey window overlooking the first floor storeroom below. So I did the only sensible thing one should do when you are scared out of your senses; I closed my eyes and pulled the covers over my head. I just lay there and listened. But I didn't hear a sound. Eventually after about an hour I went back to sleep. When I awoke in the morning, I immediately told Gordie, Ernie, and Billy all about the man in the window. We looked through the window and inspected the padlock on the door. Everything seemed as it was before.

There were no signs that anyone had been around. Therefore we all agreed that I had dreamt the entire episode. We did not believe in ghosts.

Less than a week later, I suddenly awoke during the night with that same feeling that I had sensed a few nights before. This time the first thing that I did was dive under the covers to safety. I then decided to get brave, so I turned on my side and slowly lifted the edge of the covers in order to peer at the window. There was no face in the window. I breathed a sigh of relief and flipped the covers back down and off my head. Then I saw the man. He was standing at the door to our room. It was the same man with the black handlebar moustache wearing some kind of old military uniform. For a moment I froze, not knowing what to do. Finally, I called out.

"Hello, who's there? What do you want?"

I received no reply and the man did not move. So for the second time I dove under the covers to a safe haven and listened. All I could hear was the beating of my heart. I nudged Gordie and whispered his name, but he did not acknowledge either of my prompts. So I just laid still. I wondered where Fluffy was. I wished she was under the covers with me to comfort me. This time I think it must have been two hours before I finally went back to sleep. When I awoke in the morning, I decided I was not going to tell my brothers about this latest visitation. However, I cannot keep something to myself very long, so a few minutes after everyone was awake I related what I had seen. This time they did not bother to spend the investigative time. Although they believed that I thought I saw what I saw, they still considered it a bad dream. They used the fact that I could not awaken Gordie as proof that I must have dreamt the entire thing.

"And I draw your attention to the curious incident of the dog in the night-time," added Ernie.

"Happy did nothing in the night-time," I stated.

"That was the curious incident," remarked Ernie.

But I knew that I was awake. Only Billy thought that

there might be more to the story. Later that month, Billy informed us about a weird occurrence that he had witnessed during the night. He woke up for the same reason that I had twice before. So he decided to scan the room to see if he could get a sight of the strange nocturnal visitor. He looked over at Gordie's and my bed to see a man sitting on the edge of the bed facing towards him and Ernie. When he looked again he realized it was not the mustachioed man but only Gordie.

"Gordie, what's the matter?" he inquired.

Gordie did not reply. And then Billy noticed that there were two people lying in our bed – Gordie and me. At the same time, the other Gordie started to move closer to Billy. His body didn't budge from the position on the side of the bed; however, his head edged closer and closer to Billy enlarging as it traveled across the gap between the two beds. At this point, Billy remembered my heroic response and slid under the covers and took the extra precaution of burying his head under a pillow. Then Billy, just like I had, waited for something to happen or morning to arrive, whichever came first. And the same as me, Billy eventually went back to sleep before the sun rose to signify the start of a new day.

Now we all agreed that there was something weird going on in this house that we had to figure out, and we knew the secret must lie behind the padlocked door of the storeroom. However, before we could take any action, December arrived and our thoughts turned towards Christmas. Mom had received a letter from Buddy saying that he was coming home for a few weeks to spend Christmas with us. We were all excited about seeing him again. I could hardly remember what he looked like. Buddy had been commissioned as a Pilot Officer earlier that year and had been transferred to Cold Lake, Alberta, but now he was stationed at Uplands Air Base which is near Ottawa. So he was able to come home for Christmas for the first time since he had left two years earlier. I had become very excited about Christmas and had perused the Simpsons' catalogue to choose what presents I wanted from Santa. One day I saw Mom looking through the catalogue in order to choose what items she could order for us kids. I suddenly noticed that she was going to order the present I wanted from Santa, and I questioned what Mom was doing.

"No, you don't have to order that Mom, Santa will bring it to me."

"We still have to help Santa choose, dear."

"I know why!" I cried. "There is no Santa Claus, is there?"

I went off crying to my room before Mom could answer. I finally believed what Gordie had told me much earlier that year. Now, I could believe everything he told me again.

Around the middle of December, we had a major snowstorm that deposited several feet of snow. In the schoolyard, we had created snowmen and (most importantly) snow forts. So at recess and lunch we would have snow fights between the various forts. This involved mainly the younger kids until the last day before the Christmas break, when Allan Wells decided to join the fray. I and about three other boys were in one fort, while four or five others were in another stronghold a snowball's throw away. Suddenly without warning, Allan and about six other older boys appeared on the scene and started to pelt our fort with snowballs. Henry had been recruited as one of the hurlers and I am sure the others were threatened with dire consequences if they didn't join in the 'fun'. Anyway, the force of the snow began to hurt especially when they hit us in the head, so we began to try and cover up to avoid the worse of the bombardment. Eventually, we all dropped to the ground but the barrage did not stop. We laid with our arms over our head as the snow bombs hit us all over. One boy started to cry while another shouted out for them to stop. We all expressed the fact that they were hurting us. The cry for them to cease though only increased the amount of fire and the force of their throws. They were now standing right above us and pelting us with all their strength. We just waited for the attack to end. Now we were hurting not only from the power of the missiles but from the cold as well. Just as I decided I couldn't stand it anymore, they stopped. I hadn't heard or seen anything, but Ernie and some other boys had come to our rescue. I'm not sure how they persuaded Allan and the others to halt. Probably Allan was just bored with this particular brand of torture about the time that Ernie arrived on the spot. Ernie helped me to my feet and asked how I was doing. But I could hardly catch my breath, let alone talk. I just nodded to let him know that I would be OK. Then, I noticed that Allan was still nearby.

"One last thing, don't anyone tell Evans or anyone else about any of this, or this will just seem like a picnic."

No one answered Allan.

"Do you hear?" he demanded.

"Yeah, we hear," one or two boys answered.

"Do you hear, shrimp?" Allan repeated as he looked right at me.

I still couldn't get up enough strength to reply, so I just nodded.

"Shrimp! Are you listening?"

Ernie replied before I could. "Yeah, he heard. Now leave him alone or I'll tell the world, including the police."

"Oh, you scare me," Allan responded facetiously. "You'll be next if you don't watch out."

"I'll be waiting," Ernie said as he led me back towards the school without looking back to give Allan a chance for another retort.

That night we had to go back to the school for the Christmas pageant. Mom could see that I was not looking forward to the evening.

"What's the matter, Benny? Are you worried about the play or the singing?"

"Neither, Mom. I only have a few lines in the play and I memorized those long ago. I'm not worried about singing 'Hark, the Herald Angels Sing' because Ernie, Billy, and Gordie will be with me."

"Then what's wrong, dear?"

So, hesitantly at first, I told Mom all about what had happened at school that day. Then I told her everything about the Wells. About Allan, Donna, and Max. I even told her about my fight with Max earlier that year.

"Why haven't you told Miss Evans?" Mom wanted to know.

"We can't, Mom. That will just make things worse. Allan will be even worse to me and Billy and Gordie and Ernie too. We can't tell. Besides, what can Miss Evans do? She is afraid of Allan as well. He will just cause trouble for her, too. No, Mom. Please don't tell anyone, especially The Old Man. We will just have to work things out ourselves. Don't worry about me. Ernie and Billy and Gordie will take care of me. Everything will be OK."

Mom agreed reluctantly, at least for now.

So we all went to the school Christmas show that night including The Old Man. I was not looking forward to seeing any of the Wells family; however, fortunately none of them showed up at the event. Also I was afraid that Mom might talk to Miss Evans and say something if the teacher asked how we were getting along at our new school. But that fear was groundless as well. I should have known that Mom wouldn't have said anything, after all she had given her word. The Cooper rendition of Christmas caroling went off without a hitch. I made sure that no one could hear my voice. I didn't want to ruin my brothers' efforts. The play was also a success. It was about some family and their Christmas tree. I made my appearance in the last scene. I was dressed as a cop and I had to arrest the bad guy played by the school's friendly giant, Woody. The police hat that I was wearing came halfway down my ears. I remember the laughter from the crowd as I handcuffed Woody and led him off to jail. I don't remember what else the play was about except for my small (excuse the pun) part. In the car, returning home after the evening's festivities, Sissy summed up my performance.

"You sure are funny, Benny."

"Yeah, I thought I was going to split my pants laughing when you came out dressed as a cop," added The Old Man.

"You were excellent, dear," said Mom. "All of you boys did well. I am proud of you all. It was wonderful to see the four of you together on that stage."

"I still think we should have sung 'Jingle Bell Rock'," commented Ernie. "Now that's a great Christmas carol."

The Bobby Helms' song was a big hit that winter. But I didn't mind what song we did; I just grinned and said nothing. The night had turned out way better than I had expected.

On Christmas Eve, we were all eagerly awaiting Buddy's arrival. It was ten o'clock, time for bed and he hadn't got there yet. But Mom let us all stay up, including Sissy, and shortly thereafter we saw the lights of a car come up our long driveway. It was Buddy. And he had a carload of Christmas gifts. At least it looked like a lot to me. I had never seen so many presents under the tree. This was the first time that I had seen the tree decorated with all the presents piled underneath before Christmas morning. I thought it was great. Even though I knew that Santa wasn't coming down our chimney into our wood stove, I had never been so excited about a Christmas. The Old Man had been drinking of course, but because he also had been looking forward to seeing Buddy again, he was behaving himself – so far. After the contents of the car had been emptied, it was time for bed. We hung our stockings and went up to our large bedroom. I didn't sleep a wink. Fluffy crawled into the bed beside me, but unlike me she had no trouble sleeping. I was awake all night with no thoughts about anything except Christmas morning and wondering what all those presents could be. I didn't even think about our nocturnal visitor.

We got up at six in the morning and started on the stockings. I remember a great surprise – a tangerine. I am serious; I had never had a tangerine before. I ate it right away and thought it was delicious. I've never had a tangerine since that tasted as good as that one. I'm not sure where Mom got it, she said it came from Santa. I had to go along with that story because Sissy was still a believer even if I no longer gave credence to the existence of the jolly old man. Next came the presents. In the package marked 'From Santa', there was the gift I wanted the most. The one I saw in the catalogue – a gun and holster just like Gene Autrey's. For Buddy, it was a Christmas for giving building materials. I got a canister full of little red bricks called Mini-Bricks. It also had doors, windows, and roofing so that you could spend hours constructing all kinds of different houses and other buildings. Gordie got a set of red, white, and blue bricks called Uni-Blocks. They could be used to create all kinds of different structures and forms. You could create airplanes and other vehicles, but best of all you could create robots. Billy received a set of wooden logs which could be used to build many differently shaped log cabins. Sissy received something which allowed her to play house. A small wooden dining room table with two chairs. Sorry, but I don't remember what Ernie got.

Later that day I heard an argument coming from the kitchen. I quietly went over to the door to find out what was going on. It was Mom and Buddy.

"Now, what could they be arguing about," I thought. So I listened some more. I heard Mom's voice first.

"If I hadn't had done that Buddy, there wouldn't have been any presents from Santa Claus. How do you think Sissy would have felt if Santa hadn't of come? Did you see the look on Benny's face when he opened that gun and holster? He's been talking about it for months. I couldn't disappoint him and Sissy. Maybe the others would have understood, but no, I had no choice."

"But that money was meant for you Mom. For your glasses and teeth. You've given so much to me, to all of us. I want to give something back."

"I'm sorry dear, but I'd rather go blind and have no teeth than have the kids go without Christmas. You know that."

"I understand Mom, and I love you for it. But you need your teeth and glasses. OK, I want you to promise me that you will put aside some of the money I send you each month for yourself. Promise?"

"Well, I don't know what could happen, we..."

"Promise," Buddy repeated before Mom had finished.

"OK dear, I promise. Next year I will get my teeth."

"And glasses," Buddy continued.

"All right, Buddy. I'll get both next year. I promise."

"Thanks Mom. I'm sorry I got cross with you. But you've got to think about yourself sometimes too."

I then left to go play without eavesdropping anymore. For quite a while after, I couldn't play with my gun and holster without thinking about how it should have been Mom's teeth. When I mentioned this conversation to the others, Ernie said that they already knew about Mom spending the money meant for herself on us.

"Where did you think Mom got the money, Benny?" Ernie asked. "You know that there's no Santa Claus now."

"Yeah, I know. I just didn't think about it, I guess."

I didn't tell Sissy. No use making her feel guilty, besides she didn't think Mom had to buy the gifts anyway. Santa was generous enough.

On Christmas night The Old Man got drunk again. He was located in his usual spot in the kitchen, beside his case of Red Cap. The rest of us were in the living room watching some Christmas show on TV. We had heard him mumbling to himself when suddenly his voice got considerably louder.

"Where the hell's the gray-haired old bag? Leaving me out here alone on Christmas. What the hell is she up to? Probably out whoring around again. Goddamn that old bag."

We then heard a bang and the sound of a beer bottle rolling across the kitchen floor.

"Goddamn it! Where are you, old bag?" The Old Man yelled. "Get the hell in here!"

Mom started to get up to go into the kitchen but before she was on her feet, Buddy jumped up and spoke.

"Stay here, Mom. I'll go talk to him."

He was in the kitchen before Mom could say anything in

reply. The first voice we heard was that of The Old Man's.

"Oh, Brad, Buddy. How are you doing? I love you. Come have a drink with me."

"OK, Dad. I'll sit and have a beer with you as long as you leave Mom alone."

"What are you talking about Buddy? You know I wouldn't hurt your mother. I love her dearly."

"Well, you sure have a funny way of showing it sometimes."

"Sometimes she makes me angry that's all. That fucking old bag."

"Dad! Do you want me to drink with you or not?"

"OK, OK, don't leave. Let's talk about something else. Did I ever tell you about the war, Brad? Did you hear the story about how I begged for Greg Rivers' life? A big fucking Arab was going to slice his head off."

Buddy didn't let on that he had heard the story before, many times. He just let The Old Man continue on with his anecdotes. The Old Man finished the Morocco story and then started on another tale that was familiar to us all.

"The Germans were shooting at us from every direction. I arrived on deck just in time to see a charge go off right by the big gun. We were just a merchant marine ship, so we didn't have a lot of firepower. We counted on the other ships around us for protection. But we were out- numbered this time. So I had to go man the gun. I aimed and had a perfect hit. I shot the flag right off our mast."

At this point, The Old Man began laughing. The war stories continued for a few hours as Buddy sat at the table listening to The Old Man retell events that Buddy could have told just as well. But at least this kept The Old Man occupied and away from Mom. Also it helped reduce his beer supply faster. He eventually fell asleep at the table and Buddy dumped the remaining beer and crept off to bed. Thus Christmas '56 concluded without too much more ranting and ravings from The Old Man.

A couple of months later, in late February during lunch

break, I became embroiled in another argument with Max (Mighty Mouse) Wells. I have no idea what started the confrontation, now. Not that any of the Wells needed an excuse for a conflict. They were always looking for something to happen. Anyway for whatever reason, Max had knocked me on the ground and had straddled me with the idea to punch me in the face. But before he could deliver the blow, I saw someone grab Max from behind and throw him to the ground. It was Billy.

"Why don't you pick on someone your own size, you little shit?" Billy screamed at Max.

Max looked up from his new location on the ground with the idea of shouting obscenities back at Billy, but when he saw the look of anger in Billy's face he hesitated. Before he had decided how to reply, we heard another voice shouting from a distance.

"Hey Cooper, what the hell are you doing to my brother!" It was Max's sister, Donna. The next thing I knew Donna was at Billy's side, and before Billy had answered his interrogator she had smacked him across the side of the head. I could see the fire burn brighter in Billy's eyes as he finally answered the challenge.

"You get the hell out of here, Donna, or I'll knock you down too!"

"You wouldn't dare hit a girl, Cooper. I could hit you again and you couldn't do anything about it."

"Just try it and you'll see. Besides you're no girl, you slut."

"You call me a slut again and I'll smash your brains in!"

"Go ahead, slut. Slut, slut, slut!"

Before Billy had completed this taunt, Donna whacked him across the side of the head so that her open hand struck his ear with her full force. Less than a second later, Billy reacted with a blow across Donna's face which caught her completely off guard. Donna fell backwards landing on her rear end on the still frozen ground.

"You bastard, you'll be sorry. Allan will beat the shit out

of you. You better watch your back from now on."

"Yeah, yeah, a typical Wells. None of you can finish what you start by yourself."

As Billy turned to walk away, Donna suddenly jumped to her feet and leapt onto his back, bringing him to the ground. I could see Allan coming from around the corner of the school at the same time. Not far behind I could see Ernie and Gordie. But before any of these reinforcements arrived, Miss Evans seemed to appear from nowhere.

"What's going on here? Break this up, now!" she exclaimed as she grabbed Donna by the back of her blouse pulling her up from Billy.

"Billy Cooper hit me and called me awful names. Give him the strap, Miss Evans," Donna pleaded.

"Get up, Billy. You better come inside and explain what's going on," Miss Evans demanded and then she looked at Donna and added, "You too, young miss."

"I didn't do anything, Miss Evans."

"Come along anyway, I want to hear the whole story."

At the same time Allan appeared and requested to know what was going on. Before anyone else could answer him, Miss Evans responded.

"You keep out of this, Allan. I will take care of this one. You've got your hands into too many things already."

At first I think Allan was taken aback by the fact that Miss Evans had spoken back to him. Miss Evans and the two combatants were nearly back into the school before he yelled out his rejoinder.

"Be careful, Evans. You may be getting yourself in too deep."

Miss Evans continued on into the school with Donna and Billy, without acknowledging whether she had heard Allan's threat or not.

All afternoon, I wondered what punishment Miss Evans would dish out to Billy. After all, he had hit a girl. I decided that I had to explain. So at recess, I waited until everyone had gone outside except for Billy and Donna who were told to remain in their seats. I went to the front of the class and started to explain what had happened. Before I could finish my story though, Miss Evans tried to comfort me.

"Don't worry, Benny. I know what the Wells are like. The whole lot of them. I believe Billy's side of the story. He won't get in too much trouble. I'll just make the both of them stay after school for a few days. I'm glad he stood up for you but I have to do something. He still shouldn't have hit Donna." And then her voice went lower as she added in a whisper, "Although just between you and me, Benny, she deserved it." Then she smiled. I liked Miss Evans.

Just a few days after my eighth birthday in March, four of us were playing a game of hide and seek in the house. The participants were Sissy, Billy, Gordie, and me. Sissy had trouble with the concept of the game so we always found her easily; but we would often pretend we couldn't see her even if she was, plain as day, under the kitchen table. Even when she found a good hiding spot she would either laugh out loud or shout out some comment like, "You can't find me." When it came Gordie's turn to be the seeker, I decided to hide in the cupboard under the stairs. I knew it wasn't a great hiding place but I was running out of ideas. And I was right. Almost immediately, even before Sissy was located, Gordie opened the cupboard door so that I was peering right into his face. I grinned and was just about to say something when Gordie closed the door and continued on his search. I wasn't sure what Gordie was up to, so I decided to just stay put. I had a long wait as Gordie couldn't find Sissy either. Eventually, I heard Gordie yell.

"Where the devil are you two? I give up. Come on out."

"I'm right here, Gordie," I said as I exited my hiding place. "You know that, but where's Sissy?"

"How did you get in there, Benny? I looked in there," Gordie inquired.

At the same time we heard the banging of pots and pans from the kitchen. We all walked into the kitchen in time to see Sissy crawling out of a cupboard. This was a small cupboard which seemed too little for anyone to get into.

"You couldn't find me that time, Gordie. I win," Sissy beamed.

"That was very clever, Sissy," commented Billy. "Who told you to hide in there?"

"Nobody. I thought of it all by myself. Did I win?"

"You and Benny tied. Gordie couldn't find him either."

"No you win, Sissy," I admitted. "Gordie just pretended he didn't see me."

"What are you talking about, Benny?" Gordie asked. "I never found you."

"You looked right at me, Gordie. I was in the closet under the stairs."

"Yeah, I saw you come out of there, but where were you before that?"

"Nowhere, I was in there before you had counted to ten. Stop kidding around, Gordie. Let Sissy know that she won fair and square."

"No, Benny. I remember looking in that closet. But you weren't there. No way."

"I was there, Gordie. I saw you open the door and look right at me. I smiled at you. I was going to say hello but you shut the door and went away, so I just thought I would stay there and play along with the game."

"Stop fooling around, guys," Billy requested. "You're starting to spook me out."

"I'm not fooling," I said, "I was in that closet the whole time."

"And I'm not joking either. I swear I never saw Benny."

"How could you not see me, Gordie? I'm not a ghost like that man in the uniform."

Then it hit us all at the same time. We had forgotten all about our weird experiences last fall. There was something funny going on in this house.

"Let's tell Ernie and see what he says," suggested Billy.

So the four of us went off to get Ernie and to tell him all about our latest strange escapade. Not too long later, all five of us Cooper kids plus Happy were standing outside the door to the forbidden room. Ernie was holding a screwdriver. After a few minutes, Ernie had managed to unscrew the hinge flap, which held the padlock, from the door. Slowly he pushed the door open and we all peered into the forbidden room, each of us expecting some kind of spirit to confront us. But the secret room looked the same as from the window. It was a room full of old junk.

"You better wait here," Ernie said to Sissy.

"No, I want to come in too, Can I?"

"OK, but let's stay together. And don't cry or scream."

"I'll be quiet," promised Sissy.

So the five of us bravely entered the room, but Happy refused to follow us. He just sat at the door and watched. Our eyes were peering in all directions. I looked up at the window to our bedroom, but I couldn't see anything.

"There's no way anyone could climb up to look into that window," Ernie commented, "and there's no ladder anywhere around."

We continued our investigation, but all we saw were old dressers, an old table on its side, and various other pieces of old furniture. On top of the furniture and all over the floor, there were lamps, blankets, statues, and other old artifacts scattered everywhere.

"Look there," Gordie suddenly remarked as he pointed into the far corner.

I looked towards the direction which Gordie had indicated to stare at something which startled me. At first I thought I saw someone standing in the corner, but it was just some clothes hanging on a wooden coat rack. But it wasn't just some clothes – it was the uniform. The uniform that the man with the moustache had been wearing both nights that he had decided to watch us in the bedroom.

"That's the uniform!" I exclaimed. "That's what the man was wearing. I know it."

"Holy shit, Benny, are you sure?" asked Billy.

"Yeah, I'm sure. It's got the same things on the shoulder

too."

"I'm scared," said Sissy.

"Don't worry," I said, "there's nobody here now. Is there Ernie?"

"No, there's nobody here," comforted Ernie. "Let's look around some more."

We spent close to another half-hour inspecting the rest of the room, but we hadn't uncovered anything else yet which seemed significant. I saw Billy looking through some dressers. Eventually Billy opened a drawer in one of the old dressers. I saw him take something out.

"Come here, Benny," Billy spoke softly. "Everybody come here. Have a look at this." He was holding what looked like a photograph.

I walked over to where Billy was standing and he handed the picture to me. When I gazed at the photo, I was looking at a middle-aged man with a thick handlebar moustache wearing the same kind of uniform that was hanging in the corner. I screamed.

"That's him! That's the man in the window, the man at the door! That's him!"

11 ~ Dinky Toys

Sometime in the spring of '57, we began to make frequent treks to Orangeville in order to pick up our supply of groceries. Mom had stopped asking The Old Man to drive her into town to accomplish this task, as she had tired of waiting for him to emerge from the local bar before we could return home. To say nothing of the fact that at that point he would be beyond the state that we wished to be in a car with him behind the wheel. So on a Saturday morning, we would begin the long walk into Orangeville. I'm not sure how far it was, but it took us over an hour to walk the distance. I guess it was about four miles or so. All of us, except for The Old Man, would make the trip. We would leave The Old Man at home with his twenty-four friends beside him on the kitchen floor. That was the other reason for making this particular journey. We would make a day of it and it would get us out of the house and away from The Old Man when he was drinking. As I mentioned earlier, he was getting paid once a month then, so our excursions would usually coincide with this event. Also though, I just enjoyed the chance to go for a long walk with my brothers and Sissy. The four of us boys would often run ahead so that we would have time to play by the side of the road while we waited for Mom and Sissy to catch up. We never walked back home again because of all the bags of groceries that would have had to been carted home. Therefore we always headed back home in a taxi.

When I say we would make a day out of the trip, what I mean is that we would do more than just shop at the A & P. Many times we would go to the movie theatre, for example. Each of us would have twenty-five cents to spend as we saw fit. For that you could get into a movie (15 cents) and get a bag of popcorn or a drink (10 cents). I remember seeing Audie Murphy in 'To Hell and Back'. For years, it was my favourite movie. It had been released in 1955, but as a rule it would take quite a while before a new release would come to Orangeville. One exception to that rule, was Elvis Presley's debut in 'Love Me Tender'. It came out in November '56, and yet was part of the attractions in Orangeville only a few months later. We all enjoyed 'Love Me Tender', although we couldn't believe that they would kill off Elvis at the end. I remember that it made Sissy cry. She was just about four years old at the time. I have to admit that I cried too. Although I enjoyed the movie very much, I still didn't think it could compare to the excitement of 'To Hell and Back'.

At Easter, Buddy came home for a short visit again. He drove us boys to the toy store in Orangeville and let us all pick out a Dinky Toy for ourselves. He said it was for Easter. I had never had a gift for Easter before. Except of course, the chocolates and candies that the Easter Bunny brought. No, I didn't believe in the generous rabbit by that time, but that didn't stop me from taking pleasure from a basket full of goodies just the same. Anyway back to the Dinky Toys, they became our favourite pastime for the next few years. We could spend hours and hours playing with them. For those few that don't know what I am talking about, Dinky Toys were small well-made cars and trucks, something like Matchbox toys. But way better. They were made out of metal, like Matchbox, but were bigger with far more attention to detail and realism being evident. Also they were considerably more expensive. I chose something I had always craved — a manure spreader. Because of my love of riding the fields with John Bullard, I started to collect farm machinery. Not long after, I acquired a tractor to pull my spreader. Gordie selected a large dump truck and Billy's choice was a tank. For the next few years that's how it went. I stocked up on farm equipment, Gordie built a construction empire, and Billy prepared for war. Ernie was twelve at the time and not too far away from beginning his teenage years, so he did not join the Dinky Toy craze. He opted for a model airplane that he could build and fly. It was made out of balsa wood and had an elastic band for an engine. Thus Ernie began collecting different airplane models, some wood some plastic, some able to fly and some only for display. Sissy began to complement her table and chairs with other housewares such as pots, pans and dishes. I would sometimes play house with Sissy. Sissy would be the mother of a couple of her dolls and I would be the Dad. I always made sure that when I came home from work on payday, I would give all of the money to Sissy so that she would have enough to feed and clothe the children. I would complain to Gordie that Sissy would make me play with her. That, if I didn't play house she would cry until I agreed, but in reality I enjoyed it. I thought her toys were neat, too. But I didn't admit this to Gordie or any other of my older brothers.

One thing that I have not mentioned about all the various houses that we had lived in, was the redecorating that Mom did. Some of the farmhouses that we had rented weren't too habitable when we first moved in, so Mom would paint and wallpaper much of the house. She did this mainly by herself without The Old Man's help. We boys would be the assistant wallpaper hangers. My job was mainly to fill the wallpaper trough and to sponge down the lower parts of the walls. Ernie, Billy, and Gordie would help with the hanging. Mom had not bothered to redecorate Robertsons' until that spring. Not because it didn't need it, it did. But because she had grown tired of just completing the job when The Old Man would announce that we were moving again. So she put off the chore until then as there were no imminent moves planned. We recovered the floors of much of the house with linoleum. That was the easiest and cheapest way to cover old floors and make them clean. We would help Mom choose the best pattern for the linoleum covering. We would make sure that it had decorations which could be used as a proper setting for our Dinky Toys. A straight border would become a road, a flower was a forest, and the plain coloured parts were the fields where I could do my farming. Mom sure put up with a lot from us.

This talk about Dinky Toys reminds me that I need to narrate one more incident involving Allan Wells which occurred at the school before we broke for the summer. Actually, it was on the very last day of school. I was standing with a small group of boys probably talking about the upcoming summer holidays and how we were going to spend them, when Allan, Henry and a few other boys came upon us. Allan spoke first.

"Ahh, here's some other boys. Let's see theirs as well." Then he directed his discussion to us. "We were talking about cocks and how they come in different sizes and shapes. We agreed that everyone should show their dick to each other. OK, Henry you go first."

We all wondered what Allan was up to but before any of us could react, Henry had unzipped his pants and pulled out his penis so that everyone could see.

"OK, who's next?" Allan questioned. No one volunteered. "Whoever doesn't show their pecker will get a kick in the balls. It's your choice. Now, let's go!"

So then another one of the older boys who had arrived with Allan exposed himself. And then another. Eventually it was the turn for us younger boys. Two others complied with the orders and that left only two of us who hadn't shown themselves. We were both hesitating. I knew that the only reason Allan was doing this was to humiliate us. He wanted to demonstrate his power. He could make us do anything he wanted. If he had asked us to strip nude and run around the yard, we would have been expected to follow orders without a word of complaint. Finally, he threatened the other boy again.

"Do you want a kick in the nuts? Take your dick out now!"

So my classmate pulled down his zipper and showed himself just as all the other kids had before. That left only me. I thought that I would try a diplomatic approach.

"You don't need to see mine. It looks just like his." I pointed to the last boy. He was the only other circumcised boy in the group. I was also going to comment on the fact that Allan still hadn't shown himself when I thought better of it.

"Don't get smart with me, shrimp! What's it going to be," Allan demanded, "show us your little pecker or you'll get a swift kick in the nuts. What's the matter are you afraid that we will find out that you're really a girl. Girl! Girl!"

Either these taunts made me angry or I realized that this was the last break before the start of summer and I would be safe for a few months. I don't know which. But I suddenly decided I wasn't going to play along, no matter what the cost. "Yes, now you know my secret," I answered as I turned and bolted for the door into the school. Luckily, my timing was impeccable. Miss Evans was ringing the bell.

12 ~ Peace and War

I don't recall too many happenings involving The Old Man that summer of 1957. I know that he was still drinking and was just as combative as ever. But there just weren't any occasions that really stand out. We now had a record player that he could listen to late at night. So while we were trying to sleep, we could listen to 78's of Hank Williams or Slim Whitman blasting out. We could tell when The Old Man finally passed out because the same song would keep repeating as the arm went back to replay the song after it finished. None of us would dare go down and take it off because we feared it would wake him up and cause a commotion. Eventually, I learnt to hate country music because I always associated it with The Old Man. Although I have to admit that listening to 'My Son Calls Another Man Daddy' forty-two times in a row was still a big improvement over hearing The Old Man cursing Mom and everything else all through the night.

That summer we finally got to appreciate all the opportunities that the Robertsons' farm provided for the imagination of four boys. I just say boys because Sissy got left out of most of the following fun activities that I am going to tell you about. Sometimes we let her join in our play-making but that was more the exception than the rule. Anyway to continue, we were now able to scout out the whole farm and use all of it as our own personal playground. Around the entire property there was a wooden rail fence which in some parts had seen better days. One game that we would play involved walking along the top rail of the fence as far as you could go without falling off. We would pretend that we were walking on a high wire without a net. If you fell off, you were dead. I got pretty good at the game but I couldn't keep up to my older brothers. Gordie was an expert; nevertheless, I think Billy was the champion. He could walk over half the farm before succumbing to the horrific death of a high fall. Billy would even hold a long pole to keep his balance like he had seen circus performers do. The pole didn't help me; it just made me tip over faster.

At one spot where the fence was meant to separate two fields on the farm, it had collapsed completely and scattered in every which direction. This inspired Ernie to come up with the idea of building a fort from the fallen rails. Billy's expertise in building log cabins came in very handy in this situation. Consequently, Ernie and Billy designed the plan and the four of us worked together to construct our new fort. All the rails were the same length and we didn't think we should start sawing them off, hence we weren't able to construct windows easily. So we left them out. The only opening was in the top. I thought that made it neat. It made the fort more secretive. To enter you had to climb up the side, onto the roof, and then jump down to the ground safely inside the bastion. You didn't need windows because one could peer into the openings between the rails to watch for the approach of the enemy.

Where there were less fence rails available to construct buildings, it didn't stop us from erecting other structures. They were just two-dimensional. Rails placed strategically around the ground would indicate the walls of our houses, stables, barns, and saloons. We could build an entire town for Gene Autrey and Hopalong Cassidy to ride into. We could sing the song that Ernie had taught us as we rode off into the sunset.

"On top of Old Smokey, where nobody goes.
Except Betty Grable, without any clothes.
Along came Gene Autrey, a clippity clop,
And sat down beside her, and pulled out his clock,
And said 'What time is it?'"

I guess I shouldn't let you keep on believing that we four boys always got along perfectly when we played together. That wouldn't be the truth. A few times some of us would get into arguments. But when Billy lost his temper it was best to get out of his way. If anything was laying close by, he tended to pick up whatever it was and heave it at his verbal combatant. One day during the summer, Billy and Ernie started yelling at each other when suddenly Billy reached for a shingle which was near him on the ground. Then he used the shingle to scoop up a big pie of cow shit and started chasing Ernie around the barn. Gordie and I just stood by laughing as Ernie went running by with Billy right behind him. After Billy, came Happy. He thought it was some kind of fun game. Then Billy wound up and hurled the shingle of shit and it splatted on the ground just a few inches behind Ernie's fast moving feet. At the same moment that the shit hit the ground, Billy tripped and went flying forward, landing on the ground a few inches in front of the foul smelling shingle. Happy didn't have time to stop and went running right through the stinky mess. Gordie and I started laughing even louder. We couldn't control ourselves even though we knew that Ernie and Billy weren't kidding around. All of a sudden Billy started laughing as well and before long Ernie had joined the rest of us in our uproarious state. Happy started barking while he ran around and around circling the four laughing fools. In contrast, I remember another time when Billy and Ernie fought which was not a laughing matter. Billy got so angry that he grabbed the closest object which was a hatchet, and threw it at Ernie. Luckily he missed. Just as the hatchet was released from his grasp, Billy realized what he had done.

Gordie and I didn't laugh this time and none of us ever mentioned this incident to Mom. I think at that point Billy began to see that he had to learn to control his temper better.

On a hot summer day in July, Gordie and I decided to play a game of golf. There was only one problem. We didn't have any clubs, or a golf ball either, for that matter. So we settled for the next best thing – a baseball bat and an Indian rubber ball. We decided that Gordie should tee off first. I was standing a few yards in front of Gordie and off to the side.

"You better move, Benny," Gordie warned. "I have no idea which direction this ball might go. I don't want to hit you where it hurts the most. You better stand behind me."

So I moved to the safest place that I could think of – right behind Gordie. I watched Gordie as he addressed the ball, swung back, and then hammered the ball forward. Unfortunately, I didn't compensate for the follow-through. The end of the bat came around and smacked me right on the forehead. I dropped to the ground like I had just been shot.

"Benny, oh, I'm sorry. Are you alright? Why'd you stand so close?" exclaimed Gordie.

I hadn't lost consciousness; my head was just ringing a bit.

"I'm OK, Gordie. I'll be OK. My head's just a little sore that's all." I started to stand up when I felt my legs give out and I collapsed back to the ground. "Maybe not as well as I thought, Gordie. I feel a little dizzy. Help me up." And then everything went black.

"Billy! Ernie! Where are you? Come here! Benny's been hurt! Hurry!" Gordie started to shout as loudly as he could.

I was told this later, of course. I didn't hear him. The next thing I knew I was in Ernie's arms being carried in the house. Mom was beside me stroking me gently through my hair. She saw me open my eyes.

"Oh, Benny. Are you OK? Can you hear me?" Mom spoke close to tears.

"I'm fine, Mom. You can put me down, Ernie. I'm OK now. I can walk," I replied.

But Ernie didn't listen to me. He carried me in and placed me on the couch in the living room. Mom got a cold face cloth and placed it over my forehead.

"Really, I'm fine now, Mom. There's nothing to worry about. I'll get up in a minute."

"No, don't move yet. You're going to have quite a bump on your head, I bet. Probably get black eyes too. Just stay there," Mom pleaded. "What happened?"

I lay still and listened to Gordie explain the whole story. I wasn't too active for the next few days and Mom was right. I got a bump on my forehead above my right eye about the size of an egg. And my face turned black and blue above and below the eye as well. I didn't stay in bed though. I would still get up and enjoy the summer sunshine and walk around the yard. Nevertheless I wasn't ready for the high-wire act on the fence rails just yet. I still felt dizzy for a while and suffered from occasional headaches, besides the constant sting around the egg-shaped bulge. So that was the end of my golfing career before it had even started.

That summer we began to get regular visits from Mom's first cousin, Fred Foot and his family. There was Fred and his wife, Violet, who was always called Vi. They had two children who would come with them, but they were both adults by then. There was the oldest, Ron, who was about Claudia's age, and then there was Lucy, who was around the same age as Buddy. Lucy was married and had two kids at that time. Her husband's name was Tom, Tom Locke. The kids, both girls, were called Lizzie and April. That was a funny coincidence, because Claudia's husband was also called Tom and they had two daughters now. I already told you about Lizzie who was born in Orangeville a couple of weeks after Sissy. About a year later they had another little girl who they called April. They were now stationed overseas so we hadn't seen them for quite a while. We hadn't seen April at all at that point. I say coincidence because Claudia and Lucy hadn't met and they weren't aware that they shared the same taste for names. Both of the Kilkenny (Claudia's name now, remember) girls were older than their namesakes in the Locke family. Lizzie Locke was about 3 years old at the time, about a year younger than Sissy. April Locke was a couple of years younger than her sister, so she was somewhere around a year old that summer. As you can see, there were too many names for Mom to mention when she would tell us that the Foots and Lockes were coming to visit; therefore, she always referred to her cousin and his family as 'Fred and Them'.

About a week after my confrontation with the baseball bat, Fred and Them came to visit on a Sunday afternoon. They were living in Toronto and would come to see us at least once a month on a Sunday and would spend the day. That's another reason why I don't have too many bad memories about The Old Man during the Robertson years. Between only getting paid once a month and the regular visits of Fred and Them, we didn't have to put up with his familiar antics as much, I guess. I liked it when Fred and Them would come, not only because I enjoyed the company of all of them, but also because I could usually rely on The Old Man behaving himself. Even when he was drinking and starting to get obnoxious there would be enough people around to distract him away from his usual ranting and get his mind on something else. Every time Fred and Them came, they would all play some card game called Auction. They could play it for hours. I have to admit that I've never seen this game played by anyone else. It was similar to Euchre in that there were Bowers but the Five was the highest card in the deck. I can't remember how to play it now, but it was a fun game. Sissy must have enjoyed it when they came to pay a visit as she finally had some girls to play with her. It was a welcome change from four older brothers.

When Fred and Them saw the lump on my head they couldn't believe that I hadn't been taken to a doctor. "He's got a concussion, for sure," Ron said. And the others all agreed. I didn't know what a concussion was, but it sounded serious, and exciting. I could use that as an excuse to avoid anything I didn't want to do for months. "Sorry Gordie, I can't help you. I have a concussion." It sounded great. I had something my brothers didn't have. Buddy was in the Air Force but Benny had a concussion. Seriously though, I did suffer from the occasional headache for quite a long time afterwards.

Sorry, I keep getting distracted from my story about Fred and Them. The other part I enjoyed was the tales that they, Mom, and The Old Man would tell about life in Newfoundland as they played Auction. There was the one that The Old Man used to tell about Jarge (George) that ended with the line, "Hark, what Jarge calls fruit, arrnges." I don't remember the rest of it though. But I loved that punch line. Mom would tell the story about Fred Roberts and where he hid his ten-dollar bill.

"Did you hear the one about the time Jarge saw the mirror," Fred recalled. "He was at a flea market and he saw this mirror on the ground. He picked it up and looked into the mirror and remarked, 'A picture of Uncle John, I wonder what that's doing 'ere. I've got to take this 'ome and show Martha.' So Jarge bought the mirror and took it home to show Martha. When he got home, he said, 'Look Martha, look what I got today. It's a picture of Uncle John.' Martha looked at Jarge and answered, 'Pass it over then. Let's see Uncle John.' So Jarge passed the mirror over to Martha who gazed at it and looked puzzled. And she says, 'Well, you idiot, Jarge. This ain't no picture of Uncle John. It looks like some old whore that you've been 'anging around with."

Everybody laughed, especially us boys. Then it was The Old Man's turn.

"And then there was this other time that Jarge went to the flea market. He saw this toilet seat. Jarge picked it up and said, 'I've gotta show this to Martha.' So he bought the toilet seat and took it on home to Martha. He walked in the door holding it up high and says to Martha. 'Look what I got Martha. Wouldn't your mother look great in this 'anging up in the living room?' The fool thought it was a picture frame," The Old Man continued. "Wouldn't your mother look great in this 'anging up in the living room?" he repeated as we all joined The Old Man in the laughter. "Hark, what Jarge calls fruit, arrnges," he restated again as the chortling got even louder.

I was laughing so much that my head started to throb. "Ow, my head hurts," I shouted as I continued to chuckle.

Then Mom related a story that took place back at Lowe's. I didn't tell you about it before because I didn't remember it happening. I only remember Mom talking about it years later. This occurred before I had become sentient. Anyways, I guess Mom was in the kitchen while The Old Man was outside chopping firewood.

"Then all of a sudden," Mom continued, "I heard Garf yelling, 'Look Mary, look Mary, see what I've done'. I turned around and I saw blood flying everywhere. 'What have you done?' I asked him. 'Cut my finger with the axe,' he answered. 'See.' And then he started waving his finger in front of my face and I could see that it was split like a pod of peas. It was flapping all over the place and blood was going everywhere. Then I dropped like a stone to the floor."

"Yeah, Mary fainted," added The Old Man. "So I knelt down beside her and shouted, 'Don't die on me, Mary! Don't die on me!"

"That's right," Mom laughingly agreed. "Here he was bleeding to death and the old fool was telling me not to die."

We all laughed including The Old Man. I sure enjoyed those moments when we could all take pleasure from each other like a normal family. "If only it could always be like this," I thought.

Other times The Old Man would relate his war stories to Fred and Them. Particularly when he was drinking. Later that summer, we began to live our own war stories. I mean we played war. Ernie and Billy always got to be the Allies, British and Canadian, never Americans. And Gordie and I were the Germans. I'm not sure why the two oldest would fight against the two youngest boys. Maybe Ernie wanted to ensure that the Allies always won, and they did. Their headquarters were in the chicken coop. The Germans were stationed in the gully. Ernie had built a treehouse in one of the trees in the gully. Nothing elaborate, just a few boards across a large branch halfway up the tree. So Gordie and I could be snipers. We had seen in the war movies at the theatre and on TV that the Allies never had snipers, but we were the bad guys; so we could be dirty, rotten, sneaking snipers. Wasn't that how it really was? Our guns were just usually old broomsticks. But we could cover the whole farm, trying to make a surprise attack on the Allies before they saw us. As I mentioned earlier, without too much success. Even in the odd chance that we caught Billy off guard and fired 400 rounds at him, somehow we always missed. At least that's what he would say. In spite of our casualty levels, Gordie and I always had a great time and were able to wrap ourselves into our roles with relish and fervour.

One day the war got real nasty. Gordie and I were trapped beside the barn behind a harvester sitting in deep grass. The Allies were held up behind an old pile of barn lumber about 30 yards away. The gunfire was hot and furious between the two enemy lines when Ernie noticed something in the lumber pile. There were these old wheel-shaped wooden objects that had a strip of metal around the circumference. I have no idea what they were but Ernie immediately recognized them as hand grenades. "This could turn the tide and end the stand-off," he thought. So he picked one up and tossed it towards us. But Ernie overshot his target and we heard a loud bang as the hand grenade crashed against the barn wall.

"What was that?" I said.

"Give up or we'll blow you to bits," Ernie yelled. "We have hand grenades."

"You'll never get us alive," Gordie screamed back as we both fired off another volley of fire towards our opponents.

"Have it your way then," shouted Ernie as he stood up and fired another hand grenade towards our make-do stronghold. I heard a dull thud and turned to see Gordie lying on the ground with blood seeping out of a gash on the side of his head.

"Stop firing," I hollered, "Gordie's been hit!"

"Come out with your hands up or you'll get another hand grenade blast," Billy retorted.

"No, I'm not kidding!" I stood up so that they could see that I was serious. "You hit Gordie on the head, he's bleeding. Come here quick!"

"What? This better not be a trick," exclaimed Ernie as both he and Billy came running towards our hideout. They both looked down to see Gordie still motionless on the ground with his hair now covered in blood.

"Oh, shit!" Ernie cried out. "Come on, Billy. Help me get him into the house."

As they started to pick Gordie up, I heard him moan. "Ohh, what the hell hit me. That was some powerful grenade you've got there. You British sure fight dirty. Not like us Germans."

We all smiled to know that Gordie still had his sense of humour. He was going to be just fine. As we walked into the kitchen with Gordie being held up by Billy and Ernie, Mom turned white and sighed. "Now what have you boys been up to? Can't you find something safer to play? You're going to kill each other one of these days."

But she wasn't really mad; she was just worried about Gordie, of course. Mom washed the cut and put some kind of salve on it. She said the wound wasn't as bad as it first looked. She stemmed the bleeding and wrapped up Gordie's head with a large gauze bandage.

"You look funny, Gordie," said Sissy.

"Yeah, he looks like a mummy," I added with a grin.

"Mommies don't look like that," Sissy insisted. "Gordie looks like the invisible man."

We all started to laugh including Gordie before he encountered the same problem that I had earlier in the summer.

"Ow, that hurts when I laugh."

Mom sighed again. "You boys are going to be the death of me one of these days. I'm going to have a heart attack, yet." And then she added, "But, I wouldn't have you any other way. It's great that you always see the good side in everything."

Ernie then answered for all of us. "That's the way you brought us up, Mom. Never say anything unless you've got something good to say. Right?"

She then squeezed Gordie and said, "I love you. I love you all," she continued as all five of us became recipients of her affection.

13 ~ Crash and Bang

The Repooc Club was founded in the summer of 1957. It was located at the chicken coop on Robertsons' farm and consisted of four members – Einre, Yllib, Eidrog, and Ynneb Repooc. Of course, if you haven't figured it out already, that's the four Cooper boys with their names spelled backwards. There was no Yssis (or Ylil) because this club was only for boys. Each of us had our own crest which combined together to form the Repooc Coat of Arms. I think my crest consisted of a snake entangled around a sword. Or maybe that was the same for all the Repooc members. I'm not sure now. Einre was the driving force behind the club. He constructed swords and shields for all of us. My sword even had a handle with a carved snake surrounding it. Everybody's sword had their personal designs carved on them, and every shield carried the appropriate coat of arms. He also built a powerful crossbow that sat in the clubhouse ready to defend against any attack. Just as Einre was the weapons maker, Yllib was the artist. He drew the crests and other Repooc paraphernalia such as the secret map. The secret map was hidden behind a burlap curtain in the clubhouse. It outlined the territory of the Repooc clan (Robertsons' farm). In this clubhouse, we designed our secret code. All communications and writing had to be written in this code out of fear that anything should fall in the wrong hands. Only now, can this code finally be revealed. To encrypt a message, first you spelled all the words backwards (of course) and then you replaced every second letter with its place in the alphabet. For example, 'The enemy is approaching' would be encoded as 'E8T 25M5N5 S9 G14I8C1O18P16A'. Quite an ingenious code that would even fool Sherlock Holmes. The best part about the clubhouse though, was the security features. Einre had installed an elaborate defensive system. A pail sat on the roof ready to dump a load of sand over any uninvited guest to the club. This was accomplished by a rope connected from the pail to the inside of the door. Any unsuspecting visitor who opened the door would pull the rope, thus tipping the pail full of sand down upon themselves. Before entering the club, anyone of us Repooc members would crawl through the window to disengage the trap before the rest of us could make our entrance in the conventional manner. Many rousing meetings were held that summer at the Repooc Club.

As well as the swords and shields, Ernie had created many other toys for us that summer. He had become the master toy craftsman. We all thought that Ernie's creations were far more realistic than anything that could be bought in the store. And at a much better price. He had created horses which we could ride into our various forts and towns. An old hockey stick would have a cardboard head attached. Again, Billy the artist assisted in the drawing of the horse heads. With this personal touch each of us could have a different looking horse. My mount was a roan while Gordie rode a palomino. A cloth or cardboard saddle was added and a piece of rawhide became the reins. But the special touch was the mane made from an old mop.

Speaking of rawhide, Ernie also produced Indian outfits for all of us. We would scout the surrounding evergreen forest dressed as Indians, sometimes decorated with war paint. As usual with Ernie, everything had to be done realistically. So we would be attired in two little flaps of rawhide joined by a rawhide string at the waist – and nothing else. Mom would have been worried sick if she knew that we were running through the woods in our bare feet. But that was the only way to creep silently back to camp. I don't remember playing 'Cowboys and Indians' like most boys in the 50's. We either played 'Cowboys' or we played 'Indians'. Hardly ever did we combine the two. There would be too many arguments about who got to play which. Everyone would want to play the Indian part. So two of us could be the Cheyenne or Cree and two of us could be some other tribe such as the Pawnee. Unlike when we played war, I was not always on the same side as Gordie. Often I would be teamed with Ernie against Billy and Gordie. So I had a fighting chance in this game. I almost forgot about the great bows and arrows that Ernie had crafted as well. And the quivers.

All good things must end. Therefore it was with regret that this summer came to a close and we had to return to the real world. With real battles. Back to school and back to the Wells. But before I get back to them, I have another story to tell. It was Labour Day, the day before we returned to school. We had received a letter from Buddy a few weeks before to tell us that he was going to be in the Air Show at the C.N.E. (Canadian National Exhibition) in Toronto on Labour Day. We were all regretting that we couldn't make it up to Toronto to see him, because for some reason The Old Man decided he didn't want to make the trip. Gordie and I were watching something on television, probably the annual Labour Day classic between the Argos (Toronto Argonauts) and the Hamilton Tiger-Cats. We now got Channel 3 from Barrie so the game wasn't blacked-out for us. We both cheered for the Tiger-Cats. For no other reason than we liked their uniforms best. Black with gold. We always cheered for the guys in black. Even when we watched westerns, even though the good guys wore white. Near the end of the game, they interrupted the broadcast for a news bulletin.

"A tragic accident has occurred at the C.N.E. Air Show today. A Royal Canadian Air Force jet has crashed into Lake

Ontario while performing at this afternoon's show. The CF-100 jet was carrying a crew of two. Both are presumed dead. Names are being withheld until next of kin can be notified. More details at six."

We hadn't noticed that Mom had walked into the room.

"Oh my God," she said, "That's Buddy."

"No they don't know who it is yet, Mom," Gordie said. "It was probably somebody else."

"Yeah Mom," I added, "Buddy will be OK. Just wait and see." I'm not sure I really believed it.

At six o'clock the entire family including The Old Man was glued in front of the TV to watch the news. We had switched to Channel 6 (the Toronto station), in order to get the most up-to-date information. But we didn't learn anything new other than the confirmation that indeed both the pilot and navigator had been killed. But they still weren't giving out any names.

"If a car pulls in that driveway, I think I'll die," whispered Mom.

The rest of us just sat silent not knowing what to say or do. It was almost a year to the day that Mom had received the telegram from Aunt Becky informing us about Grandma's death. Then finally, Billy broke the silence.

"There's a car coming up the driveway."

"Is it a police car?" Mom asked. Her voice was barely audible now.

"No, I don't think so. No, it's just a plain car."

"You go to the door, Garf. I'm afraid to move."

The Old Man got up without saying a word and went to the door. A few minutes later, he came back carrying a small envelope. He started to pass the envelope to Mom.

"It's a telegram. Do you want to open it?"

"No, I can't. I can't read it," Mom cried.

"OK, I'll open it up," replied The Old Man as he sat back down in one of the large armchairs.

All our eyes were facing The Old Man as he ripped open the side of the envelope, took out the telegram and began to read.

"It's from Buddy! He's OK!" The Old Man said loudly. "Listen."

DON'T WORRY STOP I AM FINE STOP I WAS ON ANOTHER PLANE STOP WILL WRITE SOON STOP LOVE BRAD STOP

"Thank God," sighed Mom in relief. "Thank God. Read it again, Garf."

So The Old Man read the good news again and then passed the telegram to Mom.

"See I told you, Mom," said Gordie. "I knew all the time that it wasn't Buddy." But he didn't sound too convincing.

As I started to tell you earlier, it was time for school again. Ernie now had the job of lighting the fire in the stove at school every morning. So I always got up early and traveled off to school with Ernie to help him (well, watch him anyway) stock the stove with wood and to begin to warm the classroom before the rest of the students and Miss Evans arrived. Gordie and Billy often would arrive later as well. They liked to sleep in. All of us Coopers had passed our grade the previous year. Thus, Ernie was now in his last year of public school (Grade 8). Gordie was now in Grade 6, Billy in 5, and I was now all the way up to 4. Allan was the only Wells that had been promoted, so he was still in the same grade as Ernie. Donna and Max remained in Grades 4 and 2 respectively. Woody had graduated on to high school. I think Miss Evans just thought it was time that he moved on. Henry was attempting Grade 5 one more time. For the first few months of the new school year, my reservations about returning were unjustified. The Wells continued to be obnoxious, but I don't recall any serious incidents. Miss Evans appeared to have a little more control of actions in the classroom as well as the schoolyard.

That September, the Cooper family finally joined the telephone age. Our telephone was a large wooden box that hung on the kitchen wall with a crank on the side. We were connected to a party line which meant that you could hear someone else's conversation if you picked up the phone when it was busy. The number of rings told us if the call was for the Coopers or not. I don't think I ever spoke on this phone. I couldn't have reached it even if I stood on a chair. The phone was mainly used for local calls, but it allowed Buddy to keep in touch with us a few times. Claudia and Aunt Becky were too far away to phone. It made much more sense cost-wise to continue for them to use the mail. However, Fred and Them could call us now from Toronto, which made arranging their visits much easier. And we could be reached a lot quicker and easier now in case of an emergency.

Speaking of visits, later that September one of The Old Man's sisters (Eleanor, I think) and her family came to visit for the day. They had a little girl about the same age as me, called Frieda. We were all sitting around the living room, as was expected when we had company. All except for Sissy and Frieda who were playing upstairs, or so we thought, until Sissy walked into the room by herself.

"Where's Frieda, dear?" inquired Mom. "I thought she was playing with you."

"She went outside," answered Sissy.

"Why didn't you go with her then, Sissy? You should play with her."

"But she's gone to the chicken coop, Mom. Ernie, Billy, Gordie, and Benny say I can't play in there. It's their secret house or something."

"Oh, I'm sure they didn't really mean it, dear. Of course, you can play in there. Can't she, boys?"

None of us immediately responded to this question. All of us four boys just looked at each other with concern showing on our faces. Suddenly Ernie replied for all of us.

"Certainly, Mom. But the door is locked. I'll go open it for them."

"I'll go too!" the rest of us responded in unison as we all jumped up and hurried out the back kitchen door towards the chicken coop. As we approached the Repooc Club, we first heard a low bang followed by a scream, and then sobs coming from the distance. Soon we saw Frieda covered from head to toe with sand. You couldn't even tell what colour her hair was anymore. It was full of the sand. Frieda just ran on by us towards the farmhouse.

"Mommy!" she cried. "Look what they did to me!"

"We're in trouble now," Gordie surmised.

"Well at least we now know that the booby trap works," Billy remarked.

"I'm glad," said Sissy. "She said she didn't like playing with me and ran off. She said we were all too poor for her to play with. She's snobby. I don't like her."

We all looked at each other and began to laugh. We decided to enjoy the moment for a few seconds before we had to face the consequences inside.

That fall we began to acquire a collection of cereal people. Let me explain. Many varieties of breakfast cereals would have different little plastic figurines free inside. We would make Mom buy whatever cereal contained a person inside. We didn't care what it was. The cereal itself was secondary. It was the 'Free Inside' that mattered. There were replicas of baseball players, football players, war action figures, cowboys, Indians, and many more. Ernie built a little house from an old phone box to put them all in. It had a hinged roof that we could open to lift them in and out. We decorated the inside by cutting pictures out of a catalogue. Gordie's Uni-blocks could be used to construct different pieces of furniture. We didn't like the people to look like baseball or football players or whatever, though. So we would get Ernie or Billy to remove their various sports or military equipment with a small penknife. One of the figures was a baseball catcher and when Ernie removed his cap, he cut a little too close to the top of his head. The former catcher ended up with a straight cut across the top of his head where his cap used to be. So we called him 'Flat'. All of the various characters were given similar colourful names. Too many to mention. Another cereal man ended up with his legs cut off at the knees. I'm not sure what equipment we were attempting to remove from his body that time. Anyway, we put him into a small green, Dinky Toy dogcart and this became his wheelchair. I wish I could remember what we called that guy. However, I recall that we began to refer to this strange collection of personage as 'Flat and Them'. Gordie had to only say "Flat and Them are coming," and I knew what he wanted to play.

One November morning, Gordie and I were playing in the schoolyard with a couple other boys when we heard loud, excited voices coming from another part of the yard. We looked over towards the direction of the ruckus to see a crowd gathered around two figures.

"Hey Benny, isn't that your brother Billy? It looks like he's fighting with Allan," one boy remarked.

"Let's go see what's happening," stated Gordie.

So off we went to find out what was going on this time. As we approached the gathering, we heard Billy's voice first.

"We're all sick of your bullying, Wells. I'm not doing a thing you say, ever again. So get out of here and leave me alone!"

"Who are you calling a bully, Cooper? You better do what I say or there will be hell to pay. Don't you try telling me what to do! Go do what I told you to do, now!"

"Fuck you, asshole!" was Billy's succinct reply.

"You little shit! You've got a lot of nerve," shot back Allan. At the same instant, he quickly stepped forward, grabbed Billy in a headlock, and wrestled him to the ground. Before Billy had time to react, Allan had Billy turned on his front with one arm twisted behind his back.

"I'll give you one more chance, Cooper. Apologize and do what you're told and I'll forget everything, otherwise I'll break your arm."

"Fuck you, you prick!"

Allan twisted Billy's arm further. "Take it back, Cooper! I mean it! I'll break your arm!"

"Go ahead. I'll sue your pants off. I'm not scared of you,

asshole!"

"Take it back!" Allan demanded as he continued to pull Billy's arm behind his back.

"I'm sorry I called you an asshole," Billy grimaced. "I meant to call you a shit-head."

"Goddamn you, Cooper!" replied Allan as he used his full force to yank Billy's arm as far back as he could. "Give up!"

Billy groaned in pain, but only answered, "Fuck you!"

"Come on, Billy. Give in" someone in the crowd spoke. "He's not worth it." It was Ernie. I hadn't noticed him before.

"Never!" screamed Billy as Allan gave his arm another tug. But suddenly, Allan let go of Billy's arm and stood up.

"You're one tough little shit, Cooper. I ought to kill you for what you said to me. But I respect you. You'd let me kill you before you would give in, wouldn't you? How's your arm?"

Billy moved slowly and sat up on the ground, all the time glancing up at Allan suspiciously, wondering what he was up to. What was coming next?

"Don't worry, Cooper. I'm done. You're a brave son of a bitch, I must admit. I won't touch you anymore. In fact, I'll take on anybody that goes near you. You're safe now. You're under my protection. Is your arm OK?"

Billy finally got to his feet while holding his injured arm. "I think it'll be OK. You're lucky it's not broken, you fucker!"

"Jesus, Cooper! You sure are hard-headed." Allan began laughing and others in the crowd joined in. Eventually Gordie and I had to laugh too, even if it was mainly from nervous relief.

14 ~ Police Interrogation

That December, we were treated to a major snowstorm. Between the snowfall and the high winds, our driveway was completely buried. The Old Man had to park his car in a small spot that he had dug out by the road. He had carved a parking space for one car near the mailbox, which had previously been completely hidden by the snow. The snow had reached up to the bottom branches on the trees that lined our laneway. I thought it was great. You could climb a tree without any effort. You were already halfway to the top. I had never seen so much snow before. While standing in the middle of the lane, facing the road, you couldn't even see The Old Man's car. The snow was higher than the roof of the car. Seeing the snow banked against the chicken coop with most of it buried reminded me of the 'Pit of Hell' many years before. At least it seemed like many years to me. Only the empty pail still attached to the roof of the coop was evident above the drifts.

A few days later, Buddy returned home for Christmas again. However this time he had brought along a surprise – his girlfriend, Catherine. His fiancée actually. Buddy announced that he was getting married the next summer. We were apprehensive about having a 'stranger' around for

Christmas; at least I was. But we needn't have been concerned, as we all warmed to Catherine right away. Catherine was Scottish and we all loved her accent and her sense of humour. Even I found that I could communicate with her. I didn't have to hide behind a chair or anything. So now the worry was The Old Man. How would he behave? Buddy must have really struggled with the idea of having Catherine face him. But he was not too bad that Christmas. Oh, he still got drunk and lapsed a few times into his 'gray-haired old bag' routine. And a few "I've been around the world; I know the score," rants. Except Buddy was able to calm him down successfully before he went completely off the deep end.

The other big change in Buddy was that he now wanted to be called Brad. He said it was embarrassing to be called Buddy in front of Catherine. So we were all to call him Brad, except for Sissy. She was still allowed to say 'Buddy'. So we all complied except for Mom. He would always remain Buddy to her.

There were more Dinky Toys that Christmas. We each got a different car. That was fine with me because my collection of farm equipment was getting quite large, as I would often purchase a different item on our sojourns into Orangeville. Now we could drive our cars on our linoleum roads to go visit Flat and Them.

Again, I heard Mom and Brad talking about Mom's teeth and glasses or lack thereof. Brad didn't say too much this time. He just shook his head and commented, "Mom, I just wish you would do something for yourself. Just once. God, it's not like you would be buying yourself anything extravagant. You need to see better. I know you have those old glasses. But they're no good. You're only making your eyes worse. And you won't wear them when you go out. And your teeth. Forget how you look. You need to be able to eat." Mom again promised that this would be the year that she would finally break down and make the long overdue purchases. I thought about my hay-rake and wagon and other toys bought from money that Mom had given me over the last year. Nothing that was worth much over a dollar or so. But money that Mom should have saved for herself. All of us had to make sure that Mom got her teeth and glasses this year.

Back at school, one day in January, Allan Wells rounded up the entire class and led us to the fence facing the road at one corner of the schoolyard.

"Everyone make a snowball and when the first car goes by, we all pelt it at one time, understand? I will yell 'when', and everybody must throw at the same time. Don't let me see anyone not throwing, or there will be trouble. OK, get ready with your snowballs!"

So we all complied and were ready for the first target to appear. We waited for about five minutes before a car finally came into view. Just as the car was passing in front of the school, Allan shouted, "Now!" My snowball went about three feet, not even making it to the ditch on our side of the road. In fact, only one snowball hit the target. Someone's missile hit the rear tire of the car as the driver continued on unaware that he had been the brunt of a full attack. Many had missed almost as badly as me.

"OK, that was pitiful. We need more weight in our shots. Everyone, grab one of those stones there, and wrap your snowball around it. Come on, let's go before another car drives by!"

Allan was indicating a pile of small stones which had been lying near the corner of the yard. So we all followed our orders again and were soon ready for the next victim to make their appearance. This time the car arrived from the other direction – our left. Just before it drove in front of where we were forced to line up, Allan once more belted out his order. "Now!" I threw a fraction of a second too early and watched my shot land even closer to the fence than before. I then looked down the line to see Billy and Gordie release their volley at exactly the same instance. I watched silently as I saw the rock-filled snowball leave Gordie's hand and make a perfect arc up and into the path of the oncoming car. I observed in amazement as at the same moment Billy's shot splattered on the grill of the car and Gordie's went right through the windshield. The passing motorist suddenly brought his car to a stop and after a few seconds of hesitation turned into the driveway of the school. We were all starting to run off in different directions, when suddenly Allan called out.

"Nobody saw anything, remember! Billy's my friend now. Anybody that squeals on him is going to get it. You didn't see him hit that car. None of us were even here. We were playing in the other part of the yard, by the snow forts. Everyone stick to that story. I warn you!"

Someone else yelled, "Nice shot, Billy," as we scattered to other parts of the yard.

"You didn't break the windshield, did you, Billy?" I asked.

"I don't know. I didn't see where my shot landed. Did you see, Benny?"

"No, I didn't see anything," I lied.

"It was me, wasn't it?" Gordie whispered lowly so that only I could hear.

"I don't know. It was too hard to tell. Everybody threw at once. It could have even been me."

I didn't want to admit to Gordie or even myself that I knew whose salvo had caused the damage. That way I could sound more convincing if anybody asked.

We all waited in trepidation as we saw the car still sitting in front of the school. Miss Evans was about twenty minutes late ringing the bell, when we finally saw the car reverse onto the road and continue on towards its original destination. Shortly after, the bell rang to bring everyone back into the class. We didn't have to wait long for Miss Evans to broach the subject on all our minds.

"Someone threw a rock at a car and broke the windshield. That was a terrible thing to do. The driver, Mr. Williams is really upset. He says his heart is still pounding. He thought he was going to have a heart attack. The rock could have hit him in the head and killed him. What were you kids thinking? He saw some people standing by the fence. So I know there was more than one involved. OK, who saw what happened?"

Her question was met by silence. After a few seconds, Miss Evans continued.

"Allan, can you shed some light on this episode?"

"No, Miss Evans. I swear. I was in the other part of the yard talking to Billy about last night's Leaf game. Wasn't I, Billy?"

"That's right, Miss Evans. I was with Allan," responded Billy.

"And we didn't see anybody by the fence," added Allan. "I don't know who it could have been. Maybe a rock just flew up from another car."

"There was no other car, Allan. This road isn't that busy. What about anybody else? Nobody will admit even seeing anything?"

Again there was complete silence.

"Well, the truth will come out. Mr. Williams is going to call the police. They will find out what happened. If someone would admit their mistake, maybe we could keep the police out of this. But if nobody is going to talk, then I guess it will have to become a matter for the police."

Miss Evans waited a minute more before speaking again.

"OK, Grade 3 and 4, let's see your homework. The others open your Speller's and study tomorrow's lesson."

The next day at lunchtime, the moment arrived that I had been dreading. The police car pulled up in front of the school accompanied by Mr. Williams. I didn't know what to do. I doubted that I could lie in front of the police. But I didn't want to see Gordie go to jail. So I had to stick to my story. I saw nothing. Although, whether I would tell about Allan making us throw the snowballs was another matter which I hadn't yet decided. They told us that the police would question us one by one, so I wouldn't get a chance to discuss it with my brothers. We were all told to sit in the classroom and not speak while each student was brought out into the entrance where the coats hung on the other side of the wall which held the front blackboard. They decided to start with the older kids. Allan was first. Then they called upon Billy. I surmised that Allan had not changed his story and that Billy was called in next to confirm Allan's alibi. Soon Billy came from the front and sat back down at his wooden desk.

"How'd it go?" Allan asked.

"No problem," whispered Billy. "I told them I didn't see anything."

"Good."

"Quiet!" said Miss Evans as she glanced towards the source of conversation.

Ernie was next. I started to worry as Ernie seemed to be in questioning for a longer time. Eventually, Ernie entered and sat down without speaking or looking at anyone. I could see that Allan was trying to get Ernie's attention, but my brother refused to look up in his direction. I watched intently as everyone took their turn to be questioned. I saw Gordie go out and return about five minutes later. I couldn't read anything into the blank expression on his face. He too ignored Allan's attempt at visual communication. Then before long, it was my turn. I walked in the front entrance to face my interrogators — two large policemen. Mr. Williams stood silently behind them. There were no seats, so I stood looking up a long way into their faces.

"Now don't worry, Benny. Benny Cooper, that's your name, isn't it son?" one of the behemoths began. I nodded.

"Speak up, Benny."

"Yes, I'm Benny."

"OK Benny, you might as well tell the truth. We know the whole story now. Someone told us what happened. We might as well tell you who told us. After all, he is your brother."

"Oh, Oh," I thought. Gordie confessed.

"Your brother Ernie told us everything," the other

policeman spoke for the first time. I did not say anything. Then the first questioner resumed.

"Did Allan Wells get all of you kids to line up by the fence?"

"Yes."

"Why did you do it?"

"Because he said he would hit us if we didn't."

"Is that usual?"

I looked confused. I didn't understand what he meant.

"Does Allan Wells often bully the school kids around?"

"Yes."

"What did he make you do this time?"

"Throw snowballs."

"At cars?"

"Yes."

"Snowballs with rocks in them?"

"Yes. Stones."

Then came the question that I feared the most.

"Did you see who hit the car?"

"No."

"Why not?"

"We all threw at once. Just like Allan told us. I closed my eyes."

"OK, you can go now, Benny. I guess we will never know who hit the car. No one saw who hit the windshield. Not that it really matters. Allan Wells is the main culprit."

"Right, bye," I replied as I turned to leave. "Thanks," I added not knowing how one should end an inquisition.

I walked into the class and sat down without even lifting my eyes from the floor. I sensed that Allan could smell a rat. Then I thought, "Thanks? How could I say that? What a dummy. Jimmy Cagney never would have said thanks to the coppers."

15 ~ Guns and the Midway

A few days later, we heard that Allan Wells had been suspended from school for a couple of weeks. After the police finished talking to the remaining children, both Allan and Billy were brought back for questioning. Allan then changed his story to blame Billy, but that didn't get him very far. Billy admitted that he might have hit the car but he wasn't sure who had done it. At that point, the police weren't that concerned whose rock had caused the actual damage. And there was no way of ever being sure. So Billy was just given a stern lecture about not telling the truth to the police. I never did admit to anyone that I knew a little more about the whole truth.

Sometime that winter in early '58, a severe ice storm struck the Orangeville area. The weight of the ice knocked down many of the power and telephone lines surrounding our farm. Although many branches broke off the trees around our farm, we were lucky that none of our trees were toppled completely; however, we lost our telephone and electrical power for a few days. The Old Man told us that he had heard that there were many people who had to suffer in a cold house. I could not understand how the loss of Hydro had caused so many people to be without heat. I didn't think that many people had electric heat. This was no major disruption to our family because we heated our home by a wood stove and a network of stovepipes, as I have described earlier. Besides, we were used to living without electricity. All that we would miss was our favourite television programs for a few days. Our biggest worry was that we might have missed something exciting on 'Leave It To Beaver'. Also the storm brought one big benefit for us. It kept The Old Man really busy repairing telephone lines for a few weeks. So much so that he didn't have time to drink, even on weekends. It was sometime during this period that The Old Man fell off the top of a telephone pole. He landed on the ground below, picked himself up, muttered something like "Oh shit!" and climbed right back up again. The other telephone workers couldn't believe it. They thought the fall would have killed him, or at least broken a few bones. Mom always said that The Old Man must have had horseshoes stuck up his ass.

Well, back to the storm, I remember thinking how neat everything looked covered in a sheet of ice. The other good part about the whole thing, was the skating rink which was created behind our farmhouse. Because of the large snowfall earlier that winter, then a partial thaw, followed by the freezing rain, a long river-like skating area had been created where no river had previously existed. We could skate a few hundred yards up and down this new natural ice surface. I had inherited skates from Gordie, as he had from Billy, and so on up the line. I spent many hours practicing my skating skills there that winter. And I almost forgot the best offshoot of the storm – no school.

That spring, everything returned to normal – sort of. The snow and ice was now a thing of the past, replaced by small ponds scattered throughout the fields of the farm. There was a large lake in the field between our house and the road which had not been there before. And then there was school, with the return of Allan Wells. He now had no fear of any authority. It was like he dared the board to suspend him again. One day he brought a small package to school. No one knew what was in the package until he eventually opened it for a group of kids which included Billy. It was a gun. Billy said it was originally a toy gun but somehow Allan had bored it so that it could now shoot real bullets. I thought, "Boy, that's just what we need." If there's anything more dangerous than a bully, it's a bully with a gun. But Allan was satisfied enough just to let us know that he had a gun. It acted as a sign that he was still in control. He kept it in his desk all that day; but he took it home that night and did not bring it back again. As far as I knew, anyway. One other day when Miss Evans was trying to teach a math lesson to the older kids, Allan became quite impatient with the whole subject.

"Why do I have to learn this crap?" he demanded.

"Because I said so," Miss Evans answered. "Now, pay attention and stop disrupting the class."

"No! This is useless shit. I'm going outside." Allan started to rise to go outside.

"Sit down! Now! And shut up, Mr. Wells! I've had enough from you."

"Go to hell! I'll do what I want."

At this point, Miss Evans whirled around and threw the eraser which was in her hand towards Allan. He reacted quickly and ducked so that the eraser soared pass him and bounced off the head of Billy, who was sitting two desks behind.

"Ow! That hurt," Billy cried indignantly as he rubbed his sore head.

Miss Evans did not get a chance to apologize to the innocent bystander. Allan was up from his seat and on her in a second.

"How dare you, you bitch! Throw something at me, will you!"

"Sit down and…" Miss Evans started to say but before she had finished, Allan had his hands around her neck. He then pulled back her head with one hand by grabbing her by the hair. His other arm was pulled back ready to strike Miss Evans with all his force.

"Allan, don't!" someone yelled. It was his sister, Donna.

He hesitated long enough that a few of the other older boys including Ernie had time to get up and try to step between the two. Even Henry had enough sense to know that what Allan was about to do was wrong.

"I don't think you should do that, Allan," he said. "You'll get in big trouble."

Allan then waited a few more seconds, before Miss Evans finally spoke.

"Go outside, Allan," she said softly, "and cool down. Do that now and I will forget that this ever happened. OK? Is it a deal?"

Allan slowly released his grip, looked around the classroom, and then walked out the door without saying another word.

"OK, boys. Everyone back to your seats. Thanks. I'm sorry, Billy. Are you alright?"

"Yeah. I'm fine. But what about you?"

"Let's just get back to the lesson. Now, where were we?"

And the math lesson continued without Allan.

Now that I had turned nine years old, I had developed a new philosophy of life. It was based on the phrase, "Don't ask me, I'm only nine."

"Whattaya wanna do today?" Gordie asked.

"Don't ask me, I'm only nine."

"Well what do you feel like doing?"

"How do I know? I'm only nine."

"Do you wanna play Dinky Toys?"

"Don't ask me, I'm only nine."

"How about Flat and Them?"

"I don't know, I'm only nine."

"Will you stop that 'only nine' stuff. You're driving me crazy."

"I can't help it. I'm only nine."

"Shut up about that nine stuff or I'll clobber you."

"You can't hit me. I'm only nine."

"Stop it! I mean it! I'll smack you a good one."

"If you hit me, I'll tell Flat and Them. After all, I am only nine."

At that point, Gordie had had enough. He jumped up and started towards me. I took off as fast as I could and ran out the back kitchen door.

"Don't hurt me. I'm only nine."

"If I get my hands on you, you'll wish you were ninety-nine, I swear."

"Don't swear, I'm only nine."

"Ahhh! I'm gonna kill you."

"I'm too young to die. I'm only nine."

And that's how my philosophy worked. It drove poor Gordie crazy. It was an even better excuse than "I have a concussion." I loved it. Unfortunately, it would only work for a year. You probably think it all sounds pretty stupid. But what did I know. I was only nine.

Later that spring, the midway came to our farm. Let me explain. A passing motorcade of trucks, carrying equipment and supplies for an amusement park or fair, had stopped at our farm one day. They were looking for a place to store everything until the Fall Fair. The Old Man had negotiated a deal with them. We were told not to tell anyone. The Old Man was afraid how the Robertsons would feel about him subletting the barn without permission. We watched as they unloaded all kinds of apparatus, tools, and supplies required to run a midway. There were large, wooden crates containing planes for some kind of flying ride. There were parts for the Tilt-a-Whirl. Then there was the machine and goods necessary to make candy floss. I can't remember what else. But it filled most of the barn. While this was going on, a girl about my age was playing in the yard. She was the daughter of one of the workers or perhaps the owner of this amusement consortium. I watched as she played with Happy. She had Happy chasing her in circles as she shouted and laughed. Happy was having such a good time, he started barking to keep up with the girl's yelps. Suddenly, the girl picked up a stick from the ground and yelled.

"Bad dog! Stop barking!" She was waving the stick at Happy.

"Don't hit Happy," I said with as much of an authoritative voice as I could manage to say to a stranger.

"Don't be silly. I'm just playing. Aren't we, doggy?"

She then brought the stick down hard, close to Happy's head. Happy backed up and looked at the girl and then started to bear his teeth. But the girl persisted in her torment. She again waved the stick in Happy's face. I could now hear a low growl coming from Happy. I had never heard Happy growl at anything before.

"Don't!" I cried. "You're going to hurt Happy."

"I never heard such a whiner as you before. I told you that we're just playing."

She then thrust the stick right into Happy's face. But Happy had enough of this game. He growled and then grabbed the stick in his teeth. The girl tried to pull the stick back and started shouting, "Bad dog! Bad dog!" Suddenly, Happy let go of the stick and lunged towards the girl, knocking her off her feet.

"Happy!" I screamed. "Come here! Now!"

Happy stopped, looked towards me and came to my side. The girl then got to her feet and ran off towards the barn.

"Daddy, Daddy," she squealed, "their dog tried to bite me!"

Not long after, the girl and her father came up to the house and knocked on the door. Mom answered the door.

"That's a vicious dog you have there, Ma'am. You oughta do something about it. It should be tied up. It attacked my daughter. If she hadn't of picked up a stick to defend herself, it could have bitten her throat."

Mom looked stunned.

"What? Are you talking about Happy? That dog wouldn't hurt a flea. It plays with all my children all the time."

"Well, it attacked my daughter."

"Are you sure she didn't do anything to scare the dog?"

I decided it was time for me to give my testimony.

"She was teasing Happy, Mom. She swung a stick at him. Happy was just defending himself."

"I never swung any stick. I was just playing, that's all, Daddy. And all of a sudden, he jumped at me, growling and barking like a mad dog. It was awful."

"You better tie that dog up, like I said Ma'am. The next time you could have real trouble. Not just a scared girl."

"OK," Mom said, "I'll keep that in mind."

"I think you better," the man added before walking back towards the barn with his daughter.

"It was the girl's fault, Mom. She scared Happy."

"Yes, I believe you, Benny. But you better bring Happy in now. OK?"

"All right, Mom. Come on, Happy. Let's go inside and play with Sissy."

I didn't see what other items were being stored in the barn until later. The next day, I couldn't find Fluffy.

"Don't worry, dear," Mom said, "she's probably hid somewhere because of all the strange people around yesterday. She'll be back before you know it. Just you wait and see."

I looked all over the barn. I found lots of things to play with, but there was no sign of Fluffy, anywhere. By the next weekend, we still hadn't caught sight of her, although I had searched every square inch of the farm. Not an easy task. I had given up hope of ever seeing her again; however, all of us were walking along the road on our way to Orangeville, when Gordie suddenly shouted and pointed to the other side of the road.

"What's that in the ditch, over there?"

I looked over to catch the glimpse of something white in the grass.

"Fluffy!" I cried as I ran over to the opposite ditch. And I stopped and stared and said nothing.

"What is it, Benny? Is it Fluffy?" Sissy asked.

I did not answer. It was Fluffy. She had obviously been

dead for quite a while. Soon everyone was standing beside me. Mom put her arm around me.

"I'm sorry, dear."

"I don't want to go to Orangeville now. Can I go home?"

"I'll go with him, Mom," Ernie said right away. "The rest of you go on. We'll be OK."

I bent down to pick up Fluffy, but Ernie said, "Wait. There could be germs." He took off his jacket, wrapped it around Fluffy, and started back towards home.

"Come on, Benny," he said. "Let's give Fluffy a proper funeral."

And we did. We evicted Flat and Them from their home and placed Fluffy inside the wooden house. Then Ernie dug a big hole back behind the barn and he gently put the box in the bottom of the hole. Ernie said the hole had to be deep so that Happy wouldn't dig it back up.

"You wouldn't do that, would you Happy?" I inquired.

We said nothing to each other as we both began the task of filling the hole back up. Happy watched the entire proceedings with a confused look. After we had completed the job of filling Fluffy's grave, Ernie placed a stone over the freshly dug earth. He then went into the barn and came out with a can of paint and a brush. He wrote 'Fluffy' on the rock. As we walked back towards the house, I finally spoke.

"Life stinks sometimes, doesn't it, Ernie?"

"Yeah, I guess so, Benny. Let's go keep Smokey company. She'll miss Fluffy too."

16 ~ A Big Shot

Not long after Fluffy's demise, Gordie got this mysterious disease. Some kind of weird red coloured circle started to appear on one of his arms by his wrist. Every day, it grew larger, redder, and more inflamed looking. This was one of those times where Mom was able to convince The Old Man the prudence of going to a doctor. So Gordie went to see Dr. McGuire in Orangeville. That was the same doctor who had brought Sissy into the world five years before. When Gordie arrived back home he told me that he had been diagnosed with a case of Ringworm. I had never heard of that before. The next day, the circle had expanded even more. It started to look more and more like someone had branded some strange circular design on Gordie's arm. Soon a second lesion appeared on the same arm, not too far away from the first. Gordie told me that if the two rings met, he would die. I wasn't sure who told him that. I started to worry about Gordie and I kept a constant watch on his arm. To me it seemed that the two ugly looking rings were getting closer to each other by the minute. However, in a few days it all started to clear up. To this day, I don't know if the story about the outcome of the joining of the rings was made up by Gordie or not. As I said before, I had complete faith in Gordie's statements and had no reason to doubt him this time. Whatever the truth, I was sure relieved to see those rings start to dissipate. And so was Gordie, and of course, Mom.

Later that spring on a Saturday afternoon, we had a visit from an Encyclopedia Britannica salesman. So far The Old Man hadn't been won over to the joys of owning your very own set of encyclopedia. He had had a few beers by this point, but the arrival of the salesman disrupted The Old Man from his ritual of finishing off the complete case of beer. The entire family was sitting in the living room listening to the discussion. The eager, young salesman said that this was a family decision and he asked for all of us to be present.

"You have four very smart, growing boys there," the sales pitch continued, "and a lovely daughter who will be starting school soon. How old is the young miss?"

I looked over at Gordie to see what he thought about the way the young salesman talked. The Old Man looked over at Mom.

"Just turned five, last month," Mom answered.

"Ah, just what I thought. Do you want your children to have a good education?"

"Yes," responded The Old Man. "I didn't get a chance to finish school, but I want my kids to get that chance, right dear?"

"Yes, of course we do," added Mom.

"Well, that's very admiral of you. Not all parents feel that way, you know. What would you say if I told you a way that you could guarantee them a head start on a good education? And it won't cost you a cent."

Mom and The Old Man both looked skeptical.

"How would we do that?" The Old Man questioned.

"With this set of encyclopedia," replied the salesman as he pointed at his shiny brochure, "your children can retrieve the latest information on any subject. They'll be way ahead of the rest of the kids in their school. Even if they end up going to university, they will continue to find these books to be an invaluable source of knowledge. They are more than books.

Much more. They represent the future. A way to show your kids how much you love them and…"

Mom cut him off at this point, thankfully. I thought he was going to go on forever.

"But what do you mean it won't cost us a cent?"

"Yeah, well that's the beauty of the whole plan. I walk out of here today and I don't need any money. Soon the Encyclopedia Britannica will arrive at your door. I just need your commitment. Your commitment to your children's future."

"You mean that they are free?" asked Ernie.

"No, not exactly. There will be small monthly payments. But you get a family allowance for the children, don't you ma'am?"

"Yes, but…"

"These books will cost you less than what you receive from the government for all these children. You don't have to spend any of your own money. That's the beauty of the plan, do you see?"

"We use the family allowance to buy food," Mom stated.

"Well, I know how much that you care about these children, so I'll give you a special deal. I'll knock a couple dollars off the already reasonable monthly fee. How's that? Sound fair?"

"OK," said The Old Man before Mom could reply, "We'll take it."

"You'll never regret this decision," the salesman replied cheerfully. "That I'm sure of. Now, if you will just sign these papers here, sir. And if I could get a cheque for a small deposit. Just to show your commitment, that's all. Here let me spread out these papers and…"

But the salesman was wrong. The next day, The Old Man regretted the whole thing.

"What have I done, Mary? He caught me after a few beers. I agreed just to get rid of him."

"I don't know how we can afford it, Garf."

"OK, I'll phone them tomorrow and cancel the whole

thing."

And he did. Somehow after a lengthy argument The Old Man convinced the company to rip up the agreement. I wondered what the industrious young man thought. But I didn't think about it too much.

Anyway, we didn't need the encyclopedia; we had found another way to get whatever it was that we wanted. We took it from the TV. This was a new game that we started. Whenever you saw something on TV that you wanted, you could just take it. Well at least as long as it was lying loose and not in anybody's hands, then you could take it. Also you had to be the first one to grab it. Obviously, two people couldn't have the same thing at the same time. We would accumulate an inventory list of what items we had acquired. This became a competition between Billy, Gordie, Sissy, and myself. I can't remember who was the most successful. Another fun game was to travel around the house without touching the floor. You had to jump from a chair, to a couch, to whatever else would keep you off the floor. We would crawl up the banister on the stairway. I don't think Mom was too fond of us playing this game.

Finally the day that I had been waiting for arrived – the last day of school before the summer break. Allan Wells had been promoted! Thus there was no more to fear from him. The other Wells would still be around, but I figured Donna and Max wouldn't be so brave without Allan around to back them up. Allan would be going to high school in Orangeville along with Ernie; nevertheless, that school was big enough to avoid anyone that you didn't want to associate with. As you can surmise, Ernie also passed his grade, as did all of us Coopers. During the morning recess, I was contemplating another summer of fun and games on the farm; however, Allan had a surprise in store for us yet. He had enlisted Henry and some of the other older boys to assist him in giving all of the boys a farewell gift. He lined us all up against the school wall and ordered Henry to punch each one of us in the face. The funny part about memory is how everyone always remembers things only from their point of view. In this case, that is definitely true. I have absolutely no recollection of Ernie, Billy, and Gordie on this day. But they must have been there. Did Allan have his new found friend punched as well? I don't know. Anyway, I remember some of the other kids getting punched by Henry, then suddenly it was my turn. As Henry swung his arm towards my face, I ducked. Henry's fist glanced off the brick wall that we had been standing against. That was a mistake. Now, Henry was mad. Now, he really wanted to hit me. He was no longer just following orders. He swung again and I felt the full force of his fist against my mouth.

"Shit! That hurt," Henry yelled.

He was right. It hurt like hell! I lifted my hand to my mouth to see if my teeth were still all there. I was bleeding.

"Someone help the Cooper kid clean himself up," demanded Allan. "I don't want Miss Evans to see Henry's handy work. You're not supposed to make them bleed, Henry."

"Thanks for thinking about me," I said sarcastically as I was helped away.

I did still have all my teeth, but I lost part of one of my front teeth. The corner had been chipped off. I had a lasting memory of Allan Wells.

In the summer of 1958, the Repooc clan declared war. Our enemy was the Milkweed. We made a pledge not to rest until they had been eliminated. We fought against terrible odds. Yllib, Eidrog, and I would invade a field full of milkweeds with our swords swinging. We would hack them down with a vengeance. Sometimes we suffered casualties. If you allowed the sap from inside the milkweed to get on your body; that meant you were injured wherever the white fluid landed. One time my right arm was badly wounded, but I just switched my sword to my left hand and bravely fought on. Another time, Yllib suffered a mortal blow to the throat. The war was going badly until we convinced the Thistles to join our side. The Pussy Willows remained neutral. The Thistles were great strategists. The taller a thistle was, the higher their rank. I specifically remember saluting a very tall thistle adorned with a huge purple flower. General Thistle, we called him. As long as we had the Thistles on our side, we never feared wading in amongst hundreds of Milkweeds. That turned the tide, and we successfully defended the Repooc Club from the Milkweed horde.

Once after a particular bloody battle, me, Billy, and Gordie stripped off all our clothes and ran nude through the pine trees at the edge of our farm. We spent several hours sneaking through the small forest, trying to stay hidden from the road. It became a game to see how far we could travel on the farm without being spotted by anyone, especially Sissy. As far as I know, we were not sighted.

One day, Gordie and I were playing with a long cardboard roll. We pretended it was a javelin and were having a contest to see who could throw it the furthest. Gordie was winning, of course. We were part way through our competition when Billy came outside.

"That looks like fun. Let me throw that thing," Billy requested.

"Later," Gordie said, "Benny and I are having a game."

"That's OK, Gordie," I said. "I'm not doing so well anyway."

"No, Billy can wait his turn."

"Give me that thing."

"Nope, not yet."

Billy tried to grab the javelin from Gordie's hands.

"Let go, Billy. I said wait your turn. You've been hanging around Allan Wells too much."

Just as Gordie got his insult out, Billy had succeeded in wresting control of the javelin from Gordie's grasp.

"Don't compare me to that jerk!" shouted Billy as Gordie took off towards the house. Billy then hurled the javelin towards Gordie's head.

"Look out, Gordie!" I yelled.

Gordie ducked just in time to see the cardboard javelin

sail over his head and right through the back-kitchen window, which was closed. Amazingly, it put a perfect round hole in the pane of glass without shattering the whole thing. Gordie just looked up towards the window and started laughing.

"Nice shot, Billy. How'd you do that?"

I looked over at Billy to see him break into a wide grin.

"It was kind of neat, wasn't it?"

And then we all joined in the laughter. Soon, Mom appeared out the back door.

"What was that noise? What are you three up to now?" she wanted to know.

"Just playing, Mom," Gordie answered first. "We're just playing."

One day that summer, we had a phone call from Brad. He wanted us all to be standing outdoors the following Sunday at 2:00 in the afternoon. He had a surprise for us. We all wondered what the surprise could be, but my bet was that he would be coming up the driveway in a new car. We knew he was to be married that August; was his surprise related to that? Thus, that Sunday we were all standing in the yard between the house and the barn waiting for the arrival of whatever was about to happen. We were all there – Mom, The Old Man, Ernie, Billy, Gordie, Sissy, and me. And Happy too, of course. Suddenly I heard a loud rumble.

"What was that?" I shouted.

Before anyone could answer, I looked upwards just in time to see a jet plane pass over my head and skim over the top of the house. It appeared to just miss the lightning rods on top of our house, although I'm sure it was not near as close as it seemed to me. The noise was deafening.

"Hello Buddy!" yelled Mom.

"I don't think he can hear you, Mom," remarked Gordie.

"I know that, dear, but that's not the point. Come on, Buddy! Do it again!"

"I don't think he'll do it again, Mom," Ernie commented.

"Yes," said The Old Man, "he's turning around. Here he comes again."

This time I had the opportunity to watch the CF-100 approach. I now knew what I was waiting for. I could see the jet coming towards us from the other side of the house.

"He's lower this time!" Billy observed.

"Hello Buddy! Hello Buddy!" Sissy began to scream as she jumped up and down waving her arms frantically. Then we all joined in the festivities including Happy, who looked up at the sky and barked in confusion. In an instance the plane sailed over the house, virtually grazing the top of the barn, and disappeared into the distance. The roar of the jet remained with us longer than the plane itself. I waited until the normal silence returned before speaking.

"Do you think Brad saw us?"

"For sure, Benny," Mom answered first. Ernie just shook his head to indicate a negative response.

"Well, I don't care what you kids think. I'm sure that Buddy could see us. I even thought that I could see him waving."

"Did you know he was going to do that, Mom?" I wondered aloud.

"I had a feeling that he was going to fly over the farm; but I didn't know he was going to be so low. What a noise."

"It was great, right Mommy?" noted Sissy.

"That was certainly exciting, that's true as light, dear."

"Yeah," added The Old Man, "except I thought he was going to hit the barn there for a second. He was low. I hope he doesn't get in trouble if anyone complains about the noise. But it was a nice surprise. It was good to see him flying, since we had missed him at the Ex."

That was one time that I had to agree with The Old Man.

The next weekend, Fred and Them came to visit again. The Old Man, Fred, and Ron decided that all the kids needed a special treat. They disappeared in the barn and not too long later, The Old Man and Ron resurfaced carrying a large silver tub. It was the candy floss machine. Then Fred came towards us carrying a large package. It contained the pink powder

124

which was used to make the candy floss.

"How do you run this thing, I wonder?" Ron asked.

"Who knows," said The Old Man. "Just throw the stuff in the tub and turn it on. It can't be that difficult."

"Does my little jockey want some candy floss?" Ron queried. Ron always said that I should be a jockey because I was so small. He was an enthusiastic racing fan and often went to the track in Toronto with Fred and Tom. I argued that I didn't know anything about horses. "You could learn," Ron would say. "I'm serious. You would make a great jockey." I would just grin or laugh and say nothing in rebuttal.

Soon there was more than enough candy-floss for the five Cooper children plus Lizzie and April. There was even some left over for the grownups. It was just like having our very own fair in our farmyard.

"Won't you get in trouble for taking the candy floss machine out, Dad?" I questioned.

"No one will know. We'll put it all back."

"Won't they notice the powder stuff missing?"

"No, we only used a little bit. Anyway, who cares? How can they complain about a few kids having some enjoyment out of that stuff? It was just sitting there all summer. Besides, we won't be here much longer. We're moving in August."

"We're moving, again?"

"Yes, I got a new job for another phone company. It's a great chance to get ahead. I'm going to buy a house too. We'll finally have our own house. I told your Mom last night."

"Oh," I said. I didn't know what else to say.

The first weekend in August, Ernie, Billy, and Gordie announced that they were going to go camping. With the help of some subtle face-screwing and whining, I convinced my brothers and Mom that I should be allowed to camp too. We went as far away as we could to spend the Saturday night. We went to one of the fields back behind the chicken coop. We even went further back than our wooden fort. We pitched our tent on a small knoll where we could view most of the Robertsons' farm. That way, we would be able to have a good, long look at our site of many wars, games, and other adventures during the last two years. It had seemed much longer. I had experienced so much, yet time did not pass by quickly. After all, I was still only nine.

Our tent was a replica of an Indian teepee. It had a tall pole in the centre which held up the canvas material to a sharp point. There was plenty of room for the four of us inside. I was really looking forward to my first night away from home. I did not count my days in the hospital with bad kidneys when I was a baby. I didn't remember that. Ernie had brought along all the necessary supplies so that we wouldn't have to return to the house for anything. In fact, I was under strict orders not to go back, no matter what. I had to pretend that we were miles and miles away from civilization. That sounded good to me. I was an expert at pretending.

Ernie cooked dinner over a campfire. We had one of my favourite meals – wieners and beans. We roasted marshmallows for dessert. After the fire went out, Ernie lit the lantern which we had brought. We stayed up until 2:00, talking and laughing. It was the latest that I had ever stayed up. It was great fun. When it was finally time to sleep, I had no trouble even though the ground was hard.

"Wake up, Benny. Wake up." It was Billy.

"What for? It's still dark."

"No, it's light out. It's almost eight o'clock. The tent fell down on us. That's why it's dark."

"Why did the tent fall down? Did Gordie kick the pole?"

"No, I didn't," Gordie answered.

"Let's get up and see what's going on," Ernie said.

So we each crawled out. I was the last one out into the open. Before I had completely crept out of the fallen tent, I heard Billy speak.

"Holy shit, look at that!"

"What!"

I stood up to face the tent to see what had attracted everyone's attention. There were hoof-prints leading from one side of the hill, right across the tent, and down the other side towards the fence.

"Look at that," said Gordie. "Those cows walked right over the tent. They must have just missed us by inches."

"Cows? What cows?" I wondered. "We don't have any cows."

"But our neighbours do," Ernie responded. "Remember the fences aren't all up around here. And look there." Ernie pointed to a recent plop of cow dung sitting right beside the tent. "What do you think did that, a bird?"

We followed the tracks down the hill to the fallen fence that divided the two farms. We could see the cows grazing off in the distance. There was a large cube of blue cow salt right beside the fallen fence. Gordie took a rock and knocked off a corner of the salt where the cows hadn't licked yet. He gave a piece to me as well.

"Come on guys," Ernie said, "I'll make you a proper breakfast."

Licking on our salt, we headed back up the hill to see what was for breakfast. Breakfast started with a small box of cereal from one of those variety packs. I chose my favourite – Sugar Pops. We opened the boxes on the side, and poured the milk right in the box. I enjoyed the fact that we got to eat the cereal this way, and not in a bowl. I was glad that Ernie brought milk along so we didn't have to chase any cows. Then Ernie started another fire and he cooked bacon and eggs. We had our eggs scrambled, that was the first time that I ever had them that way. I don't think Ernie set out to make scrambled eggs; but when so many yolks broke, he decided that scrambled was the best approach. I thought breakfast was delicious.

"Let's go for a hike," Ernie announced after we had finished our morning meal.

"Where to?" I asked.

"Back that way, through the trees."

"That's not our property back there, is it?"

"No, that doesn't matter. No one will care. Come on."

I hesitated. I was tired through lack of sleep. And I

missed Mom and Sissy. I wasn't worried about trespassing. We did that all the time when we were Cowboys or Indians. Also, I must admit that I was still a little shaken from the close encounter with the cows.

"No, you guys go ahead. I'm going back home. I want to see Happy and Smokey. I'm too tired to walk far, anyway."

So that's how it turned out. I went back to the house and let Ernie, Billy, and Gordie go off on their own.

"Hello Ernie, Billy, Gordie, Benny, whatever your name is. What are you doing home?" Mom inquired.

This was an on-going game that Mom played. Once she had called out the names of all us boys in order before she got the right one. We all thought it was hilarious. Now she would say the same thing continually, just to make us laugh. After an exchange of greetings and an explanation of my return, I told Mom all about our exciting adventures. Shortly afterward, I went upstairs to play with Sissy. It was still only about 10:00 in the morning. My three brothers did not return until almost 5:00 in the afternoon. Mom was starting to worry about them. And so was I.

"Oh, we just decided to go for a long walk, Mom," Billy stated. "Then we had to pack up the tent and things. We had a fun day."

"I think Benny was afraid that you got trampled to death. He told me about the cattle."

"Oh, Mom," I protested, "I didn't think that. I just wondered where they went. That's all."

Gordie told me later why they were so long.

"We ran into these two men hunting. They had rifles."

"What were they shooting?"

"Oh, just groundhogs."

"Were you scared?"

"Of what? No, they were real nice guys. Guess what?"

"What?"

"They even let me shoot one of their guns."

"What did you shoot?"

"I just shot a tree. It would have knocked you over if you

had shot that rifle. You should have been there."

"I don't care. I had fun at home."

"What'd you do?"

"Nothing."

"You are jealous that you weren't there, aren't you?"

"No, I don't care."

"Liar, liar, pants on fire."

Then Gordie started singing a song.

I was a big shot,

Yesterday;

But boy, you oughta see me now,

I shot the head right off a cow.

For the next little while, Gordie would keep singing that song to me, just to make me mad. I would pretend that it didn't bother me.

"What do I care about a silly old gun for? I'm glad I wasn't there." I would argue. "I don't care, I'm only nine."

I remember our last night on Robertsons' farm. There were hundreds of fireflies in the field at the bottom of our lane. It was kind of eerie. I hadn't seen so many before. We caught some and put them in jars. Billy squished one in his hand and then showed how it made his hand light up in the dark. I didn't want to come in when it was time for bed. Partly because of the fireflies, but partly because I knew that this was my last night in my own adventure-land. But eventually it was time to go to bed. Before going in, I released my fireflies from the jar and watched them fly off into the distance.

17 ~ Ice Cream All in One Place

In August 1958, we moved away from the farm to again take up life in a small town. This town was Hillsburgh, which is located to the southwest of Orangeville. So, we didn't really move that far; but, it could have been twenty miles or two hundred miles. It didn't matter. Life would not be the same. The biggest change was The Old Man's payment schedule. He now got paid every two weeks; and therefore, he would have more opportunities for drinking. The other main change (as The Old Man had told us earlier) was that we now lived in our own house. He really did buy a house. Well, at least he took a mortgage out on one. It cost $10,000. I thought that was a lot of money. We had a twenty-five year mortgage. I figured out that it would be 1983 and I would be thirty-four before the house would be paid for. That was an eternity away.

The Old Man borrowed a truck from the phone company to accomplish the move. It was really just a van, so we had to make several trips. I remember sitting in the back of the van with Gordie and Billy on one of the trips. The Old Man was in the front with Ernie. It was open behind the front seats, so we could hear The Old Man as he talked. He was talking about how things would be different now. We would have more money. We wouldn't have to worry about being poor anymore. Besides his new job and an increase in salary, he had devised a new money making scheme.

"I'm going to buy a van like this one," The Old Man started. "We can drive around together and collect bottles and return them for the deposit. Look at all the bottles at the side of the road. Beer bottles, pop bottles. Yes, that's what we'll do. We can spend our Saturday's collecting bottles. That will pay for the van many times over. You kids will have lots of extra money to buy whatever you want. Yes, things are going to be different now. You wait and see. I'll stop drinking and we can be together more. We can work together. The Cooper Bottle Collection Company. I'll get the name put on the truck. People are always throwing out bottles. We can make a lot of money. What do you think boys? Sounds good, eh?"

We all looked at each other not knowing what to say. Gordie started to grin and I could hardly hold back the laughter. Finally, Ernie broke the silence.

"How many bottles do you think we could fit in this truck, Dad?"

Hillsburgh had a population of approximately 600 people at that time. It is located in a valley with a twisting, winding road leading into the town at the south end. At the north end, there is a steep hill leading up and out of town. We lived on a side street which jutted off from the main street near the top of this hill. Our house was a two-storey building which backed onto the side of the hill. When you walked in the front door, you entered the living room. Off to the right was the dining room. However, situated in the centre of the archway which separated the two rooms, sat the oil furnace. That's right, we had finally graduated from wood heat to oil. But we still had the familiar stovepipes spouting from the furnace and circulating to the rest of the house. As you walked to the back of the house, you entered the large kitchen. A large wood stove occupied a good portion of the room. Hey, you didn't think we would abandon wood heat altogether now, did you? Off to the left was another exit door which emptied out into our driveway. On the back wall, there was another door which led into a back shed which currently served as the storage area for our wood. Turn right when you entered the kitchen and you entered the bathroom. Between the kitchen and the living room, a door hid the stairway which led to the bedrooms upstairs. The top of the stairs turned into a long hallway. On the right, the first door was Sissy's room. She had now graduated from the old crib. She had her very own single bed now. The next door on the right, led into Mom and The Old Man's room. The first peculiar thing you noticed when you looked into this room, was Sissy's bed on the right-hand side of our parents' double bed. There was no wall between the two rooms. Soon a wire and a blanket became the missing wall. Turn left halfway down the hall and you entered a bedroom which belonged to Ernie and Billy. That left the room for Gordie and me at the end of the hall. Our window overlooked the road down below and the neighbour's house across the road. This was a big improvement on the window looking into the forbidden shed with the strange nocturnal visitor.

Behind our house, there was a cut in the hill where large rocks had fallen down below. This wasn't on our property, but it was a quick fence jump to play in that area which nobody really claimed. On the right side of our house, there was a wooded lot which had been left vacant. When I say wooded lot, I don't mean any large evergreens or anything like that. There was a small orchard of apple trees and then a hilly area with a dense grove of smaller trees. I think there were some elm. I don't know what else. I just remember the amount of vines which had grown entangled between the trees everywhere. They were great for making believe you were Tarzan. In the area between the orchard and the forest (which we called it), there were a few grassy knolls. We immediately scouted out this area to continue our war battles. The Old Man said that he thought the owner of this lot lived in Toronto, so we could play in it whenever we wanted. On the left of our house there was a large stone house, but it wasn't really that close. And across the street, there lived a family which we came to know very well. They were the Smales and they had three children, two girls and one boy. The oldest daughter, Sarah was somewhere between the age of Billy and Gordie. The youngest was a girl named Jennifer or Jenny who was about the same age as Sissy. The boy who was born in between the two girls was about a year younger than me. On the first day that we arrived, there was a knock on our front door.

"It's for you, Benny," Mom called out.

"Me? How can it be for me?"

"It's the boy from next door. He wants to know if the little boy can come out to play. I think he means you, Benny."

So I went to the door to meet my new neighbour. I was met by a boy just a little bit taller than me but considerably heavier.

"Hello," he said, "do you want to play?"

"Sure. What's your name? I'm Benny."

"Sammy. Sammy Smale. But everybody calls me Sammy Snail."

"Do you like being called that?"

"No, not really."

"Then, I'll just call you Sammy. What do you wanna play, Sammy?"

"Come see my new toy gun. It shoots plastic bullets."

"OK. Let's go."

And that was the start of my new friendship. But before I tell you too much more about Hillsburgh and our new home, I need to tell you about a few other things.

The family member who had to make the biggest adjustment to the move was Happy. Mom and The Old Man said he had to be tied up outside. He had only lived on a farm and was not used to town life. They were still concerned with how he had reacted to that Midway girl. Also, one time when Fred and Them were visiting, Happy bared his teeth and growled at young April. Mom figured that Happy had become afraid of little girls. Especially when they were holding a stick. Smokey had no trouble adjusting. She still had her wooden box that she could sleep in behind the kitchen stove.

Shortly, just after we moved, Mom came home one day with new teeth and new glasses. She looked great! Like a million bucks and at least ten years younger. We were going to Ottawa in a week to go to Brad's wedding. Mom explained how she didn't want to disappoint Brad again. And she wanted to look her best for the wedding. She started to apologize for spending money on herself.

"Don't be silly, Mom," Ernie spoke for all of us. "It's about time you did it."

"I wonder what The Old Man will say," Mom wondered. But she need not have worried. The Old Man's reaction was, "You look different, dear. Did you do something to your hair?"

So the next weekend, we all headed up to Ottawa in the car. Sissy sat up in the front between The Old Man and Mom. The four of us boys sat in the back seat. I'm not sure what we did with Happy and Smokey. Knowing The Old Man, I'm sure we would have just left Happy tied up in the backyard with a few days' supply of food. Smokey would have been left out to wander the streets. Anyway, there was nothing too memorable about the drive to Ottawa. We drove up on a Friday while the wedding was on Saturday. To kill time in the back, we used to have a competition. We would each name a make of car and whomever chose the type that we saw the most would be declared the winner. I was a Pontiac man. Billy would choose Volkswagen and he would usually win with that choice. I'm not sure if there were really more Volkswagens on the road or if they were just the easiest to recognize.

We stayed at Catherine's family's place. I remember that Brad came by on Saturday morning and that really upset the family, because they said it was unlucky to see the bride before the wedding on the eventful day. I had never heard that one before. It seemed weird to me. Brad argued that he had a right to visit his mother. Brad was eventually let in while Catherine hid in a bedroom somewhere. Brad had a surprise for me and Gordie. He gave each of us new jackets which he had bought in Iceland while he had been there with the Air Force. They were reversible. My jacket was orange, black, and white on one side with a tiger on the back. I thought it looked like a Hamilton Tiger-Cat uniform. The other side was all green with a map of Iceland on the back. Gordie's was pretty similar but with different colours. I think his was blue on the Icelandic side. I thought that they were really neat. We didn't do much that day except prepare for the wedding. Sissy was the flower girl, so she had to get her hair done up. Mom put her hair in ringlets.

"Hey Sissy," Gordie said, "You look like Benny in some of those old pictures."

Both Sissy and I gave Gordie a dirty look.

"I think you look great, Sissy," Ernie volunteered.

"Yeah, you do," added Gordie. "I was just teasing Benny."

They were right. Sissy was the hit of the wedding. Everyone commented how pretty she looked when she walked down the aisle. I proudly told everyone that she was my sister.

After the wedding there was a reception in a hall on the Uplands base. We were all concerned how The Old Man would behave during the party; however, he disappeared right after dinner. We found out that he was downstairs drinking in the bar. Mom had mixed feelings about that. She was embarrassed when people kept asking where he had gone, but she was happy that he wasn't ruining the reception for Brad and Catherine. Later in the evening, The Old Man did make an appearance in the hall. While talking to one of Catherine's relatives, his voice became louder and I heard him say something about 'the gray-haired old bag'. Quickly, one of Brad's friends came to the rescue and asked The Old Man if he wanted to go downstairs for another drink. And that ended that tense moment. You didn't have to go downstairs for a drink; it was available in the hall. I remember that Ernie, Billy, and even Gordie stole a few sips of some mixed drinks. I decided it was best to remain a non-drinker for the time being. After all, I was only nine.

The next morning the five of us kids decided to go for a walk and a little sightseeing of Ottawa before it was time to make the long return car journey. Gordie and I decided that we would wear our new jackets even though it wasn't that cold. We both put them on with the map of Iceland showing on the back. We went for a long walk in order to see the parliament buildings and the Ottawa River which curved behind them. After a considerable time touring around that area, we headed down Rideau Street. We passed a man standing on the corner who seemed to be interested in our movements. A few seconds later, we heard a voice call out.

"Hello. Excuse me."

We turned around to face the man that we saw languishing by the corner.

"Do you want your ice cream all in one place?" he slurred. At least that's what it sounded like he said. All of us could recognize that the man had been drinking. We had a bit of experience in this area.

"Pardon," Ernie replied.

"Do you want your ice cream all in one place?" he repeated.

"Excuse me, I don't understand," Ernie asked again.

"Do you want your ice cream all in one place? I said."

"Yes, I know, but I don't understand what you mean."

"Oh, of course you don't. How stupid of me. Do you want your ice cream all in one place or do you want to have it in several places?"

"What? What ice cream?"

"The ice cream that I'm going to buy for you. I want to show you boys, and girl, the way we treat people here in Canada."

We all looked confused.

"So when you go back to Iceland, you'll remember how Canadians treat visitors. You've come a long way. All the way from Iceland. I want to show all of you a warm Canadian welcome."

It then clicked. We all knew what was happening. Ernie continued to be our spokesman.

"No thanks. Thanks, but you misunderstand. We're not from Iceland, we're…"

"Don't be shy. I know that you're from Iceland. I saw the boys' jackets. Come on let's go in this restaurant here. We can get ice cream here."

"I'm not from Iceland," I finally spoke up, "we're from Hillsburgh."

"Sorry, I don't know Iceland that well. So I'm not sure where that is. Come on then."

Before we knew what was happening, he had ushered Sissy into the nearby restaurant and we all quickly followed. I started to be afraid of what the stranger's motives might really be. We sat at a booth and soon we all had a bowl of ice cream in front of us. The man asked us how we liked our visit and how we liked the city of Ottawa. These questions we could answer without straying too far from the truth. Luckily he didn't ask too many questions about life in Iceland.

"Is it cold where you come from?" he wondered.

"Oh yes," Billy said, "but not too much different than here." Also not a lie.

After we finished our desserts, the stranger again asked if we wanted to go to another place and have some more ice cream.

"No thanks," we all replied.

"We have to go now," Ernie continued. "Our parents will wonder where we went."

"OK then. You better get on your way. Remember though, how we treated you here in Canada. Be sure to tell everyone about how good we are to people from other lands. All right?"

"We'll be sure to tell everybody all about it," Ernie

answered.

"Bye, good luck on your travel home."

As we headed out the door of the restaurant, an old Chinese man at the counter whispered to us.

"You're not really from Iceland, are you?"

"No," said Gordie. "We've never even been there."

"I didn't think so."

As we walked out the door, we all burst into laughter together.

"Come on," Ernie insisted, "let's get out of here before he pays and comes back out. And one more thing. The next time we go for a walk. Turn the jackets to the other side!"

And we did keep Ernie's promise to the stranger. We told everyone we knew about the day that we had ice cream all in one place.

18 ~ Good Things Come in Small Packages

The night before school began, Sammy Smale came over from next door and suggested that we go look at the new 1959 cars. I didn't understand what he was talking about. This was only 1958; how could we see cars of the future? I hadn't realized that new cars for the next year were released at the end of the summer. I wasn't used to seeing new cars in the country. So Sammy, Gordie and I went down the hill a few blocks to the local Hillsburgh car dealer. Sitting in front of the dealership was a black car with huge fins on the back – a new 1959 Chevrolet.

"Isn't it great?" Sammy commented.

"Do you think fins will get bigger every year?" I replied. "I think I like the 58 Chevy better."

"I'd take a 57 Chevy first," continued Gordie.

"Well, I love it. I bet it flies. Just look at it," insisted Sammy.

"Maybe it will just take some getting used to," I ventured.

"Nah," responded Gordie as he held his nose, "it stinks."

"You country boys are weird," expressed Sammy.

"Yup," I shot back, "where do we see the new manure spreaders?"

The first day of school, Mom accompanied us to be registered. Sissy came along as well, but just for the walk. She was still only five, and this time that was considered too young to be beginning a public education. The school was an old brick building at the south-end of town about 15 minutes away on foot. Ernie, as I told you earlier, had started high school, so for the first time he was not beginning the same school with us. He had caught a bus at the top of the hill for his trip to school in the town of Erin which was around 5 miles away. When we got to the school, we were welcomed by a woman in her mid-forties and an older British man. He had to be somewhere in his sixties. The school was divided into two rooms. The woman was the teacher for Grades 1 to 4 while the elderly man looked after the Grade 5 to 8 classes. The man looked at Billy and spoke first.

"You must be in my class, young man. What grade are you in?"

"That's right. I'm in six," Billy responded.

"Then," the woman began as she looked at an obviously younger Gordie, "you must be in my class."

"No, I'm in Grade 7," Gordie answered proudly.

"Oh, sorry, I thought you were younger than your brother."

"Yes, I am."

"Oh, then this young lad is in my class," she added as she turned her attention towards me. "That's for sure."

"I'm in Grade 5," was my succinct reply.

The woman looked doubtful as she stared at the small boy standing in front of her. Mom finally broke the confused silence.

"That's right. I have the report cards right here. Benny is going into Grade 5. He is only nine years old but he started school when he was five, you see."

"I'm only nine," I contributed.

"Oh, I see. OK don't tell me that this young miss is not in my class."

"I'm not old enough for school yet," Sissy explained.

"Oh."

So the three of us went off to meet our new classmates, while the woman proceeded back to her class with no new students to introduce. I felt sorry for her embarrassment but I was glad that I was going off to the class with the big kids. I think she thought that I was in Grade 2. I don't think she still really believed our story. Anyway, our teacher turned out to be called Mr. McKenzie. Robert McKenzie as we found out later. On the first day, the afternoon recess seemed to last longer than I was used to. I thought that maybe I had missed the bell and started to head into the class.

"Shhh." one boy whispered, "you'll wake up McKenzie."

I looked up at the front to see Mr. McKenzie asleep at his desk with his head lying in his arms folded across the desk. I then looked at the boy who had spoken.

"Yeah, he falls asleep a lot," he answered before I had even asked. "He'll wake up soon."

And sure enough in a few more minutes, Mr. McKenzie lifted his head and signaled the continuation of classes without acknowledging that anything unusual had even happened. And the other boy was right. This did turn out to be a fairly regular occurrence. Within a week, Mr. McKenzie had started to demonstrate some favouritism towards me. Whenever I would answer a question correctly, Mr. McKenzie would comment.

"See what I mean. Good things come in small packages."

I had mixed feelings about this attention. I didn't like being centred out from the other kids, however I did enjoy being complemented for my size. It was a big improvement over being called 'shrimp'; that's for sure. One day, Mr. McKenzie even made a big production of having me measured. I was 3 feet 11 and ½ inches. Not even four feet tall yet. Some of my classmates were close to six feet tall. That caused some laughter. Mr. McKenzie brought a halt to the laughter and again repeated his phrase about the proven relationship between quality and container size.

Mr. McKenzie sure had some old-fashioned ideas about teaching. No ballpoint pens were allowed. Everyone used a straight-pen and a bottle of ink to write with. I couldn't understand the reasoning. You could make a much bigger mess with a straight-pen and ink. It is true what they say about inkwells and girls pigtails. They do match. Not that I indulged in this particular fun-time. But the pens were great for chewing on. He also spent a lot of time telling us about 'the good old days' back in Great Britain. And if we ever complained about anything, he would tell us how lucky we were to be in Canada. "In Russia, they tie you to your seats," he would describe. I had a hard time envisaging all those children tied to their seats.

I don't remember too many other kids from that year. There was Richard Watson who was not afraid to speak his opinion. He was Gordie and Billy's friend more than mine though. He had a younger brother Joe that was my age; however Joe was in the other classroom. As was my new neighbour and friend Sammy Smale. Then there were two brothers named Fryman. The older brother, George, I remember because of one distinguishing feature – a glass eye. He had a habit of removing his eye to shock people. The only other boy that I remember from that first year was called Errol Flynn. Listening to all the kidding that he received about his name made me realize that being continually asked about my relationship to Gary Cooper wasn't so bad after all. At least none of us inherited the exact same name as a movie star.

About a week after school started, I was walking home with Gordie when Richard Watson came up to walk beside us.

"Hi guys. Can I join you? Sorry to hear about your dog."

"What do you mean?" I asked. "Sorry for what?"

"Oh, you don't know. I'm sorry. I guess nobody's told you yet."

"Told us what?" Gordie wanted to know. "What about our dog?"

"I guess I shouldn't have mentioned it. You'll find out when you get home."

"What happened to Happy?" I demanded. "Did he get hit by a car? Is he dead?"

"No, nothing like that. I guess I can tell you. He attacked your neighbour."

"What? What neighbour?" said Gordie.

"The Smale girl. The young one. What's her name?"

"Jenny?" I replied. "Happy bit Jenny?"

"Yes, bit her right on the neck. That's what I heard anyway."

"How do you know this?" asked Gordie.

"Billy told me. He went home at lunch-time and so did I."

"I wondered why Billy never came back after lunch," I stated. "I thought he must have got sick."

"Come on, Benny! Let's go," yelled Gordie as he started to run towards home.

I quickly ran after him leaving Richard walking by himself. We made the usual 15 minute walk in about 5 minutes although it was uphill most of the way. We quickly ran in the front door and shouted in unison.

"Where's Happy? What happened?"

Mom repeated what we had already heard from Richard Watson. Happy had indeed bitten Jenny Smale on the neck. Jenny had been taken to the doctor, but she was going to be OK.

"Why, Mom? Why did Happy do it?" Gordie questioned.

"Did she have a stick?" I added.

"No, nothing like that, dear. Happy was in the house with me and Sissy when Jenny came to the front door. When I opened the front door, Happy just jumped for her throat. I don't know why. Perhaps he thought he was protecting us. I don't know."

"Where's Happy now?" I inquired. "Is he in the

backyard?"

"No, Benny. The police took him away."

"When can he come back?"

At that point, Billy entered the room.

"Don't you two understand?" he said. "Happy's gone for good. He's not coming back. They have to put him to sleep. He did a bad thing."

"I'll watch him. He won't do that again." I argued.

"It's no use, Benny," continued Billy. "It's too late. Happy is gone."

"Why did we have to move," I cried. "Happy loved the farm. Why did we have to come to such a big town?"

At that point, The Old Man walked in the room.

"What are you crying about, Benny?"

"About Happy," Mom answered for me.

"Crying over a damn dog. That's crazy. Come on Benny, don't worry. I'll get you another dog. Any dog you want."

"I don't want another dog. I want Happy," I cried as I ran upstairs to the bedroom.

And of course, Billy was correct. We never saw Happy again.

19 ~ Follow the Bouncing Ball

I just realized that I have told you all about our games and other stuff, but I have never mentioned us doing any housework. I don't want you to think that we Cooper boys were completely lazy, so I better mention some of the things we did to help out Mom. We used to take turns doing the dishes, for example. I was usually teamed with Billy. He was the washer and I was the dryer. That means that Ernie and Gordie made up the other team. I think Ernie was the washer. I preferred being the dryer because it was the washer's job to clean the stove and kitchen counter. Still we found a way to make this chore a game. We would time each other to see what team was the fastest. We would often be faster because Billy was such a great washer. It was quite a challenge to keep up to his pile of clean dishes. We must have done other things too, but I can't think of them right now. So enough about work.

That fall at school, we were playing a softball game at recess when Billy hit a foul ball into the field adjacent to the schoolyard. This field had grass at least a foot high. Since we weren't allowed to leave the school premises without permission, someone went inside to ask Mr. McKenzie what we should do. He decided that six of the older boys should hop the wire fence and search for the missing baseball, so Billy and five other boys climbed over the fence and commenced the hunt. The rest of the boys and all the girls were ordered back into the school for the remaining afternoon lessons. We were only back into class for a few minutes though, when Mr. McKenzie, observing the futility experienced by the search team, concluded that reinforcements were required.

"Who wants to lend an eye and help find the baseball?" he asked.

"I will," someone replied.

"George, don't be a smart aleck!"

I turned around just in time to see George Fryman holding his glass eye up in the air. Finally Mr. McKenzie determined that the prudent approach would be to get all of the boys to look for the missing ball. I guess a lost baseball was more important than our education.

"Now," Mr. McKenzie explained, "I want all of you boys to spread out in a long line and hold hands, so that you cover every square inch of the field. We know that the ball's in there somewhere."

So Gordie and I with the rest of the boys hurried outside and joined the other six characters in search of a baseball. We all spread out in every which direction and began to scour the long grass, which came up past my knees, for a white, round object. Suddenly, we heard Mr. McKenzie yelling out of the school window at us.

"Come on, boys! Do what I said. Join hands in a line so that you cover the whole field."

Therefore a few boys tried to form a line across the width of the field, but the last thing that a bunch of boys ever want to do, is to hold hands. Hence, nobody did. And we formed a pitiful line. Some boys were nowhere near the rest of us. I was hunting between a couple other boys. They were not bad boys; however, I didn't especially want to hold their hands. So, I didn't. We were all laughing and playing and having a right good time when we heard Mr. McKenzie bellow out the window again.

"Get in here, now! All of you! On the double! Let's go! Right in here this minute!"

"What's the matter, Mr. McKenzie?" someone shouted. "We haven't found the ball yet."

"I don't care. You heard me. Get in here!"

So we all made our way back inside the classroom to see what was up. As we walked into the school through the door at the back of the classroom, Mr. McKenzie spoke right away.

"Don't bother sitting down. Come up to the front, all of you. Line up in a row at the front. OK, is that all of you? What did you boys think you were doing out there? It wasn't recess. I didn't see anyone looking for the ball. You were just playing. You all deserve the strap. In fact, that's what I'm going to do."

He reached into the top middle drawer of his desk and brought out a long, leather strap. Mr. McKenzie went to the far end of the line from where I was standing. I was the last one in the line at the opposite end. Then he ordered each boy to hold out his hand as he struck them across the palm and wrist with as strong a blow of the strap as he could manage. One of the boys, I think it was Richard Watson, moved his hand away just as Mr. McKenzie's arm was coming down towards the target. This caused the strap to strike Mr. McKenzie right on his thigh.

"Damn you, Watson. Put your hand up again. And this time don't move it until I say so."

Richard then got two lashes but still it didn't stop him from smiling. Mr. McKenzie continued down the line towards my end.

"Ow!" Billy yelled when he was hit. Gordie just grimaced and said nothing. As each boy received their corporal punishment, I feared the pain that I would be facing in a matter of seconds. Then it was my turn. Billy said he saw tears in my eyes, but I don't remember that part. I looked up at Mr. McKenzie as he brought the strap up into the air. And then suddenly it came down and very lightly tapped my hand.

He had stopped his arm before the blow was struck. The whole classroom groaned.

"I didn't strap Benny because he was the only one that was seriously looking for the ball," Mr. McKenzie explained. "The rest of you were just playing around."

More groans were heard.

"I told you that good things come in small packages."

I heard the chants of 'Teacher's Pet' all the rest of that day and for years later. Especially from my brothers. We never did find the ball.

A couple of weeks later, the entire class received the gift of a free book – the Bible. Actually, it was The New Testament only. However, I felt quite proud to have my very own copy of the Bible. I liked the nice leather binding and I wrote my name in the front. Excitedly, I took it home with me and that night I kept leafing through it. Then I began to read it from the beginning. After a few verses, I soon realized that I didn't understand a single thing. So I flipped through the pages some more. I then felt the cover, put it down, picked it up, and thumbed the pages one more time. Eventually after wondering what I should do with my new gift, I took it back to school and placed it inside my desk.

Around that time, Mom and us five kids started to attend church most Sundays. Sometimes, The Old Man came too. We belonged to The United Church. I hadn't remembered going to church before, so I didn't understand why we were going now. Gordie said that we used to go to church before, but I couldn't remember any of it. He said we hadn't been for a while because it was too difficult in the country. Now we just had to walk down into the village at the bottom of the hill. I had about as much luck understanding the minister's sermons as I did at my attempts to read the Bible. So I just sat there and said nothing and daydreamed. I would sit between Mom and Sissy. I didn't want to sit by Gordie, because he would kick and punch me in order to get some reaction from me. Never hard enough to hurt me, mind you. He was just trying to make me laugh. And I knew if I had looked at Gordie's face, we both would have broken into laughter. He would make faces as he imitated the screwed-up looks that I was making.

Also at that time, we started attending Sunday school. We went downstairs right after the sermon. We would all sit in a circle as one of the parishioner women taught us some of the Bible stories. These I could understand, but I never remembered them. I would sit quietly and not say a word unless I was asked a question. Then I would say "Hmm, umm,…, umm,…" until someone else answered for me. My favourite part was when she would tell us that it was time to go. Gordie showed the same interest in Sunday school as I had. Sissy seemed to enjoy it though. Somehow, Ernie and Billy didn't have to participate in this particular brand of religious education. They were too old for Sunday school, I guess.

Georgetown is a small town about twenty-five miles south of Hillsburgh. When I say 'small town', I should qualify that statement with the fact that it all depends on your perspective. At that time going into Georgetown was like going into the city. It made Hillsburgh seem like an anthill in comparison. We would travel into Georgetown on the Friday that The Old Man got paid. At least it seemed like every second Friday, although it probably wasn't that often. But what the hell do I know now? Memory plays tricks on you. In order to get to Georgetown, we had to drive to the south-end of Hillsburgh, past our school, up the twisting road, and across Highway 24. If you turned left on Highway 24, you were heading into Erin (where Ernie went to school, remember) and if you turned right, you were off towards the city of Guelph. However, if you went straight, you went up another winding hill and on towards the direction of Georgetown. So this is the route that we took twice a month or so. The Old Man would drive us into Georgetown where Mom would do the shopping at the local A & P. The best part about this journey, was that Gordie and I each got a dollar to spend however we saw fit. I can't remember how much Sissy got to spend, but at that time she still thought money grew on trees. That's what we told her, anyhow. Ernie and Billy would remain at home. I would use my new found fortune to purchase some new toy. I recall buying a bow and arrow set that shot a rubber-tipped arrow towards my enemy (not a patch on what Ernie could manufacture), and I had bought a few toy cars. Not Dinky Toys, even then a dollar couldn't purchase a Dinky Toy. But a large friction-powered car was in my price range. Like the three-wheel vehicle I once bought, with the clear plastic cockpit (similar to those on fighter airplanes) attached to the top. Gordie and I would often buy chocolate cigarettes. They were better than the candy ones because they had real paper around the chocolate tobacco. So they looked like the real thing. We would eat them without removing the paper. I don't think that I've mentioned yet that The Old Man smoked. He used to roll his own cigarettes from a big can of Player's Navy Cut tobacco. Mom didn't smoke though. Anyways, I digress, those were the good things about our trips to Georgetown. The bad part was the return home. More often than not, we sat in the car parked in the parking lot of the grocery store while we waited for The Old Man to decide that it was time to head out. He would disappear into the local bar of course. We could smoke a whole pack of chocolate cigarettes while we waited. A few times he returned very drunk, and we had no choice other than to sit quietly in the car and hope that we could make it home safely. Miraculously, we always did. I would close my eyes and sit in sheer terror as we traversed the two winding gradients. More than once I thought we were going over the edge. But no, we never did. And no, my life never passed in front of my eyes. I thought more about the future and the possibility of not having the opportunity for enjoying one. I didn't want to die; after all I was only nine.

In November 1958, I watched The Wizard of Oz on TV for the first time. It had made its debut on television two years earlier (November 3, 1956 to be exact), but somehow I had missed that eventful premiere. I was enraptured. We were still seeing it in black and white and I had no idea that things turned to colour in the Land of Oz. I never knew that until many years later. But that didn't take away from the magic of Oz. Also, I didn't catch on until the end that the people in Oz looked a lot like Dorothy's acquaintances at home. In fact, by the time I watched it the following year, I had forgotten that all over again. I had never seen anything as frightening as flying monkeys before. It was great! This became a tradition over the years. Come November, The Wizard of Oz would be shown once more. I can't remember how many times I have seen it, but I could watch it again.

A few weeks later, The Old Man brought home an early Christmas present. It was something that I said earlier that I didn't want, but I was delighted when I saw what it was – a dog. A puppy actually. He was a jet black spirited mutt that somewhat resembled Happy. Naturally, we called him Blackie. Blackie took an instant liking to Billy and would follow him everywhere, except to school. He would provide good company to Mom and Sissy during the day while we were all away there.

That was the winter that I started collecting hockey cards. You know – the kind you paid five cents for in order to get four cards and a piece of gum. We used to flip them at school. You would hold them at your waist and flip them to the ground. You would win cards from other kids by playing such games as 'Heads or Tails' or 'Odd man wins'. I was a pretty good player, probably because I was closer to the ground than any other kid. I was eventually able to collect most of the Toronto Maple Leaf roster including Horton, Stanley, Baun, Brewer, Mahovlich, and my favourite George Armstrong, only to name a few. Ultimately, Mr. McKenzie decided to put a stop to this fun. He thought it was gambling and not fair to the poor children who had spent their hard earned nickels on their sports heroes only to fritter them away shortly after. We quit playing for a short time, but in due course we returned to our gambling ways in clandestine parts of the schoolyard. There I was able to complete my

Leaf collection.

Later in February '59, Claudia and Tom came to visit. It had been so long since I had seen my older sister that I could hardly remember her. I remembered things about her and various incidents, but I didn't really remember her at all. Tom I didn't know from Adam (whoever he is). Their oldest daughter, Lizzie, I hadn't seen since she was a newborn baby. Now she was 5 years old. The same age as Sissy, remember? Their youngest daughter, April, none of us had ever seen before. Then there was a new addition, a son Tommy who was close to two years old, that we obviously had never laid eyes on before. To avoid the confusion with the two Tom's, we called my uncle 'Big Tommy' and referred to my new nephew as 'Little Tommy' Thus it was quite a family reunion to have them come visit us. They had just returned from France and would shortly be on their way to Montreal as the Air Force had transferred Tom back to Canada again; and they had a couple weeks free to see the family before it was time to move to their new home.

It didn't matter that we hadn't seen them for so long or not at all. I better reword that. Of course it mattered. What I meant to say, was that it made no difference to how we reacted to seeing them. It was like we had just seen Claudia a few days ago. We had a great time talking about the past and she laughed as she told the story about me saying, "That's not the way Mom does it" over five years back. And Tom fit right in. He was great. I felt like I had always known him. I thought that if I ever grew up and got married, I wanted it to be like Claudia and Tom. I loved the way they kidded and joked with each other. Sissy was only two weeks older than Lizzie, so they had a great time together. And April was only a year younger than them both, hence she could join in their play.

On the Saturday afternoon after they arrived, The Old Man came home with his usual case of 24 Brading's Red Cap and placed it at his feet by the kitchen table. He asked Claudia and Tom to drink with him, consequently they agreed mainly so that there would be less for The Old Man to drink. Tom

152

drank a few bottles and so did Claudia. However, they couldn't keep up with The Old Man. But this didn't stop Claudia. She started pouring beer into a nearby plant as she pretended to be consuming more than she actually desired. I think it was an African Violet. But still The Old Man drank close to a dozen beer, if not more, before it was time for dinner. Nevertheless, he had behaved himself so far. I assumed with company The Old Man was trying to be at his best. Wrong assumption.

As dinnertime approached, Mom went to the basement door (I think I forgot to tell you about this door off the kitchen earlier) to bring up the potatoes.

"Let me help you," Tom volunteered.

Tom went downstairs and was just approaching the top to give Mom the potatoes when The Old Man started.

"I know what's going on. Do you think I was born yesterday? The two of you going down in the cellar together. What do you take me for? I wasn't born yesterday. I'm no goddamn fool."

"Dad!" Claudia shot back in amazement. "What are you saying?"

"What do you think I am? An eight-day clock or a sewing machine? I've been around the world; I know the score. The gray-haired old bag is screwing around again. I'm sorry, Claudia; but that's the truth. She'd fuck anything and she's fucking around with Tom right now. I know that bitch – your mother – better than you do. I wasn't born yesterday. I know…"

"Garf," Mom interrupted, "behave yourself. The kids are right here and what would…"

"Behave yourself! You're telling me to behave myself! You, you gray-haired old bag! Screwing everybody in sight and telling me what to do!"

"Come on, Garf," Tom spoke quietly. "I just helped Mary get the potatoes, that's all. There's nothing to…"

The Old Man swung his arm knocking his half-full beer bottle across the room and under the wood stove. It landed a few inches from Smokey's wooden box.

"Do you think I'm afraid of you? I can take you with one hand tied behind my back. Come on, you bastard. Fuck with my wife, will you? I'm not afraid of you. I'd take a whole army of dirt like you. You're nothing but dirt. All of you. Nothing but dirt, dirt under my feet."

The Old Man started stamping on the kitchen floor to emphasize his ravings.

"Dirt, dirt under my feet. That's all. The gray-haired old bag and everyone else in this fucking house. Dirt! Dirt! Dirt!"

At that point, The Old Man headed towards Mom and grabbed her by the arm.

"I'll teach you a lesson, you old bag!"

Then Tom stepped in between Mom and The Old Man and tried to force the release of Mom's arm. "Leave Mary alone, Garf," Tom requested softly but authoritatively. I saw The Old Man's face turn red with rage and his one hand clench into a fist as his other hand started to twist Mom's arm. His free arm swung back to swing at Tom when all of a sudden, Claudia stepped forward and knocked The Old Man over the head with something which was now in her grasp. It made a thud-like sound, but The Old Man did not fall. He just turned around with a stunned look on his face, not quite believing that Claudia had struck him. He looked towards Claudia to see her holding a large ceramic dog statue (we called it Lassie) over her head.

"Leave Mom alone, you bastard, or I'll hit you again!" Claudia demanded.

The Old Man slowly released his grasp and finally spoke. "What's going on here? Why is my family turning against me?" he pleaded. "I didn't do anything wrong."

"Let's get out of here," Claudia exclaimed.

And we did. Claudia, Tom, Mom, Sissy, Lizzie, April, and Little Tommy went somewhere in the car. Ernie and Billy (with Blackie as well) went downtown to someone's place. I'm not sure who. Gordie and I went next door to the Smales. As we left, we again heard The Old Man stomping and yelling "Dirt! Dirt! Dirt!" This was the worst I had ever seen him. I'm sure he must have been just as bad before, but I don't remember ever having to escape from our own home any other time. I must have appeared upset because Sammy asked what was wrong. So Gordie and I told him the whole story. Sammy told his Mom and she told us that we should come to their place if something like this ever happened again. We were welcome anytime of the night or day. And we were invited to stay for dinner. Dinner was liver which I hate. But I ate the whole thing and didn't complain, I was just thankful to be away from the turmoil. What will Tom think of us? I wondered. Why can't I have a normal father like the rest of the world?

After dinner, we played with Sammy's toy Jaguar car. It was great. You could take it apart and reassemble it. And it had a friction engine. Sammy had great toys. I almost forgot about The Old Man, but not really. I was afraid he might come to the door looking for everyone, but he never did. Later in the evening, Mom, Claudia, Big and Little Tommy and the 3 young girls arrived. Sammy's mother invited them all in for coffee. They said thanks but they wanted to get back home and go to bed. So, soon we were walking across the street and back into our house. As we walked in the front door, we heard the television blaring. However, The Old Man wasn't in the living room. He must have been in the kitchen. We didn't hear a sound from the kitchen and we assumed he was asleep. Thus, we all went quietly upstairs to bed. Claudia, Tom and their kids were sleeping in Ernie and Billy's room. Ernie and Billy were already home and were sleeping on the floor in my and Gordie's bedroom. Ernie told us that The Old Man was passed out at the kitchen table. He had another 24 Red Cap in the car and he had already made good progress in finishing it off. I went to bed but I didn't sleep. I just lay there with my eyes wide open awaiting the next outburst.

I must have finally gone to sleep, because I remember awakening in the middle of the night and I could hear the hum sound that the television made when the test pattern was showing. Then I heard the footsteps of someone stumbling up the stairs. It was The Old Man going to bed. He was mumbling something under his breath, but I couldn't hear what he was saying. I laid awake for another hour afraid of what I might hear coming from the main bedroom. But, eventually I went to sleep without hearing anymore uproar.

In the morning when I went downstairs to the kitchen, Mom and Claudia were laughing about something. I couldn't figure out what they could be laughing about.

"What are you laughing at, Mom?" I asked.

"Take a look at the plant over there in the corner."

I looked over to see the African Violet drooping to the floor. It had definitely seen better days.

"I guess it doesn't like Red Cap," Claudia laughed, "but then who does, except for The Old Man."

"Does he have any left?" I queried.

"There were only three bottles left," Claudia replied, "so I threw them down the sink."

"Won't he be mad?"

"He won't remember what he had left. And if he does I'll tell him I got thirsty and drank them. Anyways, who cares? He can't be any worse than he's already been. I would rather him mad and sober than mad and drunk."

Claudia was right. When The Old Man finally surfaced at lunchtime, he never mentioned how much beer he had left. He was in one of his "butter wouldn't melt in his mouth" phases, apologizing for everything he said and did. He also promised that he would never drink another drop again for as long as he lived.

"Or payday, which ever comes first," Claudia whispered so that only Mom and I could hear.

A few days later, Claudia and Tom left for Montreal to get settled in their new home before Tom had to return to duty. I think they cut short their visit by a few days. They said they had lots of packing to do, but I'm sure the experience with The Old Man influenced their decision, no one could blame them.

20 ~ The Hedgehog and The Whitewash Woman

And Claudia was right! A few weeks later, on a Saturday afternoon, The Old Man was drunk again. He had been sitting in the kitchen screaming about something or other again while the rest of the family sat in front of the TV trying to concentrate on whatever was being broadcast at the time. Eventually he quieted down and in a pleasant voice asked Mom if she could come into the kitchen to see him.

"Stay here, Mom," Ernie pleaded.

"That's all right, dear," Mom replied. "I'll go see what The Old Man wants before he starts up again."

And before Ernie or any others of us could argue, Mom went on into the kitchen. Surprisingly, we never heard any sudden outburst. The kitchen remained quiet. About five minutes later, Mom came back into the living room.

"The Old Man wants me to go upstairs with him," Mom informed us. "So I said yes. At least it will give you some peace and quiet for awhile."

"Oh, you don't have to do that just for us, Mom," Ernie reasoned.

"That's right, Mom," Billy concurred. "Don't go up to

bed with that bastard. Not while he's drunk like that!"

"No, I'll go on up. Don't worry, it won't be the first time that I've gone to bed with your father when he's in that condition. I told him I would. Now, I better stick to my promise. Just keep watching television. I'll be fine."

And off Mom and The Old Man went, up the stairs. I was confused.

"Why are they going to bed in the middle of the day?" I wanted to know. "Are they tired? I don't understand."

"I think The Old Man wants to kiss," Sissy explained.

Billy looked at me and laughed. "Benny," he said, "I'll explain it to you someday. Sissy knows better than you."

I shuddered when I thought of Mom kissing The Old Man when he was drunk like that. And in the same bed as him too. Although things remained quiet for the rest of the afternoon, I still couldn't concentrate on the TV program. I guess that's why I can't tell you what show we were watching. I usually remember useless stuff like that. A couple of hours later, just before dinner, Mom reappeared to tell us that The Old Man was now fast asleep. I felt guilty because I was glad that Mom had stopped the harangue that we had heard previously. But I knew that I should feel bad for what Mom had to put up with just for the sake of peace. However, I still didn't understand the true nature of her sacrifice.

Not long after, while walking to school one day with Gordie, I produced my small Bible out of my pocket and started to thumb through it.

"What've you got that for?" Gordie wanted to know. "I didn't know you were reading that."

"I'm not," I responded quickly. "I forgot that I stuck it in my pocket before leaving school yesterday. We were supposed to memorize the Books of the Bible, remember? The Bible teacher is coming to the school today. I forgot all about it. Let's see. There's Matthew, Mark, Luke, John, and then I'm lost."

"I think it's Donner, Dancer, Prancer, and Blitzen next, isn't it?"

"Come on, Gordie be serious. Did you learn the Books?"

"No, I didn't. Do you believe in that stuff?"

"Well they told us we had to learn it, so we should, right?"

"I don't mean that. I mean do you believe all that stuff in the Bible?"

"You mean all those miracles and stuff like that?"

"Well, not just that. Do you believe the stuff about Jesus being the Son of God? That he arose from the dead. You know. All that kind of stuff."

"I'm not sure, Gordie. What do you think?"

"I don't believe any of it."

"So you don't think that God had anything to do with Jesus."

"I don't think God has anything to do with anything. He created the world in seven days! Adam and Eve! No Benny, I don't believe that stuff. I don't even believe in God. There's nobody watching over us. If there is, he's not doing a great job. What did Mom do to be treated the way she is? She's never shown anything but love to everyone she's met, including The Old Man. You know, The Golden Rule? 'Do unto others as you would like them to do unto you.' That's what she believes. And she has to put up with that asshole excuse for a father that we have. No I don't believe in God. I doubt if a single thing in that Bible actually happened. It was written by a bunch of guys just like us. No big hand of God came down to write it."

"Oh," I replied with a long pause before continuing. "What about heaven and hell?"

"Nope. I don't believe in that, more hogwash. When you die, you're dead that's all. I'm sorry Benny, but Happy, Lucky, Fluffy, Snowflake, Snowball, none of them are in heaven. They're just in the ground, that's all."

"No, not Snowball, she's living on another farm. She just didn't like our place. The Old Man was too noisy for her."

"OK, OK, that could be true. But you know what I mean. What do you think about all of this, Benny? Come on;

give me your opinion. This time, don't just believe what I tell you. What do you think?"

"Well, I guess I agree with you about heaven and hell. That's always sounded a bit hokey to me. Did I show you that comic that I got in Dubble Bubble the other day? Remember, where one kid says, 'Do you believe in the devil?' And the other says, 'No, it's just like Santa Claus. It's your father.'"

"That's a good one," Gordie laughed. "I don't think I saw that one."

"And Adam and Eve seems crazy. And some of the other stories are not as believable as a man flying around delivering presents to every kid in the world in one night. But I'm not sure about God. I thought that I believed in that. I'm not sure, I guess."

"All right, Benny. You've got to make up your own mind. I can't do it for you."

"OK, Gordie. I will. Not just yet though. After all I am only nine."

"Benny, don't start that again. And you're ten now, remember. Your birthday was a few weeks back."

"I know, but 'Don't ask me, I'm only ten' just doesn't seem to have the same ring to it. So I don't say that. I don't know any better. I'm only nine, you know."

So that's how my first theological discussion with Gordie went. Or with anyone else for that matter. When we got to school, the Bible teacher never showed up for the weekly class. Something to do with his car breaking down or something. So I had another week to learn the Books. So maybe someone is watching over me, I thought.

On the way home, Gordie and I had passed the church and the hotel and were just at the bottom of our hill when he took off running and jumped clear over the hedge in front of the next house. So I followed him and just cleared the top of the hedge. My back foot may have brushed the top of the hedge. If it did, I wasn't aware of it. All of a sudden, we heard a door opening and then heard a loud, high-pierced screech.

"You kids get away from my hedge! I spent a lot of time

growing that! I'm going to call the police on you!"

I turned around to see an old woman walking down the front steps of the house and heading our direction. "Let's get out of here, Gordie!" I yelled. And off we ran as fast as our legs could carry us.

"Don't do that again! The police will put you two in jail. You can't destroy property like that! You two little devils!"

We ran until we got to the top of the hill. There we stopped and even though we were out of breath we both burst into laughter.

"Put us in jail!" I repeated. "Like the police care about her hedge. I never touched it anyways. Who does she think she is anyway?"

"She's a Queen I guess. No, no. I know who she is," Gordie answered. "She's the Hedgehog."

"The Hedgehog! The Hedgehog!" I chortled. And Gordie and I both burst into uncontrollable laughter.

At the top of the hill where you turned down the street to our house, the sidewalk was lower than the road. So there was a stone wall around that corner that was higher than my head. Higher than Gordie's head too. As we laughed, I fell against the stone wall. Suddenly, I heard another door opening. I looked up to see another old woman heading our way. Gordie and I thought about fleeing again, but we could hardly get up enough strength after our recent escape and our sidesplitting laughter.

"Hey, you boys! Careful with my wall. I spend hours on that wall. I don't want any stones to fall. See how it's nice and white. I come out here and whitewash it all the time. Do you know what whitewash is? Come on in my house and I will show you. That's what makes it look good. See, some paint has fallen off over there. I will have to whitewash that spot again. It's an endless task. Kids go flying by here on bicycles and scrape it off. I'm always at it. Not you two. I know you. You live just around the corner, don't you?" We didn't have time to answer, so we nodded. "Some kids are so reckless. I watch you go to school and come home every day. You're

OK. Just be careful, that's all. Look at this wall here. Doesn't it look nice? Feel it. It's smooth. It wouldn't be like that if I didn't keep on top of it all the time. Do you want to see the whitewash? I've got some in the front porch. Come on, don't be shy. I'll show you. I'll get some and fix that spot over there. Let me show you. It makes you feel good when you keep it nice. It looks nice, doesn't it? Here, let me get the pail of whitewash and my brush. Don't move. No, come with me I mean. Just to the front porch."

This conversation went on for about fifteen minutes. Gordie and I never got the chance to respond to any of her questions. She just kept on talking. We couldn't get away, so we watched her get her pail and reapply the whitewash to the rocks that she said were in need of repair. They looked fine to me. I couldn't see much difference. But Gordie and I played along and nodded and grunted our approval in all the right spots. Finally, after what seemed hours we made our excuses and headed back towards our house.

"The Whitewash Woman," I muttered.

It was a sunny, Saturday afternoon in late April of 1959 which was like a lot of other Saturday afternoons. The Old Man was well on his way to getting drunk again when we heard someone knocking at the front door. I was going to answer the door assuming it was my friend Sammy; however, before I could make it halfway across the room, The Old Man jumped up from where he was sitting on the couch and headed to the door. The Old Man opened the front door revealing a young man dressed in a suit and tie. And before I could surmise who it was, The Old Man was inviting the stranger into the living room. I noticed that he was carrying a magazine or newspaper in his hand. I couldn't read the cover but I could make out part of the title. It was 'Watch' something or other. I saw Mom waving to me from the kitchen trying to get my attention. Just then the door from upstairs opened and Gordie appeared. I used this opportunity to exit from the living room and head into the kitchen with Gordie. At the same time, I heard the stranger ask The Old

Man a question. It sounded like he was asking him if he had thought about Jesus much lately.

"Come here, Benny, Gordie," Mom whispered from the far corner of the kitchen. "If The Old Man asks for me, tell him that I've gone next door to see Mrs. Smale about something. Go get Sissy from upstairs and bring her on downstairs. She can go with me."

"OK, Mom. I'll get Sissy," I replied.

"What's up?" Gordie wanted to know. "Why is everybody whispering?"

"There's some strange man in the living room with The Old Man," I answered. "Is it an encyclopedia salesman, Mom?"

"No, dear. It's a Jehovah's Witness."

"What the devil's that?" I questioned.

"I'll tell you later. Just get Sissy."

So I did as I was told and soon was coming back down the stairs and heading into the kitchen when I heard a voice say, "Isn't that a lovely little girl!" I grabbed Sissy by the hand and kept walking to where Mom and Gordie were standing. Before I could blink an eye, Mom and Sissy were out the back door. Just in time, too.

"Mary! Mary," The Old Man yelled, "come here for a minute. Someone wants to meet you."

I tried to push Gordie into the living room. And he tried to push me. Eventually, we both made our way into the living room as The Old Man shouted for Mom one more time. Gordie then explained that Mom had gone next door to see Mrs. Smale.

"That's two fine looking boys that you have there, Mr. Cooper," remarked the stranger. He then turned his attention to us. "You boys sure are lucky to have such a fine father. I bet you thank God every day. Bless you both."

"I gotta go to the bathroom, Dad," was my quick response. A few seconds later I was safely enclosed behind a locked door. I didn't give Gordie a chance to escape with me. I waited for about an hour before finally deciding that I should make my reappearance. There was The Old Man at the door making his farewells to the stranger. Gordie was sitting on the couch giving me a real dirty look.

After The Old Man shut the door, he started laughing. "I thought I would never get rid of him. That's the last time I invite one of them in. Your mother was smart. I should have hid too." This surprised me. I thought that The Old Man would be really angry with Mom for leaving. At that point, Mom and Sissy walked back into the room. The Old Man continued his laughter. "How's Mrs. Smale, Mary?" he asked.

"I thought that guy would never leave," Mom answered. "Sissy and I were hiding in the wood shed the whole time. What did you talk about for so long?"

"I didn't get a word in edgewise. That man never shut up. I finally told him that I had to take you to the doctor to get rid of him. The next time that I invite a Jehovah's Witness in the house hit me over the head with something to bring some sense into me. Will you, Mary? And the next time that someone else asks me if I thought about Jesus lately, I'll say 'Yes, just a few seconds ago when I saw you coming up the walk. I thought to myself, Oh Jesus, here comes another Jehovah's Witness.'"

A few weeks later, we had a new student start at school. He was from Scotland and nobody could understand a thing that he said. Except for Mr. McKenzie. The boy's name was John Brooks and he was placed in Grade 7, the same grade as Gordie. He was a soccer fanatic. I had never seen anyone who could bounce the ball around like he could. Off his feet or head. I never mentioned earlier that we would play soccer at the school. It was Mr. McKenzie's favourite sport. I was glad about that because I wasn't that bad of a player. Nothing compared to John, but I was just as good as the rest of the local kids. It was one sport where you didn't have to be a giant to play well. I was hopeless at baseball and football. Whenever we played baseball and the team captain's took turns choosing players, I was always invariably the last boy chosen. Let me correct that. I was always the last person chosen – male or female. At soccer, I was chosen in the middle rounds somewhere. One day, I actually scored two goals. Both nicely setup by John, where I couldn't have missed if I had wanted too. "Brilliant!" John would shout. I'm not sure how John was doing in his schoolwork, but he got along well with Mr. McKenzie. The two of them could talk about soccer all day. Except during Mr. McKenzie's naptime, of course.

That Mother's Day, Gordie, Sissy, Mom, I and The Old Man were sitting in the living room watching TV. Ernie and Billy were out with some friends downtown somewhere. I think they were with Richard Watson and his older brother Phil. Blackie was with them too. Smokey was lying on Sissy's lap. This Sunday, The Old Man wasn't drinking. It wasn't pay week. That alone was a good present for Mom. We were watching the long episode of The Lone Ranger. The one that explained how he first became the 'masked man' and met up with Tonto. The story was just about over when we heard the front door open. Shortly Billy entered into the room. We all immediately recognized that something was wrong. Billy was crying. There was no sign of Ernie.

"What's wrong, Billy?" Mom asked as she rose from the couch to go to Billy's side. "Where's Ernie? What's happened?"

"Blackie's dead!" Billy sobbed. "I watched him get hit by a car right at the top of the hill. I called him and he ran right in front of a car coming down the hill. It was my fault." Billy paused for a moment and then continued as Mom placed a comforting arm around his shoulder. The rest of us remained silent. "Ernie's taken Blackie into the backyard. Can we bury him, now?"

"I'll get the shovel, Billy," said The Old Man, and with surprising sincerity added, "Don't blame yourself, Billy. Dogs have a mind of their own. You can't help where they run. Let's go."

Then we all went outside and saw Ernie standing over the lifeless body of Blackie spread out on the ground. We watched as Ernie and Billy took turns digging a deep hole which would soon become Blackie's final resting-place. It was just like that Mother's Day only three years before. It had seemed like a lifetime. I'm sure that earlier incident was on everyone's mind. As Blackie was lowered down into the hole, I looked at Gordie and spoke.

"You're right, Gordie. There is no God."

21 ~ Hey Poncho, Hey Cisco

That spring, we started visiting a family that lived in the country somewhere between Hillsburgh and Georgetown. The Old Man and Mom had become acquainted with them through the Bullards – the family whose farm we had lived on many years before. I'm not sure if they were related to the Bullards or not, but they had one main thing in common with them. They had no electricity. This seemed really peculiar to me now. I couldn't imagine anyone living in these modern times without lights and especially without television. What could they possibly do for entertainment on Sunday nights without Ed Sullivan? And this clan had absolutely no desire to join the electrical age either. They preferred the simpler times where you didn't have to rely on anyone else for anything. That included power. Have you noticed that I keep referring to this family as 'They'? I can't seem to recall their last name now. Whenever we went there, Gordie and I would spend the whole time outside. They had a whole field full of wrecked cars. It was great! Gordie and I could play in those cars for hours. We could pretend that we were driving and we didn't have to worry about anyone saying, "Leave that alone. That's not a toy you know." There were two sons in the family but they were too old to play with. They were around

Brad's age, I think. I remember that one son had a girl's name – Alice. That was weird. But I liked him. He reminded me somewhat of my old tractor mate – John Bullard. Mom said that the older couple were a bit unusual but she still enjoyed visiting them. At the very least it was a chance to get out of the house, and best of all, they never had any alcohol in their home. And The Old Man had always adhered to their rules. I wonder what The Old Man found to talk to them about.

Did I mention that since we had moved to Hillsburgh we had no telephone again? Well we didn't until that spring and then we joined the modern age. We got a dial telephone. That was the reason that The Old Man got the job in Hillsburgh actually. That area was just getting converted from the older crank phones to the modern rotary-dial phones. It seemed funny to have a black telephone sitting on a small table in the dining room rather than the big, wooden box hanging on the kitchen wall. Now one of those wooden boxes was only a home to Flat and Them.

In late May, Gordie got sick. He had a high fever and the skin on his hands and elsewhere started to turn red. Once again, The Old Man was convinced to take Gordie to the doctor. And again it was Dr. McGuire in Orangeville. This time, Gordie had Scarlet Fever. I moved out of my room and slept in Ernie and Billy's room since Gordie was contagious. Gordie missed the rest of the school year due to this illness. As he started to get better, the skin on his hands and face started to peel off revealing tender, pink, baby skin. Although we felt sorry for Gordie, this didn't stop the rest of us from making fun of the way he looked. He would even laugh along with us.

One day, when Richard Watson was at our house, I heard him refer to Ernie as 'Little Garf'. I thought that was quite amusing until Richard advised me that we all had nicknames. Billy was 'Littler Garf', Gordie's name was 'Even Littler Garf', and my unfortunate designation was 'Littlest Garf'. It didn't bother me too much. Actually I liked it because it made me part of the group of Ernie, Billy, Gordie, and Richard and Phil Watson. It made me feel like a big kid. Ernie hated that nickname though. For one main reason. He wanted no part of any identification that compared him in any way to The Old Man. But this didn't stop Richard from continuing to call Ernie 'Little Garf' every time he saw him.

Speaking of nicknames, there was a guy who lived a couple of blocks from our place who everybody always referred to as 'Tweety Bird'. He was about twenty years old but lived in a house by himself. He had a high head of hair which was slicked back by a tube of Brylcreem into a 'duck-tail'. He loved cars. One of his cars was a '55 Chevy with a continental on the back. It had a 'V6' sign on each fender; however, in reality it was powered by a large V8 engine. This caught more than a few drag competitors by surprise when the V6 Chevy pulled quickly away from them. Tweety Bird also owned a '57 Chevy. I'm not sure what he did for a living. It didn't seem to be much. But he always had money for his cars. I don't think he spent a cent on anything else. He did all the work on the cars himself at his place. Right in his house. Usually if you entered his living room, you would be greeted by an engine sitting on the floor. When you first saw Tweety Bird, you thought of him as a very tough customer. Someone that you should stay away from. But that wasn't true at all. He was a friend to almost everyone in Hillsburgh. At least to the younger generation. However, he was definitely someone you wouldn't mind on your side if any trouble ever did blow your way. Ernie and his friend Phil Watson used to spend a lot of time with Tweety Bird. As I said, everyone called him Tweety Bird, so it was quite a while later before I learned his real name – Gordon Springfield. Somehow it didn't fit. I never did hear how he came to be called after the pest who forever got poor, old Sylvester in trouble.

When school ended, we found out that we had all graduated except for Gordie. He blamed it on the Scarlet Fever and missing the last month of the school year. This time Mom didn't bother going to the school to argue like she had done years earlier for Billy. Gordie asked Mom not to bother. He knew that there was no changing Mr. McKenzie's mind once it was made up. Well at least, he and Billy would be back in the same class again. I mean the same grade. We would still be returning to the two-room school with four grades in one class in the fall. We had just learned though that a new school was being built and construction would soon begin. The rumour was that it would be a four-room school. We didn't know for sure yet.

A few days after school ended, The Old Man came home with a graduation present. You guessed it! Another puppy. This one looked different than our other dogs. It was a she to begin with. All our other dogs were always male. Also, although she was a mutt like our other dogs she looked different. The others either looked like collies or beagles. This one was golden-brown and had short legs on a chubby body. She looked something like a wiener dog, but not quite. She wasn't long like one of that breed. I guess what I'm trying to say is that I haven't the foggiest idea what made up her pedigree mix.

"What should we call her?" Mom queried.

"How about Goldie?" Sissy answered.

"No! No way!" Gordie demanded. "Not another name that ends in 'EE'. Like Happy, Lucky, Blackie, Sandy, and whatever else. It's bad luck. It must be. It was a sad ending for them all. Let's choose something different, maybe it will change our luck. Most of our cats had names like that too. Let's be different for once."

"Our names, too," Ernie reflected.

"I still like Goldie," Sissy insisted.

"Yes, that's a nice name, Sissy," Mom agreed. "Why not Goldie?"

"No, I agree with Gordie," Ernie replied.

"Me too," said Billy. "It's time for a change."

"Me too," I stated. I then, although I'm not sure why, said, "She looks Mexican."

"How about Cisco, then?" Billy asked.

"Yuck," commented Sissy.

"I got it," said Gordie. "Poncho!"

"Hey Poncho!" I exclaimed.

"Hey Cisco!" responded Gordie.

So we all settled on Poncho as the name for our new family member. Sissy still argued that she preferred the name Goldie for a few days but she soon came around to liking the name Poncho as much as the rest of us.

In the early summer, we returned to the drive-in theatre in Orangeville. Ernie didn't go. He had another engagement. But Billy, Gordie, Sissy, and I went with The Old Man and Mom. Sissy sat in the front between the grownups. I sat in the back seat between my two brothers. That was my choice because there I could see over Sissy's head, which was below the back of the seat. We went to see an older movie. One that had been released three years earlier in 1956, Godzilla. We all loved it! Sissy found it scary but she still really enjoyed it anyway. On the way home, as we were travelling along the dark country road, we three boys in the back were discussing what we would do if Godzilla suddenly appeared in our path.

"What would you do, Dad?" I eventually asked.

"I would take one look at him and say, 'Get out of here you great big monster! You don't scare me!' That's what I would do."

Dad then laughed. And all of us joined in the laughter.

A week later, we went to the drive-in again. But this time the circumstances were completely different. We saw a new movie and we didn't go with The Old Man. Let me start at the beginning. This weekend was the pay weekend for The Old Man. The night before, we had gone into Georgetown and it was one of the few times where we didn't have to wait for The Old Man to exit from the bar. No, this time he didn't want to waste his money on draught at the local. When we got home, we watched as The Old Man carried in the groceries followed by two cases of 24 Red Cap. That night, I lay in bed awake half the night listening to The Old Man down in the kitchen.

"Goddamn that gray-haired old bag! Where the fuck is

she? What does she take me for? Who's that old bag screwing now? Goddamn it! I wasn't born yesterday. I know what's going on here."

At any rate, you get the picture. In between those tirades, I heard either the television blaring some old movie or the record player blasting out some Slim Whitman songs. I couldn't sleep even when things got quiet. I just lay there shaking as I waited for the next outburst to come again. And it did. The Old Man never did go to bed that night.

Morning finally arrived. Usually after an all-night binge, you could count on The Old Man being passed out. Not this morning. Somehow he was still going strong. He was still working on the first case but he was on the last few bottles. I had a nice warm greeting.

"Hey, Benny. How are you doing? The old bag's not here. She's gone downtown to the store. That's what she said but who knows with that bag. She's probably off whoring again. Get me another beer, will you."

I didn't. I never even acknowledged that I had heard him. I just went straight out the door and across the street to visit Sammy. It was just after nine o'clock. I hoped someone would be up. I left Gordie in bed. I assumed Billy and Ernie were still in theirs. I noticed that Sissy was no longer in bed. I supposed that she was with Mom. When I arrived at Smale's place, I was greeted by Sammy's mom.

"Sammy's still in bed, Benny. Why don't you come back later?" I guess she then noticed the look on my face. "No come in now, Benny. Don't be shy. Come on in. Have you had breakfast yet?"

Mrs. Smale was the only one up yet. Mr. Smale was away at the time. He was a transport truck driver, so he was often away for long stretches as he drove to places like Florida. Sarah and Jenny hadn't yet arisen for the day either. I sat quietly and ate my cereal with Mrs. Smale. She didn't ask me what was wrong and I didn't volunteer any information. I figured she understood. After I had finished my Trix, I decided it was time to head back across the road. Mom would soon be back and wonder what became of me. Just then, Sarah came down the stairs in her pajamas.

"Hi Benny. What brings you here so early in the morning?"

"Oh nothing," I answered. I lowered my head so I wouldn't feel so embarrassed about seeing Sarah not yet dressed. "I just wanted to play with Sammy, that's all. I better go now, though."

"Listen Benny," Mrs. Smale pronounced as I was starting to leave, "you come back again. Sammy will want to see you. And you tell your Mom that she's welcome too. The whole family's welcome. I don't care when. Like I told you before, if you need help or just need to get out of the house, then come on across the road. OK, remember that."

"Thanks," I said softly. And then I reluctantly left for home. I looked into the windows to see if I could see Mom or Sissy. I wasn't going back in if they weren't back yet. I noticed that Sissy was sitting on one of the big chairs in the living room. So I went back in. The Old Man had finally fallen asleep at the kitchen table. I told Mom where I was and explained the offer from Mrs. Smale. My brothers were all up and at it by eleven. No one else had slept much either. Things remained quiet until shortly after noon, when The Old Man woke up. It didn't take him long to take up where he had left off.

"Where's my lunch, Mary? What are you trying to do? Starve me!"

"OK Garf, what do you want?"

"I don't care, anything. I just need something to eat. I take you to the store in Georgetown and this is the thanks I get."

"We had hash, beans, and fried egg. Do you want that?"

"Yes, Mary. That sounds good. Just make it quick, eh."

So that's what Mom made for The Old Man. In about ten minutes, after The Old Man had started his second case of beer, Mom placed the full plate in front of him at the kitchen table."

"What's this shit!" he shouted.

"It's the lunch you asked for," Mom replied.

"I don't want this fucking shit! Get me a decent meal, you bitch!" This invective was accompanied by The Old Man throwing the plate across the kitchen where it smashed against the far wall only inches from Mom's head.

"What's going on in here?" someone questioned. It was Ernie.

The Old Man banged his fist down on the table with his full force. "That's what I want to know! Do you think that I'm afraid of you? I could take the whole bunch of you on with one hand tied behind my back!" He jumped up from the table. "I'll break your fucking neck. All of you!"

I heard Sissy crying in the living room. Billy was standing in the kitchen now too. He had that angry look on his face that he gets sometimes. Mom saw it too.

"Let's go," Mom urged. She then walked out of the kitchen directing Ernie and Billy in front of her. I didn't need any direction. Gordie was already in the living room with Sissy. Mom walked us right out the front door and across the street. All of us went to the Smales. Sissy went up into Jenny's room to play. Billy, Gordie, Sammy, and I played on the kitchen floor with Sammy's electric train set. Ernie sat at the kitchen table with Mrs. Smale and Mom. Sarah had gone somewhere by this point. Mom didn't want Ernie to leave because she was afraid that The Old Man would come across the street looking for us. None of us really relaxed. We all had the same fear. Around four o'clock in the afternoon, we heard a large Mack truck outside. It was Mr. Smale arriving home from his latest delivery destination. What a relief! The Old Man wouldn't try anything now. At least that was my logic. Wrong again. Around five, there was a loud banging on their front door.

"Stay here and be quiet as mice," Mr. Smale said. "I'll send him away."

We overheard The Old Man asking if we were there and Mr. Smale reply that we were there earlier but had left a couple of hours ago. He didn't know where we had gone, he said.

"I know they're here," The Old Man replied. "Tell them it's OK now. If they come home, I'll be fine. It's dinner time."

"They're not here," Mr. Smale repeated.

"Damn you! May you all go to hell!"

Then The Old Man returned across the road. Mr. And Mrs. Smale could see how nervous Mom and the rest of us were. So they suggested that we go somewhere. Consequently, Ernie and Billy went to some friends in downtown Hillsburgh, while Mr. And Mrs. Smale, Mom, Gordie, Sammy, Sissy, Jenny, and I went to the drive-in theatre in Orangeville. It was kind of crowded in the car, but it was still far more relaxing than staying so close to our place. The movie that we saw was 'The Shaggy Dog'. It had just been released a few weeks before. It was just the kind of movie that we needed. It enabled us to forget about the day and enjoy some laughter.

On the way home, all of our minds were on the same thing. What would we come home to? But when we got home, The Old Man was fast asleep on the couch. And the house remained quiet for the remainder of the evening. The next day, The Old Man only asked whether we had a good time or not. Butter wouldn't melt in his mouth that day.

22 ~ Little Green Apples

That summer there were certainly more circumstances where The Old man got drunk and caused a ruckus. But I'm not going to mention that for a while. I'm tired of talking about it and I'm sure that you've listened to enough right about now. So I'm going to talk about some other things that we did in the summer of '59.

First I'm going to talk about hockey, an unusual thing to talk about in the summer, I know. Gordie and I got this table hockey game and we started playing tournaments on it. This was the type of game where the players only turned around on a fixed peg. They didn't go up and down the ice at all. The puck was a black marble. The funny thing was that the two teams that came with the game were the Boston Bruins and the New York Rangers. And we bought the game in Canada! Why no Leafs or Canadiens? Gordie selected the Boston Bruins as his team. Why not, they had finished in second place the year before. That left the Rangers for me. They were a fifth place team. So I had to switch my allegiance from the Leafs to the Rangers. We would collect the hockey cards for those two teams and line them up on the table to indicate which line was currently on the ice. But we decided a good idea would be to change the names of all the players. For example, Lorne 'Gump' Worsley became Warn 'Stump' Worstley and Johnny Bucyk was re-christened as Junky Buick. We would play whole seasons and then have playoffs for the Stanley Cup. Since Gordie was still suffering from the leftover effects of the Scarlet Fever, he could not turn the players very fast with his fingers. So he used his forearms. This was still effective enough to beat me most of the time. Over the ensuing years, Boston and New York became the two worse teams in the NHL, but don't lay the blame for that one on us. That's just a coincidence. Anyways, I just remembered we weren't the Bruins and the Rangers. Oh no, we were more original than that. We were the Boston Beans and the New York Riders.

Another game that I started playing that summer involved my next door neighbour, Sammy. We would sit in the big, red Mack truck that belonged to his dad and pretend that we were driving across North America. Sometimes Mr. Smale would remind us that it wasn't a toy, but mainly he would let us play in the cab as long as we wanted. Sammy usually got to be the driver and I was his driving companion. When there was a trailer attached to the cab, we could play in that as well. Playing in that cab was like owning a giant Dinky Toy. Speaking of Dinky Toys, Sammy was also a fan of that brand of toy. We could play it for hours. He, naturally, collected trucks. I had a huge, yellow dump truck that impressed Sammy. Gordie had a large, car carrier transport. And yes, the linoleum in our upstairs hall had an ideal pattern for playing with our Dinky Toys.

I told you about the empty lot next door which was comprised, among other things, of a small apple orchard. This summer we got to sample the apples on the trees. We wouldn't wait until they got red or large. We would pick them when they were small and green. The greener the better. I recollect sitting with Gordie and Billy and a whole basket full of green apples. One of us would bring the salt shaker. We would sit in the empty field next door and eat the whole basket in one sitting. We would sprinkle salt on our apple before each and every bite. They were delicious! This would drive grownups nuts. Every one of them would warn us that we would get a terrible stomachache. Actually they would say 'tummy ache' in case we didn't understand big words like stomachache. I think Mom gave up with the warnings. She knew that we were addicts and it was useless to try and stop us. When Fred and Them came to visit, you could definitely count on Fred, Vi, Ron, Lucy, and Tom all counseling us about the dangers of eating green apples. But we never listened. And none of us ever got a tummy ache either.

While I'm on the subject of the lot next door and Fred and Them, I should tell you about The Old Man's great plans. This was something other than the Cooper Bottle Collection Company. The Old Man would tell people (most often this was Fred and Them) about his future dreams. When he made a bit more money (I suppose this is where the bottle collecting came in), he would buy the next-door lot. Then he would have it graded and flattened out and build a brand new house on the recently acquired land. And we would live happily ever after. I'm not sure why his dream included that particular plot of land. It was the antithesis of being flat. There were gullies, hills, bushes, trees, mounds, stumps, and the like everywhere. That's what made it such a great play area. I couldn't imagine it any other way. But none of us ever spoke negatively about this to The Old Man. As far as his dreams went, it sounded pretty good.

The other field that I need to tell you more about is the one right behind our backyard. Just like the empty lot next door, only a quick jump over our wire fence was required to access this specific playground. I think I mentioned that there was a large cut in the hill behind our house. At the bottom of this geological incision there was an abundant pile of massive rocks. In the summer these boulders could be explored and enjoyed in many ways. I recall finding quite a few fossils among the various stones. Ernie explained to me what fossils were. I thought it was really neat to hold a piece of a history of the earth in my hands. We even found one that looked like a fish. The boulders themselves also made a good source of entertainment. We could sit behind them and pretend that we were sitting behind the wheel of a racing car. For some reason, Gordie's car was always faster than mine.

If you climbed the hill and ventured on further into the adjoining fields, you came to terrain that looked much like our farm at Robertsons'. There were even old rail fences that could be constructed into two-dimensional western towns. Gordie and I would often go back there with Sammy and continue our games of cowboys that had begun years before. I still had my Gene Autrey guns and holster. The extent of our range was back a few fields until we reached a farmer's lane. This would be the Wells Fargo trail. I was glad to have a friend like Sammy to join in these adventures because Gordie was starting to lose interest. I could tell that it didn't seem as much fun to him as it used to be. Or maybe he just missed the freedom and expanse of the Robertsons' ranch.

Everything wasn't always fun and games when I played with Sammy. A few times we would start arguing over something stupid. It could be as silly as the following exchange.

"You're dead!"

"No, I'm not. You missed."

"Did not!"

"Did too!"

And then it would end with Sammy heading home. "I don't ever want to play with you again, Benny! You're not my friend anymore!"

I would wait about a half-hour and Sammy would return asking, "Do you want to play at my place?"

"Sure," I would answer. And the previous fight would never be mentioned.

That summer also marked the beginning of the Great Cereal Wars. That's right, war was declared and Flat and Them were conscripted. We would throw a handful of the various cereal people into a pile and then Ernie or Billy would attack them with a sharp knife. They would start carving and slashing without looking at who was being injured. Whoever lost his head or other vital body part was declared dead. Any who lost an appendage such as a leg or arm could be fixed up with a little paint applied to the stump. During the war that summer, quite a few lives were lost. Even the poor guy in the wheelchair, whose name I still don't remember, became one of the fatal casualties. Flat's best friend lost his right arm. We started calling him 'Lefty'. Even Flat did not come through the war uninjured. He lost his left foot. I think I better explain what would make a group of kids manufacture such a strange battle scene. This macabre amusement started because we thought that we were getting too old to play with little men. However, we couldn't quite give it up. Flat and Them had become part of the family. So this was a way to slowly pull ourselves away from that pastime without giving it up all at once. In any event, that's my excuse.

A few weeks later, Flat departed from us in a more spectacular matter. Inspired by 'Sputniks', we thought that it was time for manned space flight. First we took one of the green, plastic, rocket-shaped, whatever they are called things that are used on telephone poles. Then we jammed a large firecracker in the bottom. The brave volunteer was then strapped to the side of the rocket. The spaceship was then placed on a hand-made launcher. The launcher was placed on top of the well in the backyard. Billy, Gordie, and I then sang 'God Save The Queen' and the wick was lit. It was a huge success! The rocket flew straight up in the air and then disappeared. I am serious. We never found any sign of the rocket or Flat the Rocket-man again. He most certainly went into Outer Space.

Besides hockey, Gordie and I started a baseball league. We each had a team. He was Guelph, and I was Ottawa. We chose our player names and team colours and everything. I remember that I chose Green and Orange for Ottawa. I couldn't think of two colours that contrasted each other as much as those two. I think Gordie's colours were Yellow and Purple. This was not a table game. We played in the backyard with a real baseball bat and ball. I can't recollect how we managed to play with just the two of us. But one thing for sure, I never stood anywhere near Gordie when he swung that bat.

Until that summer, I had never really experienced the death of someone I knew well. There were lots of animals, for sure, but not a human being. I'm not counting the loss of Grandma because at the time of her death, I couldn't really remember a lot about her. And since we heard about it from such a long distance it never in effect seemed real. One afternoon, Richard Watson came by to advise all of us 'Garfs' that Mr. McKenzie had died in his sleep the night before. They assumed that he had suffered a heart attack. Richard could tend to be a bit of a prankster so it took some time for him to convince us that he was telling the truth. He told us that Mr. McKenzie would be on view the next day. I had never heard of someone being 'on view' before. I didn't know that people wanted to look at a dead body. It seemed kind of weird to me. Subsequently, when the following day came, Billy, Gordie, and I were entering some strange house on the main street about halfway between the top of the hill and the school. When we first walked into the front room, I thought that we had set foot in the wrong house. I didn't recognize a single soul in the place. They were all older people. Not a single student was in sight. But we hadn't made a mistake. We were welcomed by two older women who introduced themselves as Mr. McKenzie's wife and sister. They thanked us for coming and led us into another room which was being used as the viewing room. The first thing that I noticed was other kids that I knew. Among them were Richard Watson and his younger brother Joe, the two Fryman brothers, Errol Flynn, and John Brooks. And then my eye caught the casket along the far wall. It was open and I could see a body reclining in it. After saying my hellos to everyone, I finally got up enough nerve to venture over towards that side of the room. I expected to be shocked. After all, I had never seen a dead body before; however, to my surprise I didn't feel anything. Mr. McKenzie resembled the way that I had seen him many times in the last year. That is, he looked like he was just sleeping. As we were leaving the house, Gordie nudged me with his arm and whispered, "Didn't it look like he was just sleeping?"

In August, I encountered another new experience. Mom, The Old Man, and Sissy went away for a few days to visit one of The Old Man's sisters in Detroit. Ernie had talked them into leaving us four boys alone at home. I felt grownup now. I was now ten. No longer was I only nine. I could now be trusted on my own, or with a few older brothers to be correct. Ernie was now fifteen so he was definitely pleased that Mom had agreed to his idea. And Mom needn't have worried. Ernie kept us all in line. At the high school in Erin, all male students had to belong to the army cadets. There was no option. So Ernie had already completed a year of training. He ordered us to do various things like make our beds, the dishes, and other house cleaning chores. He and Billy looked after the cooking. There wasn't much time to get in trouble after you had completed all your duties. The only thing I remember that we did, which we wouldn't have done otherwise, involved the telephone and Sammy. Sammy showed us a new amusement. He phoned the local grocery store in downtown Hillsburgh.

"Do you have Robin Hood by the bag?" he inquired. "Well, you better let him go! Ha, ha, ha!"

Now it was Gordie's turn. He phoned the other store. Believe it or not there were two general stores in that small town. Sammy told him what to say.

"Do you have Betty Crocker by the box? Yes. Then, you better get your hands off of her! Ha, ha, ha!"

I didn't partake in this particular brand of entertainment, but I had a good laugh just watching and listening to Sammy and Gordie. In spite of what I said about Ernie acting like a General, we had a great time during those few days. We just liked to kid Ernie, but he was actually a lot of fun.

One Sunday in August, we discovered a new play area.

The Old Man drove the whole family to Stanley Park in Erin. This would have been a Sunday when 'butter wouldn't melt in his mouth'. There we could swim in the river, walk through some woods, play in a playground, or eat in the picnic area. Mom had made a picnic lunch for us. There was even a small, sandy beach by the edge of the river. Gordie and I were playing in the water by the edge of the river with Sissy. None of us could swim. In the meantime, Billy was on a small inflatable raft, Ernie was off walking somewhere, and Mom and The Old Man were sitting on a blanket in the grass just above the line of the sand. When Gordie, Sissy, and I got tired of wading in the water, we went back to play in the sand. Mom then came towards us with a worried look on her face.

"Where's Billy?"

"Oh, he's just floating around on the river," I responded.

"Where? I don't see him."

"Right there, Mom," Gordie replied as he pointed to the last spot where we had seen Billy. The trouble was Billy wasn't there anymore.

"I don't see him either, Gordie," I added.

We all went down to the riverbank and scanned the river more closely. Billy was nowhere in sight.

"Benny, get your father, real quick! Gordie, see if you can find Ernie."

Both of us were gone by the time Mom finished speaking. Sissy stayed with Mom. The Old Man ran straight into the river with his clothes on, searching and calling for Billy. Mom and Sissy were both yelling his name as loud as they could.

"I'll cross the bridge and look on the other side of the river," I said trying to comfort Mom. "He probably just floated over to the other side."

"OK, dear. But be careful. I don't want two lost boys."

"I will, Mom."

And off I went. But Billy wasn't on the other side either. By the time that I got back, Ernie was now there too. He had his bathing suit on and was diving under the water to try and catch sight of Billy or the raft. But neither was anywhere to be seen. By now, half the people in the park were involved in the search. No one recalled seeing what happened to Billy or the raft. This frantic search went on for about ten more minutes before Mom finally admitted her worse fears.

"He's gone, Garf. He must have drowned. Oh my God," Mom sobbed.

"Where's that raft though?" The Old Man asked. "It's not around either."

"Is this your son?" we suddenly heard someone shout.

We all turned around and looked down river to see a man walking towards us with one hand holding Billy's and the other the raft. Billy was walking with his head down, afraid to look up at us. Mom ran towards Billy and picked him off his feet and embraced him as hard as she dared.

"Oh, Billy," she sighed, "where have you been?"

The rescuer replied first.

"I found him way down the river, still floating on this thing." The stranger waved the raft. "He was oblivious to everything around him. I had to coax him into the shore. I think he thought he was Tom Sawyer floating down the Mississippi without a care in the world."

"You scared your mother to death, Billy," The Old Man reprimanded. "What were you thinking? You scared all of us."

"We thought you were drownded," Sissy voiced.

"I'm sorry," Billy finally spoke. "I was just floating and before I knew it I was heading down the river. I didn't know how to stop. I was scared too. Don't be mad at me, Mom."

"Oh Billy," said Mom, "We're just happy you're here. How can we be mad with you?"

On a few other occasions, we went back to Stanley Park but that raft never accompanied us anymore.

On Labour Day weekend, Brad came to visit us. Catherine wasn't with him though. She was at home with their young daughter Cheryl who had been born earlier that spring. Brad was on his own because he was returning back to Ottawa after being at the base in London for a week. That's London, Ontario not England, so Brad was driving back east and we were on his way. Brad had a new car. A white Cadillac convertible. It looked brand new, but it was actually a 1951 model. Brad said that a few people had mistaken the Cadillac for a current model. We all watched with interest as Brad lowered down the top and fastened on the cover.

"Who wants to go for a ride?" asked Brad.

"Why don't you all go ahead? I'll stay here," Mom answered. "I've got to start getting supper ready and who knows when The Old Man will be home."

This was Saturday afternoon and The Old Man had gone somewhere that morning. So we all jumped in the car. Ernie and Sissy sat in the front seat with Brad, while Billy, Gordie, and I took up the rear. Brad drove us all around town. I felt like a millionaire riding in a Cadillac convertible with the wind blowing our hair into our faces. I was hoping to see one of my friends so that I could wave to him from the back of the open car. I felt like I was in the Grey Cup parade. But the town was dead. We didn't see a single person that we even knew, let alone a friend.

Just after we got back from our drive, The Old Man arrived home. It was about four o'clock in the afternoon.

"Hello, old bag! I'm drunk again," was his greeting as he walked in the front door. With this entrance, I watched Poncho back into the dining room and crawl under the china cabinet in the corner. He remained there for the next hour watching The Old Man at all times.

"Garf," Mom spoke next. "Buddy's here!"

"You think that scares me?" was The Old Man's response. "I can take him with one arm tied behind my back. I'm not afraid of Buddy or the whole damned Air Force!"

"That's not what I meant, Garf. Who's talking about being afraid? I just thought that you would be happy to see him, that's all. Can't you even say hello?"

"Hello Dad," said Brad.

"I knew you were here. I saw you driving around downtown in your fancy new car, thinking you're King Shit, the King of fucking France. You're too good for us now, is that right? You think I'm afraid of you? Just try it! I'll knock your ass flying across the room. Don't think I couldn't do it either. I once held a car on my back. In Halifax, it was. A jack had broken and the car fell on this poor bloke. I told my friends to just lift the car onto my shoulders. I held it in place while they got the other guy out. That's the truth. Did I ever tell you that story before, Buddy? That's true, isn't it Mary?"

"Yes, Garf."

"No, I never knew that story," Brad lied. We had all heard it hundreds of times. "Tell me more about it."

So The Old Man became temporarily distracted from his ravings and began telling all of us this story in detail. And then came the usual war stories. We couldn't relax, though. We all knew that The Old Man's temperament could just as easily turn back to rage as quickly as he had turned away from it. The rest of that evening he lapsed a few times into 'that old bag' routine, but generally he didn't show any of the anger that he had demonstrated that afternoon. Until we had all gone to bed. I was half asleep and half awake as I listened to The Old Man talking to himself down in the kitchen.

"I need something to eat! Where the hell's that old bag? Hey, gray-haired, old bag! Get up and get me something, fucking to eat. Will you? I'm starving." I then heard quick fumbling steps up the stairs and The Old Man's voice was much louder. "Get the fuck up, I said! Get me some goddamned food will you, old bag!" I then heard some rustling sounds.

"Don't Garf," Mom pleaded. "I'm trying to sleep. It's three o'clock in the morning."

"Get the fuck out of this bed, now!" That was followed by more noise.

"Garf, you're hurting me!"

"Daddy, don't hurt Mommy!" cried Sissy. And then came a large thud.

186

At the same time I heard other feet hitting the floor, including mine. Gordie and I arrived in the hall to see Brad, Ernie, and Billy all outside the entrance to our parents' bedroom.

"What's going on here?" Brad demanded to know. "Oh, God. Are you all right, Mom?"

I peered in the door to see Mom sprawled on the floor with the sheets half wrapped around her. The Old Man had one hand on the end of the curled sheets and the other was holding Mom's arm by the wrist.

"Let go of Mom!" Brad shouted.

"Yes, you bastard. Don't you dare hurt Mom!" That was Billy.

"What the hell's everybody looking at me for? I just want something to eat, that's all. Now, go back to bed. Come on you gray-haired, old bag."

"You're hurting my arm!"

Before anyone could say anything else, Brad was on top of The Old Man. He had taken him completely by surprise and had him straddled on the floor. I heard a crunch as Brad's fist connected with The Old Man's face. And then again.

"You bastard!" Brad screamed. "I'm not taking this shit from you any longer! How do you like getting hit back? You're good at picking on women. Take this!"

Brad punched The Old Man once more. I could see blood coming from somewhere on The Old Man's face. Then Brad just sat there on top of The Old Man and no one spoke. It was probably only for a second, but it seemed much longer. Mom had got herself back on the bed and was hugging Sissy who was crying frantically. I heard Billy shout, "Hit him again, Brad!" Ernie, Gordie, and I stood in silence. I could hear my heart pounding and I couldn't stop shaking. Finally, The Old Man spoke.

"OK, Brad. I've had enough. I think you broke my teeth. And my nose. I'm sorry. I don't know what got into me. You can let me up now. Come on, Brad."

Brad looked at Mom and she merely nodded. Slowly, Brad started to stand up.

"Be careful," Ernie warned. "Don't trust him, Brad."

The Old Man sat up and felt his face. "Mary, please get me a cloth. I'm bleeding like a pig. Please, dear." He then removed his upper dentures from his mouth along with some blood. His plate came out in two pieces. "My teeth are broken, too."

Mom got out of the bed on the side by Sissy's bed and headed downstairs to the bathroom. "I'll get a wash basin and cloth, Garf."

"Thanks, dear," said The Old man as he remained sitting on the floor beside the bed.

When Mom returned, we all just stood and watched as Mom cleaned up The Old Man's face.

"It's not as bad as it looks. Nothing's broken except for your false teeth. You just have a nosebleed. That's all. And your mouth is bleeding a bit. You have a small cut from the teeth. Nothing too bad."

"Thanks, dear. I'm sorry. Is your arm OK?"

"A little sore. It's been twisted so many times I can't tell anymore."

"OK kids, Brad. You can all go to bed now. I'm going to bed too. Brad, you broke my teeth. I didn't even see you coming at me. Why did you do that?"

"If you don't know, I can't tell you," answered Brad.

"I don't know why you hit me, Brad. I don't…"

"Come on, Garf," Mom interrupted. "Get into bed, now." She looked at all of us. "Go to bed now. I'll be OK."

I watched as The Old Man got into bed with the cloth on his face. I also noticed the bloodied water in the basin on the floor. I almost began to feel sorry for The Old Man. But I forced myself back into reality by recalling what precipitated the entire incident, and the many previous similar sleepless nights. I lay awake all night waiting for something to happen again. But nothing did.

The next day seemed weird. This was one of those

Sundays when The Old Man was on his best behaviour. He never really mentioned the fight, but he continually inspected his broken dentures so we knew it was on his mind. Brad and The Old Man spoke to each other, but you could tell that neither was very comfortable with the situation. Eventually, we all said our farewells to Brad and he continued his journey home.

"I guess I'll have to get new teeth, Mary," The Old Man stated.

Somehow, I knew that he wouldn't have to wait as long as Mom did.

23 ~ At Least the Speeches Are Finally Over

It was time to head back to school, and now Sissy was old enough to attend as well. Except she didn't want to be called Sissy anymore. She was now too old for that. Mom asked us to refrain from using that moniker, especially at school. Sissy didn't want the other kids to hear that name and end up getting stuck with it for the rest of her life. So from now on, it was Lily. Thus I better correct myself and say that now Lily was old enough to attend school.

We were still at the old two-room schoolhouse, so Billy, Gordie and I remained together in the same class while Lily began her education in the other classroom. I was now in Grade 6 while Billy and Gordie were once again in the same grade (Grade 7). Meanwhile, Ernie was beginning Grade 10 at the same high school in Erin. Of course, we had a new teacher. His name was Mr. Woodrow. To start the day, each of us had to stand and tell our name and grade. When it was my turn, I did my usual mumbling routine.

"Benny, Grade 6," I mouthed.

"Pardon? Speak up," said Mr. Woodrow. "I didn't catch your name and it sounded like you said Grade 6. That can't be true."

"That's my brother Benny," Gordie answered before I could. "Yup, he's in Grade 6."

"Let your brother speak. I wasn't talking to you Mr. Gordon Cooper."

"Benny," I spoke loudly. "Benny Cooper. Grade 6."

"All right then. That's better. Next!"

"John Brooks, eight," replied John.

"Speak English, son. I can't understand a word you're saying."

"I am speaking English, sir," said John indignantly in his strong, Glaswegian accent. "I said John Brooks. Grade 8."

"All right, Mr. Brewks, is it? Have I got that right?"

"Brooks, sir! B-R-O-O-K-S."

"Oh, Brooks. Why didn't you say so? Next!"

Everyone was grinning over this exchange. I still hadn't got over Gordie being referred to as 'Mr. Gordon Cooper'. At lunchtime, a few of us were discussing our new teacher.

"What an idiot!" commented John Brooks. "Useless. A complete waste of space."

"This is only his first day," Gordie remarked. "Maybe you'll grow to like him, John."

"Nae chance! That Woodpile is absolutely useless. Dogs in the street can see that."

"Did you say 'Woodpile', John?" Richard Watson asked. "That's it! That's his name from now on. 'Woodpile'. I like it."

"Brilliant!" I remarked. And 'Woodpile' he remained.

That fall, a new television show started on Sunday evenings following 'The Ed Sullivan Show'. It was 'Bonanza'. And we all loved it. From the moment the four Cartwrights rode up during the opening credits, I was hooked. It was the first network series broadcast in colour, but that didn't matter to us. We had a black and white set and would for many years to come. But we wouldn't miss the show nevertheless. Mom and Lily liked 'Little Joe' best. Billy liked Hoss while Gordie and I were fans of Adam. Even The Old Man would watch this show with us. I'm not sure which character was his favourite.

Speaking of The Old Man, that September he finally lived out his dream. He borrowed a van from the telephone company and the Cooper Bottle Collection Company was born. That Saturday, Billy, Gordie and I joined The Old Man on his quest for fortune through the search for bottles alongside various highways and back roads. We started early in the morning and didn't return until late in the afternoon with a van chock full of empty bottles. Some were beer bottles and others were pop bottles. Soon after we got home, The Old Man left again to cash in all the bottles for refunds. We didn't see him again until late that night. It turned out that he received just enough money from the bottles to treat himself to a case of 24 beer and several draughts at a tavern in Erin. Boy, was Mom ever mad! I had never heard her tell off The Old Man so much before. She said that no way was she ever again going to allow us kids to work all day, just so that The Old Man could spend it on beer. Hence, ended the saga of the Cooper Bottle Collection Company.

That also was the fall that I eventually decided to join the 50's, although that decade was almost over. I decided to use Brylcreem. I'm not sure what influenced me the most. My older brothers, especially Ernie who sported a very prominent ducktail, or the television commercials. You probably remember the ads with the catchy slogan, 'A little dab will do ya'. Ernie had an addendum to that phrase, 'but a big dab will do ya even better'. I have to admit that I liked to use a fair-sized dab myself. And I too formed a ducktail. Now all four of us boys carried that fashion statement. I know that I was influenced by ads, because I still remember that long-winded statement about Crest toothpaste. 'Crest has been proven to be an effective, decay preventive dentifrice, of significant value, when used in a conscientiously applied program of oral hygiene and regular professional care.' I loved all the big words that they used. What a way to say, it works if you brush! I used to recite it to Gordie just to drive him nuts.

However, I still couldn't name the Books in the Bible.

The Erin Fall Fair was on the Thanksgiving weekend in October. The Old Man drove the whole family to the festivities, all except for Ernie who got a ride with one of his friends. I was looking forward to the event because I hadn't had the chance to attend a real fair before. The closest I had been was the candy-floss seconded from our barn at Robertsons'. I have to admit that I was disappointed. I enjoyed the few rides, but other than that, I wondered what all the fuss was about. You could look at prize pigs or bulls, and watch them being auctioned. But after you've lived with a pig (Curly, remember him?) and been nearly trampled to death by a wandering herd of cows, it's no big thrill to gaze at livestock. Then there was the big barn full of local 'crafts'. The crafts mainly consisted of things created at all the nearby schools – pictures, drawings, knitting, and the like. Some were good, I guess, but not my cup of tea. Where were the dinky toys? In order to not appear too spoiled, I have to admit that I had a good time meandering the grounds with Gordie and running into a few school chums. When it was time to go home, we couldn't find any sign of The Old Man. We could guess where he was though. So Mom decided that we should walk home. After all, it was only five miles to Hillsburgh. Therefore, Mom, Billy, Gordie, Lily, and I began the long trek home. Ernie wasn't ready to leave yet. He said he would get a ride home with someone later. The walk home reminded me of our walks into Orangeville for the monthly shopping sprees. Billy, Gordie and I spent more time in the ditch than we did on the road. Actually, Lily did as well. We had a good time. Shortly after we arrived home, The Old Man made his appearance.

"Why didn't you wait for me, Mary?" he wanted to know. "How did you get home? With your boyfriend? I can't trust you for a minute, Can I? You gray-haired, old bag!"

This abuse didn't last long though. The Old Man didn't have any beer, so he soon fell asleep. When Ernie arrived home he told us about his adventure. He and Phil Watson were getting a ride home with Tweety Bird, when a car suddenly came upon them from behind hogging the middle of the road and drove them right off the road. The driver kept on flying by and didn't acknowledge that he had driven a '55 Chevy in the ditch. It was The Old Man. Luckily no one was hurt. And Tweety Bird was thankful his car survived undamaged as well. This added to Mom's theory that The Old Man must have had horseshoes stuck up his ass. If that had happened to anybody other than Tweety Bird, The Old Man would have had a visit from the police. Also, this revelation made us even gladder that we had decided to walk home without waiting for The Old Man to show up.

A few weeks later, it was Halloween. This was my first Halloween in a town. At least that I could remember. It was fun to 'trick or treat' by walking from door to door. I was used to being driven from lane to lane and taking one hour to visit five houses. Now you could hit five houses in a few minutes. I was dressed up as Zorro, I think. Gordie and I took Lily out trick or treating and then went off on our own when it got too late for her. We then went to the houses downtown at the bottom of the hill. Even the general stores were giving out goodies. I refrained from asking if they had Robin Hood by the bag. We even tried the Hedgehog's place. We assumed she wouldn't recognize us in our costumes. I don't remember what Gordie was dressed up as. However, she didn't answer the door. We then decided to stick a firecracker in her keyhole. Gordie lit it and we ran like hell. We were hidden well out of sight when we saw the Hedgehog come out the front door to investigate the cause of the explosion. She glared in every direction for what seemed liked fifteen minutes before finally going back inside. But just before she did, this warning was issued.

"I know you're out there somewhere, you little brats! I've called the police! You're going to get it this time!"

"We better get home," I said to Gordie. "Do you really think she called the police?"

"Nah, she's just trying to scare us. Even if she did,

they've probably got other things to do on Halloween. OK, let's go. Anyways, I don't think she knows who did it."

We went home and I quickly went to bed. Whenever a car went by the window, I wondered if it was the police. But, they never did come to arrest us or take us away to the reform school in Guelph.

A few days later, I told John Brooks about the incident with the firecracker and the Hedgehog. He said that we should try the old trick that he used to use in Glasgow. He would stick some envelopes partway through the mail slot with a string attached to the other end. Then when the resident tried to collect their mail, he would tug on the string pulling the mail back through the door and down the sidewalk. That wouldn't work in Hillsburgh though. Nobody had mail slots. We had to go to the Post Office for pickup and delivery. Another trick of John's involved attaching a string to a wallet conveniently placed outside a pub. He and his friends would hide in a bush, and they would await for some poor, unsuspecting (and intoxicated) patron to emerge from the pub. Then they would watch in amusement as he tried to pick up the wallet. I briefly thought about using this trick on The Old Man but soon thought better about it.

Many of the girls in our class used to have Autograph Books. These were the little books that you passed around to your classmates to write some inspirational writing or creative poetry. One of the popular classic lines was "Yours 'till Niagara Falls wears rubber pants." Another favourite was "Yours 'till the U.S. drinks Canada dry." What you wrote wasn't really that important. The idea was just to fill your book with something from all your fellow students, so that you could look back at it years later and say, "Who are all these idiots?" One day in November, Woodpile grabbed the books off the desk of two girls and carried them to the front. They belonged to Mary Brooks (John's younger sister whom I have failed to mention so far) and Rhea Kressman (her family had just migrated to Canada from Germany during the previous summer).

"I've been noticing some of the things that you have been writing in these books," Woodpile began. "Listen to this."

"Roses are red, orchids are black.

You'd look better with a knife in your back."

The entire class laughed. I looked over at Gordie because I recognized it as his work.

"This is not funny!" bellowed Woodpile. "This is disgraceful. These young girls come to Canada and this is how you treat them. What must they think about us? This is bad enough to put in anybody's Autograph Book. But to write this drivel in the books of an immigrant is really insulting. I am ashamed of all of you. Not just Mr. Gordon Cooper, the author of this, this, whatever you call it. Certainly not literature."

"We're just having fun," explained Richard Watson. "It doesn't really mean anything."

"If I wanted your opinion, young man, then I would ask for it! This is not fun. Here's another example."

"Your teeth are like stars, they come out at night."

"I am disgusted. There's others here that I won't even read in class. That's how bad they are. Let's show some respect for each other. You should be able to do that."

I immediately thought of the sequel to the last line.

"Your eyes are like two piss-holes in the snow."

I wondered if anyone had written that one in either book. Perhaps that was the line that Woodpile wouldn't read. He recited a few more and got more upset after each reading. Eventually it was time for recess and we got a break from the lecture. At recess, we were all talking about Woodpile's tirade.

"What an idiot!" exclaimed John Brooks. "What gave him the right to read someone else's book anyway? Like I said before, a complete waste of space."

"Was your sister Mary upset about what people wrote in her book?" I inquired.

"No, of course not. She'd be upset if everyone treated her differently than the rest. She thinks that the sayings are funny. She's only upset that that moron took her book. I'll be glad when we move into the new school. I hear that Grades 7 and 8 will get someone new. I'm afraid Benny, that you'll still be stuck with Woodpile. I feel sorry for you."

"Thanks a lot, John," I responded, "I guess I'm just lucky."

It was a cold, snowy day in December. Billy, Gordie, Lily, and I were walking home together. At times, we could hardly see where we were going. The snow was blowing into our faces and all around us. As we got part way up the hill, we could make out someone standing at the next corner. It appeared that whomever it was, was waiting for us to catch up.

"Did you guys hear anything about a bus accident?" It was Sammy Smale.

"No," Gordie answered first. "What accident?"

"Someone said that a school bus got hit by a train."

"Where, Sammy," I asked, "in Ontario somewhere?"

"Here in Hillsburgh, Benny. At the tracks at the other end of town."

"How'd you hear about it already?" asked Billy. "We just left school. The bus probably only left a few minutes ago."

"No, not a bus from our school. It was a high school bus, I think. Coming back from Erin."

"A bus from Erin, coming to Hillsburgh. Are you sure, Sammy?" questioned Billy.

"That's what one of the kids said. I'm not sure, but I think that's what I heard."

We all looked at each other. We were all thinking about Ernie.

"Come on, let's get going," Billy ordered. "Ernie should be home by now. Let's go see."

The four of us hurried home as fast as we could travel. I think we left Sammy standing in his tracks. Before we were all in the front door, Billy yelled out, "Ernie! Ernie!"

"He's not home yet," Mom answered from the kitchen and then walked into the living room as she continued to speak. "What's going on? He's usually home by now. I was starting to worry. But I figured you'd just say I was being silly."

"I'm not sure, Mom," Billy replied hesitantly, "but Sammy says he heard that a school bus had been hit by a train. A bus coming from Erin."

Mom turned totally white and appeared to sway a bit on her feet. "Oh God. That's Ernie."

"We don't know for sure yet, Mom," Billy repeated. "I think there's two or three different buses that come to Hillsburgh from Erin. It could have been a different one. Or maybe Sammy just got the story all wrong."

"Ernie is late though, dear. Oh God, I wish your father was home." I couldn't remember hearing Mom say that before. "We need to go see what happened," she continued. "Where? Where did Sammy say it happened?"

"At the other end of town," Gordie spoke this time. "I guess at the tracks on the road to Erin."

"How serious was the accident? Was anybody hurt?" Mom asked as the reality of the situation started to sink in more.

"We don't know, Mom," said Billy. "We don't have any details, just a rumour. We don't know."

"Don't get undressed," she said to Lily and I, as we started to remove our boots and coats. "We've got to go now even if we have to walk. I'll get my coat."

Just then we heard a car pulling in the driveway and Mom rushed to look out the window.

"It's your father. Thank God. I'll grab my coat now."

By the time that The Old Man came into the kitchen door at the side of the house, we were all standing there with our boots, coats, hats, gloves, and mittens on. I expected him to wonder what the devil was going on, but he spoke first.

"Get ready, oh, I see that you are. A bus has been hit by a train at the south end of town. I'm not sure but I think that it's Ernie's bus. Someone from the telephone company was working down there at the time repairing some lines from the storm. He saw the whole thing. Ralph told me."

"How bad is it, Garf? How bad?" Mom asked fearing the answer.

"Come on, let's get going. I'll tell you everything I know in the car."

"How bad?"

"Not good, Mary. It exploded, caught on fire. I think some kids have been killed."

"Good God. We're ready let's go."

Lily and I hadn't spoken during this entire exchange. We all climbed in the car without anyone saying a word. We all knew what was on each other's minds. Finally Lily broke the silence.

"Ernie will be OK, Mom. You'll see. Don't worry."

"I hope you're right, Lily. I pray that you are right."

During the car ride The Old Man shared all the knowledge that he knew about the incident. As he mentioned earlier, a telephone worker or workers repairing lines at the other end of town witnessed the accident. The bus was crossing the tracks, when a train rammed into it broadside pushing the bus far down the tracks. It caught fire after the gas tank exploded. Some kids got out of the bus. He wasn't sure how many. But not everyone escaped. The phones weren't working so someone had to drive to Erin in order to phone Guelph for an ambulance. It had all happened well over an hour ago. The Old Man had just heard the story from another worker before he had hurried home.

When we first arrived at the scene, I couldn't see anything other than a lot of parked cars. Then I noticed that a train was stopped in a field on the other side of the road. As we walked along the track, I felt an eerie feeling in my body as no one spoke or even looked at each other. We were all surveying the surreal scene around us. I could see something black off in the distance but I couldn't make out what it was. It was surrounded by a crowd of people. As we got closer, Mom broke the silence.

"Oh my God, that's the bus."

At first, I couldn't see what Mom was referring to until I realized that the black shape that I was staring at was all that remained of what used to be a bright, orange school bus. We worked our way past a few people to see that the entire side of the bus had been smashed in so far that it appeared that the two sides were touching. And it now appeared black because the whole thing had been completely burnt out. No windows remained in the bus. The back emergency door was hanging wide open, serving as a clue of how some may have escaped from the twisted wreckage. My first thought was that no one could have survived. How could they have? I glanced back towards the road and realized that we had walked over a hundred yards down the track. The Old Man and Billy went off in different directions looking for any sign of Ernie or anyone that knew what may have happened to him. We overheard other people talking. Three or four students had been killed. The driver had been taken to the hospital. He had pulled many kids from the burning bus. Many had suffered severe injuries. Some had been taken to the hospital in Orangeville; some had gone to Guelph. Others were still lying in snow banks recovering from the smoke, the flames, and the shock. A lot of parents seemed to be wandering around looking for their missing sons or daughters. Everyone else seemed as confused as we did. I saw a couple volunteer firemen carry something from the bus. It appeared to be a burnt log.

"Look, they're carrying out another body," I heard someone in the crowd say. "That's three now, I think."

Suddenly I spied Richard Watson. Gordie and I went to see if he knew anything more than us. But he was just as lost as we were. He was still searching for a sign of his older brother Phil. I then looked back towards Mom and Lily just in time to see The Old Man come up to them. Billy wasn't far behind. The Old Man was talking to Mom and pointing at something or someone on the other side of the bus. I looked towards the direction he was indicating and saw the object of his attention. It was Phil Watson. Before I could say anything,

I saw Richard run off towards him.

"Benny, Gordie," Mom called. "Come here!" Before we were halfway back, Mom cried out again. "Ernie's been taken to the hospital in Guelph. We think he's going to be OK. We're driving there now. Hurry up."

The Old Man had got all of this information from Phil Watson. It turned out that he wasn't on the bus. He had got another ride home. He came when he heard about the tragedy just as most of Hillsburgh had. Somebody had told him that Ernie and another one of his friends, Ken Arden, had been taken to Guelph in someone's car. He thought Ernie would be OK but he wasn't sure. As we were walking back to the car, I noticed one of my classmates sitting beside another car. A woman was holding him and he was crying. I didn't have time to stop and talk to him. The ride to Guelph seemed a lot longer than usual that night. And when we got there, we found out that Ernie had already been discharged. He had already got a ride back to Hillsburgh with another family. This last part was told to us by Ken Arden's younger brother, Larry. He also informed us that his brother was going to be fine as well. He had only a broken leg. And he knew more. Three girls had been killed. One was a girl that lived at the other end of town, another was the older sister of my classmate that I had spotted earlier, and the third was the daughter of one of our neighbours. I had seen her in the neighbourhood many times. Many other students were still in the hospital and so was the bus driver. We then headed home back along Highway 24 to the Hillsburgh road. This time the ride seemed even further.

When we got home, Ernie was sitting in front of the TV waiting for us. I think he was just as relieved to see us, as we were him. He was more concerned with us (especially Mom) worrying about him than he was anything else. After the obvious reunion hugs and kisses, Ernie explained more about the afternoon and evening. There was an assembly at the school that day which had run late due to various speeches by the school staff, so the buses had left later than usual. Phil

Watson had decided to curtail the speeches and left early and got a ride with someone else, rather than wait for the departure of the buses. He had asked Ernie but Ernie thought it would be faster to wait for the bus, as Phil wasn't quite sure how he was getting home. Anyways, it had been a normal bus ride home with singing, yelling, and the usual ruckus that happens on a school bus when someone spotted a train through the snow and yelled out. The next thing that Ernie knew was that Ken Arden was telling him to hurry up and get off the bus. He remembered Ken coaxing others out the emergency door as well.

"I heard crying and screaming. Some of the kids were on fire and were jumping in the snow. I saw two girls at the front. They were on fire. There was no way to get to them. People were screaming at me to get away from the bus. They thought it would explode. Only those at the back could get out quickly. We were running in every direction, just trying to get as far away as possible. When I stopped and turned around the whole bus was in flames. I just sat down in the snow and waited for help. I didn't know what to do."

Later that night, I asked Ernie what he thought when he first knew that they were going to be hit by a train. Did his life flash in front of his eyes?

"Nah, nothing like that," he said. "All I could think about was all those damn speeches. At least the speeches are finally over, I said to myself."

24 ~ Screams At Night

The entire town of Hillsburgh (and many others) attended the funeral services a few days later. There were so many people they installed loudspeakers outside the church. We were among the crowd that was standing outside in the cold listening to the service. But we didn't mind. Nobody even felt the cold. That morning we had heard that the bus driver had died as well. He had suffered severe burns during his repeated attempts to free as many people as possible from their fiery trap. The entire tragedy had a lasting effect on me as I'm sure it did on most of the town. For me, it was my introduction to the realities of death. It comes sudden and indiscriminately. Death does not make sense. I still hear people talk about instances such as the demise of some television character and comment, "How could they kill him/her off? There was no reason." Who said death has a reason? That's what hit home for me anyway. It can happen anytime, anywhere, to anyone. Not just the elderly or someone else. Ernie could have just as easily been one of the youngsters buried that day. I now realized that we all could be killed, maybe in a car ride back from Georgetown one Friday night. And for the first time in my life, I was afraid of dying. I guess everybody else already realized this. We had a few telephone calls from different relatives. One was from Aunt Becky. Like the rest she had heard about the accident on the CBC national news, caught the name Hillsburgh, and wondered if one of us were on the bus. Aunt Becky also announced that she would be coming up from Newfoundland to visit us in a few months. Mom had not seen her sister since Grandma passed away, so she was excited by this news, as we all were.

For Christmas that year, all four of us four boys received new pajamas. I can't remember who gave them to us now, but I think it was Claudia and Tom. I mention this because I thought they were really neat. They were like uniforms. They were made of some stretchy material and came in two different colour schemes. Mine and Ernie's uniform, I mean pajamas, had a yellow pullover top with brown pants. Gordie and Billy were dressed in light blue tops with navy blue bottoms. They were really comfortable and warm. I wanted to wear them all day. Lily must have been jealous of our new fancy attire. And yellow is still my favourite colour.

When we went back to school after the Christmas break, we did not return to the old two-room schoolhouse. To commence the new decade, we now had a brand new school with four modern classrooms and a new name. It was no longer just Hillsburgh Public School; we were now students of the Robert J. McKenzie Public School. That made me feel old. To be attending a school named after someone that I knew. I thought buildings were only named after old, dead people. I was now once more in a class without my brothers. They of course were in the Grades 7 and 8 class, while I was a member of the 5 – 6 group. And John Brooks was right. I still had Woodpile. Their teacher was brought in from one of the country schools which were closed down in order to consolidate us all together in one larger school. His name was Dan Clark and he was also made the new principal. Everyone soon referred to Mr. Clark as 'Danny'. Billy and Gordie both told me that Danny was a big improvement over Woodpile.

Shortly after, I started having this recurring nightmare. Nothing to do with being the only Cooper in my class again.

At least not that I know of. I think I was over that traumatic experience by now. You might think it was connected to the effects of the bus accident. But I don't think so. That thought never occurred to me at the time. Anyways, if I tell you my dream then maybe you can advise me of its meaning. One night while sleeping soundly in my new yellow and brown pajamas, I was suddenly transported to this field in somebody's farm. The field had grass about six inches high. I thought that I could see something gray moving in the grass towards me from a distance. I soon realized that it was a wolf. And its intentions were not friendly. I started to run as fast as I could, but of course I couldn't get myself to run very fast. I then caught sight of a rail fence. If I could just make it over the fence then I will be safe, I thought. Eventually, I did arrive at the fence and began to crawl through it. I thought I had been successful in escaping when the wolf's teeth sunk into my right leg which was the only part of me still on the field side of the fence. And I screamed. I mean I screamed not just in my dream but out loud. I woke up and I was sitting up in my bed covered with sweat. Gordie was still sound asleep beside me. I expected Mom to run in any second to see what had happened, however the only sound that I could hear was my breathing and my heartbeat. Both of these alone seemed loud enough to awaken Gordie. But no one else stirred. So I surmised that I hadn't screamed for real at all. A few days later, I had the exact same dream with the same abrupt ending. Again I was sitting up wearing a sweaty pair of yellow and brown pajamas. And a few days later, it happened once more. And again. Then finally a few weeks after the first dream, I screamed for real. And awoke the whole house. Gordie thought that I had been bitten by a snake. Mom wondered if I was being murdered. Billy and Ernie suspected the return of the mustachioed man in uniform. Lily asked if flying monkeys were after me. And The Old Man couldn't understand why I was yelling over some stupid dream. That night I told Mom and Gordie my entire dream. All of a sudden it didn't seem so bad anymore. I had the dream again a few more times but now I recognized it as just a dream. So I wasn't frightened. I just stood my ground and said, "You don't scare me wolf. I know that this is just a dream. So you can't hurt me." That would make him lose interest and I could go back to dreaming about something more pleasurable. Then I started dreaming about falling off cliffs. I told Gordie about this one a lot sooner. I was learning. OK, what's your prognosis? Do I have deep problems or what? I'll leave it with you to think about it while I go on with other things.

That winter we had a ton of snow. Isn't it funny how there always used to be more snow in years gone by? The little cliff behind our house, where the large rocks like racing cars were situated, was completely covered in snow banks. No boulders were to be seen anywhere. There was so much snow, Sammy and I could toboggan down the side of the cliff for our first and last time. When we reached the bottom not only did we discover the hidden stone mammoths, but we took the snow down with us. We were completely covered in an avalanche of snow. We were scared to death for approximately two seconds, and then we popped out of the snow and started laughing our heads off. We wanted to do it again, however we decided the cliff edge was no longer covered in enough snow for another exciting run. So that was the end of that game.

In February an inquest was held concerning the train-bus collision. Ernie and his friends including Ken Arden had to testify. This was held in the small town hall located downtown near the United Church. The train tracks where the accident occurred intersected the road at a level crossing with no barrier or lights. Apparently the county had approved the installation of warning lights at that crossing a few weeks before the tragedy. So of course one of the recommendations from the inquest was the placing of warning lights and bells at all major crossings. Also it came out that it was too noisy on the bus to hear the train whistle. Thus the other proposal was that all buses stop in front of train tracks before crossing and open the doors to look and listen for the approach of an oncoming train. So every time you see a school bus stopped at a railway crossing or read the procedure on the back of a bus, think about the four casualties, Ernie, and all the other people affected by that terrible incident in Hillsburgh. That's what I do anyway.

When the snow started to melt as spring approached, we began to discover items in the schoolyard, which were leftover from the construction. For example, I and some others from my class found some empty paint cans and lids one recess in March. I decided to pick up one lid and throw it underhand to see how well it would fly. I watched as it soared through the air in a perfect arc. It went up fairly high and then turned back towards the school in a parabolic curve and crashed straight through our classroom window.

"Oh shit!" I exclaimed as we all started to run to the other side of the school.

"If Woodpile asks, nobody say anything," one of my classmates suggested. "We'd probably all get in trouble. So don't admit anything."

The others all readily agreed. As we all nonchalantly returned back into the classroom, we encountered Woodpile inspecting the damaged window while grasping the evidence in his hand. He did not look too pleased.

"Who did this? Who saw who did this?" Nobody answered. "Come on now. Somebody must have seen something. This didn't come in here by itself. Now speak up. It won't hurt anyone to tell me what they saw. I just want to find the culprit that's all." Again he was greeted by silence. "What's the matter with you people? Somebody has damaged school property without any regard for authority. Now, let's get the truth!"

"We didn't see anything, Mr. Woodrow," someone finally responded. "Most of us were on the other side of the school. Weren't we?"

"That's right, Mr. Woodrow," another boy agreed.

"I saw some of you outside digging in the snow. This is

still a construction site. You can't be playing with everything you find in the yard. It is not your property. That's school property. You must have regard for other's property. Now I know nobody in this class threw this," Woodpile continued as he waved the paint can lid to us all, "as no one in this class would be strong enough to throw it with that much force. It had to be someone in Mr. Clark's class. I know that. So just tell me who it was." More silence. "Well, you will all stay after class then."

"That's not fair!" one boy protested.

"Too bad! You must be shown respect for order. One last chance, does anybody have anything to say?"

During this entire exchange I expected someone to tell the truth and point me out but no one did. By this moment though, I was feeling guilty and decided to own up.

"I did it, Mr. Woodrow," I blurted out. "I threw the lid."

"Don't be ridiculous, Benny Cooper. How could you have done it? Who are you protecting? Was it one of your brothers? Billy or Gordie? Is that it?"

"No, it was me."

"Nonsense, now that's enough. I don't want to hear anymore. Everyone stays after school and that's it. Now let's get back to our lesson."

I found out after school, that Mr. Clark had only commented to his class that they should be more careful in what direction they toss things to avoid future accidents. When I told Billy and Gordie my story, at first they didn't believe that I was the discus thrower either. But eventually I convinced them and they thought Woodpile's reaction was hilarious.

"You're turning into quite a trouble maker, Benny," Billy joked. "I'm glad I'm in a grade ahead of you. I wouldn't want to be misjudged by teachers because of the bad reputation of my brother."

Even I had to laugh at that prospect. So that's the true story of how the Frisbee was invented. Some smart aleck just stole my idea, that's all.

As promised, Aunt Becky came to visit us in the spring. We hadn't seen her for so long I couldn't really remember too much about her. She resembled Mom in many ways especially since Mom had acquired her teeth and glasses, but as I mentioned much earlier in this long, rambling narrative, they were also as different as night and day. It didn't take long to realize that Aunt Becky wasn't used to being around a lot of children. She was now used to living alone, so we must have been as big of an adjustment for her as having her around the house was to us. She didn't understand any of our ideas of a good time. When she saw Lily and I playing the game where you traverse the house without touching the floor, she told us to get off the furniture. When Gordie and I each sat on one of the arms of the living room chairs and pretended we were Gene Autrey and Hopalong Cassidy, Aunt Becky spoke to us.

"Oh my Blessed Father, what are you two up to now? That's furniture not a hobbyhorse. Why can't anybody stay on the floor in this house?"

However, Aunt Becky always meant well and she showed us a lot of love and kindness while she was there. Now as far as her and The Old Man went, that's a completely different story. She had absolutely no time for him. Aunt Becky stayed for about six weeks, and for the first couple of weeks The Old Man had not gotten drunk. He was quite hospitable to Aunt Becky actually. But she wasn't fooled. By the third week, on a payday weekend, The Old Man purchased his usual case of 24 beer and proceeded to drink himself into a drunken stupor. Before long the 'gray-haired old bag' taunts had begun.

"How do you put up with that man, Mary?" Aunt Becky questioned. "If it was me, I think one of us would have been dead long ago. Forgive me Lord for saying so, but I think I would have killed him by now."

Mom just shrugged and tried to explain. "If I say or do anything, then he just gets worse. I only think about the children. I try to ignore him as much as possible and hope we'll all still be here in the morning. If I did anything silly and got hurt or hurt The Old Man, then where would the children be? Not only would they be without a real father, they would lose their mother too. No, Becky. I just have to turn the other cheek as the Bible says. What else could I do?"

"I don't understand why you haven't left him, Mary. Just get up and go."

The Old Man was of course at the kitchen table while this conversation was taking place in the living room. I could hear 'old bag', 'whore', and the other usual slurs coming from the kitchen at the same time.

"I can't do that either, Becky," Mom replied. "I still have five kids at home to clothe and feed. Where could I go? What could I use for money? I know that you help out, as do Brad and Claudia. But you can't have me and five kids showing up at your door. It wouldn't be fair to you. Or to the kids. I'll leave him when they are all grown up. When Lily is old enough. But for now, I don't see any other option."

"Well, you know that I'm always there, Mary. I still don't…"

"Hey, what the hell's all this whispering about?" It was The Old Man now standing in the living room. "What are you two gray-haired old bags talking about? I wasn't born yesterday, you know. I've been around the world. I know the score. What do you think I am, an eight-day clock or a sewing machine?"

Before The Old Man had finished, Aunt Becky jumped up from her seat and left the room and Poncho crawled under the china cabinet in the dining room corner. I assumed, as I'm sure we all did that Aunt Becky was just escaping from the abuse. But a few seconds after The Old Man stopped talking, she was behind him with the large iron frying pan over her head.

"You call me an old bag once more and you'll be a dead man! I don't have to take that from you. Nobody does. Now get back in the kitchen and act like a normal husband! If you can."

The Old Man looked at Aunt Becky and the frying pan. I thought that he would go berserk. But I was mistaken.

"Yes, dear" he said.

"And don't call me dear either! I'm not your dear."

"Yes, dear. I mean Becky. Don't worry. I'm going back into the kitchen. You sit back down and watch TV. Don't mind me." And he left the room.

"See what I mean, Mary?" Aunt Becky said after The Old Man had left. "You shouldn't stand for his insults and blasphemy. No sensible person would."

Mom hesitated and then finally answered. "That may work for you, Becky. At least this time. And the night is not over. But if I tried that." Mom stopped for a few seconds again before continuing. "I would pay for it in more ways than one. Look at my arms. Twisted black and blue. That's from last month. I told Garf to be quiet. And he grabbed me. He went nuts. I thought that he was going to kill me."

"You never told us this, Mom," Gordie protested. "When was this?"

"Two weeks ago."

"I didn't know he was that drunk that last time," Billy stated.

Mom began to speak slower and lower. "That's just it. He wasn't. He's getting worse. He now gets drunk just thinking about drinking. I don't trust him at all. I dare not give him any reason to jump at me or any of you. I only think about you kids. That's the only reason that I live. If it wasn't for all of you than I wouldn't care if The Old Man killed me tonight."

"Mom, don't say that," I pleaded.

"Is Daddy going to hurt you tonight?" asked Lily.

"No, no," Mom responded. "I mean what I said, Benny. You and Billy and Gordie and Lily and Ernie, plus the rest. That's all I care about. You're my life. And I'll continue to do what I feel is best for you all. Do you understand, Becky?"

Aunt Becky just nodded and continued to look at Mom's arm. She was still gripping the frying pan in her right hand.

"Let's watch the hockey game now," Billy said.

"OK," Mom replied. "Let's hope that we can watch it without any more interruptions."

"Mary," Becky finally spoke, "whatever you do. I'll try to help you. That's all I'll say. That bloody fool just better not hurt you. Oh my Blessed Father, now he's even making me swear. I think it must be contagious."

For the rest of that night, The Old Man stayed in the kitchen. And I never heard him call Aunt Becky a gray-haired old bag again. Not to her face anyway. Oh, by the way the Leafs won the game.

A few days later, Billy, Gordie, Lily, and I were once more traversing the living room and dining room without touching the floor. There were alligators there, you must understand. Suddenly we heard the distinctive steps of Aunt Becky coming down the stairwell.

"Aunt Becky's coming!" warned Billy.

I reacted so fast that I started to slide off the large armchair headfirst. To save me from severe head injury, Billy attempted to grab me in order to ease me to the floor. Unfortunately he grasped me by the waist of my pants and I kept falling to the floor while my pants (including underpants) ceased their descent. In other words, I ended up on the floor naked below the waist with my pants down around my knees. I immediately clutched the waist of my pants and tugged them back up to their rightful location in order to restore my lost dignity in front of Lily and the fast approaching Aunt Becky. Just as I had pulled my drawers back up over my exposed body parts, I looked up to see Aunt Becky staring down at me. She just shook her head, said not a word, and walked on into the kitchen. I looked at my brothers and sister and they all burst into laughter at once. So I joined them in their frolics.

"Aunt Becky's coming! Aunt Becky's coming!" repeated Billy.

And we all laughed harder than before.

"Aunt Becky's coming!" said Gordie.

And we rolled on the floor.

"Aunt Becky's coming!" added Lily.

And my sides started to hurt.

"Aunt Becky's coming!" I said too.

That was the cue for the real chortling to begin. I never was sure what Aunt Becky witnessed. The others told me that she saw everything or nothing depending on the reaction they wanted to incite from me. However, for a long time we needed only to recite those famous three words in order to cause any of us to break into instant hysterics. Aunt Becky's coming!

The weekend before Aunt Becky was set to return home to Newfoundland, The Old Man got drunk again. We were all sitting in the living room watching television while The Old Man was situated at his favourite drinking spot – the kitchen table. Eventually he stumbled into the living room.

"What's this shit you're watching? Why aren't you watching hockey?"

"It's not on yet, Dad," explained Ernie. "Not for another half hour. This is just some movie with Boston Blackie."

"Well it looks like shit to me. Is there nothing else on other than this fucking shit?"

"Garf!" protested Aunt Becky. "Your mouth is getting more foul all the time. Look at you! You drink so much. One of these days you're going to drop dead from all the drinking."

"Drop dead! Drop dead! Me drop dead? What are you talking about? Have you ever seen me drop dead? Don't you worry about me."

"I'm not worrying about you. That's for sure," Aunt Becky responded quickly.

"You've never seen me drop dead, have you? Have you ever seen me dead?" The Old Man continued.

I looked at Mom and she was smiling. And then I looked at Gordie and we started laughing. And then Ernie and Billy joined in. And finally Mom couldn't stop herself from giggling either. Soon we were all laughing except for The Old

Man.

"What the hell is everybody laughing about?"

"Did you hear what you just said?" asked Mom as she kept laughing at the same time.

"I don't know what you're laughing about. All I said was, have you ever seen me dead?" And then The Old Man stopped talking for a few seconds. I could tell that he was thinking. Suddenly he started laughing as well. "Have you ever seen me dead? That's a good one! Of course, you haven't seen me dead, have you Mary?"

"No," replied Mom. "Not yet anyway."

"Have you ever seen me dead?" restated The Old Man again. "That's a good one. I better go for another beer. Have you ever seen me drop dead?" he echoed as he disappeared back into the kitchen.

25 ~ The Great Fire

Just before school broke for the summer of 1960, I noticed a large, luxurious car parked in the driveway of our new school. A few of us checked it out and realized that we were looking at a Rolls Royce. The first time that I had seen one live and in person.

"Whose car is this?" I inquired. I was standing with my friend Sammy and Richard Watson's younger brother Joe.

"Someone said it belongs to the school architect," Joe informed us all.

"The architect," I said. "Well that's what I want to be when I grow up."

So that's how I decided my career choice at the age of eleven. Later that day, I found out that I had been promoted to Grade 7, so everything was developing as planned. All of us Coopers passed their grades. So it was goodbye to Woodpile, now I would be in the same classroom as Billy and Gordie once again.

That summer the Cooper family discovered fire. It all started when Billy showed me a new trick. "Watch this," said Billy as first he squirted some lighter fluid on his hand and then lit the flammable liquid with a match. "This won't hurt because the fire will just burn off the lighter fluid and then it will go out." And it did, but not before Billy yelled, "Ow! That hurt. It didn't hurt last time." Billy shook his hand and examined it closely. "Good, no burns. Just a little too much heat, that's all. I must have used too much lighter fluid. Don't you try it, Benny. I don't want you burning the house down."

"Don't worry, Billy. I've already learnt that fire burns. I don't need to prove it again."

"Very funny. I'm serious. Don't try this."

"OK, I won't."

But I didn't promise that I wouldn't try it on something other than my body. Remember how we decimated the Flat and Them entourage by engaging in 'Cereal Wars'? Well similarly we thought it was time to stop playing with friction cars and Dinky Toys. Again we didn't want to withdraw 'cold turkey'. So we thought of ways to play and reduce our collection at the same time. It started with the friction toys. We staged demolition derbies. We smashed the vehicles into each other, against walls, down stairs, and out windows until the cars and trucks were no longer drivable. And then we threw them in the garbage. Some were so sturdy that we had to speed up the destruction process with hammers. Mom was not too fond of our new source of entertainment. She thought it was a great waste of perfectly good toys. Although we were having a good time, we decided not to destroy too many of our cars this way. So in reality we probably only wrote off three or four cars and those were the ones in the worst shape anyways. At least that's our story.

So then we turned our attention to the Dinky Toys. Anyone that knows anything about Dinky Toys knows that you can do pretty much anything to them and still not cause any noticeable damage other than a few paint chips. So we came up with a new plan for them. Fire. But we couldn't bring ourselves to really wreck a Dinky Toy, so this is where the lighter fluid experiment comes into play. Sammy and I engineered a multi-car pileup with about six Dinky Toys on the sidewalk in front of his house. Then we squirted lighter fluid on them and set them on fire. It worked beautifully.

Other than a few black marks, the cars were still in excellent condition. When Sammy went home for lunch, I decided to demonstrate the procedure to Gordie. We chose the empty lot beside the house as our crash site. We were situated in some grass beside the apple grove section of the vacant property. We placed about three cars together, applied the lighter fluid, and then struck the match. The whole thing went up in flames. Before we had even realized what was happening, the fire had spread about a foot in radius around the cars. And it was spreading fast. The grass was brown and dry and was quickly engulfed in the flames.

"Oh shit, Gordie! What are we going to do? Should we call the fire department?"

"No, help me! Let's try to stamp it out."

Unfortunately that plan had little or no effect other than burning the soles of our shoes. The fire was now about three feet square.

"I think we better go phone the fire department!"

"No not yet, Benny. The Old Man will kill us. No, find something quickly that we can use to smother the fire."

"OK, let's look, fast!"

With one eye I was scouring the area for anything. For what, I didn't know. My other eye was continuously following the course of the fire. It was now covering a six-foot by six-foot area. I was envisioning the whole lot burning, and then our house, and then the Smale's, and then all of Hillsburgh. Gordie and I would be infamous for life. The two boys that destroyed a whole town. Only because they didn't know better than to play with matches. I could feel my heart pounding. I finally spotted a small piece of lumber. I was so scared, I grabbed the lumber ran to the edge of the fire and started pounding the ground. I actually managed to put out one small part of the flames.

"Gordie, it's working! Help me!"

Then I saw Gordie start walloping the earth with a large, thin metal sheet. He was hitting it everywhere as hard and as fast as he could.

"Keep it up, Gordie! We're putting some of it out."

"You too, Benny. Don't stop until every inch is out!"

So for the next few minutes, which seemed like hours, we attacked the flames and the ground with as much power and speed as we could muster. And then I noticed Sammy beside us. He was striking the ground with another piece of wood.

"What are you two trying to do, burn down the whole town?"

"Almost," I yelled. "Almost!"

Eventually, the three of us were standing exhausted staring at a large black patch of burnt out grass, which must have been about ten feet wide and fifteen feet long. For a few moments nobody spoke. We were all too tired. And relieved. Finally I broke the silence.

"I really didn't think we'd get that out. I thought that we would be in big trouble."

"What are your parents going to say?" wondered Sammy.

"Who's going to tell them?" Gordie questioned. "Not us. And not you, right Sammy?"

"No, not me. But won't they see the grass all black and burnt?"

"No," Gordie reasoned, "they never come over here. The Old Man dreams about owning this property but he never comes here."

"But what if he does?" I asked. "Then he'll find out."

"Let's cover it up," Gordie suggested. "Come on help me."

Then Gordie started pulling long grass in other parts of the lot and threw it on top of the evidence. So Sammy and I joined in the cover-up and before long the scarred part of the field was barely visible. Unless you looked.

"What about our Dinky Toys?" I just remembered.

Gordie went over to where the fire started and retrieved the three cars which had caused this whole eventful near disaster.

"That's the end of these," he said. "Look!"

I looked in Gordie's hand to see three cars with the paint completely removed, the windows popped out, the interior melted to a glob, and the tires no longer in existence. One car used to be one of my favourites – the two-toned '57 Plymouth.

"I don't know about you guys," I admitted, "but I'm never touching that damn lighter fluid again."

"Me either," said Gordie.

"Don't look at me," replied Sammy. "I didn't start this. I never liked the idea in the first place. I still want to play with Dinky Toys like we always did. In your upstairs hall."

"OK, it's a deal," I readily agreed. "Come on let's go. Dinky Toys in the hall it is. Coming, Gordie?"

"Sure, why not?"

"And then we can go play in my dad's new truck," advised Sammy. He should be home soon. He's got a new Kenworth truck with a bed in the back and everything."

"Neat!" I exclaimed. "Let's get out of here and have some fun."

I told you earlier about the fields directly behind our house where we would wander back as far as the Wells Fargo trail. That summer we started going even further. Not only straight back but off to the right as far as the next concession road. And sometimes even further. We would make a whole day of hiking and exploration. We had no concern about whose property we were on. And nobody seemed to take notice of us, or if they did, they didn't mind our intrusions. These hikes usually involved me, Sammy, and Gordie but sometimes we were joined by Billy or Lily or even one or both of Sammy's two sisters, Sarah and Jenny. Once we walked all the way to the dump a few roads away. I enjoyed the visits to the dump. You always found something interesting even if it was just bottles to smash on the rocks. However, the best part of the hikes was just the exploring, discovering new fields, streams, forests, springs, and animals. And not just cows. A few times we saw foxes. It was the freedom that we enjoyed. The freedom to walk wherever we wanted without worry. I felt like Davey Crockett crossing the Appalachians for the first time. When we had fully scouted out those fields, we started crossing the main road at the top of the hill and headed west to new frontiers. Going that way we could circle back and end up at the other end of Hillsburgh. We had endless possibilities and all the time in the world. We thought we did anyway.

One day The Old Man brought home two old, crank telephones. And to our surprise, he installed one in Gordie's and my room and the other in Ernie and Billy's room. Then he stapled a line along the hallway wall between the two rooms. And then we had an internal communication system. Gordie and I could phone Billy or Ernie and they could phone us. It was also a good source of fun when Sammy came over and we played different games. I thought it was one of the best things that The Old Man had ever done for us kids. That phone installation was a step down for him. He had just installed the new dial phone for Conn Smythe. And The Old Man would tell anyone and everyone about that proud moment. He said that Connie had even spoke to him. That was at the Smythe household on Highway 10 near Caledon, and close by the gravel pits that made his riches. I knew that he was rich because he had a white, wooden fence around his property. Also his racehorses were clearly visible in the fields.

That was also the summer that Gordie and I decided to become writers. We had read many comic books and children's stories and reached the conclusion that anyone could write that stuff. The comics came first. We based our stories on some of the DC Comics. I remember creating a little comic about a large monster that terrorized a city. Not a monster exactly; actually it was a giant haystack. It would swallow up large crowds of people, cars and all. It was really scary. I drew the pictures and put in the balloon dialogue and additional narrative. Its name was 'Gorgon'. It would say to its enemies, "Who dares to defy Gorgon!" Gordie and I both noticed that every successful monster story included that particular interrogative phrase. The Armed Forces attacked Gorgon with soldiers, planes, tanks, and artillery without any success until finally the hero of the story got the innovative idea of throwing a lit match into the haystack. "Ahhhhh, I'm burning! How could you destroy Gorgon? You awful, awful man." Quite original, eh. There were a few more but that's the only one that I remember. Somehow, I can't remember Gordie's comics at all. Then we turned our attention to books. I wrote a long story about the travels of a squirrel and a raccoon. I wish I could remember what I called it. It was inspired by books like 'Wind in the Willows'. It was a masterpiece, but alas I can't share it with you today. A few weeks later, Mom saw what looked like scraps of paper under our bed. She burnt them in the wood stove. The scraps were of course our comics and storybooks. We were devastated.

"How could you, Mom?" I asked.

"I thought it was junk, I'm sorry, dear."

"It was our books," Gordie explained. "We wrote them ourselves."

"Why didn't you tell me?" Mom questioned. "I would have liked to read them."

"Well," I said, "I'm not sure you would have liked them. But we spent a lot of time on them, didn't we Gordie."

"I'm sorry, dears. You must really be upset."

"Oh that's OK, Mom." I felt guilty now for making Mom feel bad. "They were just junk."

"That's right," said Gordie. "We can just write them again."

But we didn't. I couldn't rewrite my squirrel story. It just didn't seem right. So we both gave it up. I never attempted to write another book again until I started this opus many months ago. If I could only remember that damn squirrel's name, I would somehow insert him into this story. After all, who dares to defy Benny Cooper!

26 ~ And They're Off

That summer was the first time that The Old Man was so violent that we called the police. At least this was the first time that I remember. I don't really remember what started it all. I could make something up, but I can't bring myself to envisage something that I have been trying to forget. Anyways, it doesn't really matter. I'm sure it was nothing at all. The Old Man was just drunk and was looking for Mom to feed him. Yeah, that's probably it. And he didn't like the look of his food. I imagine he said something like, "What the hell's this? It looks like my hass'ole!" And it would have been something that he had asked for a few minutes before. And this time Mom explained that to him. That's when all hell broke loose. First the plate went flying across the room just missing Mom's head and smashing to pieces against the opposite wall. Then the kitchen table was turned over on its side with everything which had been on top of it scattering throughout the kitchen. This time not only did Poncho vacate the room for the safety of the dining room corner, but also Smokey went skittering out of her box beside the stove and ran up the stairs to Lily's room. Well, I guess I remember more than I want to after all. The Old Man than jumped up and surged towards Mom.

"You goddamn gray-haired, old bag! Don't get smart with me! I'll break your fucking neck!"

Then he shoved Mom back against the wall, pinning her there with the full force of his body.

"You fucking, old bag. I think I'll just kill you now; you're no good to anyone," The Old Man sneered.

"Don't Garf, you're hurting me," Mom pleaded.

Then he grabbed Mom by the neck. Lily and I screamed simultaneously.

"Don't Dad! Don't hurt Mom!"

"What do you care about this old bag for? She's nothing. She's dirt under my feet!"

He started to squeeze his large hands around Mom's neck with greater force. That's when Gordie entered the room with his baseball bat. Both Ernie and Billy were not home when this all occurred.

"Let go of Mom, right now!" Gordie demanded. "Or I'll smash your head in."

The Old Man looked at Gordie. I could see that The Old Man's face was full of hate. I feared what would happen next. However, this was just enough of a distraction to allow Mom to squirm from The Old Man's hold on her.

"Let's go!" she said. "Out the front door. Come on everyone. You too, Gordie."

"What the hell's going on here?" The Old Man bellowed. "My whole family is turning against me. You goddamn, old bag! Now you've turned my own children against me. You love me, don't you Gordie? I wouldn't hurt your mother. You know that. I just lost my senses for a minute. That's all. That old bag just makes me mad sometimes."

Gordie didn't bother to reply. We were all going out the front door.

"Come on. You come too, Poncho," Mom spoke softly.

"What about Smokey?" I said.

"He'll be OK, dear. He's smart enough to hide somewhere and keep out of The Old Man's way. Hurry."

As we walked out the door with Poncho, we could still

hear The Old Man.

"Where the fuck do you think you're going? Don't ever come back if you want to live. Fuck you! Fuck you all! I don't need any of you. This house won't be standing when you come back."

Then we heard the sound of something smashing. It sounded like more dishes. Then we ran. We ran until we had turned the corner to head down the hill.

"Where are we going, Mom?" I inquired. "Why don't we go to Smale's?"

"We can, Benny. I just didn't want The Old Man to see where we were going," explained Mom.

So we circled around the block and carefully approached the Smale household from behind. We knocked and entered the backdoor. Mr. Smale wasn't home. He was on a truck trip somewhere again. The rest of the Smales were home though. It was Mrs. Smale's suggestion to call the police. Mom was at first hesitant because she feared the consequences.

"How can he be any worse?" Mrs. Smale questioned. "You won't even be able to go home. You'll be afraid of what he will do. Come on, let's call."

So we did. And then we waited for what seemed like a long time for a police cruiser to arrive. Eventually, we saw it pull up in front of our house. And two large police officers went up our front step to the door.

"Everybody stay here," said Mom. "I better go back across the street. The police will want to talk to me."

"Do you want me to come with you, Mary?" Mrs. Smale asked.

"No, I'll go alone. I don't want to involve you. I'll come back soon."

We watched as Mom crossed the street, climbed the front steps, and entered the house. About fifteen minutes later, the police walked out of the house followed by Mom. For a fraction of a second I thought that they had arrested the wrong culprit. They were taking Mom to jail.

"What's going on?" I asked. "Why aren't they taking The

Old Man to jail?"

"Let's watch," said Gordie.

The police then got back in their cruiser and watched Mom cross the street to return to Smale's. Then they drove off. The Old Man was nowhere in sight. We all had a million questions for Mom when she returned. But we let Mrs. Smale do the talking.

"What did they say? How's Garf now?"

"The Old Man, Garf, has quieted down for the minute. He couldn't understand what the police were doing there. He said he didn't do anything. Luckily, the police could see all the mess in the kitchen. But they say that they can't do anything. He didn't do anything wrong."

"What do they mean? Look at the bruise on your neck. He could have killed you. They should have taken him away until he sobered up."

I agreed whole-heartily with Mrs. Smale. What good are they, I thought. Now The Old Man will just be worse. He'll really be mad about Mom calling the police.

"I know," answered Mom. "But they say their hands are tied. They can't interfere in a family matter. The one policeman told me not to worry. That they spoke to Garf and he's fine now. He said he will behave and he's sorry. He just lost his temper for a minute. He told me that I should stay in the house to show him my support."

"I don't believe it! They don't have to live with him, do they? Don't you listen to them. You can stay here all night. We have room."

So we did. We watched for Billy and Ernie's arrival and directed them to Smale's as well. Gordie and I slept in Sammy's room. Actually I didn't sleep too much at all. In the early morning, we all returned home. The Old Man was passed out on the couch in front of a blaring television. All of his beer was gone. We found Smokey under Billy and Ernie's bed. We helped Mom clean up the kitchen and let The Old Man sleep until butter wouldn't melt in his mouth.

That summer, Billy and Gordie got to go on a trip to

Montreal to visit Brad and Catherine. That's where Brad was stationed now. And I was jealous. I didn't let on to Billy and Gordie that I cared though. Why wouldn't I be jealous? Not only did they get to have a vacation, see Brad again, and visit Montreal; they were far away from The Old Man and his antics. Billy was a paperboy for the Toronto Telegram at that time. So while he was away, I had the job of delivering the papers for him. My first job! The best part of that was collection day. I got a few good tips that Billy was kind enough to let me keep. Billy and Gordie were gone for close to two weeks. When they returned I was filled with envy when they described all of their adventures. The part I remember the most was that they visited Granby Zoo. I couldn't forget that fact because they both had a pennant to commemorate their trip to the zoo. And they both hung them on the wall above their bed. Gordie must have now known how I felt because he constantly pointed out the little, green Granby Zoo flag to me. That flag represented not only a zoo that I wished I could go to, but a vacation from Hillsburgh and The Old Man as well.

Towards the end of the summer, I got to experience some holiday time too. I went on a day trip with the Smales to Niagara Falls. We had a picnic with Colonel Sander's chicken. But my real vacation was a two-week visit with Fred and Them in Toronto. Mom probably had heard enough of me whining about not getting to go to Montreal, so she probably convinced Fred and Them to take me away. Anyway, I remember it as a really good time. I was away from my entire family for the first time and I had a ball. Ron, Lucy, and Tom were all a lot of fun and they kept me busy. The highlights included a trip to the Eaton's College Street store (the escalators were especially thrilling) and more than one excursion to Old Woodbine racetrack. To get there, we drove partway along the new concrete, elevated highway along the lake. At the racetrack, I would wander around the grandstand and collect all the tickets that people had discarded in disgust after not seeing their choice cross the finish line either first, second, or third. Ron taught me all about Win, Place, and Show. I even learned what a 'Quinella' was. Ron would help me check every ticket to make sure that I wasn't holding a winner that someone had dropped in error. No luck there. I still kept the large bundle of tickets though. It was something that I could show Gordie whenever he brought up the Granby Zoo.

27 ~ NOBS

When we started school in the fall of that year, I was excited to be back in the same classroom as Billy and Gordie. For those not keeping track, I was now in Grade 7 while Billy and Gordie were in Grade 8. And we all shared the same teacher – Danny Clark. Lily was now in Grade 2 and Ernie had gone on to 11. John Brooks was now in Grade 9, so he was now a fellow passenger with Ernie on the bus to Erin. Richard Watson though was still in our class in Grade 8. But it was a new student that I remember the most that first day. He had just recently moved from Toronto to Hillsburgh. His name was Randy Bush and proud of it. When Danny Clark called out our new classmate's name as Randolph Bush, Randy was very quick to correct him.

"It's Randy, Mr. Clark. Randy Bush. There's no Randolph here. I'm Randy Bush."

"OK, OK. I get your point." Then Danny Clark quickly went on to the next name.

A few days later while we were singing God Save The Queen, the anthem was suddenly interrupted by the unmistakable sound of a large fart.

"Excuse me," Randy immediately blared out.

"Mr. Bush!" responded Danny Clark. He still wasn't

calling him Randy. "Please mind your manners!"

"What?" replied Randy indignantly. "I said excuse me."

"Yes. You would have done better to stay quiet."

"Well my father always tells me. Wherever you are, wherever you be, always let your wind blow free."

"Enough, Mr. Bush. Let's get on to our first lesson."

The class was breaking up in laughter and Danny Clark was trying to get things back to normal. The rest of us now knew that it would be an interesting year with Randy Bush in our class.

September 30, 1960 was a historic day in television. A new show was premiering and we all rushed home to watch it. We had all read about it or heard about it. And now the day for its first showing had finally arrived. We were all sitting around the TV set in the living room, including The Old Man. Richard Watson was there too. The new series was 'The Flintstones', the first primetime cartoon. And we weren't disappointed. It was great right to the closing credits when Fred got locked outside after putting out the 'cat' and started banging on the door yelling "Wilma!".

Also that fall, Gordie and I started a new experience. We joined the Cubs. Our meetings were once a week in the upstairs of the Town Hall at the bottom of the hill. I envisioned that we would get to go on lots of camping trips and other such adventures. However, so far our sessions had consisted of exercising on old mats, learning to tie and identify different knots, and mastering semaphore – flag signals. Not exactly what either Gordie or I had in mind. I couldn't see where I could apply this new knowledge unless I found myself on an enemy boat in the middle of a war and had to wrestle my captor on a mat, tie him up in a lovely knot, and then signal for help. But we decided to give it a year and see what happened. Eventually we should go on a camping trip.

One thing that we didn't learn in Cubs that I thought might come in handy someday, was how to split and chop firewood. I remember watching Billy one day in the backyard cutting up wood for our stove in the kitchen. I was quite impressed with the force that he exerted every time that he brought the axe down upon a fresh log. Before long I noticed that as Billy struck the wood he was also muttering something. It sounded like, "Take that you bastard."

"What are you doing, Billy?" I finally asked.

"I find it a lot easier to cut this wood if I use my imagination, Benny. And more fun, and it goes a lot quicker."

"What are you imagining, Billy?"

"Watch me, Benny. See that log? That's The Old Man's head. Now watch this."

The axe came down with all the strength that Billy could muster and split the log into two pieces.

"You won't hurt Mom again, will you? You piece of shit!" Billy spoke to the splintered wood which had fallen to the ground. "That's what I'm doing, Benny."

"Oh," I said not knowing what else to say. I just knew that I wouldn't want to be The Old Man on the day that Billy decided it would be a good idea to live out this fantasy. Billy must have noticed the look of worry on my face.

"Oh Benny, don't worry. I'm not really going to do this to The Old Man. As Mom would say, he's not worth going to jail for. But it sure makes me feel good to take out my anger on this pile of wood."

"Do it again," I said.

"Die you bastard, die," yelled Billy as the axe came down once more.

Not long after, we had one of those days that I imagined would drive Billy out to the back shed to retrieve the axe. The Old Man was sitting at the kitchen table (where else?), drunker than a skunk again. Mom and I were the only other ones in the kitchen at the time. He was calling Mom every name in the book and had eventually started uttering his death threats one more time. This was an occurrence that was coming far too common to my liking.

"I ought to kill you, you gray-haired old bag. Who the hell would miss you? I could grab a knife and kill you right now and no one would give a shit?"

"I would," I answered. "We all would. But we wouldn't care if you dropped dead tomorrow."

"What did you say, Benny?" The Old Man demanded to know.

I didn't bother to repeat what I had said. I knew that The Old Man had heard me.

"Jesus Christ! The whole goddamned family has turned against me. The fucking old bag has turned the whole family against me. Goddamn it! I think I'll kill that bitch right now!"

At that point, The Old Man started to stand up. I didn't know what to do. I couldn't hide behind the big living room chair anymore. I couldn't put the covers over my head. I couldn't join Poncho behind the dining room china cabinet. But before I could decide how to react, my body started reacting for me. I started to cry. And I couldn't stop. I was sobbing more than I had ever remembered. And I was shaking.

"Now look what you've done to Benny," Mom complained. "I hope that you're proud of yourself."

I wanted to tell Mom that I was OK, but the words wouldn't come from my mouth. Only more sobs came out.

"Benny, don't cry," The Old Man spoke soothingly. "You know I didn't mean what I said. I just get crazy sometimes. It's not me; it's the beer. You know that. I'm sorry. I wouldn't hurt your mother. I love her. Come here and stop crying."

I stepped to go towards Mom who was heading towards me; however The Old Man picked me up and placed me on his lap. And he hugged me and rubbed my back to console me. But I kept crying.

"Benny, Benny," he continued, "please stop that crying. I am sorry. I love you. Please believe me. I'm OK now."

But I didn't stop. But the funny part was that I believed that I could stop whenever I wanted. I felt like I was continuing to cry in order to get The Old Man to cease his hostilities. I experienced the eerie feeling that I was standing in the kitchen watching myself sitting on The Old Man, that it wasn't me at all. Or if it was me, then I was just play-acting. However, the weeping persisted. And the shaking did not desist. But I knew that I could stop if I really wanted. Couldn't I? This scene continued for about ten more minutes and finally Mom suggested that I go to bed and she volunteered to tuck me in. I readily agreed through my tears.

So Mom walked with me up to the bed. The crying stopped as I climbed in between the sheets. Smokey jumped on the bed beside me.

"I'm fine now, Mom," I argued. "Don't worry about me. I have Smokey here to keep me company."

Smokey started purring while Mom hugged and kissed me.

"Just try to get some sleep, Benny."

"OK, Mom. Goodnight."

"Goodnight, dear."

I lay there awake thinking that I had fooled The Old Man. I had got him to stop his belligerent attack on Mom by pretending to cry. But then I thought, could I have really stopped at any time? I wasn't so sure. I listened for further outbursts and eventually went to sleep. I didn't even hear Gordie when he came to bed.

Actually before I went to sleep, I did something else. Something that I haven't told anyone about before now. Not even Gordie. Especially not Gordie. I prayed. I didn't believe in God; we didn't go to church anymore (I failed to mention that earlier. Mom got tired of explaining the absence of The Old Man, so she gave into our complaining about attending service). But I still prayed. I prayed only that The Old Man would behave himself the rest of the night. And it worked. At least it worked that night. I tried it a few other nights over the years while lying in bed listening to The Old Man downstairs. Sometimes it worked; sometimes it didn't. When it didn't work, I cursed myself for believing that it might. And I cursed God for failing me. Then I criticized myself for cursing someone that didn't exist. Then I would try it again. I wished so much for some peace for Mom. It was worth a try, just in case.

One day, Randy Bush came to school sporting a large button that had the letters 'OFI' on it. We all wondered what that stood for.

"Official Falsie Inspector," Randy proudly informed us.

After someone explained to me what a 'falsie' was, I realized why Randy was beaming when he showed it to all the girls in the class. Before long, Danny Clark asked Randy the meaning of the button. Now, as you may have gathered, Randy was a forthright and honest to a fault kind of guy. So he admitted the significance of the button.

"Take that button off, Mr. Bush," was the predictable reaction.

After much arguing, whining, and complaining Randy eventually complied with the order. He never wore the button in class again, but we would often see it pinned to Randy after school. I'm not sure if the 'OFI' title ever gave him the opportunity and licence to conduct any inspections.

Speaking of sex education, it was around then that I found myself walking home alone with Richard Watson when he asked me an unexpected question.

"How big is your dick, Littlest Garf?"

"What?" I asked.

"How big is your dick?"

I hesitated and then eventually thought of the appropriate response.

"It changes size. Sometimes it's really small; other times it's bigger."

"When does it get bigger? When you see a good-looking girl? When you think about girls?"

"I don't know. I never thought about that. Perhaps."

"That's when mine gets bigger. Like when I see Betty Lake. Now, she's nice. Right, Littlest Garf?"

"Yes, I guess so. I never really thought about her."

"You should. She'd pass Randy's inspection for sure. Nothing false about those. Let me tell you."

"I never noticed."

"Don't worry, Littlest Garf. You soon will. Soon you'll be interested in girls. Just like your older brother Gordie. He notices, I tell you. He's hot for Betty. You just wait. Your little pecker will be growing for lots of girls before long. You'll see."

"Does Gordie really like Betty?"

"You bet he does. Ask him."

"OK, I will."

I remember watching one of the four Nixon-Kennedy debates on TV with Ernie, Billy, and Gordie. It was probably the last one on October 21. I recall that Ernie was really happy that John F. Kennedy appeared to be the winner of the debates. He thought that Richard Nixon was an idiot. Since I was new to politics, I went along with Ernie's point of view. As did everyone else in the household. So on election night, we stayed up half the night waiting for a winner to be announced. It wasn't until the next morning though that we knew for sure that JFK had beaten Nixon. I found it exciting to watch. I had never known that elections (in another country at that) could be so interesting. Nothing compared to a good Leaf game, but entertaining nevertheless.

In December, Lily became very sick. She would lay on the couch, covered with a blanket and try to pretend that she was not that bad. But she had a cough that wouldn't go away and a high fever. After a few days of assuming that Lily had contacted some kind of flu bug, Mom was able to convince The Old Man to come to the realization that this was one of those times that a doctor was required. So Mom called Dr. McGuire and he drove from Orangeville to check out Lily's condition.

"Lily's got pneumonia," Dr. McGuire advised.

"How serious is it, Dr. McGuire?" asked Mom.

"She needs to go into the hospital in Orangeville. I'll arrange it so you can take her in today."

"Today? Then she'll miss Christmas at home. Can't we wait until after Christmas?"

"If you wait any longer, Lily won't be having anymore Christmases." Mom didn't speak. "She needs to go to the hospital right now."

"Will she be OK, Doctor?" Mom inquired. I'm sure she was thinking about 'dear little brother' Philip who had succumbed to the same disease long before I arrived on the scene.

"Yes, I think so. As long as we can get her attended to right away. She'll be fine."

So that Christmas was very strange and not so joyful. Without Lily at home, nothing seemed right. Mom cried when she got up on Christmas morning and none of us could get into the spirit. For Christmas dinner, Mom had agreed that Ernie could invite Gordon Springfield (better known as Tweety Bird). He had no family and Mom couldn't stand the thought of someone having Christmas dinner alone. If Lily had to spend Christmas in a hospital bed then at least she could help someone else have a better Christmas. I had never seen Tweety Bird in this kind of setting before. It was weird to see him being so polite ("Thanks, Mrs. Cooper. This is a great dinner, Mrs. Cooper.") I was used to the tough exterior that most of the town saw. He seemed more like a 'Gordon' and less like a 'Tweety Bird' that day.

Dr. McGuire's assessment of Lily proved to be correct and she was finally able to come home on New Year's Eve. That made it a great way to start 1961, with Lily once more at home.

One night, Mom, The Old Man, Gordie, Lily and I went to Randy Bush's house to play Monopoly with Randy and his parents. The Old Man had met Mr. Bush somewhere and had arranged that we all get together. I can't remember who the big winner was but one incident has stayed in my mind over the years. Mr. Bush had landed on one of Mrs. Bush's properties without being detected before Randy began to take his move.

"Wait!" Mrs. Bush exclaimed. "Your father owes me rent. Don't move yet."

"It's too late," Mr. Bush argued. "Randy's thrown the dice."

"But he hasn't moved his piece. Come on pay up. You owe me $450."

"No, that's the rules. You missed it. Too bad."

"But Randy grabbed the dice before you had even finished moving. Give me $450."

"Kiss my ass," Mr. Bush said with a smile.

"Produce it," Mrs. Bush demanded.

"OK, if you insist." And Mr. Bush stood up, turned around, and pulled down his pants to display his bare rear end.

None of us could believe it. The Old Man started laughing. Mrs. Bush picked up one of her hotels and threw it at the inviting target.

"That's all you're getting from me tonight, Mr. Bush," she said as the hotel bounced off his backend just before the pants were back in place.

Then we all started laughing. To me it explained a lot. I now understood Randy a lot better. When we left, The Old Man asked Mom if she had a good time.

"Yes, the game was fun."

"What did you think of Randy's parents?" I asked.

"Interesting," was all Mom would say. "Interesting."

Randy introduced me to two new forms of entertainment. The first was Mad magazine. I had never seen one until Randy showed me some of his issues. I thought they were great. I recall seeing the classic comic with the Lone Ranger and Tonto in a Mad pocketbook that Randy also owned. You know the one I mean. The Lone Ranger and Tonto see hundreds of Indians cresting a hill to surround them. "What are we going to do now, Tonto?" says the Lone Ranger. "What do you mean, we, white man?" is Tonto's famous reply. Before I discovered Mad, my main reading materials were the Hardy Boys. I had read every one that I could get my hands on, which was practically all of them. So now I had something else to read and I started to purchase

Mad myself every month. The other source of enjoyment that Randy acquainted me with was the Toronto radio station CHUM. I had never listened to it before. After many weeks of having to listen to Randy talk about CHUM, I ultimately became fascinated with the Top 30 and began to listen to the countdown on the radio every week. Gordie and I would try to guess the order each week. We would write down the song titles and save them. I found it a big improvement on the Slim Whitman records that were forced upon me in the middle of the night.

That winter The Old Man came up with another quick moneymaking scheme. This was far better than the now defunct Cooper Bottle Collection Company. He bought chickens and raised them in the back woodshed. I guess you could say that we were now the Cooper Chicken Coop Cooperation. I know that Mom wasn't too fond of the noise and smell from all those chickens. Some we ate ourselves. I recollect a chicken scurrying around our backyard after The Old Man guillotined it with the axe. So I learnt that they really do run around like a chicken with its head cut off. I thought that was just a saying or an old wives tale. Some of the chickens The Old Man was successful in selling in order to get enough money to buy beer. The rest he gave away to fellow drunks that he picked up at the bar after spending his earlier profit.

The Old Man got in the habit of bringing strangers home from the tavern. Some weren't so bad, but usually they were just as drunk as him. I remember one such visitor who kept telling us how lucky we were to have such a generous father. The Old Man was very popular at the bar because he would often buy drinks for the other patrons.

"Garf here," he said, "is the greatest guy that I ever met. He'd give you the shirt off your back if you asked. Mrs. Cooper, Mary, may I call you Mary? You're so lucky to be married to this man. He's the best. I hope you realize that. You kids sure are lucky to have Garf – your dad – for a father. And don't you forget that."

This really pissed Mom off when she heard this. Not only did she have to listen to what a great guy that The Old Man was, but she had to hear how he threw money around to strangers while we often didn't have enough to make ends meet. If we didn't have credit, we wouldn't have been able to eat. The Hillsburgh grocery store would let Mom buy our weekly groceries on credit. She would pay some when she could but the outstanding balance never got down to zero. Except for when all the various bills got too much and Mom and The Old Man would go to Household Finance to arrange a consolidation loan. Or another car loan. I never quite understood how finance companies worked. We would borrow $1,000, then pay $50 per month for a year, and at the end of the year owe $1,100. It didn't make sense to me. I fantasized about Robin Hood stealing the money from the lending companies and giving it back to the borrowers. A fantasy shared by many families probably.

Also around then, we had another visit from an encyclopedia salesman. I was going to tell you all about it then I thought why bother. Just go back and reread the part I wrote earlier when we were at Robertsons' farm. The exact same scenario was played out. The salesman talked about how we the children needed these books. How it was the only thing to do if our parents loved us. How they wouldn't cost anything except for a small deposit and minimal monthly fees for eternity. And again The Old Man fell for it hook, line, and sinker. He signed on the dotted line. It was a few days later, probably after looking at the bill from Household Finance, that The Old Man realized he had committed another blunder. And once more, he somehow had the contract nullified even though they had his legal endorsement. So I never did get an encyclopedia. No wonder my grammar is so bad.

In March, after I turned twelve, I became a member of the NOBS. The NOBS club was started by Randy Bush, Richard Watson, Billy, and Gordie. Also part of the group were two other classmates that I haven't mentioned before –

Johnny Wheeler and Henry Donaldson. Johnny and Henry were both good friends of Gordie. Johnny lived next door to the Watsons. What I remember most about Johnny was the time that Gordie and Billy went to the Wheeler household to get him.

"Is Johnny home?" they asked his mother.

"There ain't no Johnny here," she replied. "His name is Jonathan. There's no Johnny. Do you want Jonathan?"

The NOBS had a clubhouse that the aforementioned boys built in a field near the Watsons' home. We used to say that NOBS was an acronym for something. Maybe it was the National Organization of Boy Students. Or did the 'O' stand for Ontario? And 'Students' doesn't sound right. I don't remember, because every time we would say it stood for one thing, we would come up with something else. Anyways, it didn't really stand for anything. We were just NOBS. We took white T-shirts and wrote NOBS on the front in large black letters so people would know who we were. One day Randy wore his NOBS shirt to school, but Danny Clark was not too fond of it. Randy was told not to wear it again. So we just wore them around the clubhouse. What did we do at the club? Mainly we just sat around and talked, told jokes, and read Mad magazine. And smoked. I didn't smoke though. Not yet anyway, more about that later. I was the youngest one in the club; however, I felt older just hanging around with the rest of the group. After all, I was almost a teenager.

One day at school the Grade 8 students were given a Math test which almost half of the class failed. This included all of the NOBS except for me. They argued with Danny Clark that the test was much too difficult and that he should adjust all the grades upward.

"What do you mean, too hard?" Danny Clark refuted. "I thought it was easy. A Grade 7 student could probably do it better than you did. In fact, that's a good idea. Just to prove my point, I'll get a Grade 7 student to write the same test. Benny, I want you to write this test."

So I did. I got 98%. I made a stupid mistake on one

question. That result did not make me too popular with the Grade 8 kids. Billy and Gordie wanted to kill me.

"What did you do that for, Benny?" Gordie complained. "You made us all look stupid. Now Danny won't adjust our marks."

"I couldn't help it," I reasoned. "I thought it was easy."

"You could have answered them wrong," Billy added.

"I'm sorry. I just answered them. I didn't think of that."

"What do you think, Billy," said Gordie, "should we kick Benny out of the NOBS?"

"No," I pleaded, "I'll try to be stupider from now on. I promise. I'll be a real NOB."

At any rate, somehow I did avoid being purged from the association.

On Mother's Day afternoon, Mom told us not to worry about keeping her company and to go off and play if we wanted. The Old Man was drunk the night before, but this being a Sunday she said that he wouldn't have anything more to drink. Hence, Billy, Gordie, and I headed off to the NOBS club for fun and relaxation. Ernie went somewhere with his friends, while Lily stayed home to play with Jenny Smale. A couple hours later, we were sitting in the clubhouse reading and exchanging jokes with Richard, Randy, Henry, and Johnny. Suddenly we heard a dog barking.

"That sounds like Poncho," I observed.

"Yeah, it does," agreed Gordie. "What's she doing here?"

We opened the door to see Poncho looking up at us. And not too far behind was Mom and Lily. I couldn't figure out what they were doing there. This was just for us boys. How did Mom even find the club? I followed Billy and Gordie to greet Mom. I could immediately see that Mom had been crying.

"What's wrong, Mom?" Billy asked.

"It's your father. Somehow he got more to drink. He was awful. He was smashing dishes and cursing. He even called Lily names. I decided to get out of there. As I was leaving, he warned me to stay. He said that I wouldn't have a house to come home to. He would burn it down."

"That bastard," said Billy. "He called Lily names, too?"

"He won't burn the house down, will he Mom?" I asked.

"I don't think so, I hope not, dear."

"How come you didn't go to the Smales?" I questioned.

"They're not home. Jenny didn't come to play. They went to Niagara Falls, I think. Don't you want me here, Benny? I didn't know where else to go. Are you embarrassed for your friends to see you with your mother?"

"No, of course not," I replied quickly. "I just…"

"Come on in and sit down, Mom," said Gordie. "We'll check out the house in a little while. You know Richard and Randy. I'll introduce you to our other friends."

"Hello, Mrs. Cooper," yelled Richard. "Are you coming in to see us?"

I felt like an idiot. How could I have felt that Mom was intruding on us? And on Mother's Day, at that. What an ingrate I was. I now was glad that she and Lily had come to us. I still didn't know how they found us, but I wasn't going to ask. It might sound like I didn't want them there again. I saw how the other boys responded to Mom. With respect. And she returned the same attitude. Randy even said that Mom and Lily could be honorary NOBS. I was so proud of Mom. And I loved her more than anything else in the world.

We made several scouting trips back home and eventually returned after dark when The Old Man had exhausted his beer and had passed out for the night. The house was still standing and unharmed except for broken dishes. Smokey was once more safely hidden under a bed.

28 ~ Nine-Year-Old Bicycle Gang

In the spring of 1961, I got struck with my first case of spring fever. In other words, I became interested in girls. My first indication was when I was at a birthday party for Joe Watson. This was a coed celebration and eventually someone decided to play 'Spin the Bottle'. I was terrified that the bottle might end up pointing at me and a girl would have to kiss me; however, when it did inevitably happen I found out that I kind of enjoyed it. Now I don't even remember the name of the girl that gave me that first kiss. I was quite happy when I had to kiss another girl later in the game. I had to leave the party early and I was disappointed when I heard that a game of 'Post Office' had broken out later.

The second incident that I remember was when I was playing across the street with Sammy Smale. A girl who was a classmate of Sammy's came to play with us. I can't remember what game we were playing, but somehow we were wrestling and I ended up under Sammy's friend. Then she kissed me. I remember her name – Brenda. That was also the time that I discovered that Richard Watson was right about the correlation between girls and the size of a certain body part.

One of my other interests that spring became bicycling. I had received a new bicycle on my twelfth birthday and I enjoyed riding it everywhere. One day we had a torrential downpour that flooded many of the streets. Sammy and I rode our bicycles all around town to survey the damage. Some roads were covered in a couple feet of water. Basically half the town at the bottom of the hill was flooded. We rode our bikes through a large pool of water which covered the road that led into the baseball park. That was a lot of fun.

When the school year ended and I was promoted to Grade 8, I felt so much older all of a sudden. I was a senior now. I was ready to act a lot older. So the first thing I did was quit Cubs. And so did Gordie. There still had not been a field trip planned. Maybe in the fall, we heard. We hadn't made it out of the upstairs of the hall. So we gave up. The NOBS was more fun anyways.

The other decision I made was to start smoking. I was the only one of the NOBS who hadn't given it a try. So why not, I thought. Hence at the age of twelve, I became a cigarette smoker. Rothmans was my brand. I would take a drag and then cough but I thought it made me look and feel older. I knew that if Mom found out she would kill me. Well OK, she wouldn't have but she would have been very disappointed and it would have hurt her. So I didn't want her to find out. Thus I mainly smoked at the NOBS club or in a back field a long ways away from civilization.

We also kept up our bicycling. One night Gordie and I were riding around town when a few other boys joined us on their bikes. There was Sammy and a few of his classmates including a boy named Ben Jones. Although Ben was in the same grade as Sammy, he was actually my age. I had never had much contact with him before. But that night we became friends. Not real close friends but he started hanging out with Gordie and I. Anyways, that night we rode our bikes around the town and declared ourselves a 'bicycle gang'. We never did anything but cruise around but as more and more boys grabbed their bikes and joined us we laughed that we had started a gang. However it wasn't a real gang. We didn't even ride around the town any other night. Definitely not with more than three or four of us.

One day, Gordie, Sammy, and I decided to ride our bikes to Guelph. We started out early in the morning and headed down the hill and past our school. We were singing as we passed the sign that invited us to 'Please Come Again'. It was a good travelling song.

I'm Popeye the sailor man,
I lives in a garbage can.
I loves to go swimmin'
With bare-naked women,
I'm Popeye the sailor man.
Eahh, Eahh.

We only made it to the top of the first steep, winding hill when Sammy advised that he had gone far enough. He was too tired to continue. He was angry that we didn't agree to head back home yet. Consequently he took off back down the hill in a huff. Gordie and I continued on and were almost at Highway 24, when we decided to turn back and catch up to Sammy. We didn't have the desire to go to Guelph anymore now that Sammy wouldn't be with us. I was also feeling guilty about parting company on such a sour note. We caught up to him before he reached the 'Welcome to Hillsburgh' sign. As I should have guessed, he acted like nothing had happened and was as friendly as ever towards us. Good old Sammy. We could always count on him.

Not long after, The Old Man had a car accident on that very same hill. He was driving back from a night of drinking in Georgetown and missed one of the sharp curves. He rolled the car over and over down the side of the grassy slope. The car was absolutely demolished but The Old Man walked away from it without a scratch. And walked on home. Proof again about the existence of horseshoes up his butt. Or the other explanation was that he was so drunk that he stayed relaxed and didn't tense up, thus avoiding breaking any bones. I preferred the horseshoe theory myself. Further evidence to support this theory was that somehow he only received a small fine from the court. That for leaving the scene of an accident. He was not charged with impaired driving. He claimed the hood flew open and blocked his view. I guess that story was believed because the hood of the car was ripped completely off. We also considered ourselves to be very lucky. For we had declined to go to Georgetown with The Old Man that night. Usually Mom, Gordie, Lily, and I would have been with him. I'm not sure what was the inspiration for that good choice. The good thing about the accident was that it scared The Old Man and stopped him from drinking for a month. That is to say, for one pay.

As I mentioned earlier, Gordie and I started to hang around Ben Jones on a regular basis. We found that he could be a fun guy to be with. I remember one of the jokes that he told us that left me in stitches. This guy went into the general store to buy some condoms (Ben called them 'safes'). He was frightened but he managed to tell the man behind the counter what he was looking for. "What colour do you want?" asked the clerk. Now, the guy didn't know that they came in different colours. "What colours do you have?" he questioned. "Red, blue, or green," was the reply. The customer couldn't decide. "I'll have one of each," he said. So he bought one of each colour. A few months later the same guy went in the same store and the same clerk was at the counter. Again the guy was nervous. "Excuse me, do you have a maternity blouse?" he asked. "What bust?" the clerk asked back. "The blue one," he answered.

I was going to tell you something else before I got sidetracked on that joke. I guess I didn't really want to tell you. It's not one of my proudest moments. You see. Gordie, Ben, and I were hanging around the baseball park one day. No one else was anywhere in sight. We were standing in front of the concession stand (a wooden shed with a locked shutter) when I commented that I was hungry.

"There's food in there," volunteered Ben. He was pointing at the concession stand.

"That's no good to me. It's not open."

"So," he answered. "Look down there." He was pointing

at a small square opening below the locked shutter which was boarded up. I still didn't get what he was hinting at until he elaborated. "You could kick that in pretty easily, I bet."

"No thanks, I'm not that hungry."

"Chickenshit!"

"Don't call us that," demanded Gordie. "We're not afraid. We just don't want to."

"Chickenshit! If you're not afraid then prove it. Kick it."

"You kick it then. If you're so smart," said Gordie.

"All right, I will," Ben responded. And he stepped forward and gave the board a quick kick with the heel of his shoe. The board cracked but did not crash in. "OK, Gordie. It's your turn. Let's see if you're afraid or not."

"I'm not afraid. Watch!" Then Gordie kicked the board twice until it completely gave in leaving a small opening into where the food was stored.

"Now who has the guts to go inside?" Ben said.

"Not me," I replied.

"I don't think I could fit in that hole," Gordie observed.

"Then it's you, Benny," Ben added. "We kicked it in. Therefore you should crawl in. Come on."

"No, I don't think so."

"Chickenshit!"

"Don't call me that."

"You might as well go in," Ben continued. "We're already in trouble if we get caught. We still broke in. And you were with us. You're just as involved as Gordie and I. So get on in there."

That tactic of reasoning worked better than the name-calling. I surprised myself and crawled into the small entrance and stood up on the inside of the concession stand. It was pitch dark.

"What do you see, Benny?" Gordie wanted to know.

"Nothing, it's too dark. I'm coming out."

"Just wait," Ben said. "Your eyes will adjust."

He was right. Soon I could see bags of chips, chocolate bars, cartons of cigarettes, licorice, and other typical concession foods. I told Gordie and Ben what I could see.

"Pass out some chips, I'm hungry," Ben requested.

So I shoved three small bags of chips through the opening. And then three chocolate bars. And then two cartons of cigarettes. It was too dark to see which brand.

"Aunt Becky's coming," Gordie suddenly shouted. "Aunt Becky's coming!"

For a fraction of a second he fooled me. Then I realized she was a couple thousand miles away in Newfoundland.

"Very funny, Gordie," I said sarcastically. "Very funny." But that little scare was enough to make me want to get out of there. Right that instance. I'd had enough. I was scared shitless. "I'm coming out," I told the two lookouts.

"Not yet," Ben said. "Pass out more food."

"No, if you want more you'll have to get it yourself." I was climbing back outside at the same time that I was answering. "I'm finished."

I expected Ben to crawl in next, but his reaction surprised me.

"Let's get the hell out of here. I can't believe you guys stole that stuff. I'm going home." Ben then took off running towards home with one bag of chips, leaving Gordie and I literally holding the bag. "Remember not a word of this to anyone. If they find out, it's off to Reform school in Guelph."

Gordie and I ran home, ate our chips and chocolate bars, and hid the cigarettes. We hid them in the bushes and then went in the house where we found a plastic box. We opened all the cigarette packages and lined the cigarettes up in the box. We then hid the box in the empty lot in amongst all the vines. We placed the empty packages, bags, and wrappers in a paper bag which we then proceeded to bury. Not until we opened the cartons did I even notice what brand of cigarettes that we had stolen. Matinee and DuMaurier. Not even Rothmans.

For the next week every time that I arrived home from somewhere, I was afraid that I would see a police car in front of our house ready to take Gordie and I away to Guelph. But so far no suspicions were cast our way. Gordie and I were slowly working our way through the secret cache of cigarettes. He never showed anyone the complete stash. Not even Billy. We didn't want anyone to know. As far as we knew there were only three people who had knowledge of the culprits. Me, Gordie, and Ben. One day Gordie and I had quite a few cigarettes on us at the NOBS club. Randy Bush asked us where we got all the smokes. We told him something original and brilliant.

"We found them," I declared. "A few packages were lying on the ground. Someone must have dropped them."

After that close call, we never had more than a half-dozen cigarettes on us at any one time.

Shortly thereafter, Mom, Lily, and I went to Montreal for a couple of weeks to not only visit Brad and his family but also to see Claudia, Tom, and their kids. As I mentioned earlier, Tom as well was stationed in one of the suburbs of Montreal. Ernie, Billy, and Gordie had to stay home with The Old Man. I finally got back at my brothers for going to Montreal without me the previous summer. The first week we stayed with Brad and Catherine. They now had two daughters – Cheryl who at that point was two years old and 'Small Catherine' who celebrated her first birthday while we were there. We had a good time in spite of having to listen to Brad's Mario Lanza records. They weren't so bad really but not exactly my kind of music. The second week we stayed with Claudia and Tom. I told you about their two daughters previously – Lizzie who was the same age as Lily (eight years old) and April who was one year younger – and their son 'Little Tom' who was now four. However there now was a new addition to the family. A one-year-old son named Matthew. I recall that I slept on the couch and was awakened most mornings by Little Tom and Matthew getting up to watch the cartoons. Many which were in French. A new experience for me. I couldn't believe how much all of Tom and Claudia's kids had grown since I had last seen them. They would soon all be taller than me, I thought. That was another enjoyable week. I loved listening to Mom and Claudia talk about the incidents many years before. I heard all over again about the destruction of the Christmas tree at the hands of The Old Man and my verbal reaction one year later. I also relived the "That's not the way Mom does it" stories. It's a wonder Tom didn't get bored with it all. I was sad when it was time to go home. I hadn't even thought about my new life of crime and the fear of the consequences. Not until we were heading home on the train.

When we arrived home, Gordie quickly advised that nothing was new on the crime front. He had heard a few kids mention the break-in, but never in the same sentence as our names. I was relieved and figured that we were probably now in the clear.

So it was now time for some serious playing again. We used to play cowboys in the upstairs of our house. By we, I mean Gordie, Sammy, and myself. Billy never played but he helped by drawing Wanted Posters of us. Billy was always a good artist, even in school. We would dress up different ways, a different hat, maybe a pencil moustache, assorted guns and holsters, left-handed or right-handed, and then Billy would draw us on a poster. We would make up appropriate sinister sounding names for each of our characters. Each of us could have more than one role to play. One of Gordie's personalities carried a small derringer just like Yancy Derringer did. He would hide it in his boot (shoe actually). The scene was set as follows: the hall was the outdoors, my bedroom was the saloon, Billy's bedroom was the bank, and a large closet was the jail. What does that leave for our parents' room and Lily's? You figure it out. I can't remember now.

In the bank was realistic looking money that we had made. A whole skate-box full of hand made money. Bills that we had painstakingly drawn (Billy's skill again) and then coloured the appropriate colour for a Canadian note. Far better than anything you could buy at the store. You know what I mean — those ugly, tiny green bills. Ours were authentic looking even in size. So if you liked, you could rob the bank and then head off to the saloon for a stiff drink. One day I did just that. I was a mean son-of-a-gun. Just like in that ad that was popular at the time. "Men so mean that they made noise with their straws." So there I was standing at the bar, when murderous Sam "Itchy-Finger" McGraw stepped up beside me. I said something that he didn't like and he threw a drink in my face. I pulled out my gun and shot him through the eyes in cold blood. Boy, was Sammy ever mad. He had spent hours coming up with the idea for this particular identity. He had stood still for half an hour while Billy drew the Wanted Poster. And two minutes after his initial creation, he was lying dead in a pool of blood.

"It's not fair!" Sammy cried. "You can't kill me already. No one would kill someone just for throwing a drink in his face. I'm not dead yet."

"I would kill for that. I'm Benny 'The Killer' Walton. I've left a trail of blood throughout the West and you're just a punk kid looking for a reputation."

"It's not fair! I'm going home. You're not my friend anymore."

Furthermore Billy wasn't too happy that we were killing off people faster than he could draw them. So for that reason and to appease my friend, I eventually relented and let Sam "Itchy-Finger" McGraw ride once more. There just wasn't room for the both of us in the same town, that's all.

One August day, Sammy and I went for a long walk in the fields. We were gone most of the day and were coming up the street past Sammy's house when he spoke.

"I wonder what's going on at your house, Benny."

At first I didn't understand what Sammy meant but I looked up to see a police car parked directly in front of our house. My heart sunk. I didn't say a word.

"I guess your father is acting up again," Sammy surmised.

"I hope so," I muttered with no explanation.

"What! What do you mean, Benny?"

"Nothing, Sammy. I guess I better go check it out. I'll see you later."

I walked slowly up the steps and in the front door. All I could think about was what life would be like in Reform School. Would I go on to Grade 8? Could I watch the Flintstones and Bonanza? Would Mom ever speak to me again?

"Is that you, Benny?" Mom queried from the kitchen.

"Yes, Mom."

"You better come on in here," The Old Man said.

I entered the kitchen and my worst fears were realized. Standing in the kitchen, besides Mom and The Old Man were two policemen, Gordie, Ben Jones, Ben's father, and a man I didn't recognize at first. Then I realized the man was the town barber. Also he was the owner of the concession food stand at the baseball park. Gordie and Ben were standing facing the rest of the cast. I went and stood beside Mom. My head was hanging low. I avoided eye contact with anyone. I was shaking like a leaf. "Reform School, here I come," I thought. The Old Man spoke first.

"The police want to ask you a few questions, Benny. Just tell the truth."

My head stayed down. I said nothing and did nothing.

"OK son," the first policeman began, "we know about the break-in. These two have confessed. So there's no use denying that. We just want to make sure we have the story straight. So as your father said, just tell us the truth. Do you understand?"

"Yes sir."

The second police officer checked his notes and then took over from his colleague.

"Were you in the park on the day that your brother Gordon Cooper and this other boy, Benjamin Jones forced their way inside the locked premises owned by Mr. Wyecroft of Hillsburgh?"

"Yes."

"Did you assist in the break-in in any manner?"

"I crawled inside."

"No, I mean did you help in smashing down the small entrance into the structure?"

"No."

"Did you witness who forced the entry into the premises?"

"Yes."

"What did you see, son?"

"Ben kicked it first. And then he dared us to kick it right in."

"Yes and then."

"Gordie, my brother, kicked it and it broke open."

"Are you sure it happened like that, boy?" the first policeman asked.

"Yes."

"What would you say if I told you that Benjamin Jones has another story?"

"I don't know. Maybe he can't remember."

"They made me do it!" Ben exclaimed.

I looked up for the first time and stared at Ben. His arms were crossed. The second policeman continued his fact-finding.

"Benjamin Jones says that you and your brother coerced him into cooperating with you. Is that true?"

I hesitated because I couldn't believe what I was hearing. I thought Ben was our friend. The police thought I didn't understand the question.

"Did you and your brother force Benjamin Jones to help you break into the food stand?"

"No, it was his idea."

"He's lying," Ben insisted. "They made me do everything."

"Yeah, I guess Benny held you while I punched you," Gordie interrupted sarcastically. Ben was much bigger than me. "Is that it?"

"You two stop it and let the police ask their questions," The Old Man demanded.

"Yes," Mom agreed, "let Benny tell his side of the story. We've heard yours. Go on, Benny."

"It was Ben's idea," I repeated. "He kicked first, then Gordie."

"OK, let's go on," the policeman with the notes stated. "Who went inside?"

"I did."

"Did anyone make you go inside?"

"No, Ben just dared me that's all."

"Ben didn't try to stop you?"

"No. He called me a chicken. He dared me to go in."

"Why did you go inside the building?"

"I don't know. I was the only one small enough to fit in."

"But why?"

"I don't know."

"You thought it would make you older, part of the group," said Mom. "Right, Benny?"

"Yes, I guess so."

"What did you take from the concession stand?" asked the note taker.

"Chips, chocolate bars, some other stuff."

"Three bags of chips. Three chocolate bars. And two cartons of cigarettes. Is that correct?"

"Yes."

"You ate the chips and chocolate bars. Where are the cigarettes?" Before I answered, the policeman answered his own question. "You gave some away. And threw the rest away. Is that correct?"

"Yes," I lied.

"OK, I think we can stop now," the first policeman observed. "We know the story. We have the two ringleaders standing over there. It was their idea. They kicked open the door. This young boy was just one of their instruments to complete the theft." I thought I contributed more to the crime than that but I didn't bother to correct the investigator. "Now, Benjamin Jones. Your father must be disappointed in you for making up that story about being threatened and coerced into this robbery."

"I was," Ben still insisted.

"Give it a rest Ben," his father spoke for the first time. "We've heard enough of your shit. Now, shut up and listen."

"Mr. Wyecroft has decided not to press charges so no action will be taken against you, but don't underestimate the seriousness of this incident. You're all very lucky that there aren't other consequences. You could have gone to Reform School for this. You all better stay squeaky clean and out of trouble. I don't want to hear about any of you again. You should all apologize to Mr. Wyecroft, and thank him for his leniency. Your parents will have to pay for the stolen goods. Benjamin Jones and Gordon Cooper, you two are especially lucky that no other action will be taken. OK. Let's hear those apologies."

I was so relieved. I wasn't going to Guelph. Then I looked at Mom. The relief disappeared. She looked devastated. I had hurt her so much. I could tell just by the look on her face. She didn't have to say anything. She would be so disappointed in both Gordie and I. Why did I do it? I will never get over this, I thought. I had never felt so much shame. Anyways, we all apologized. And thanked Mr. Wyecroft. When everyone had left, I wondered what would come next.

"How could you do that?" The Old Man said. "Didn't we bring you up to be smarter than that? You better say you're sorry to your mother as well. You won't be going out for awhile. I can't believe it. My own sons are thieves. You better stay away from Ben Jones, too. He's a bad influence on you. What have you got to say for yourselves?"

We both said that we were sorry. And promised that it wouldn't happen again. We agreed to stay away from Ben Jones and accepted being grounded for as long as deemed necessary. That was about the extent of the punishment from The Old Man. Just the one lecture. He never mentioned the episode again. Even when he was drunk. Now Mom was a different story. She didn't say much at all. But I was right. She was very hurt. She could not believe that we would have done what we did. How could her sons get in trouble with the police? In a few words, she summed up her disappointment.

"Why? How could you do this? I get enough trouble from your father. I count on you for support. Not more hardship. I hope you've learned your lesson. I still love you as much as ever but you've made me feel like I've failed you in some way."

"I'm sorry, Mom," I repeated. I was just about in tears. "We'll be good from now on. You'll see."

"That's right, Mom," Gordie agreed. "I'm sorry, too."

And that was that. Our life of crime was over. Mom didn't speak about it anymore, but we knew she did not get over the incident for quite a while. We got bigger lectures from Ernie and Billy than we did from Mom and The Old Man. They were really mad at us. They even made us feel worse. "How could you hurt Mom like that?" That's what they both argued. We didn't have a good answer. Lily wouldn't let us forget it either. "Why did you steal cigarettes? Are you going to jail?" I don't know about Gordie, but I was looking forward to school starting in a few weeks. I needed a distraction. But I certainly had learned my lesson. The same lesson that I saw on Gunsmoke once a week. Crime does not pay.

A few days later Gordie pointed out a story in the local newspaper. It went something like this:

Nine-Year-Old Bicycle Gang Disrupts Quiet Village

Police report that the normally quiet village of Hillsburgh has been disturbed from an unusual source this summer. A group of nine-year-old boys has recently been taking to the streets on their bicycles at night and causing many disturbances. This self-proclaimed gang has been linked with some minor acts of violence and even some robberies. One downtown resident who wished to remain anonymous stated that these boys had violated her front lawn and had even resorted to setting off fireworks. They call themselves the

NOBS. At press time we could not determine the significance of this malicious sounding moniker. Jeffrey Franklin, a longtime resident of Hillsburgh, says that most of the boys aren't locals. "The local lads are pretty good boys. It's the outsiders that come from the big towns like Erin that are bringing in the trouble," he maintains. There is a happy ending to this strange tale though. Police have ensured that the 'ringleaders' of the gang have been apprehended and that the village should return to its normal, peaceful setting. The inhabitants of Hillsburgh only hope that they are correct.

I reread the story several times. I couldn't believe it. They didn't even get our ages right. That story, as you can imagine, caused the need for a few explanations to Mom.

Before the new school year started, I decided to turn over a new leaf. I wanted to distance myself as far as possible from my previous life of crime and gangs. I didn't want anything to remind me of the entire episode, so I made the decision to quit smoking. It was obvious to me that cigarette smoking soon led to a life of misdeeds, infractions, and felonies. And who knows what else? So at the age of twelve, a few days before I began Grade 8, I was transformed into a former smoker. Also the NOBS club was abolished. Actually, it sort of just faded away. All the other members were going on to High School in Erin and were losing interest in the coterie. Besides, that newspaper story kind of ruined my attachment to the NOBS organization. As I said I didn't want any links to the sordid past.

I recall one last thing that summer. A sign that I was now making the right decisions. Sammy asked me what my favourite number was. I didn't know; I had never thought about it. So I made one up. Seven was too common. So was eleven. So I sort of combined the two and came up with seventeen. It had a good sound to it. A couple of days later, Randy Bush showed me a map of Hillsburgh. It had street names and numbers on it that no one even knew existed. Not me, anyway. I don't remember the name of our street. But I do recollect our house number. You guessed it – seventeen.

29 ~ Do Not Pass Go

When school started, I now got to sit in the row by the window. I was in Grade 8. My teacher was still Danny Clark. But I no longer had my brothers or any of my closest friends in my class. Billy and Gordie were now travelling each morning on the bus to Erin with Ernie (Grade 12) and John Brooks. Joining them in Grade 9 were Richard Watson, Randy Bush, Johnny Wheeler, and Henry Donaldson. All of the ex-NOBS. My best friend Sammy and Joe Watson were in Grade 6 so they weren't there to keep me company either. Lily was now in Grade 3. But I didn't care that none of them were with me. That wasn't on my mind at all. I had something else to think about. The occupant of the third seat in the far row by the opposite wall. Wendy Monahan. I wasn't sure if she even knew who I was, but I was immediately interested in her. Wendy was new to the school, having been transferred from a one-room country schoolhouse which had recently been put out of service. I'm not sure what attracted me to her. Maybe it was just the look of her friendly face and short, dark hair. I looked forward to the times that she would put up her hand to answer a question. Then I had an excuse to look at her without being too obvious. Eventually I got up enough nerve to talk to her. I was a brilliant conversationalist.

I would say, "Hi Wendy. How are you today? I'm fine. See you later." That was about the extent of it for now. But I was happy just to hear Wendy say, "Hello Benny."

In early October, The Old Man crashed his car again. A different one. A week before he had bought a '51 Hudson from some older woman in Hillsburgh that he knew. He was coming home late at night from Georgetown again. This time it was the winding hill south of Highway 24 that got him. He went off the road, sheared off a tree, and rolled to the bottom. And again he walked away. He walked all the way home. I heard him arrive back at three o'clock in the morning.

"Mary, please wake up. I've done it this time. I've hurt my back. I can hardly move. Help me get into bed. Will you, dear?"

The Old Man got up early the next morning. A friend drove him back to the accident scene. And he towed the now destroyed car back to our house. It was quite a sight. The Old Man had his friend put it as far back in our yard as possible so that it wouldn't be in sight. He thought that he had got away without anyone knowing about the accident. He had a sore back and no mode of transportation, but at least the police hadn't found out. However the luck of his horseshoes must have finally worn out or else they fell out when he was ejected from the car. Because the police appeared at the door later that day. Someone had witnessed The Old Man removing the car from the accident site. This time the judge wasn't as lenient. The Old Man was sentenced to three months in jail. Which was in Guelph.

So we had to live without The Old Man being at home for the next three months. Hip, hip, hooray! The funny thing was that others didn't see it that way. Everyone would tell us how sorry they were to hear about our father. People would ask if there was anything they could do to help us. The United Church minister came by our house to offer his sympathy and prayers. Some parishioners bought boxes of food. We also got some clothes. Mom wouldn't let us have the clothes. She said they weren't fit to wear. We managed OK because of three main reasons. The first was The Old Man's pay cheque that came just as he went to jail. That lasted a lot longer than usual because The Old Man wasn't there to spend a good portion of it on beer for himself and other assorted bar patrons. The second reason was the family allowance cheques. And the third was credit. We would have been quite happy if The Old Man had been sentenced for a lot longer.

On Halloween, we were supposed to wear costumes to school. I didn't know what to wear. Mom suggested my old Cub's uniform. I couldn't think of anything else so off I went the next morning with that uniform in a shopping bag. When it came time to change into our costumes, I realized what a ridiculous outfit I had for Halloween. We had to prance around in a circle in the centre of the classroom so that we could be judged. And Wendy would see me. I got so nervous that I started to stumble and a few kids laughed, so I had an inspiration. I grabbed an empty Flip (a drink that only cost a nickel) bottle and started to act like I was drunk. I swayed and waved myself around the circle. Believe it or not I won best original costume. I guess no one had seen a drunken Cub before. Wendy even commented on my performance.

"You were great, Benny. You made me laugh. How did you come up with such a great idea?"

That definitely made my day. I didn't tell her about my extensive experience in observing the behaviour of someone drunk.

While The Old Man was in jail, I went to a 'Father and Son' banquet in the basement of the United Church. My temporary father was a man that lived in Hillsburgh and had no son of his own. He asked Mom if I would be his 'son' for the day. You will never guess who it was. Mr. Wyecroft. That's right, the barber and owner of the baseball park concession stand. I felt very guilty the entire night, but Mr. Wyecroft was very pleasant to me. He told me that he was very proud to have me for a son even if for only one night.

He had always wanted a child of his own. I never mentioned how embarrassing it was to enter the barbershop to get our hair cut. For some reason, he was always very friendly to Gordie and I. It made us feel like real jerks. Here was a guy that really believed in 'forgive and forget'.

In early December, The Old Man was released from jail. One month early on account of good behaviour. He was a model prisoner we were told. And well-liked by everyone including the guards. While The Old Man was away, Mom was very careful about the amount of firewood that we burned. She didn't want to go through all the wood in the back shed because she feared the reaction from The Old Man.

"Where the hell has all the wood gone? What have you been doing? Up all night partying and whoring. You old bag!" Mom said impersonating The Old Man.

So we made sure that we didn't burn too much wood in the kitchen stove. We would sit in the living room at night and let the kitchen get cold. When The Old Man arrived home he was completely sober as he had come straight from the jailhouse. We watched as he went directly to the back shed. We all looked at Mom. The Old Man walked right back into the kitchen and bellowed.

"Why the hell is there so much wood left? What have you been doing? Out all night partying and whoring. You old bag!"

"You just can't win," Mom said half-laughing as she glanced at all of us. The Old Man didn't get the joke.

In spite of that initial outburst, The Old Man soon announced that he was a changed man. He had quit drinking for good. He would attend regular meetings of the AA. Sitting in a jail cell for two months had shown him the error of his ways. He had a great family and would appreciate how lucky he was from now on. He had learned his lesson.

"I know I've said that before, Mary. But this time I mean it. No more beer or any alcohol for me. I'm finished for good. Just you wait and see."

When the next payday arrived, The Old Man surprised all of us and turned his earnings over to Mom without spending any on beer. And he started attending AA meetings just like he said he would. He explained how everyone stood up and declared that they were alcoholics and then proceeded to describe how their lives had been destroyed by the bottle. Mom asked The Old Man if he said anything.

"No, I didn't want to stand there and tell everybody my troubles. Anyways I'm not an alcoholic. I'm just a drunk. I don't crave it during the week. I can live without a drink. I just like to drink that's all. I could stop anytime I like. And I have. I just can't drink. It drives me crazy. Some explained how they've lost their families, homes, everything. I'm the lucky one. I still have a great family, a home, a job. I had nothing to tell. I'm a drunk, not an alcoholic."

The Old Man went to another meeting the next week and then decided it wasn't for him. But he still hadn't fallen off the wagon. The United Church minister came to see us once more. And prayed for us again. He told us to have faith in the Lord and The Old Man. He was a changed man, we were told. He needed our support and love if he was going to successfully shake off 'this horrible disease' and be the loving father and husband that the Lord knew that he could be. Then a member of the AA came to our house to visit The Old Man and he gave us the same speech.

"Alcoholism is a disease just like any other. You must continue to support and love your husband, Mrs. Cooper, regardless of the success of this treatment. If he had cancer or was physically disabled, you wouldn't reject him. Right now the best cure is the love of his family and the comfort of his home. Garfield is a good man, Mrs. Cooper, and deserves this second chance."

Mom didn't say too much. She agreed to give The Old Man the benefit of the doubt and to help him stop drinking in whatever way she could. I thought to myself, "What does he mean second chance? This must be chance 4,321 and counting." My other thought was that if The Old Man had cancer, that wouldn't cause him to berate, abuse, and beat Mom. Frankly I couldn't see the comparison. But I didn't voice any of these concerns. I too was willing to wait and see what happened and I actually started to believe that maybe The Old Man could really change.

We had a good Christmas. Things were peaceful, if you know what I mean. A couple of days later The Old Man was late returning from work. We all wondered if he had returned to his old ways, but then thought, wouldn't we feel bad if something had happened to him. He returned home at nine that night. A strange car pulled in the driveway. The Old Man hadn't purchased another car yet. First, a man we didn't recognize got out of the car. Then we saw The Old Man. They came in the door off the kitchen.

"Hello old bag! I'm drunk again. Come and meet my good friend Arnold. We're hungry. Where the fuck's my dinner? Come on, you old bag. Get us something to eat, will you. What do you think I am, an eight-day clock or a sewing machine? I work my ass off and this is the respect I get. I installed Connie Smythe's phone for Christ's sake. What are you doing? Off whoring with your boyfriends again? I know the score. I've been around the world. Where the hell's my dinner, you gray-haired old bag!"

Poncho crawled under the china cabinet in the dining room corner. Life had returned to normal.

In January 1962, Smokey surprised us all by giving birth to five kittens. We thought that she was too old for that. This time I witnessed The Old Man drowning the babies in a pail of water. I was only able to rescue one dark gray kitten that looked a lot like a baby Smokey (except for the fact it was a boy). Lily and I decided to call him Pepper. I had forgot how wild and crazy kittens got after a few weeks. Pepper was a lot of fun. I remember that he would jump on Mom's back as she was trying to cook in the kitchen. Pepper used to sleep on Lily's bed while Smokey continued to use the wooden box by the kitchen stove as her bed.

At the beginning of February, Aunt Becky came to stay

with us for four weeks. I don't recall any incidents involving The Old Man and Aunt Becky during that visit. I'm not sure if that's because The Old Man behaved himself or if the drunken occurrences just became too common to stand out in my memory. There definitely weren't any major confrontations during this stay or else I surely would have some recollection of it. I know that I was afraid that she would find out about me and Gordie's run-in with the law the last summer, but if she did it was never mentioned. I know that Mom would have never brought up the subject with her older sister. The one thing that I do remember was that every time we heard Aunt Becky's feet on the stairs, one of us would say, "Aunt Becky's coming!" And the rest of us would break up in laughter. One day Pepper jumped on her back. He must have thought that Aunt Becky was Mom. "Oh my Blessed Father," she exclaimed, "someone get this animal off of me. I don't mind cats but not when they get on you like that." Lily had to rescue Pepper (or should I say rescue Aunt Becky) and take him upstairs. This time Aunt Becky made some different meals that we had never had before. For example, she made a dinner with a stuffed eggplant. None of us had tasted eggplant before and we weren't really looking forward to the meal. But it was delicious. Even The Old Man liked it. After supper, Mom commented, "As Reg Carter used to say, I'm sufficiently suffonsified, if I had anymore I'd be superfluous." This was a comment that Mom would often make after a hearty meal. And she would always pronounce the last word the way that Reg Carter did – 'super-fluous'.

In those days, on Valentine's Day you gave everyone in your class a valentine. Male or female, whether you liked them or not. It was expected of you. You would buy these large packages of valentines which you had to cut out and then sign the night before. There were about thirty cards that I had to prepare that year; however, I decided that I would get Wendy something more. I couldn't just give her the same card that I gave Marsha White. Marsha was twice my height, a few years older, and not the sharpest pencil in the case. One day Marsha was asked to point out the United States on the globe and she couldn't locate it. So I went to the store and bought a special card for Wendy. It was about a foot high and six inches wide and had a cute squirrel on it holding a large red heart containing the words 'Please Be My Valentine'. I got really creative and brave on what I wrote inside. I decided on the direct approach and wrote 'To Wendy' followed up by 'From Benny'. The next day when it was time to distribute the cards to everyone, I slid the large card for Wendy on her desk without her noticing. She was busy passing out her cards. When I sat back down, I tried to watch Wendy's reaction without her being aware. I saw her look at it and then immediately put it down and look at another card. "Oh, what an idiot I am," I thought. "She doesn't even like me." At recess, Wendy came up to me outside. "She's going to ask me why I gave her such a big card. I know it," was what crossed my mind. After all, Wendy had given me a card similar to the one that she had given to the rest of her classmates. First she showed me a broad smile and then spoke.

"Thanks for the nice card, Benny. That was very sweet."

"You're welcome, Wendy," I managed to mumble.

"I'm going skating on Saturday," she informed me. "Are you going? Perhaps I'll see you there."

"I wasn't planning to… Yes. I'll be there for sure. I'll see you around one o'clock."

"All right. Thanks again, Benny. See you later."

I couldn't believe it. I actually had a date. I thought about it all afternoon. I was going skating with Wendy. I was wondering if I would get up enough nerve on Saturday to actually skate with Wendy, when I was suddenly awakened from my daydream.

"Benny Cooper," Danny Clark remarked, "if I can get you to stop staring at Wendy Monahan for a minute and pay attention, then maybe you could answer my question for the class."

"What? Sorry, Mr. Clark. Could you please repeat the

question," I replied sheepishly amongst the chuckles of the entire class. I thought that I had blown it completely until I caught Wendy smiling at me a short time later. I attempted to pay attention to the lessons for the rest of the day.

On Saturday, I arrived at the Hillsburgh Arena at the bottom of the hill a few minutes before one o'clock. I didn't see Wendy anywhere. So I went into the boy's dressing room and laced up my skates. When I skated out onto the ice, I still could not catch any sight of Wendy. I started to skate around in circles when finally, I saw her skate onto the ice surface. She was with another girl from our class, Sharon. I kept skating around and around with one eye on Wendy and Sharon who were skating beside each other. I was pondering how stupid I was to think that I had a date. Wendy just wanted to skate with a friend and only asked if I was going to be there, that's all. She didn't mean anything else by it. As these thoughts were crossing my mind, I hadn't noticed that Wendy had come up beside me. "Do you want to skate with me?" she asked. Then she took my hand and we skated together around the rink. I was speechless. Eventually I got up enough nerve to start a small conversation. The day continued in this manner. I skated alone for a while and then with Wendy again. Wendy asked if I minded if her friend Sharon skated with us for a song. She didn't want to leave her alone too much. I readily agreed. Before I knew it, they were announcing the last skate. It had finished so fast. For the rest of the winter, the events of that day became the regular routine for a Saturday. Each time, we would skate more and more often together and less and less alone. Sometimes Sammy would come with me but that didn't deter me from skating as much as possible with Wendy. Somehow I got up enough nerve one day to ask Wendy if she was doing anything after the skating ceased. We then started going to the Hillsburgh Hotel afterwards. OK, wipe that smirk off your face. It's not what you think. There was a snack bar in the hotel. We would sit there at a table, eating French fries and drinking Coke. And listening to the jukebox – songs such as Palisades Park, Big Bad John, or Runaway. Or we might play on the pinball machine. Sometimes it was just us. Other times, Gordie, Sammy, Sharon or some other friends might have been with us. Whatever we did, I didn't care. As long as it gave me the opportunity to be with Wendy as much as possible.

30 ~ The Long Goodbye

One particularly cold, late February day, Sammy and I got a ride to Erin and went skating at the arena there. We lost track of time and before we realized it, it was getting close to dark and time to head back to Hillsburgh. The other thing that we lost track of was how to get home. We soon realized that there was no one left at the arena who was heading back to our hometown. So we walked up the road to the turnoff for Hillsburgh and stuck out our thumbs. And waited, and waited. Eventually we were getting so cold that we decided it would be better to walk home. Something we had done a few times before, but not in the dark and never when it was that cold. We had probably walked about one-half of the five-mile distance when I realized that my feet were freezing.

"Are your feet cold, Sammy?" I inquired.

"Cold? They're frozen stiff. I don't think I can walk much farther. They feel like they're going to fall off if they get any colder."

"Me too. What are we going to do?"

"I think we better call my Dad," said Sammy, "and see if he can pick us up. Let's stop at the next farmhouse and ask if we can use the phone."

"Good idea."

I had no idea who lived at the next farm or how they would react to two strange, half-frozen boys knocking on their door in the middle of the night. But I didn't care. I was dying. So we eventually made it to a laneway with a mailbox out front after what seemed like another two miles, but what obviously was only a few hundred yards. We slowly limped our way down the long lane up to the front door of the house. Sammy knocked on the door right away. An older gentleman answered the door.

"Sammy Smale, what are you doing here? You look frozen stiff. Who's this with you? Come in; come in out of the cold. I have a nice warm fire going. Ruth, we've got company."

It turned out that the farm couple were acquaintances of Sammy's parents. I was too cold to talk yet. My feet hurt so much that I was crying in pain. We went to the fireplace and started to warm ourselves up. Our host was afraid that we had frostbite. He called Sammy's dad and he said that he would be there to get us shortly. When my body had heated up enough that I could talk again, I found out that the farmer also knew The Old Man. He didn't tell me what a great guy my father was though; he only said that he knew him. I was thankful for that. Before too long, Mr. Smale arrived to take us home. By then I realized that my feet were probably not going to fall off. Sammy's feet had also survived the ordeal. Everyone said that we were extremely lucky to not have suffered permanent damage. Still that was the last time that I walked that route.

A few days later, I did have an accident where I suffered permanent damage. It was during lunch at school. We were playing that game 'The Fox and the Hound". That's where someone (the fox) makes tracks in the snow and another (the hound) chases the leader around through the same tracks. Wendy was the fox; I was the hound. I started to run very fast so that I could catch up to Wendy when I suddenly lost my footing and went headfirst into the snow. Unfortunately, there was a sharp stick in the ground which had been hidden by the accumulation of snow. The point of the stick went into my chin just below my lower lip and entered my mouth. There was blood everywhere which was quite evident contrasted against the white snow. I was helped into the school by Wendy and a few other kids where Danny Clark applied first aid. After he had cleaned the wound and stopped the bleeding, Danny Clark asked me how I had managed to injure myself. After I explained the story without mentioning who the fox was, he laughed. "Well Mr. Benny Cooper, if you're going to chase girls you're liable to get hurt sometimes." He was no fool. The permanent damage (besides my pride) was a scar on my chin that remains to this day.

In March, I became a teenager. I was now thirteen and a reformed ex-smoker and a rehabilitated ex-thief. And I was very happy. Why shouldn't I be? In April, the Leafs won the Stanley Cup by defeating Chicago in six games. Hip, hip, hooray! That was the first Stanley Cup win that I remembered. I was too young in 1951. I didn't even know who Bill Barilko was; Dave Keon was my hero. Then two things happened to change that mood of happiness. The first occurred in late April. Our bathroom sink was clogged and Mom put Drano down the drainpipe. A little while later I saw Smokey under the sink putting her nose in something. There was a small puddle there. After close examination, Mom realized that the pool of water came from the drainpipe which was leaking and that it was not just water, but water with Drano dissolved in it.

"Was Smokey drinking the water, Benny?" Mom asked.

"I don't know Mom. I think I picked her up before that. I think she was just smelling it."

"I hope she had sense enough not to drink it."

"What do you think would happen Mom if she did drink it?"

"It would eat her insides right out, dear. That's what it does to the junk clogged in the sink. It burns when you get it on your skin."

"Then she wouldn't drink that, Mom," I said confidently.

Not long afterwards though we noticed that Smokey had trouble walking. The poor creature was falling against the wall and looking up at us with a painful expression on her face. She attempted to meow however it came out like a low squeaking sound.

"Let's take Smokey to the vet, Mom," I pleaded.

"OK, dear. But we have to wait until your father gets home in a half-hour or so." He had a car again. I didn't mention that earlier. "I'm not sure Smokey will last to then," she added.

"What can we do, Mom? We need to do something."

"I don't think there's anything we can do, dear."

All the family except for The Old Man was home at the time. Ernie, Billy, Gordie, Lily, and I, all felt as hopeless as Mom. We couldn't do anything. Pepper was looking at his mother and crying too. And Poncho was nosing around trying to figure out what the matter was. Before The Old Man got home the pain stopped. Smokey died. We were all relieved that her suffering was over, but we would surely miss the old girl.

And then we got the other bad news. We were moving again. The telephone company had finished their installation of dial telephones in the area, so it was time for The Old Man to go to a new location and help perform the same task there. I should have expected it. You probably did. We had been in Hillsburgh for four years now. Far too long for us to stay anywhere. Still we were all shocked. Nobody wanted to move. Ernie had spent all his high school years in Erin and wasn't eager to change for his last year. Billy and Gordie had met new friends (many of the opposite sex) in the first year at school in Erin, so they had no desire to move away. Lily, however, was the one who reacted the strongest against the move. She had only known school in Hillsburgh; she had met her first real friends in the town as well. Previously we had lived on farms and she had to rely on her brothers for company. She was sad and angry. She declared that there was no way that she was leaving Hillsburgh. And then there was me. For obvious reasons I didn't want to leave, but I didn't say too much. At least not to Mom. What could she do? But I complained to Gordie a lot. I told him that I wasn't going anywhere. The only good point about moving was that I wouldn't be going to school in Erin. What's wrong with that? Army cadets. It was still mandatory and I couldn't really envision enjoying that. I had grown out of playing war games. What about Mom? I'm not sure how she felt for herself, because she was too busy being concerned about us. Alas, none of it mattered because we were destined to move that summer regardless. We were moving to a new burgh. Literally. Our new home would be Newburgh, a small town at the other end of Ontario, near Kingston. When we told anyone that we were moving to Kingston (there was no use telling them Newburgh), they always mentioned the same thing. "Oh, you're going to Kingston Penn." That's all anyone knew about Eastern Ontario, including me.

Back to the story, there are a few more things to relate before we head on down the road. It was June 1962 and the school year was winding down. Danny Clark advised the class that we were all going on a trip to Toronto to see the Toronto Maple Leafs in action. Being June, the Maple Leafs that I am talking about was obviously the baseball team. He was looking for volunteers among the parents to assist by driving some students to Toronto. Somehow it was arranged that me and three other boys got chauffeured by someone who wasn't a parent – Tweety Bird. So we had a great time! From the beginning, it was fun. We got to ride to Toronto in Tweety Bird's '55 Chevy. There was a scary moment when we arrived at Maple Leaf Stadium and we were informed that the tickets were for the previous game the night before. But Danny Clark convinced the ticket collectors that it was raining in Hillsburgh the night before, and therefore we thought that there had been a rainout. It wasn't the truth and the Maple Leaf staff probably knew that, still they took pity on us and honoured the tickets for that evening's contest. The game which was against Buffalo was entertaining, but I was more interested in the stadium itself. I had never been in such a large baseball facility. A few of us, including Wendy, wandered around on all the levels to check things out. Oh yeah, the Maple Leafs won the game too. On the way home, all of us boys were feeling high. Not on anything but excitement. We hooted, hollered, and sang all the way home. I couldn't believe that Tweety Bird put up with us, but he seemed to enjoy himself as well.

On the last day of school, we had a 'track and field' day. At the end of the events, we were informed that the winner of the award for the highest marks for a student graduating from Grade 8 was Benny Cooper. I was to get my name put on a plaque that was named after the school which Wendy used to attend. Many of the other students cheered the announcement and I was lifted up on their shoulders and carried around. I could not believe their reaction. Having my classmates recognize my small achievement that way meant more to me than any plaque ever could.

There was another class excursion later that night – the last night of the school year. This was a hayride. A tractor pulling a wagon loaded with hay bales picked us up at the school after dinner and drove us all around the Hillsburgh area. We traveled many of the roads that Gordie, Sammy, and I had covered on foot over the years. I remember that all the other kids were telling me to sit closer to Wendy. That I managed to do, although I was embarrassed because so many people were advising me what to do. Then I was coached to place my arm around Wendy. I eventually got up enough nerve to do that when we were five minutes from her drop off location. And lastly, I was encouraged to give Wendy a goodnight kiss. This may be my last chance, I was informed. They all knew that I would be leaving Hillsburgh before long. But I was too shy. Wendy disembarked from the wagon and we exchanged only goodnights without the accompanying kiss. And I didn't see Wendy again before our departure to our new home.

As June came to a close we were still in Hillsburgh. We

hadn't sold the house yet so we were accorded a one-month reprieve from our forced relocation. The Old Man had to start work in Newburgh, thus he left without us and stayed at a boarding room in our soon to be new hometown. While he was there, The Old Man was to arrange a new house and hope that there was some action on the realty market back at our end. But I got ahead of myself again. Before he left The Old Man had to do two things for Ernie. The first was to laugh at the red socks that Ernie wore one day and accuse him of being a 'poof'. "What's with those poofy socks, Ernie?" The Old Man laughed. Ernie was not amused. Billy, Gordie, and I were though. Then on the weekend before he left The Old Man drove Ernie to Ipperwash in order to attend army camp. What I recall about that trip was the car breaking down and Ernie hitching a ride on alone while The Old Man got a ride to the nearest service station. The rest of us spent half a day sitting in the hot sun in the car by the side of the road. We never even got to say a proper goodbye to Ernie who we wouldn't see again until after we had arrived in Newburgh a month later.

That July, it was kind of quiet and subdued at the Cooper household what with The Old Man being a couple hundred miles away. One night all of the old NOBS went camping by a small pond at the south end of town. Besides Billy, Gordie and myself, the ex-NOBS included Randy Bush, Richard Watson, Johnny Wheeler, and Henry Donaldson. We stayed up until 6:00 in the morning at which point I had been up twenty-four hours. That was my new longevity record. I remember singing one particular song half the night.

"Does your chewing gum lose its flavour on the bedpost overnight?

When your mother says don't chew it; do you swallow it in spite?

Do you catch it on your tonsils and then you heave it left and right? Ooh, ooh.

Does your chewing gum lose its flavour – on the bedpost – overnight?"

Then Gordie would sing:

"A dollar is a dollar and a dime is a dime.

I'd sing another chorus but I ain't got the time."

And then we'd start all over again. Ad nauseam. It was a great campfire song.

The only other two things that I remember about that July were going swimming with Sammy in this dark pond in the middle of one of the backfields that we wandered. The water was so dark you couldn't see your legs once they entered the water. I guess it probably wasn't that ecologically safe. What did we know? The other new experience for me that summer was working. I worked for a week on somebody's farm (I have no idea whose farm it was now) helping with a few chores in the fields. I couldn't understand how I ever wanted to be a farmer. Yes, an architect was definitely the job for me.

Before the eventful day of departure, there were some other hard decisions to be made. We had to organize all our toys, clothes, and other stuff which we had collected over the years and throw out what we didn't need anymore. The Old Man did not want to move all the junk with us. I remember a few things that I foolishly discarded that I regret to this day. Some of those things were comic books. I had the one which explained how Superboy became Superman, the one which told the story of Bruce Wayne's decision to transform into Batman, another story about Batman going to London and swinging from the Tower Bridge, and so on and so on. I'm sure many others made the same regretful decisions. The other item that went to the garbage was a shoebox full of bubble gum cards. There were baseball cards. I only remember Warren Spahn. There were hockey cards. Although we did keep the Toronto Maple Leafs (for all of us), the Montreal Canadiens (for Billy), New York Rangers (for me), and Boston Bruins (for Gordie). In other words we threw out the Chicago Blackhawks and the Detroit Red Wings. But what I think about the most now, are the TV Western cards that ended up in the pile of garbage. We had cards for all the great TV Westerns of the 50's and early 60's. How many of these do you remember? 'Yancy Derringer', 'Laramie', 'Rawhide', 'Maverick', 'Bat Masterson', 'Wild Bill Hickok', 'Have Gun Will Travel', 'Wagon Train', 'Wyatt Earp', 'Gunsmoke', 'Wanted: Dead or Alive', 'Riverboat', and 'The Rifleman'.

Then came the actual day for the move. The Old Man had returned from Newburgh to take us back with him. He had rented a truck and had recruited a friend to drive our car on the trip. We still hadn't sold the house yet, but we left anyway. The Old Man let the house go back to the bank just like he had done when we left Halifax twelve years before. We said our sad farewells to the Smales and then it was time to go. The Old Man, Billy, and Gordie went in the truck. That left The Old Man's friend to drive Mom, Lily, me, Poncho, and Pepper in the car. Pepper was in a cardboard box. We were all very quiet during the journey. Partly because of the stranger in the car and partly because we all wondered what lay ahead for us at the other end of the 401.

Oh My Blessed Father – Book 2
"Dum Dum"

Be sure to follow along with Benny Cooper and his sometimes tumultuous yet loving family as they struggle through adversity while living and growing up in Southern Ontario during the highly turbulent '60s.

The following is an extract from the continuation of Ted Burton's coming of age novel
Oh My Blessed Father - Book 2
"Dum Dum"

By Schooner Publishing
Ottawa, Ontario, Canada

1 ~ Another Dam Place

Mom always said, "If you don't have anything good to say about someone, don't say anything at all." But she never said anything about writing. So after a short break, I've decided to keep on with my narration. To begin with, I will describe my first impressions of my new hometown. Newburgh had more in common with Hillsburgh than just the name. The population of both towns was around 500 to 600 people at that time, and Newburgh too had a large hill at one end of town. The hill in Newburgh was even steeper than the one in our former village. But we didn't live at the top of the hill this time. No, we lived at the other end of the town on the street farthest from the hill. And we no longer owned our home; instead we were renting once again. But we were still living in a town; our farm days were over.

We were renting the house from a family called Chance. So of course, we only referred to this abode as Chance's Place. At first inspection, I was quite impressed with the house. It had lovely hardwood floors and French glass doors dividing the living room from the hallway and the stairs leading up to the bedrooms. There was a large kitchen and a separate dining room. When you went up the stairs, you came to the top of a small hallway with four doors opening onto it. The first door on the right was Lily's bedroom. She now had her own bedroom with real walls, no more blanket partition. This fact helped to appease Lily somewhat about the move. The other door on the right became Mom and The Old Man's room. On the left, the one door led into a large bedroom which was assigned to Ernie and Billy. It had a door off of it which led into a smaller bedroom (but still a fair size) that was left for Gordie and I. So Gordie and I had to walk through Ernie and Billy's room to get to ours. The last door directly straight ahead at the top of the stairs – where you would expect a bathroom to be – was actually just a large walk-in closet. The bathroom? It was in the backyard – an outhouse. That was a first for us, at least that I could remember. A lot of people in Newburgh still had outhouses. I couldn't believe it. I felt like we had moved away from civilization. And the phone? We still had one but once more it was a large wooden box hanging on the wall with a crank handle on the side. Nobody in Newburgh had a dial phone yet. Hence, that accounts for The Old Man's transfer to this town. To introduce them to the modern era of communication. But the bathroom was another matter.

On the first night in our new home, we were awakened by the sound of a large explosion followed by what sounded like an air-raid siren that continued wailing for a long time. I thought the town was being bombed. I was close. In actuality, a U.S. Air Force plane crashed in a field just south of town killing the crew (Was it two or four? I can't recall). That was the explosion. The fire alarm to alert the Newburgh Volunteer Fire Department into action was what sounded like the air-raid siren. That was our welcome to Newburgh. The next day some of the other kids told us about their experiences during the night accompanied by all the gruesome details. I was sort of glad that I remained in bed and missed all of the 'excitement'.

In short order we became aware of the two most distinctive features of Newburgh. Other than the hill, that is. The first was the dam. It is situated on the Napanee River which runs from town towards the town of Napanee seven miles away. The dam towered about 10 to 15 feet above the water depending on the time of the year and which end of the dam you were standing on. In the summer when the water was fairly low, the dam actually worked like one. In the spring, water rushed through it because of the large tunnel in the middle. I was amazed to see kids dive off the dam into the water below. I already told you the height of the dam, as for the water it was at most five feet deep in the deepest spots. You definitely had to know how to dive shallow. Not that you had much choice. If you dove straight down, you would hit your head on a large rock protruding from the aforementioned tunnel. But everyone seemed to know what they were doing and I never saw anyone get hurt. I'll have much more to say about 'the dam' as this story unfolds.

The other main feature of Newburgh was the nicknames. Practically everybody had one, well at least the boys anyway. And they weren't necessarily complimentary. But nobody seemed to mind that much. I'll give you some examples now. At the top of the hill lived the two brothers Top Cat and Big Boy. Partway down the hill there were three brothers – Schroeder, Linus, and Pigpen. At the bottom of the hill, Sneezy and Maynard (I thought that was his real name for the first year) took up residence. On the road towards the dam lived Flip (Flip the Sausage) who I was told was aptly named. Further into town, there were another two brothers – Pooh and Birdbrain – who lived with their father Great Elk. Just to confuse things, a father of one of the boys was also called Sneezy. However, we were still just Billy, Gordie, and Benny. Whoops, no we weren't. I almost forgot. Billy now insisted that he be called Bill and Gordie followed that up with his own demands to be referred to as Gord. 'Bill' I could manage most of the time, but 'Gord' just never seemed to roll off the tongue easily. Ernie was still Ernie (call him Ern at your own peril) and Lily was of course still Lily (not Sissy, remember). Me, I was still Benny or as Mom often would call me – 'Dear Little Benny'. I think that was started by Lily when she was two or three. "Oh look, Mom. Here comes Dear Little Benny home from school," she blurted out one day. The handle stuck.

There were three other facets of Newburgh that I should tell you about. One being the hockey arena – there wasn't one. Right in the middle of town, at the bottom of the hill, sat a large, low building on a fair-sized lot. On first glance I thought it was an arena. What gave it away though, was the large sign on the front of the building which said 'Newburgh Sales Barn'. I didn't know what that meant at first. At least not until I attended my first cattle auction there. Not exactly the place to take your first date. Another significant building in Newburgh was right beside the sales barn. There sat an old tar-papered structure that looked ready to burn down at a moment's notice. Which would have been scary because Dorchester's Service Station was situated right on the other side of it. This ominous edifice was a factory. The Kitchen Brush Factory. For the first year I always wondered what a 'Kitchen Brush' was until someone explained to me that it was just a brush factory and Kitchen was the name of the owner. And the third highlight of Newburgh that I want to tell you about is another industry – the cheese factory. It was at the end of town near where we lived. You couldn't miss it, even with your eyes closed. Because you could smell it. This disgusting looking stuff would dump out of the factory, right into the little stream beside it. In keeping with Newburgh traditions, this stream will hereto always be referred to as 'Shit Creek'.

A few days after we arrived in our new residence, a boy came to the door to introduce himself and to see if I wanted to play baseball. He was a little younger than me but not by much. His name was Brendan Casey. I agreed and off I went to meet his friends. Also playing the game were Schroeder, Linus, Sneezy, and Flip. As well there was another boy that I haven't mentioned yet – Very Dorky. That's what everyone called him, I swear. I eventually determined that his real name was Barry Dorchester. Very Dorky originated from the way that Barry's older brother Brian used to pronounce Barry's name when he was a baby. Brendan Casey and myself were just about the only kids there that went by our real names. All of the participants in the game except for me attended the Newburgh Academy, the local public school. At first they didn't believe that I was going into Grade 9 and would be going to the high school in Napanee on the bus. I was the smallest one there – no surprise. When the game started, I was positioned at second base which scared the wits out of me. I was no Ty Cobb when it came to baseball. I was used to languishing in the obscurity of the outfield. Sometimes I had been inserted at shortstop. Why? Because I was short. I never understood the connection. Anyways, when the first ball was hammered my way, I made a brilliant catch and tagged out the guy on second.

"Boy, not only is this kid smart, he's an athlete too!" commented Sneezy. I just blushed.

Not long after, Sneezy and the rest of the competitors soon realized the error in their judgment. I never stopped another ball that came my way.

"Maybe he's not so smart either," somebody suggested. But it was all good-natured jesting. And I soon became good friends with many of those players.

That night Gordie (see I told you I couldn't get used to Gord) and I met a couple of local girls. We were just at the end of our street in front of a church when they introduced themselves to us. I don't remember now who they were anymore. I only remember what one of them asked us.

"What religion are you?"

"None," replied Gordie.

"What do you mean, none? You have to be some religion," she replied.

"Well we used to be United, but we don't go to church anymore," explained Gordie.

"Thank God!" the girl exclaimed, "You're not Catholic. I hate Catholics."

Both Gordie and I didn't know what to say to that. I was shocked. That was my first real experience with religious bigotry like that. I wondered what she would have said if we had told her that we were atheists. I assume that would have been OK compared to Catholicism.

When I say that was my first experience with prejudice based upon religion, I am not being entirely truthful. When The Old Man was drunk he used to sometimes rant against Roman Catholics. But that was different. The Old Man said many things when he was drunk. Both Claudia's husband Tom and Brad's wife Catherine were Catholic. And when The Old Man was sober, I never heard him make a big point of it. Besides this was coming from someone my own age. I couldn't understand the reaction at all. I thought to myself, "What the devil difference does it make what building people sleep in on Sunday mornings have to do with anything?" That's absolutely true. That's how naïve I was about those things. I remembered Brendan Casey was Catholic. I only knew that because he told me that he was going to be going to school in Brockville to become a priest. I finally got up enough nerve to answer.

"I like Catholics. They are just the same as us."

That was the extent of the theological discussion. I never talked to that girl about religion (or anything else, for that matter) again.

ACKNOWLEDGMENTS

Thanks to John Brooks, Barb Burton, Chris Burton, Gary Burton, Gillian Burton, Marilyn Burton, Meghan Burton, Sam Burton, Scott Burton, Wayne Burton, Jean Delaney, Gord Delaney, Eric Dennis, Sabrina Dennis, Arlene Déry, Christina Evans, Bob Rainone, Annette ter Stege, Anna Webster, and Wayne Webster for encouragement, suggestions, and story ideas. Special appreciation must be added for Meghan and Gillian Burton for reading, re-reading, editing, and proofreading my manuscript while attempting to curtail my excessive use of commas and semi-colons. As well, I would be remiss if I did not mention my thankfulness to Christina Evans, who not only provided constructive criticism, but also inspired me to keep writing whenever I reached a creative impasse. I must also extend extra gratitude to Gary Burton and Scott Burton who continually provided input to much of this book and never seemed to be bored, although I never stopped talking about it. But most of all, I would like to express my indebtedness to Wayne Burton. Without his continuous support, advice, criticism, prodding, narrative contributions, and enthusiastic interest, this book would never have been finished.